Paradise Court

Jenny Oldfield was born in Yorkshire in 1949 and studied English at university. She has had stories published in magazines such as *Bella*, *Woman & Home* and *Cosmopolitan*, and has written crime novels, and books for young adults. She lives in Leeds with her two children.

JENNY OLDFIELD

Paradise Court

PAN BOOKS
IN ASSOCIATION WITH MACMILLAN

This edition first published 1995 by Pan Books Ltd

an imprint of Macmillan General Books
Cavaye Place London SW10 9PG
and Basingstoke

Associated companies throughout the world

ISBN 0 330 33886 2

3 5 7 9 8 6 4

A CIP catalogue record for this book is available from
the British Library

Typeset by CentraCet Limited, Cambridge
Printed and bound in Great Britain by
Cox & Wyman Ltd, Reading, Berkshire

For my mother and father

Part One

SHAME
November 1913

Chapter One

Tommy O'Hagan waited in the dark alley for a signal from his sister Daisy's dressing room. His worn jacket gave no protection against the swirling November wind. 'Come on, Daisy,' Tommy muttered through chattering teeth. He was starved as well as freezing, and this waiting was getting him down. 'I can't stay here all day!' In the dim, grey light he looked no more than a huddled bag of bones.

At last a shapely hand and wrist emerged through a window and beckoned him. Tommy nipped down to the stage door, Daisy opened it and he slipped in out of the cold afternoon.

'Thanks, Daisy,' he said, though at first he couldn't swear it *was* her under all that muck on her face. Then she spoke.

'Get a move on, Tommy. If they catch you hanging about backstage my name'll be mud!' She propelled him forward by the shoulder. He blundered down a long, cream corridor with open doors to left and right through which he caught the heady impression of feathers, frills, silky dresses and limbs, and the heavy scent of greasepaint and powder. He paused to breathe it all in, but Daisy gave him another hefty push. 'And don't never say I don't do nothing for you!' she cried, shoving him through a narrow door at the far end of the corridor.

Tommy heard it thud shut behind him. The muggy

warmth hit him and he waited for his eyes to get used to the huge, dark auditorium. Better than hanging about the street-corners, he thought. Not that he'd have paid tuppence to see Daisy prancing about up there. But seeing it for free was different. Practicality, not principle, gave Tommy this cast of mind for he'd never in all his fifteen years had the tuppence in his pocket to pay for a ticket.

Daisy hurried back to her crowded dressing room to finish fixing her hair.

Hettie Parsons caught her friend's reflection in the mirror as she pinned a cockade of purple ostrich feathers into her own dark coils. She felt a tiny stab of envy; though she was only twenty-five herself, Daisy's youthful figure seemed to her to be hour-glass perfect. 'Who's it this time, another new gentleman friend?' she asked casually. Her long fingers clipped the head-dress firmly in place. Daisy would be getting into bother one of these days.

Daisy snorted. 'I should say so! No, that was my little brother, Tommy.' She sat alongside Hettie and stole a couple of hairpins. Expertly she wound her long auburn hair into full, soft folds on top of her head.

'You got to be more careful,' Hettie warned. 'One of these days someone's gonna tell Mr Mills and then you're done for.' She'd seen it happen before. If one of the other girls got it in for you, they could easily go telling tales to the manager.

But Daisy just shrugged. 'Here, have one last pull at this lace of mine, will you?' she asked, standing up and turning her back. She breathed in deeply to let Hettie pull the bottom stay holes as tight as they would go.

'If you get much thinner round your waist, you'll vanish,' Hettie warned. But she pulled hard, as requested. Though Daisy's waist was slim, her stays showed the round fullness of her breasts.

'Thanks.' Daisy gave a pert glance at the mirror; chest out, stomach in. Then she went and struggled into her costume, stuffing yards of white petticoat inside the bustled, frilled confection of purple satin and lace.

Up in the gods, Tommy O'Hagan lounged against a brass rail and watched the curtain go up. The lights came on and he squinted down at the stage for a sight of Daisy, but since it was too far for his short-sighted eyes to see he soon gave it up. It was warm and dry, an ideal place for a kip. He slumped in his corner on this, his one shot at luxury, and caught up on some sleep.

Hettie and Daisy stood side by side in the chorus line in their low-cut frocks. They swayed to the music. This wasn't exactly the Alhambra or the Empire, and they weren't Marie Lloyd. So what? They were young and pretty and sang like larks. The Southwark Palace lay open beneath them; row upon row of upturned faces sitting in their plush new velvet seats. They saw the tiers of balconies and boxes, all carved into grapes and cherubs, and painted gold. The heat of the coloured electric lights at their dainty feet and the curling cigarette smoke beyond made them light-headed. They drank in the applause from the galleries. They sang their hearts out before they left the stage to give way to the mother-in-law jokes of Archie Small, resident comic and ladies' man.

Hettie's feet were killing her inside her pointed boots, and her ribcage felt bruised and sore from the rigid whale-bone stays. Her own figure was wearing well; still round in the right places, still slender at the waist. Her luxurious, dark, wavy hair was one of her best points. She held her head high, knowing she could still put on a good show against the likes of Daisy O'Hagan and Mr Mills's newer recruits. And she knew her way around better than they did.

5

Gratefully she eased out of her costume and changed into her street clothes, eager for an hour or two at home with her feet up in front of the fire before they had to come back for the evening show.

A couple of stage-hands came down the corridor, one with a ladder, the other with coils of cable slung over his shoulder. They leaned in at the dressing-room door and winked at the girls.

'Daisy, Daisy, give me your answer do,' they crooned.

Daisy had a sharp retort ready for each of them.

'We going to be here all day?' Hettie asked irritably. Sometimes she wondered why she'd got in with Daisy O'Hagan. After all, she was only a kid of nineteen, new to the halls and too cheeky by half. Though there were only six years between them, Hettie herself was very steady by comparison. Perhaps she felt Daisy needed keeping an eye on. Anyway, she lived close by, just down the court from Hettie, with that ragged family of hers. They shared the same tram ride home.

At last Daisy put on her thin, shabby outdoor coat and she and Hettie stepped through the stage door into the cobbled alleyway and the cold November afternoon. The lamplighters had already been by and brought their small cheer to the main street, so the girls jumped the dark puddles and hurried up there. They soon caught a tram and rode home together past the new Town Hall, across Park Road into the maze of closes and courts just south of London Bridge.

Here they alighted and once again braved the narrow streets.

'Your dad in work just now?' Hettie asked. She buttoned her collar tight and walked quickly past a row of tenements where the gangs hung out.

Daisy shook her head. 'It's been three months since he

6

lost that last job washing bottles. He says it's women's work and wild horses wouldn't drag him back there again. You should've seen his hands though. Cut to shreds they was by that job.'

'And what you lot living on?' Hettie demanded. She knew Daisy was the oldest in a family of six or seven kids. She'd lost count. With old man O'Hagan out of work, there couldn't be much money coming in.

But Daisy stuck her chin out. 'We manage!'

Hettie stopped on the pavement. 'You'll come in and have a cup of tea then?' she asked kindly.

They stood under the lamp at the corner of Duke Street and Paradise Court. Daisy would carry on into the court to reach her home three floors up in one of the old boarding-houses, where she shared just two rooms with her mother and father and all those brothers and sisters. Hettie would step through the double doors of the Duke of Wellington public house, advertising its fine ales in big gold letters and offering a bright welcome to all the thirsty carmen, dockers, railway workers and builders who lived hereabouts. For Hettie and the Parsons tribe, this was home.

Daisy, pale without her make-up under the gaslight, nodded gratefully. 'Don't mind if I do,' she said grandly, taking up the hem of her skirt and sweeping past a group of young lads lounging on the doorstep.

'S'nice night, Ethel!' one cawed, his Adam's apple working up and down his scraggy throat. He wore a peaked cap, but no neck scarf around his collarless shirt.

'I should shay sho!' Daisy called back, unabashed.

The boy's mates went wild with delight. 'You clicked there,' they shouted in a raucous band. 'She your bird?' and, 'Hey, Smudge just got off!' they cried.

Daisy stepped inside the swing doors of the pub into a room full of mahogany tables and shiny mirrors. There was a strong smell of mingled beer and sawdust. The boys' catcalls drifted through. 'Bleeding monkey parade,' she said, her grin as bright as a button. 'Who do they think they are?'

'Did you see that one with the big belt and the white silk scarf?' Hettie giggled. 'Really loves himself, he does.' But she pulled her face straight when she caught her father's severe eye behind the bar. 'Come through,' she whispered quickly to Daisy. 'Come upstairs and put your feet up.' And she led the way.

Arthur Ogden, lounging against the bar, watched them go and heard the boys' surge of raw laughter outside. He hunched over his porter and beckoned to the landlord, Wilf Parsons, known as Duke. 'That girl of yours still working the halls?' he asked. 'Can't you get her into decent work?'

Carefully Duke dried and polished the glass in his hand. He breathed on it and rubbed it sparkling clean. He wasn't going to rise to Arthur's easy bait. Arthur Ogden was a work-shy wastrel with two kids of his own just growing old enough to begin to cause him a problem or two. Duke would defend his own to the hilt, but he didn't want a scrap. So he went carefully. 'Thought you went about for a bit with a girl from the halls?'

Arthur's dull eyes lit up. 'Did once, and that's the God's honest truth. Lovely looking girl, she was, by the name of Maisie.' He sank into reverie.

'Would that be before or after you hitched up with your Dolly?' Duke put in. Arthur Ogden was all hot air as far as women and work went. Besides, mention of his wife, Dolly, was guaranteed to shut him up.

Where Arthur was small and weedy, Dolly was ample. Where Arthur shirked, she grafted. While Arthur boasted and boozed, Dolly would stand and nod with a grin on her wide face until it cracked in two. 'Arthur Ogden,' she'd yell down the street in perfect good humour whenever she

8

heard of his shenanigans, 'that's sixteen women you've had since we tied the knot to my certain knowledge! And according to you every one a stunner!' And Arthur would have the grace to look at his boots and grunt guiltily. 'It's no wonder you nod off by the fire when you get home nights,' Dolly would tease.

Upstairs, the kettle sat singing on the hob. Daisy O'Hagan warmed her feet by the fire and sighed. 'Didn't see hide nor hair of our Tommy after the show,' she grumbled. 'Cheeky little hooligan, ain't got no manners.' She stretched her long legs luxuriously and hitched her skirt well clear of her slim ankles.

'Leave the poor little blighter alone,' Hettie said. She too settled comfortably in a chair on the far side of the hearth. 'Looks as if he could do with a slap-up supper, he does.' Though things had sometimes been tough at the Duke, what with their mother dying when Sadie was born, and their dad being left to cope, the Parsons kids had never gone short of a good square meal at the end of each day.

Hettie felt sorry for kids like Tommy. You saw them everywhere; without so much as a decent pair of shoes to their name, dressed in jackets three sizes too small, ragged-arsed and skinny. Only last week she'd seen young Tommy, desperate to earn a penny, chasing rats for Annie Wiggin down the bottom of the court. Annie hated rats and was prepared to part with real money to be rid of them. 'I'll give you a penny for a pair!' she declared. 'They've got to be still warm, mind you, and none of that rigid mortis. You bring them to me hanging by their horrible little tails. I don't want no stinking old ones you dug up to try and trick me with! Fresh ones, you hear!' And she'd stumped off into her front room to dust, clean and box the stuffing out of her one easy chair.

Hettie waited until Daisy had finished her mug of tea

9

and the doorstep wedge of bread and dripping that she'd given her before she made a move away from the cosy fire. She checked her hair in the mirror over the mantelpiece, and smoothed and tucked her lacy white blouse inside the tiny waistband of her skirt. 'Ain't you got no home to go to?' she grumbled softly. There was no sign in the house of either her older sister, Frances, or of young Sadie. 'Well, it's either get yourself off home or help me with the spuds,' she said. She went through to the kitchen to begin making supper for her father and the boys.

Daisy leapt up, scattering crumbs and swigging down the last of her tea. 'Better go.' She winced at the chilblains on her toes as her warmed feet made contact with the Parsons' hearthrug. 'Ma wants me to mind the little ones. Ta for the tea.'

She was already on her way downstairs when she bumped into Robert Parsons.

'Steady on, where's the fire?' he called. He grabbed her round the waist as she half fell against him. 'Or has our Frances been having a swipe at you two lovely girls again?' He grinned and took a second or two longer than he needed to set Daisy back on her feet. 'She's a bit strait-laced, is Frances. Is that why you're in such a rush?'

With the way down blocked by Hettie's brother, Daisy retreated coyly upstairs. 'Frances ain't in. Hettie's cooking supper,' she reported breathlessly. She felt herself colour up under Robert's brazen gaze. His handsome, moustached face was still grinning below her as she backed off. Beyond him, she caught sight of poor Ernie, trailing after.

'And you mean to say you was on your way without so much as saying hello to me and Ernie?' Robert put his arm around her waist again and swept her back into the living room. 'Even knowing how it makes our day?'

Daisy was reduced to blushes and giggles. Robert Parsons overwhelmed her with his teasing, though she was bold enough with other men. He did it to all the girls, but Daisy was half in love with his hazel eyes and bristling dark moustache.

Hettie marched in from the kitchen, knife in hand. 'Robert, you put Daisy down, you hear. You're a rotten flirt and she has to go and help her ma!' She flashed her brother a cross look. 'And, Ernie, I need some help if anyone's to get anything inside their bellies tonight.'

Ernie set off to obey and follow Hettie back into the kitchen, when Robert stuck out an arm to stop him. He winked. 'Here, Ernie, come and say hello to Daisy first.' There was a broad grin on his face as he loosened his stiff collar. He stuck two fingers inside it and unhooked the metal studs. 'Come on, Ernie, don't be shy.'

Daisy blushed and smiled at slow, awkward Ernie. Though he had Robert's sturdy build and wide brown eyes, and was as good-looking as the rest of the Parsons, he had none of their quickness of mind and speech. He moved forward at half speed, darting glances at his older brother. Daisy thrust out a hand. 'Hello, Ernie,' she said in her animated way, and she gave him a brilliant smile.

Ernie took the hand. It was small and slim. He looked up at Daisy's smooth face, at her grey, dark-fringed eyes and thick auburn hair. 'Hello,' he mumbled, wide-eyed and nodding furiously.

'That's right, Ern,' Robert encouraged. He'd rolled back his shirt-sleeves and now slicked back his hair with his fingertips as he watched Ernie's greeting in the mantelpiece mirror. He turned to Daisy. 'Ernie's always going on about you,' he said. 'He thinks you're a dazzler!'

Daisy's glance was suspicious. 'You're having me on,' she said.

'No, honest.' Robert crossed his arms and studied Daisy.

'He does.' And he began to hum, 'He's half crazy, all for the love of you!'

Ernie stood, enthralled.

'Not funny, I don't think!' Hettie yelled from the kitchen.

'Well, bring him along to the show, why don't you?' Daisy suggested. 'I think he'd like that.' She made a move to go.

Robert nodded slowly, still standing his ground. 'Maybe I will,' he agreed.

Hettie emerged from the kitchen threatening dire consequences if Ernie didn't manage to tear himself away from the lovely Daisy, and Robert sent him up to help while he escorted Daisy back downstairs. He parted with her in the public bar. 'Mind how you go,' he said, holding the door with exaggerated courtesy.

'Here, Robert, there's three barrels standing here waiting for you to tap,' Duke called gruffly from behind the bar. 'Never mind the girls, just for once in your life.'

Robert went off grinning to help his father hammer the brass taps into the new barrels. He took up the heavy wooden mallet they kept on the top cellar step and inserted the first tap with a sharp, expert blow. Then he tapped gently at the bung on the top which would let air into the barrel when they began to draw the beer. It was a skilful job, to be done without loss of liquid and without disturbing the sediment newly settled at the bottom of the barrel. Duke watched and grunted with satisfaction as Robert finished the job.

'I only hope it tastes better than the last lot!' Arthur Ogden said sourly, as he slammed his pint pot on the counter for a refill.

Chapter Two

By 1913, Wilf Parsons, known to all his customers as Duke, had run the pub on the corner of Duke Street and Paradise Court for almost a quarter of a century. He'd seen service in India as a farrier, chosen because of his massive build and his long-time knowledge of horses. His own father had driven a hansom cab, and his father before him. Wilf had been brought up to the ring of iron shoes on the cobbled yard below, and he'd sat alongside his father through the dirty black fogs of many a London winter.

At seventeen the strong lad had joined the army for adventure, and left it at twenty-five with the usual conviction that the sun never set on the British Empire. Army service had impressed upon him the values of orderliness over impending chaos, sternness in the face of insurrection, and a belief in polishing, spitting and polishing again against all the combined forces of darkness.

The army had turned him into an upright, impressive young man who didn't question things deeply. But afterwards he sought a situation minus the constant 'yes, sir, no, sir, three bags full, sir' of life in the army. He knew enough to be his own boss now.

First he must find a wife, and through his father's family he was introduced to a girl in service with a Chelsea property owner. She was the cousin of a cousin, named

13

Patience, and that was her nature too. Pattie, as Wilf called her, was a drudge to the Chelsea family; a tweeny who was as badly treated by the housekeeper and the other servants as she was by the mistress of the house. Up before five each day, she had to clean and lay fires in twelve different rooms before the rest of the household had risen. It was her job to provide hot water for the bedroom pitchers, her job to cart away the lukewarm slops. If a coal scuttle was ever found empty, Pattie felt the housekeeper's stick. She scrubbed and brushed and polished until midnight seven days a week. Bed was a box in a garret.

Duke rescued his Pattie from this slave labour by marrying her. She was just nineteen. He was twenty-six. He found work as a cellarman in a pub in Spitalfields, where his size and muscle came into their own once more. He rolled the great barrels down chutes and up cellar steps with enviable ease, and hoisted the empty ones like toys on to the dray carts. Besides, he never fell sick and he never missed a day through drunkenness, unlike so many in his trade.

While Pattie gave him children to dote on; first Frances, a solemn, round-faced baby with her mother's pale colouring but her father's striking dark eyes; then gurgling, smiling Hettie, so Duke worked his way into the esteem of the pub owner. And when, in 1889, Jess was born, a third daughter and so a cause of disappointment to the burly cellarman, the offer came of a pub of his own.

It meant moving across the water and leaving behind all Pattie's family for new neighbours, new streets. But they went eagerly to set up home above the run-down Duke of Wellington public house at the corner of busy Duke Street and dingy, ramshackle Paradise Court.

Five years on, the family had grown to be as much a part

of the place as the bricks and mortar. Indeed, Wilf had already come to be called 'Duke', and the name had stuck.

When the Parsons moved in with their young family, the Duke itself was one of the old-style beer houses; disreputable home to King Beer and Queen Gin. But the neighbourhood was a warm, closely connected one of men who'd built the underground railways, or who worked the markets and the docks, and women who'd begun to go out to work in the factories and shops. A problem shared was a problem halved, they said. And the Duke was the place to meet and give vent to troubles after work. This was true for the men at least. The women often preferred to stay at home to gossip, or else they chatted on street-corners in fine weather, while their hordes of children played at marbles in the gutter.

Wilf Parsons, or Duke as he now was, wanted to provide a place a notch or two above the standard in the working men's own homes. To that end he painted and spruced the place up with cast-iron tables with glossy mahogany tops. And when money allowed, he lined the walls with beautiful bevelled and etched mirrors and fancy brass brackets for the gaslights. Electricity failed to impress him, however, and he clung for many years to the familiar hiss of gas and the gauzy white mantels.

Meanwhile, Duke's family had increased in size. Robert was born, his pride and joy. The boy was perfect in looks and temperament; impossible to upset and with a ready smile for all the coos and caresses bestowed by his older sisters. Duke felt his heart would burst with pride whenever he took an hour off on a Sunday and walked at the head of his small procession across London Bridge and under the stern white walls of the old Tower.

It almost burst with a more painful emotion before long,

15

however, when he nearly lost Pattie as she bore him their next child. Never strong, she found the complicated labour was almost too much for her, and poor Ernie himself was damaged in some unseen way; not perfect like Robert.

Duke thanked God that Pattie was spared, and for a time they were careful to have no more children. Then, in a kind of gentle, autumn affection, a baby was conceived. It was another troubled pregnancy, and this time Pattie was too weak and worn out to survive the labour. Sadie, another girl, was born, but her mother died to give her life. Duke almost went under from grief, but his own sister, Florrie, stepped in. She pulled things together, and brought up the children while he worked on behind the bar, steadily serving the drinkers of Duke Street and Paradise Court.

Business never slackened and time lessened the hurt, though it never entirely healed the wound. After Pattie's death a strange thing happened to Duke. As if angry with her for dying, he turned to disliking all women. A mild, slightly amused distrust of their fussy, gossipy ways developed, and he could never rid himself of the suspicion that a woman would, given half the chance, worm her way under your skin and into your affections, where she would not be welcome. There was no place there except for Pattie; Duke was adamant about that. It meant he even kept his own daughters half at bay, as if Frances, Hettie, Jess and Sadie would insinuate themselves and coax and steal away a little part of his heart.

Now with Sadie aged fifteen, the rest were practically off his hands. Frances held down her steady job at Boots the Chemist, Hettie had found herself a good life and income treading the boards. Jess was comfortably in service over in Hackney. Robert used a mixture of brain and brawn to pick up any well-paid work that was going in the docks. And Ernie, poor Ernie was at least happy in his own way. All in all, Duke felt that his motherless family had managed to stay on top.

As for himself, he still cut a fine figure. Nearly sixty, respected up and down Duke Street, and in the court, life dealt him little blows, it was true. But nothing serious, nothing he couldn't manage to shrug off.

Now he looked balefully over the top of the shelf he was wiping down as Annie Wiggin marched through the swing doors. Annie was one of life's little blows.

She came up to the bar in her scuffed, unlaced boots and rapped her jug down. Steadily Duke wrung out the rag he was using. Rattle, rattle went Annie's earthenware jug. 'Ain't no one round here got a pint of porter?' she demanded. She rested her elbows on the bar. 'As if my money's not as good as the next man's!' she declared.

Arthur Ogden shuffled a yard or two further down the bar. Annie's sharp tongue was to be avoided. A couple of other young drinkers looked on in casual amusement.

'Men!' Annie proclaimed again. 'All the bleeding same! All over you when they want something from you! Like bleeding December any other time! Freeze to bleeding death standing waiting for any of them! Here, ain't no one going to serve a person!'

Every tea-time Annie shuffled down Paradise Court in her lost husband's cast-off boots. They were the only things he left behind when he went, telling her he was off to sea on another trip and would be back in two weeks. Two weeks soon stretched to two months, and still the old boots dried and curled at the hearthside. After two years to the day, Annie declared him lost at sea and began a life of her own running a haberdashery stall at the local market. She bought and sold vast yards of virginal white lace, bags of beaded, pearled and silvery buttons that sat in their boxes like buried treasure. Her stall was decked with blue and white and cherry-red ribbons, and it was stocked with hooks, needles, pins, scissors and skewers like a miniature torture chamber. And yet Annie herself trudged everywhere in her faithless husband's boots. 'I fell in the cart good and proper marrying him,' she would grumble. 'Still, it's a gamble you have to take.' And so life went on.

As she stood and rattled her jug in Duke's deaf ears, Hettie swept downstairs and into the pub, on her way out to the evening show. She gave Annie a smile and tutted at her father. 'Here, Annie, pass us your jug,' she volunteered. 'I'll fix you up.'

'And tell your dad from me he's too slow to catch bleeding cold,' Annie moaned. Then she looked critically at Hettie's green velvet coat and matching hat, all adorned with feathers and a kingfisher-blue bird's wing, intact and standing proud of the crown. 'Where you been buying your bits and pieces?' she asked suspiciously, with narrowed eyes.

Hettie kept on smiling as she handed back the full jug. 'From you mostly, course!'

'But not that blue item sticking up there.' Annie pointed an accusing finger. 'You never bought that from me!'

'I said "mostly"!' Hettie answered defiantly. 'As a matter of fact, I got this from Coopers'.'

'Ooh, la-di-da!' Annie shrieked. '"As a metter hof fect . . .!" Go on, tell us what you paid for that bit of dead pigeon, Hettie Parsons!' She made fun of Hettie hob-nobbing in the big department store.

'Calm down, Annie.' Hettie came round to the front of the bar and took her by the elbow. 'Got your jug safe? Right then, I'll walk you home. I need to talk to you about some jet buttons I seen on your stall last time I passed.'

'Jet buttons?' Annie heard the words through her dis-gruntled haze. She allowed herself to be propelled smartly between the swing doors and out on to the street. Through

years of practice, the beer stayed in the jug as Annie shuffled
down the cobbled street. Hettie steered her past lamp-posts,
across the court to one of the houses at the bottom. 'Jet
buttons don't come cheap,' she told Hettie as the younger
woman opened her front door. 'But I might be able to do
something special, seeing as it's you,' she promised.

'Thanks a lot! I'll drop by at the stall some time soon.
Night, Annie,' Hettie said good-humouredly. She pulled
her collar high, winked at Tommy O'Hagan in residence
under a nearby lamp-post and stopped to ask him where
Daisy was.

'Gone,' he said darkly. 'Gawd knows where!'

'To work, you ninny!' Hettie told him. It meant she was
late, so she set off up the close at a trot, regretting the
plumage on the green hat after all, for it caught in the wind
and made negotiating the shallow tram step into an art
form that a working girl in a hurry could well do without.

At the tram stop Frances descended as her sister, Hettie,
got on. The women had only time for a quick hello.
'Something up?' Hettie called through a side window.
Frances looked even more serious than usual. And she was
late back from work.

'I've been to see Jess,' Frances replied.

'And?' Hettie craned her head sideways. The feathers in
her hat flapped furiously. She held it on with one hand as
the tram wheels ground, sparked and rattled off.

'Tell you later!' Frances waved. She stood on the pavement in her slim grey jacket. Her fur hat, pulled well down,
was practical and warm. Her gloves were good kidskin
leather. People would take her for a teacher perhaps, or an
officer working for the Relief Board, and they wouldn't
notice the attractive symmetry of her oval face, the fine
brows, the chestnut tint in her hair. She made herself too
severe and plain for that. At twenty-eight, Frances was

considered a long-term spinster. She'd put herself on the shelf by choice at first, and now she was stuck there.

No boys called out to her at the corner of Duke Street, and Arthur Ogden felt unaccountably guilty as she came quietly through the public bar. 'Evening, Miss Parsons,' he said politely. Then he picked up his cap and pulled it firmly on to his head. 'Best be on my way,' he called out to Duke.

Frances smiled and went on up.

Blow it, Arthur thought after she'd gone. What am I saying? Time for another one at least! And he took off his cap again.

Robert had told Frances time and again that she was bad for business.

'How can you say that?' she said, alarmed rather than amused. 'I don't say anything! I don't do anything to make you say that, do I?'

'Exactly!' Robert said, grinning. 'You just are, Frances! Respectable, that's what you are!'

'And that's bad for business?' she retorted. 'Well, then, I'm glad!' She would storm off, unable to take Robert's jokes.

Now she went upstairs with a preoccupied look. As she paused at the top step to take off her hat, she sighed. But the sight of Ernie through in the kitchen, his broad back turned, his figure full of studied concentration as he stood at the sink to wash the dishes, filled her with a rush of warm feeling. She went in quickly and gave him a bright hug of greeting. 'Now tell me about your day,' she said. 'While I toast some cheese here at the fire. Go on, Ernie, who have you seen?'

'Daisy,' he said slowly. He sounded unreasonably happy.

'Good. And what have you done?' Frances relaxed as she knelt by the fire. She held a slice of bread and cheese at arm's length on a long toasting fork.

'Brought up three barrels from the cellar with Robert.'

'Good again! And where's Sadie?'

Ernie plodded on through the pile of dirty plates. He was meticulous about the washing up. 'Don't know,' he decided. 'She's not here.'

Frances nodded. The heat began to send her into deep thought. She remembered the note Jess had sent to the chemist's shop the day before yesterday. 'Dear Frances,' it read. 'Come and see me on Saturday afternoon. I need to talk to you. Love from your sister Jess.'

She'd gone along, puzzled and fearful. Jess had been with the Holdens for three years or more, with no trouble, no complaints. Like everyone else, she had to work hard, but that didn't trouble their family. They'd all been brought up to work. No, it couldn't be that. Frances had opened the iron gate and trodden up to the tradesmen's entrance with increasing worry. She rang the bell. Jess herself came flying down the corridor to answer the door. Frances went in, spent ten minutes with her sister, listening hard.

Then, feeling leaden and slow, she'd come back home on the tram. Now she heard her father's heavy footstep on the stair. Ernie still worked quietly and methodically in the kitchen. Duke came in.

'Joxer's behind the bar for ten minutes,' he said. He sighed and sat down. 'Is there any tea up here?' Duke was practically teetotal and never drank beer or spirits when he was working. Ernie heard, came through for the kettle and took it away to fill it at the tap. 'Good boy,' Duke said.

Frances was still crouched by the fire, but the toasting fork lay on the hearth neglected. The firelight caught her face, flickering shadow then warm red light across it. There were glints of red-gold in her light brown hair. 'Dad,' she sighed, then stopped.

Duke sat in the chair behind her. 'Trouble?' he guessed.

She turned and saw the lines on his face, the years of hard work. She could hardly bear to be the bringer of bad news. 'It's Jess,' she said quietly. She'd promised, she reminded herself. She was the oldest sister and she took the family's troubles squarely on her own shoulders. She would have to tell him. She looked up again at the light of the fire flickering over her father's face.

He looked down at her and guessed the truth. 'She hasn't, has she?' he said sadly. There was no need to go into any details; he just knew.

'She has.' Frances nodded.

Duke sat and looked for a long time into the fire. 'And?' he prompted at last.

Frances swallowed hard. 'She wants to know will you take her back?' she said. 'Jess asked me to ask you, can she come home?'

Chapter Three

Duke soon went downstairs again to take over from Joxer at the bar. He had given no definite answer to Frances's anxious question on her sister Jess's behalf.

'Don't rush me,' he said. 'Jess has got herself into this mess. She ain't the first and she definitely won't be the last.' He went straight down and gruffly told the cellarman to get off home. He served beer to his customers in his usual steady way. So, his third and troublesome daughter was in a spot of bother. He wouldn't be pushed into a rash decision, he'd told Frances. Maybe she could come home to have the child, maybe not. But then he thought of the gutter women, clutching ragged bundles to their thin chests, who sold themselves for sixpence to put bread in their little ones' mouths. He saw them down the dingy back courts, white-faced flotsam of the city. No daughter of his must come to that. Duke held a glass up to the light and polished it for a third or fourth time.

'Fill 'er up.' Arthur Ogden was into the slurred phase of his night's drinking. 'Make it 'alf an' 'alf.' He grinned across at Sadie Parsons, who seemed to his bleary gaze to be a golden angel in a halo of gaslight. She stood by the door, having just come in, heralded by a gust of sharp, cold air.

'About time,' Duke called sharply to her. 'Where you been till this time?'

23

'I been at Maudie's like I said.' Sadie took off the tartan beret perched jauntily on the back of her head, walked over and threw it down on the shiny bar top. She ducked under the counter to join her father amidst the bottles and barrels. 'Remember, I said I was going to Maudie's house.' She gave him a bright, conciliatory peck on the cheek.

'Yes, and missed all the chores,' Duke grumbled. 'Hettie had to make supper with no one around to lend a hand.'

'What about Frances?' Sadie settled unconcerned on to a high stool behind the bar. Her bright, thick hair tumbled in a loose plait to her waist, chestnut brown against her white blouse. She was the prettiest of the Parsons girls, with all the shine of undimmed youth. Her face was a small triangle of pleasing features; dark eyes widely set and heavily lashed, a small, straight nose and soft, full mouth whose pouts and smiles would soon storm the stoutest hearts. And she flitted between school and friends' houses and home with a carelessness that her sister Frances had never had, an innocence long since gone from Hettie's life, and the delicate beauty shared by all the sisters, Jess included. 'I thought Frances would be here,' she repeated. Her father was in a bad mood about something, so she must sit and humour him.

'She had to go to see Jess,' Duke said, short and sharp. 'It's too much to get Hettie to do everything, what with her going out again at night.'

Sadie nodded. 'I'm sorry, Dad, I never thought.'

'You never do, you young ones. That's your trouble. Just you wait till you're finished with school and working in the rope factory down the road. See how you like it.' He grumbled on. The rope factory was his worst threat, but he was serious in his own mind about being stricter with Sadie, to make up for the mistakes he'd made with Jess. Jess had always been headstrong, and look now! If she could get herself into trouble as easy as this, without Sadie's looks, think what might happen to the youngest girl in a year or two!

'I'm not working in no rope factory!' Sadie protested. 'I'm gonna work in a hat shop.' She swung her legs off the stool and landed daintily on the floor.

'Course you are,' Arthur Ogden encouraged. 'Pretty as a picture, she is, Duke. Can't send her to work in no factory.' He hunched over the bar and peered at Sadie. 'Just like my Amy. She's gone into hats!'

'She never!' Sadie went up to him to learn more. Amy Ogden, Arthur's daughter, had been a year or two ahead of her at school. She'd worked for a time on Annie's stall straight after she left, but that meant being out in the cold in all weathers and she didn't take to it. Sadie hadn't heard this latest development. 'Is your Amy in a big store up the West End selling hats?' It was Sadie's own dream come true.

Arthur frowned and shook his head, slopping his beer in the process. 'Not exactly. Dolly found a place for her at Coopers'.'

Coopers' Drapery Stores was at the top end of Duke Street by the railway line. Still, it was one up from a job on the market. Sadie pictured her working with ribbon and lace. She'd be selling those huge, frothy hats you saw in Coopers' big plate-glass windows.

'Dolly works in "Hosiery",' Arthur explained. 'So she got a place for Amy in "Hats".'

'She makes them, does she?' Sadie was still eager to know more about the latest fashions worn by the better off ladies.

Arthur nodded. 'Top hats. My Amy puts the greaseproof band inside to stop the oil on their heads from staining the silk lining. Very posh hats, they are.' He looked pleased with his daughter's achievements and smiled sloppily into his drink. 'Mind you, she works long hours, and it's only seven pence for two dozen hats.'

'It's a job, ain't it?' Duke said. He wiped the stains around Arthur's glass as he kept an eye on the door. Chalky White and his gang had just come in. 'Go up and get something to eat,' he told Sadie. 'And no messing.'

Sadie made a face. She ducked under the counter, too late to avoid the bunch of new customers advancing on the bar.

Chalky White was well known on Duke Street and down the court, where he lived in a squalid corner in one of the cheapest rooms rented out to workmen. In his late twenties, he worked as a warehouseman on Albion Dock, but this was only a front for the many dodgy deals he was involved in. Everyone knew Chalky cheated his way along the waterfront, earned plenty, then blew the money on the clubs and halls. He was over six feet tall, kept fit at Milo's, the local boxing club, and had a reputation for knowing how to handle himself in a fight. He was a flashy dresser and didn't mind spending the easy money on the string of women he went around with. But they didn't like his temper. 'You never know where you are with Chalky,' they said. 'He'd as soon hit you in the gob as give you a kiss.' They quickly dropped him, and afterwards every one had a tale to tell about Chalky's drunken rages. Yet when he was sober and dolled up for a night out, he could be hard to refuse. 'He's got a way with him,' they warned. 'You have to watch out.'

He swaggered in ahead of four or five mates and caught sight of Sadie. 'Oh my, what lucky fellow's walking out with you?' he called with a low whistle. He jostled his pals with his elbows.

Sadie stopped in her tracks. She blushed and looked back at Duke.

'Go on up,' he repeated.

'What's the rush?' Chalky said. He leaned against the door. 'I only want to know who's her beau. It's not one of them little ikeys hanging around out there, is it? You're too good for any of them, you know!'

Sadie blushed a deeper red. 'I'm not walking out with no one,' she said, gathering her dignity. 'And if I was, it wouldn't be with any of them hooligans.'

'Quite right. Like I said, a girl like you can afford to be a bit choosy, can't she, Arthur?'

Chalky got one step bolder, reached out and took Sadie's arm. Then he advanced her with mock gallantry towards the bar, surrounded by his friends. Arthur grabbed his cap and prepared to leave. If there was trouble brewing he wanted to be well clear of it. 'Don't ask me,' he mumbled. There was an inch of beer left in his pint glass. He gulped it down, jammed his cap on his head and called out his farewells. Duke was getting up a head of steam back there behind the bar at the way Chalky was messing his girl about. 'Night all!' He threaded his way to the door between smoky tables. Everyone had a wary eye on the Chalky White gang. They knew Duke wouldn't stand any nonsense.

But as Arthur scuttled out into the street, Robert Parsons came in. Quickly he sized things up, threw his cigarette to the floor and moved in on Chalky. Stockier than the glib warehouseman, but smaller by four or five inches, Robert squared up. Both his hands were clenched into fists, resting at hip height. He thrust out his broad chest and his dark moustache seemed to bristle with anger. White looked down at him, a superior smirk stretched across his thin lips. 'Watch it, boys, I think we got trouble,' he sneered.

Sadie had backed off against the bar into the space afforded by Arthur Ogden's hasty exit. She felt hot tears of

27

shame brim and prick her eyelids. 'Leave off, Robert,' she pleaded. 'He ain't doing no harm.'

'No, and if you'd done as I told you and gone upstairs when you was asked, we could all have been spared this blooming circus!' Duke snapped.

Sadie fled, her cheeks wet.

Duke leaned forward on the bar, his hands spread wide. He didn't mind Robert showing Chalky White who was boss if necessary, but he cast a worried eye over the empty glasses ranged along the bar top. Quickly he removed them to a safe place in the stone sink. Other customers cleared a space around the two men and an air of tense expectation spread through the room. One or two of the boys hanging about on the doorstep crept in to watch the fight.

'That's my little sister,' Robert began slowly. His eyes swivelled from Chalky to the heavy mob ganged up behind him. He'd already clean forgotten his own flirting with Daisy O'Hagan earlier that evening. In his book that was innocent fun, whereas Chalky White was a dirty-minded lout who couldn't even keep his foul mouth and hands off a fifteen-year-old girl. His fists were raised to chest level now, thrust out in front of him. He'd fight the lot of them if he had to.

'You don't say!' Chalky's insulting grin stiffened. He pulled at the white cuffs of his best shirt, then back went his shoulders. He cleared his throat. 'Now look,' he said. 'No point taking this any further, is there?'

A disappointed sigh went round the room like a great barrage balloon beginning to deflate and sag. Chalky's mates backed off. Chalky himself thrust his hands into his trouser pockets. 'I'll give you a fight any time you want, down at Milo's that is. But just now I'm busy and my mind's on other things.' He grinned, still casually twisting the knife. 'And I got all my best clobber on.'

Robert's glance ran over Chalky's grey silk necktie neatly knotted between the peaks of his high white collar. He wore a dark waistcoat fully buttoned, with a fancy gold watch chain slung in two loops across his chest. A long fitted jacket over lighter grey trousers and soft leather shoes completed the outfit. It was best clobber all right. Most East-Enders would never hope to own a suit of clothes like that. If they had one once for their own wedding day, it was in pawn by now and only got out for funerals. Robert snorted in disgust. He turned on his heel. Chin thrust out, he headed straight upstairs to rant at soft-headed Sadie.

Chalky winked at his mates. He turned and leaned on the bar. 'Six pints of best bitter,' he said to Duke, staring him out without flinching. 'And have one for yourself.'

Duke nodded. He drew from the barrel into a jug, then poured the beer with expert ease, giving each pint a good head. His own gaze was steady as he took Chalky's money. 'You lot heading somewhere special?' he asked.

'Up the Palace,' Chalky replied, smooth and easy.

'Best be quick. Show's started.' Duke slammed the coins in the till and turned back. 'They won't let you in if you're late.'

Chalky swatted the air and grinned. 'I'm best pals with Fred Mills, the manager,' he explained. 'He always lets us in, no bother.' He paused. 'Reckon we can still get an eyeful of one of your girls up there without being flattened by your Robert. And very nice too.'

Duke watched the froth from the beer stick to the sides of Chalky's glass as he downed his pint. He stood his ground, like one of the cart-horses his father had driven. Scum like Chalky didn't deserve an answer. He lived like a pig in his filthy room so he could squander all his money on women, booze and clothes. Down any court, in any tenement block, you could find a bad penny. Chalky was that penny in Paradise Court. Only when he finally swaggered out through the doors and tossed a coin to the waiting gang of boys could Duke breathe freely in his own pub.

Dolly Ogden glanced at the clock on the wall as her husband's unsteady footsteps clattered down the passage towards the back kitchen. He fell down the three steps into the room. She didn't look up again until she'd put the finishing touch to the seam on the stocking she was busy with, then she added it to the creamy pile on the table. By this time Arthur had staggered to his feet.

'Gawd's sake, man, stand up!' she said, as Arthur flopped into the wooden rocking-chair she'd just vacated. But she sighed as she assessed his condition and gave up the struggle. Instead, she shook a pair of stockings free of the silky pile, rolled them up from the toes and tucked the top band of one around the whole roll to secure them together. Then she stacked them at the far end of the table for Amy to count.

Amy, at seventeen, found her father's drunkenness more difficult to bear. 'He stinks of the pub!' she whispered, standing with her back to him.

'Yes, and he's your father,' Dolly reminded her.

Amy shook her head fiercely at this lack of logic. She felt a hairpin or two loosen and a broad swathe of blonde hair threaten to fall free. She fixed it back in place. 'How can I ever bring anyone back when he comes home in this condition?' she demanded in a high and mighty tone.

'Why, who do you want to bring back here?' Dolly went to the fire to swing the battered tin kettle on to the hob.

'I'm just saying *if. If* I wanted to bring someone home!' Amy said exasperated. She was a younger version of her mother, already slightly plumper than was fashionable, but with a developing sense of her own style and grace. She wore her waist nipped in tight, and made sure that her dark-blue day dress made the most of her full breasts and hips. Her arms, which she considered too heavy, were carefully draped with full, lacy sleeves, but the plumpness showed at her wrists and ankles. Still, her blonde hair was naturally thick and wavy. She didn't need to pad it out with wire frames like some girls did.

'Well, until you do,' Dolly said with raised eyebrows, 'just count these stockings for me and count your blessings while you're at it.' And she went across to bang about at the sink in the corner, rinsing cups, straining out tea-leaves from the cracked brown pot to see if they could be reused once more.

Among the blessings Amy felt she could count were the recent attentions at work of the boss's son, Teddy Cooper. She thought of him now as she stacked up the stockings.

Teddy was always coming and poking his nose into the hatters' workshop. He pretended to check the work, but really he came to stop and chat with some of the better looking girls. 'Hats' was way up in the rear attics above Coopers' shop, up the back stairs and loosely supervised by Bert Buggles, who was as silly as his name suggested.

Bert always had his long, thin nose stuck into the racing papers. He didn't care tuppence what the lads and girls under him got up to, unless Mr Cooper himself stepped up with an especially important order. Then he became suddenly strict in a mincing sort of way. Hat trade was generally poor, and Amy certainly hadn't found the pressure of work too great since she'd come to Coopers' last autumn, unlike her poor mother in 'Hosiery'.

When Teddy Cooper put in his daily appearance in 'Hats', he didn't usually affect Bert's interest in the winner

31

of the Epsom 2.30. The girls were free to spoon with the young man to their hearts' content. And it seemed to her that she, Amy, was his chosen one. He singled her out for special comment, praising her hair and pretty blue eyes. Once he even put an arm around her waist and popped a chocolate from his coat pocket into her surprised mouth. Yesterday he had whispered a promise to take her to the Balham Empire if she was good. She'd never been to the cinematograph.

Amy cast a sideways glance at her sleeping father. She'd already decided to keep quiet about Teddy Cooper, since there was never any risk of having to bring a young gentleman like him home to meet her ma and pa. Still, she'd go out to see *The Perils of Pauline* with him since he'd asked, and she'd have a good time on the quiet. A girl deserved to be given a chance.

It was all right for her brother, Charlie. He was a boy. They'd always thought Charlie would amount to something, right from the start. Now, with his scholarship and his big ideas, they'd been proved right. As for Amy, they thought the hatters was good enough. The local women blessed the ground Mr Jack Cooper trod on for keeping them all in work. Teddy, though, called his old man a pompous prig. Amy stifled a laugh at the memory.

'What's up now?' Dolly asked. She woke Arthur and practically ladled the weak tea down his throat.

'Nothing.' Amy wasn't telling.

'You don't laugh at nothing, leastways not if you're right in the head. Must be something,' Dolly grumbled on. 'Just tell Charlie to come down here a minute, will you. I want him to run up to the Duke to ask how much the old man's put down on the slate tonight. He'll only lie to me if I ask him straight.' She took it all for granted. Arthur would drink. She'd sew stockings. She'd pay for his beer and hope there was money left over to pay for a shoulder of bacon or some sheep's liver a couple of times a week. If not, well, there was no point losing sleep. Dolly's broad face rarely registered emotion, but she laughed uproariously when she got the chance, usually at puny Arthur's expense.

Charlie came down and took on the errand, ungracious as only a fifteen-year-old boy can be. His head hung down, his eyes stared at the dark stone flags. 'You know I hate going up to that place,' he moaned.

'Oh, la-di-da!' Dolly mocked. 'That place, as you call it, is home from home for your pa. And Duke Parsons is a decent sort. Now you get yourself up there and find out how much we owe him, or else!' Her voice rose to a bellow. Charlie scuttled off.

'Ma!' Amy protested as the door slammed shut.

'Well!' Dolly pulled off Arthur's worn-out jacket and slung his inert arm around her broad shoulder. 'What is he when all's said and done? A little stool-arsed jack, that's what! Here, Amy, be a good girl, help me get your pa to bed.' Dolly brooked no argument in her own house. Amy and Charlie did as they were told.

Chapter Four

The gang of boys hanging around the front steps of the Duke was one reason why Charlie loathed this errand. Though he was older than most of them, it was hard to hold his own against the insults they chucked at him. And he usually had to dodge the odd hob-nailed kick.

'Go boil your head!' he muttered. He wrenched himself free from the grasp of a little O'Hagan, no more than nine or ten years old and desperate to rise in the gang's estimation.

The kid tried to link arms with him again.

'Ooh!' the others cried. 'Shall we? Shall we stroll 'cross the Common?'

They swung their hips as girls did, mimicking a woman's walk. 'Get lost!' Charlie yelled. He freed himself and practically fell forward into the passage leading into the bar. Quickly he made his way through the groups of men standing and sitting in the smoke-filled room. 'How much does my pa owe?' he asked. He had to raise his voice and yell over the sound of the pianola playing away in a far corner. The tune broke off before Duke had time to reply.

Duke consulted the slate. 'Well, young man, he downed five pints of Bass and two pints of half and half. Tell your ma she owes nine pence three farthing.' His answer sailed loud and clear across the room. Charlie nodded his thanks. He felt the hairs at the nape of his neck prickle with embarrassment. He would never get used to this. All he could hope now was that the gang outside would be off down the street on a game of knock-down ginger, hammering on the door of some helpless old woman. As long as they found someone else to annoy he didn't care. Stopping in the passage by the door to button his jacket and steel his nerves, he looked up and saw Sadie coming downstairs.

'Hello, Charlie.' She hugged a big cast-iron pan in front of her, but still stepped swift and sure through the door which he held open for her. She wore her tartan beret, a dark coat and a big blue woollen scarf wound high around her neck. Her long plait and short skirts swung as she turned down the street. 'Are you on your way home?' she called back.

Charlie fell in beside her. 'Yes. Where are you taking that?' The gang had melted away; no fear of being kicked and put down in front of Sadie. It was because he stopped at school and studied instead of hopping the wag with the rest. That's why they called him names; he wouldn't join in with the crowd.

Sadie sighed and raised her eyebrows. 'Frances says I have to take it down the court to the O'Hagans. One of the little ones ain't right. I dunno.' Her lace-up boots tapped along the stone pavement. 'It's a pan of broth,' she explained. 'Frances boiled the ham bones with some pearl barley. She says it's good for you when you're feeling under the weather.'

Charlie strode along. He glared at the little O'Hagan kid, who scuttled on ahead of them now, barefoot, heading for home. He was skinny as a whippet in his threadbare rags. 'Must've smelt the broth,' Charlie noted. He stopped by the door of his own terraced house. At least the steps were clean and scrubbed. His ma did her best, not like some.

'You going straight in?' Sadie asked. 'Why not come down with me instead?' She felt she had to be bold with Charlie Ogden. He was too slow to take things up on his own account, with his nose always glued to a book.

Just lately she'd noticed that behind the buttoned-up jacket and serious manner lurked something interesting and attractive. He was a good head taller than she was, with what she called a nice face. His features were fine and regular, unlike most of the lumpy-skinned, misshapen faces of many of the boys at school. She'd decided to set her cap at him.

'No,' Charlie said after a moment's hesitation. He stared at his ma's whitened steps. She made a border down each side with carefully applied donkey-stone. 'Thanks.' He took the three steps at once and disappeared through the door.

'Thanks for nothing!' Sadie huffed. She tip-tapped on down to the end of the court.

'What's that?' Tommy enquired, sniffing the air. He'd appeared from the cellars of the tenement block like a jack-in-the-box. Now he poked his nose at Sadie's pan and lifted the lid with a grimy hand.

She smacked it smartly. 'Leave off, Tommy. It's broth for your sick brother, that's what. Anyhow, what you got there?' She pointed to a big square object sticking out from behind his back.

He side-stepped, angling to get past without showing what he had hidden. But a tiny, pitiful cheeping sound gave his game away. 'Cage birds,' he said, giving himself over to a couple of minutes' delay. Girls went soft over cage birds.

'Oh, Tommy!' Sadie said. Her face lit up. She put the soup down on the black, greasy pavement. 'Let's have a look. Oh, they're pretty. Where did you get 'em?' Inside Tommy's wire cage, with its bent and battered ribs, perched two ruffled larks. Their breasts sagged mournfully, their round, black eyes blinked with shock.

Tommy held up his property for inspection. 'Railway embankment,' he told her proudly. 'I limed 'em myself.'

'Oh.' Sadie's voice was less enthusiastic. 'Poor little mites. But will someone buy them?' She hoped the pathetic things would last the night. Knowing Tommy, he'd have no food to give them.

He nodded. 'I'm off back up the Palace to catch the crowd coming out. There's always a lady there can get her beau to buy her a songbird.'

Sadie sighed and picked up her pan of broth. 'Best of luck then.' She turned and went on her way. He was never short of ideas, but then you had to look out for yourself in a family like that. Funny, she thought, Tommy's the same age as me and Charlie, but you'd never guess it. He had the face of a fifty-year-old stuck on the body of a runty little kid. She was still shaking her head as she climbed the narrow stairs with the broth, up to the top floor of the block. This was what Tommy called home.

Mary and Joe O'Hagan and their family lived in two rooms at number 48 Paradise Court. It was a bleak, bare-fronted tenement of blackened bricks and grimy windows, butted up against a blank stretch of factory wall and facing out on to another identical block across the narrow cobbled street. Their two rooms, a kitchen and a bedroom, lay at the back of the building, shut off from fresh air and sunlight. Down on the ground floor they shared an earth closet with a dozen other families in the block. Up here in the garret, Mary O'Hagan brought in washing and stood at the wooden tub all day and most of the night with her board, her scrubbing brush and soap.

Sadie tapped at the door and went straight in. Joe O'Hagan sat at the bare table, an empty look in his eyes. He was small and thin, with a hangdog bearing, as if kicks were all he ever expected from life, and all he ever got. Beaten down in body and soul, terrible things took place around him. It was as much as he could do each morning to stumble into his worn trousers and button up his frayed shirt. Then he would sit, bent over the table, vacant and listless, while Mary thumped at the washing-board. Meanwhile, Daisy would smarten herself up at the piece of broken mirror propped on the bedroom sill. Tommy would be out early to beg and scrounge, while the little ones swarmed from kitchen to bedroom, and up and down the dark stairs.

Sadie put the broth on the table. 'Frances sent it,' she said quietly. Peering through the door into the bedroom, she saw a small child lying on a bed under an old blanket. 'How is he?' she asked.

Mary came forward. She wiped her red hands on a coarse apron and shook her head. The pan lid rattled as she lifted it to peer inside. Again she said nothing, but took it to the mean fire in the grate and set it to heat there. Sadie bent and lifted a little one from the floor. She set the child against one hip. Another came and tugged at her skirt.

'You heard the tale, did you?' Joe O'Hagan opened his mouth and the flat, Irish voice drifted across the room. The silent, round-eyed children turned curiously towards him. 'I expect that's why you was sent.'

'Joe, Sadie doesn't want to listen to all our moans and groans,' Mary reminded him. 'We're just waiting on the few shillings Daisy gives us each week, then we can fetch the doctor,' she explained.

Sadie nodded uncomfortably. The child in the bed coughed and turned.

'Aye, but I went before the Board today.' Joe insisted on telling the whole story, his peaky face pale and set. 'I've lost three kids to Paradise Court, and I'll be damned before it's a fourth. We need a doctor. So I went before the Board. "My child has to see a doctor," I tell them. "He has the fever bad. He sleeps five to a bed with the other children. Without a doctor I doubt he'll last the weekend."' Joe paused to study the wood grain on the table. '"And have you no money at all coming into the house?" they ask me. "Nothing to pay for the care of your own child?" I explain we're waiting for Daisy's few shillings. They look me up and down. "And have you no better off family to help you?" Where would I have better off family? My three brothers are all in Dublin, and I wish I was too. I've been here fifteen years, in work and out. Why did I come to the Board if it wasn't necessary, I say?' Joe raised his fist and thumped it weakly on to the table. Mary raised her apron to hide her face. Sadie hugged the child.

'So they turn me away at last. "Wait for your daughter to come home tonight with the money you need to pay your own way." One of them marches me out of the office. "And next time you come before us, I advise you to wear a suit," he says. I say to him, if I had a suit, I'd *pawn* it and pay for a doctor myself. I wouldn't go to the likes of him.'

A hush fell on the room as Joe stopped for breath. It was broken by the child coughing and Mary sniffing. 'Daisy will bring us the doctor,' she promised.

'Aye, not those nice bastards over there.' Joe sat, wrapped in misery.

'Joe!' Mary remonstrated. She turned and took the child from Sadie, then went and bent over the pot on the fire. Strands of greying hair fell forward on to her face. With a weary gesture she pushed them back. She was worn out.

'Daisy's a good girl, and she's good to us,' she told Sadie as she stirred the broth.

'Oh aye,' Joe said, hollow-voiced. 'Working in a place like that!'

Sadie left them while Joe issued dire warnings about the consequences of working at the Palace and Mary took a shallow bowl of broth through to her sick child. When she got back to the Duke, she ran straight upstairs to Frances, fell against her shoulder and cried her eyes out. Life was hard down Paradise Court.

Hettie and Daisy came off-stage for the last time that night, just as Archie Small went on for his final session of wisecracks and songs.

'Hello, girls!' He winked as their paths crossed backstage.

'I'm melting!' Daisy gasped. 'Gawd, them lights don't half give off some heat!' She still held the smell of hot dust and metal in her nostrils.

'I'll soon cool you down,' Archie leered. 'Just you wait!'

Daisy glanced at Hettie and mirrored her friend's expression of disgust. 'Ugh!' She gave a little shiver and they ran for the dressing room, jostled by the other girls, crying out their exhaustion.

'Let's have a bit of hush down there,' the stage-manager warned. 'Get yourselves off home before Mr Mills comes and catches you making all that racket.'

'No need to tell us,' Hettie called back. 'You won't see me for dust.' She staggered ahead of Daisy into the room, jockeyed for a chair and fell backwards into it. 'My poor feet!' She moaned. The place was swirling with discarded silk dresses and petticoats, reeking of hot bodies and face powder. The amount of female flesh on view would fill fifty seaside postcards. Hettie bent double to pull off her heeled boots, snagged a nail on her stocking and sent a ladder shooting from ankle to thigh. 'Oh gawd, bang goes my wages!' she cried.

'Come on, Hettie, help me out of this.' Daisy stood over her, demanding help with the tight bodice. 'I gotta get home.'

'That's a turn-up.' Hettie hoisted herself out of the chair to loosen the lace that kept Daisy's waist nipped in so tight. She heard Daisy groan. 'Why, what's the rush?'

'Nothing.'

Both women vanished for a few seconds beneath yards of crimson silk. They emerged, hairstyles miraculously intact. Then they hung the dresses on the rack and scrambled for their street clothes.

'Anyone seen Freddie?' Daisy asked.

'Freddie' was what they called Mr Mills when his back was turned. 'Hasn't he got them wages down here yet?'

'Not bleeding likely,' someone muttered. Greasepaint came off left, right and centre, leaving pale, tired faces in the mirror. 'When did he ever rush down with the wages, you tell me!'

Daisy shrugged herself into her dowdy jacket and set her hat at a sideways angle. She rubbed at her cheeks to encourage a faint pink glow. 'Ready?' she asked Hettie.

'Blimey.' Hettie eyed Daisy. 'I said, where's the fire?'

'Nowhere. Only, I have to get back.'

Hettie vaguely remembered Frances mentioning a little brother ill at home. She knew, too, that Daisy's wage was practically all that kept body and soul together at number 48. Suddenly the rush to get off home made sense. 'Half a tick,' she said. 'And I'll be with you.'

But they were still standing inside the stage door twenty minutes later, waiting for Freddie to show up. Archie Small was already off-stage, pursued by raucous laughter. He bounded down the corridor towards the bunch of girls who were kicking their heels by the door.

'Still here, darling?' He slid up to Daisy and snatched her by the waist. 'Just waiting for Archie.'

Daisy wriggled free. 'Leave off, you horrible little man!'

Archie wore a loud checked suit, with spats and patent leather pumps. His bow-tie nestled against several spare chins, and his waistcoat buttons strained against a large belly. His hair was slicked to one side to conceal a mottled bald patch. 'She only says that because she likes me!' He winked at the other girls.

Daisy jabbed him hard with her elbow.

'Hush, here comes Freddie!' someone warned.

They quietened down as the manager approached, and Archie went off to lounge in an alcove, where he lit up a cigarette. 'Bleeding nuisance!' Daisy muttered to Hettie. She stood anxiously in line to receive her wages.

Fred Mills took his time. He made the most of the power of his position. Tonight he'd brought along some friends to 'meet the girls'. Everyone knew what that meant. Most backed away, sullen and offhand.

'Hettie, I'd like you to meet Mr White.' Mills pressed a few coins into Hettie's palm and drew her forward by the wrist.

Hettie had already recognized Chalky and his gang. Just our luck, she thought, knowing that Daisy was keen to be off. It could mean having to stay behind for a drink at least. She wished she'd taken less care with her outdoor dress. The blue feathers on her hat winked and shone.

'We already met,' Chalky said. 'In fact, we're neighbours, you might say. Hello, Hettie.' He glanced at his pals to measure their approval. 'We was just having a chat with your Robert earlier, wasn't we?' As he turned back to study her, she felt every stitch of her clothing being removed in his mind's eye. But she wouldn't drop her gaze, not for a king's ransom.

'And Daisy!' Chalky oozed the famous charm. He passed a hand through his hair, and when Daisy felt her own hand raised to his lips, she could smell the sickly sweet macassar oil that darkened and slicked down his short cropped style. He hung over her, standing much too close, as bandy-legged Mills passed on down the row of girls. Still, she'd got her wages clutched tight in her other hand.

Jealousy was too strong a word to describe the sensation Archie Small felt when he saw Chalky and his mates ogling fresh-faced Daisy O'Hagan. But he was peeved. He'd set his own mind on that little girl. Anyway, he pushed himself clear of the cold brick wall and strolled towards the group. He approached warily. His difficulty was that Chalky White was a friend of the manager. Even Archie had to mind his p's and q's if he wanted to go on cracking jokes at the Palace alongside the performing Jack Russells and the fez-wearing conjurors. He couldn't risk antagonizing Fred Mills. 'I found us that taxi-cab, girl,' he said, sidling between Daisy and Hettie. 'I got it waiting for us up on the street.'

Chalky's grin tightened. Daisy frowned. Hettie dug her in the ribs. 'Come on!' she whispered. This was their chance to get straight off. Once outside, they could ditch Archie and head for the tram.

'What you girls want with a taxi-cab?' Chalky wheedled. 'We can walk you home, can't we, boys?'

A chorus of agreement followed.

'See. We're even going your way.' Chalky looked down at Archie. 'Run along to your old lady, why don't you? Let a dog see the rabbit.'

Archie felt his forehead break out into a sweat. He clenched his teeth. Daisy was a fool. She'd been slow to catch on and Chalky had got the better of him in full view of all the other girls. Well, she'd be sorry. He backed off in a foul temper, glaring at Hettie as if it were her fault.

Hettie shrugged. Daisy *was* a fool if she thought Chalky White was any better than Archie Small. Hadn't she heard the stories about him?

'Ain't you supposed to get straight back home, so they can fetch the doctor?' she reminded her.

'That's right.' Daisy still met Chalky's bold gaze. 'Another time, maybe.'

But Chalky wouldn't let it drop. He'd made up his mind that Daisy was his girl, for tonight at least. 'Who's sick?' he asked, as he took her by the arm.

'My little brother, Jim. Ma says he's bad.'

'He ain't croaking, is he? Anyhow, what doctor would turn out at this time of night?' Chalky winked at Fred Mills and turned Daisy around towards the door. 'Now just be nice, Daisy girl, and keep a poor man happy!'

The manager glared at Daisy.

She sighed and shrugged. 'Just for half an hour then.'

Little fool, Hettie thought again.

But Chalky paraded Daisy up to the stage door. He winked at Mills again, and glanced back to check that someone else had grabbed Hettie and the pair were following. Hettie found herself on the arm of a small-time crook called Syd Swan, who grinned at her like a lunatic and dragged her along.

Outside, the cold air blasted them. Further up the alley, she saw the tall figure of Chalky White already pressing against Daisy, one arm over her shoulder, the other roaming over her body. He kissed her long and hard. Hettie stared at Syd. 'Don't you try nothing!' she warned, and marched firmly ahead of him up the alley, past the spooning pair.

At least Daisy had the sense to keep up. Two minutes

later, Hettie heard rapid footsteps. Chalky passed by, linked up with Daisy. He sang a cocky little song about taxi-cabs:

'To newly wedded couples, it's the best thing that is
    out,
It fairly beats the hansom cab, without the slightest
    doubt.'

Daisy laughed and ran ahead, like a little flirt. Her laugh showed her even, white teeth and she poked out her pink tongue at Chalky. Hettie looked on as he swung Daisy in the air and landed her again with both hands round her waist.

'When driving to the station to go on honeymoon,
The driver can't look through the top to watch you
    kiss and spoon.'

He sang in a raw voice but Daisy laughed on delightedly. They had to walk all the way home in the drizzling rain through the still crowded streets. 'One last drink,' Chalky said, as the Duke came into view. 'Come on, girls, one last drink never hurt no one.'

Daisy looked doubtful. She glanced down Paradise Court to her black tenement at the bottom. Inside the Duke, the pianola thumped out a tune. Lights glittered through the fancy scrolls and lettering of the etched glass doors.

'I never ask twice,' Chalky said, one hand on the giant brass handle.

'Right you are,' Daisy agreed. She swept in ahead of the rest. 'One last drink!'

She enjoyed all the eyes on her as she flounced up to the bar with Chalky White.

Chapter Five

The pub was crowded out with dockers, carters and market traders all having a fling after a hard week. If you had a few coppers to enjoy yourself you came out. Back home, your old woman would moan on about the cost of this and that, with a long face and a surefire tendency to make it look like your fault if bread had gone up by a farthing a loaf that week. Here at the Duke there was music, a decent place to sit, or the chance to have a knees-up if you felt in the mood. Besides, coming out with your mates was a sign you were getting work, holding your own. It was a bad week if you didn't make it down the Duke on a Saturday night.

The men crowded round the bar. They'd come through another bad year, with more strikes on the docks and down the markets. Nothing had moved through the East End for months as the fruit and veg lay rotting in great piles in the warehouses. You had to live hand to mouth then and your family nearly starved. During August they'd even cut off the water and gas, and then there were hundreds of rats running through the uncollected rubbish.

Now, at the onset of winter, things were better, though union pressure rumbled on and the bosses still didn't give an inch if they could help it. You still queued on the waterfront for your day's work, slipping someone a back-hander for a better chance. But at least the food moved out of the docks now and on to the markets. The dockers, the carters, the stall-holders had backed off from the threatened riots. The system creaked on.

Duke poured pints steadily all night long, with Robert on hand. He relied on this extra help on busy nights; Robert was good for keeping an eye on the barrels and clearing off the empties. He was popular with the customers, many of whom he knew from his dock work. Duke watched him now, mingling with his mates. He shared a joke, throwing his head back to lead the laughter. He was a strong, handsome lad, his foot just on the first rung of life's ladder.

Robert brought two fistfuls of empty glasses to the bar. A cigarette hung from the corner of his mouth, one eye closed against the drifting smoke. 'Watch out, Pa,' he warned. 'Here comes trouble.'

Annie Wiggin had just put in another appearance with some of her fellow stall-holders on the market. They'd gone down the court specially to bang on her door and persuade her out for a natter; four or five skinny women with big voices and loud laughs. Their kids were in bed, minded by the eldest. Their old men were already here, drowning life's sorrows. So they'd donned their bits of finery; their hats decked with ostrich feathers, their long fringed shawls, and they paraded themselves down to the Duke for a bit of a laugh and a singsong. 'Come on, Annie, for gawd's sake. Can't have you moping about all on your own!' They were family women and they took Annie's case to heart. If their man walked out on them, like Annie's husband had done, they wouldn't half give him what for. If they could lay hands on him, of course; which Annie couldn't with hers.

'You're not wearing them old boots again, Annie!' Liz Sargent protested when she answered their knock. 'Them's your working boots!' She glared down at the offending articles; misshapen, boiled, resoled and stitched until they resembled old kippers.

'Them's my only boots,' Annie muttered. 'They was his boots, and I wear 'em in his memory.' She put on a dark jacket which she grabbed from a peg in the gloomy passage. She turned her key in the lock and thrust it down her bodice. 'Well, what we waiting for?' she demanded.

The women made their way back up the court towards the gaslight at the corner. 'What you want to remember him for? That's what I'd like to know.' Liz thought badly of Annie for not putting her best foot forward, so to speak. 'He was a rotten old bugger, so they tell me.'

Annie sighed. 'He was. But he's the cross I have to bear, and these old boots remind me.' She would say no more, but she marched ahead of her spruced-up friends, straight into the public bar.

'Now then, Mrs S.' Duke addressed Liz, deliberately ignoring the bothersome Annie. 'What'll it be?'

The orders went out; a sharp cry for a pint of porter or a drop of gin from each of the market women. If their menfolk were present, they kept well hidden, leaving the women to their own devices. Liz Sargent adjusted a small length of fox fur around her shoulders and grabbed her drink. 'Any rate, I see you put your best hat on to come out with us.' She nodded her approval at the bunches of fake cherries bedecking Annie's black straw boater. 'I suppose that's something.'

'And it ain't even bleeding Sunday!' Annie scowled sarcastically.

'So who died?' Nora Brady winked at Liz.

'No one died. What you mean? This ain't my funeral hat!' Annie glanced at herself in the fancy long mirror behind Duke's broad shoulders. She tucked a wisp of hair behind her ear.

'Who got spliced then?' The women gave wicked, knowing looks.

'Leave off, why don't you? Can't a woman have a bleeding drink?' Poor Annie grew fed up with their teasing and sank her face into a pint of porter.

The women made a great show of leaving her alone. They told Duke to be sure and take good care of her, before they drifted off in pairs to different corners of the room. 'She's all on her ownsome,' they cheeked, thrusting bold faces across the bar at him and pouting their lips. 'Poor lonesome Annie!'

'Silly cows,' Annie grumbled. But she stayed put. If he did but know it, Duke *was* the reason she came in night after night with her earthenware jug, and she didn't care who noticed it.

Underneath the profusion of cherries and regardless of old man Wiggin's boots, Annie wasn't a bad-looking woman. Past her best, it had to be admitted, but sprightly. Well into her forties, her hair had lost none of its auburn tinge, though she hid this good feature by scraping it back from her forehead and twisting it into a tight bun as severe as any workhouse warden's. Her face had a fine, birdlike quality, with rapidly changing expressions. In repose, her eyes were big and dark, the skin tight over her high cheekbones. But seeing herself as the scourge of all errant men had served to fix frown lines on Annie's forehead, and the corners of her mouth were set down. No man alive would have called Annie Wiggin attractive, but a *woman* might stop to look at her and declare she was wearing well, considering.

Duke caught Annie giving him the eye as usual and shuffled off down the bar. He never knew why she bothered, since he gave her not one word of encouragement.

'What'll it be, Annie?' was the longest sentence he'd

addressed to her in all the years she'd been patronizing the establishment; through his being married to Pattie and the mourning period after, through her own marriage to Wiggin, who scarpered without paying his bills, and through all the years since he ran off. 'What'll it be, Annie?' he said as he reached for her empty jug in the early evening. 'What'll it be, Annie?' when she called in by herself late at night.

Yet whenever he glanced her way, Annie had her eye on him. He alone of all men must have been excluded from Annie's list of hopeless cases. She sat there rolling her eyes and smiling; an unusual expression for Annie on the whole. If Arthur Ogden attempted so much as a remark on the weather as he passed round the back of Annie's stool, she'd spit at him like a cat. A broad-shouldered navvy lodging in the Ogdens' spare room would feel the lash of her tongue, and she reserved special venom for anyone bearing the look of the sea. They were the happy-go-lucky, often handsome and feckless men who drifted in and out of the tenement rooms, sometimes American, sometimes Polish, with dark walrus moustaches and heavy brows.

Why then in God's name did Annie Wiggin roll her eyes at him? He was Duke Parsons, a decent widower of sixty, weighed down by family care and struggling to keep business afloat during the strikes and troubles. Duke shook his head and backed off in search of Robert, Frances, even Ernie. Anyone would do. He ducked out the back way into the corridor and yelled upstairs. It was Ernie who appeared on the landing, a smile on his face.

'Come on down, son, and give us a hand with the empties,' Duke said. 'It's last orders, so look sharp.'

Ernie nodded and came eagerly down with his flat-footed, heavy gait. He hadn't developed the controlled, springy stride of the average youth. Instead, his legs straddled an invisible ditch, and he thrust them forward like an awkward toddler as he rushed along the corridor into the bar.

Duke grinned and stuck his thumbs in his waistcoat pockets. He was a good son, young Ernie, without a bad bone in his body. But his great, open features made your heart ache in this wicked world.

'Clear the bar for me, Ern,' Duke said, pointing carefully. 'And mind how you go.'

Ernie took each glass between his two large hands as if it was the football cup. He gently deposited them in the sink. Annie sat and watched him. She drank her own glass to the dregs and held it up. 'Here, Ern, take this one from me.' She gave his hand a tiny pat as she handed it over.

But both Annie and Duke noticed the shine go from Ernie's face when his chore took him along the bar towards the corner with the pianola. He'd just lifted another glass when he spotted Daisy with Chalky and his crowd. They were singing their heads off.

Hettie had managed to give Syd Swan the slip and head straight upstairs as they came into the pub. So Daisy stood alone surrounded by young men, head high, face flushed. She'd taken off her coat and wore a blouse as white and thin as any Ernie had ever seen. It was adorned with tucks and frills, and curved in at her tiny waist over a skirt of shiny purple. Ernie sighed as he stared. Somehow he knew he'd never get to sing with Daisy like that, and hold her round her slim waist, no matter how much she smiled and petted him.

Suddenly Chalky broke off singing. He'd noticed Ernie's long, lingering stare. His laughing face narrowed and turned mean as he fixed the boy with a look. Syd's gaze followed. Even Daisy, her throat flushed above the snowy white blouse, stopped singing and put a hand involuntarily to her cheek. Chalky moved a fraction of an inch in Ernie's direction, head on one side, scowling.

'Stop gawping, Ern, for gawd's sake!' Robert broke out of a nearby crowd and seized the glass from his grasp. 'Don't you know you look like a bleeding idiot standing there!' He gave his brother a hefty shove back towards the sink.

Chalky checked his stride, shrugged and turned his attentions back to Daisy.

Robert took a long drag on his cigarette, immediately regretting what he'd just said. There was nothing Ernie could do about it; that was just the way he was, standing there with his mouth open, ogling the girl. He meant nothing by it. But Robert jutted his chin and bounced back Duke's meaningful glare. 'What you looking at, you silly cow?' he muttered at Annie Wiggin as he went past with a handful of empties.

He'd go round in a second and talk to Ern; he'd fix up that trip to the Palace with him. They'd sit together in the plush seats and Ernie would be able to gawp at Daisy to his heart's content. It'd be Robert's treat. After all, the poor kid never went out and it would do him good.

After a few minutes swilling glasses in the sink, Robert had restored himself to good humour. Ernie was plodding around the bar once more, lifting stools on to table tops as gradually customers packed up and went home. Robert stopped for a few words with Walter Davidson on his way out.

'You been down the club lately?' Walter asked. He and Robert sometimes met up at Milo's for a spot of boxing.

Robert nodded. 'I been to see a man about a taxi-cab.' He grinned. 'Wants to sell it. I told him we was interested.'

Walter laughed. 'Blimey, Rob. We're interested all right. Did you tell the geezer we'd have to pay 'im in washers?'

He was a regular at the Duke, spending too much of his meagre wage from Coopers' on beer and cigarettes. Like all the young men round about, he was ambitious to be his own boss. He'd talked often to Robert about the dream of running their own taxi-cab together. Horses were finished in that line of work these days; too messy and slow by far. Both men wanted to be part of the future in the shape of a shiny black, purring automobile. But neither earned more than a pittance; Robert on the docks and Walter in one of Coopers' sweatshops. They were past the boyhood stage of swaggering down the street calling after the birds, but they were still a million miles away from achieving their ambition. Walter thought ruefully of the shilling he'd just squandered pouring beer down his gullet. 'I hope you didn't promise him nothing stupid, Rob.'

'Would I? I said we could pay him bit by bit, on the never-never,' Robert reassured him.

'What did he say?'

'He said we could have the taxi bit by bit an' all; one wheel at a time, with the engine bust up into little pieces.' He winked at his friend.

Walter laughed and went out.

'Silly beggars,' Duke muttered. He'd overheard. 'What you thinking of buying one of them newfangled things for, then? What's wrong with the old hansoms?' He turned on the last, lingering drinkers, including Annie Wiggin. 'Ain't you got no homes to go to?'

Annie fixed her cherry-laden hat further on to her head. 'All right, all right, I'm on my way.' She gave Duke a pert look and shuffled off.

'C'mon, mate,' he grumbled at Chalky White. But he went warily. Chalky had had one too many as usual, and his temper turned nasty when he was drunk.

''E-wants-ter-gerrid-of-us,' the tall, dangerous-looking

man slurred. He leant forward in front of Daisy and grabbed Syd's arm. 'You 'ear?'

Daisy extricated herself from his long reach. 'Well, it's time for me to say ta-ta, at any rate,' she said brightly. As she stood up, Chalky overbalanced and fell. He crashed against Syd, then made a grab at Daisy. As he caught the sleeve of her blouse, it ripped slightly. She turned on him. 'Here, watch what you're about!'

Chalky wasn't too drunk to feel put down by Daisy's cry. 'Very sorry, miss,' he sneered. He launched himself towards her. 'Very sorry, I'm sure.'

Daisy smoothed herself down. 'That's all right.' She tried to meet his gaze, but then looked away and began to search for her coat. There was something about Chalky that made her feel trapped. She wore an uncertain smile as he advanced again, but she felt breathless. 'Gotta go,' she said.

'Not so fast.' He held her by the arm. His hand easily circled her slender forearm. 'You're going my way, any rate.'

'I gotta get back home,' Daisy explained. 'My brother's sick, remember.'

'Aah, poor little mite.' Chalky propelled her out of the pub on to the wet pavement. 'What are you, all of a sudden, bleeding Florence Nightingale?'

'I told you; he needs a doctor!' Daisy felt lousy. The story about Jim was all too true. And she'd been larking around all night instead of getting home to her ma with the money for the doctor. She pictured Jimmy lying under the blanket coughing. She could kill herself for ignoring the poor little thing. Her pa had even been up before the Board; a thing he only did when a kid was at death's door. 'Listen, Chalky, it's true. I gotta go!'

She wrenched herself free and ran off round the corner,

down the straight stretch of unlit cobbles to the far end of the court.

Well, she thought, what difference does an hour or two make? Ma can't fetch a doctor till morning. I'll go up, give her the cash, and she can go straight up Duke Street in the morning.

She was almost sobbing by the time she arrived home. Her attempts to excuse herself had failed. She felt in poor shape as she climbed the dark stairs. She was a wicked, selfish girl with not an ounce of fellow feeling, she told herself. She delved into her pocket for the long-awaited shillings, gritted her teeth and opened the battered, half-rotten door.

Chapter Six

Frances waited for the lull of a Sunday morning in late December before she tackled her father once more about the problem of Jess. This time, he wouldn't be able to claim the distraction of pub work, and he would have had more than enough time to absorb the news. She wanted to play her cards right. Jess needed to be out of that place in Hackney and home with the family before Christmas, when her disgrace would be growing obvious for all to see. That would still give them time to plan ahead.

A pale sun struggled through watery clouds above the grey roofs of Duke Street. Duke stood at an upstairs window, looking down at Dolly Ogden dragging an unwilling Charlie and Amy off to church. She did her best to smarten them up, sending Charlie down the pawn shop on a Saturday tea-time to redeem his Norfolk jacket for Sunday best. Come Monday morning she'd be sending it back, bundled up with her one decent pair of boots and a couple of china dogs from her front-room mantelpiece. That bit of money was vital to see them through the week since Arthur had lost his job at the glass factory. But Dolly was canny; she'd never see them go hungry, and she was bent on putting Charlie through school until his scholarship money ran out. So she sailed up the street to church every Sunday with her kids, one on either side, like a battleship in full regalia, escorted into port by two dutiful tugs.

'Pa,' Frances began in her quiet voice, 'did you hear, they're recruiting for jobs in the Post Office exchange?' She sat in her upright chair by the table, where she kept her sewing basket with its never decreasing pile of socks and stockings for darning. That's how she kept herself busy now, weaving her needle in and out as she sidled into conversation about Jess.

'Listen here, it says I can buy a motor car for only one hundred and thirty-three pounds.' Duke held up his newspaper and pointed to an advertisement. 'One hundred and thirty-three pounds! Rob needs to think again, I say. Taxi-cabs. Motor stables.' He snorted and rubbed the end of his nose with his forefinger, then thrust his large head back between the pages of the paper.

But Frances was not one to be deterred. Her long fingers dipped and bobbed as the needle sped in and out. 'It's women they need to work the switchboards. It'd be a definite step up from tweeny work.' She held her breath and let the idea sink in. 'The Post Office is an up-and-coming job for a woman nowadays.'

'Switchboards.' Duke insisted on missing the point as stubbornly as Frances persisted in making it. 'Telephones. Newfangled nonsense.'

'Now, Pa, telephones are quite common and I'm always on at you to get one for here, you know that. But listen, most women want to come out of service these days. Everyone wants the Post Office jobs and you can't blame them. Look what happens when you stay in service all your life.'

'No need to tell me.' Duke stared stolidly at the advert for the Model T. Then he broke the silence. 'How can you work on a switchboard when you're carrying a babe in arms? That's what you're on about, ain't it? It's Jess. But you tell me how she can have a baby and go working for the Post Office!' He was angry. Frances must be wrong in the head, thinking that Jess could go applying for jobs in her condition, and unmarried.

Frances sighed. 'Look, Pa, Jess is having this baby, we know that. But it ain't the end of the world. It don't have to be. We've got time to think about things, ain't we? First off, she either has the kid, or she don't.'

Duke left his newspaper and came and banged the flat of his hand on the table. The veins in his neck stood out. 'No, you look. The girl's a fool!' he cried. 'Getting herself into this mess!'

'How do you know she had any choice?' Frances looked up at him with her steady gaze. 'From what Jess told me, there wasn't even a by-your-leave.'

'Who was it, that's what I'd like to know?' Duke backed off, stunned.

'The Holdens' son, Gilbert.'

Duke leaned on the table, covering his forehead with one broad hand. Then he breathed deep and stood up straight. If you got a wound in the war, or a kick from a horse, you went and had it cleaned up. A few stitches saw you right. But no one knew how to stitch up this kind of blow.

'Any rate,' Frances went on, 'without the kid she could go about getting a job straight off. If she decides to have it, well, there's plenty of us around here to help her look after it. She can still go out to work and earn her keep.' She kept steadily at her darning. What she wanted was for Duke to take it for granted that Jess would come home, where she belonged. 'That's why I'm telling you, Pa. There's plenty of jobs for women around these days. And the sooner Jess is out of service the better.'

'If there's plenty of jobs around, why's young Amy Ogden sweating away over them top hats in Coopers'?' Duke demanded. 'If there's plenty of jobs, why's our Ett parading herself half-naked in front of them dirty-minded little bleeders at the Palace every night of the week? Tell me that. If there's jobs, why are them poor bleeding women walking the streets out there? Don't talk daft, Frances!'

Duke had raised his voice, but now he halted. That last remark had hit a nerve with him. He turned away, shaking his head. That's what had struck him the night Frances first told him about Jess; what if she ended up like those skeleton-women, clutching her bundle of rags that was really a baby starving to death? He walked to the window to gaze out. Then he took a deep breath. 'Tell her she can come home,' he said.

Frahces nodded without showing any reaction. But she was satisfied. She finished off her work, snipped the thread and rolled the socks into a pair. 'I'll go and fetch her this afternoon then.'

Duke's head had sunk to his chest.

'Will you tell the others, Pa?'

'Yes. Go and fetch her home, there's a good girl. Quick as you can.'

Frances went to him, reached up on tiptoe and kissed his lined cheek. She'd been thirteen when her mother passed on. Never since that time had she seen her father look so bad as he did this moment. 'Don't worry, Pa, we'll manage.'

'I'll knock his bleeding head off if I get the chance!' His voice was cracked and hoarse.

She nodded and went to put on her coat and hat. She stepped straight downstairs and out of the house, her heart heavy. She only hoped Jess would be good and co-operative now, since Duke had relented. She'd better realize what it

59

had taken out of the old man; this arrow of disgrace in his respectable heart.

The tram took her up Duke Street, along Bridge Road to Southwark Bridge. Over the river, she stepped out of the cold drizzle down into Cannon Street underground station. She headed north-east to Hackney, feeling the train rattle and shudder, blind to the attractions of Van Houten's Cocoa and Nestle's Milk Chocolate. To outsiders, she was the schoolteacher figure in her high-necked grey costume with its fur collar and matching toque hat. She sat severely, hands crossed over the black leather bag on her knee.

Frances had always been called Frances, never Fran, even within the Parsons family. One look at her told you she warranted the use of her full name if you wished to avoid the risk of receiving one of her somewhat haughty stares. She didn't invite intimacy, with her straight-backed carriage and fastidious manners. She didn't invite suitors either, since she lacked the easy banter of her sister Hettie, or Daisy O'Hagan from down the court.

Her cool appearance might be something she regretted but couldn't do anything to alter. She'd lost her mother at precisely that age when a girl needs some role model in her budding relationships with the opposite sex. She'd no one to turn to when she needed to know the details of how to behave after a man began to show interest. Not a natural flirt, her uncertainty converted at first into shyness, then into a distinct air of reserve. At the age when most girls walked out on the Common or went cycling into the countryside with the boy of their choice, Frances turned to books and study. This was an unusual thing for a girl, even then. She filled her head with novels, with images of Mr E. M. Forster's elegant young ladies touring round Italy or showing up in India to be married. And she turned her back on the Chalky Whites and Syd Swans who drifted in and out of the tenements or who propped up the bar in the pub downstairs.

If she was lonely she didn't show it. Her one disastrous experience in life came after she'd finished with Board School, where she'd won prizes and praise from all around. 'Frances should go and train as a teacher in college,' her own teachers informed Duke. 'She's very able.' But the family was poor, with different expectations. So she submitted to being sent into service much against her will. At seventeen, she wrote home to Hettie in her beautiful copperplate hand that the work for her Mayfair family was dreary and disgusting. She skivvied from dawn till dusk. But worse, the children of the house persistently bullied and cheeked her in front of their parents, much to everyone's amusement. 'There's an old dog called Bob in the house and he's not too bad, I suppose. Otherwise I hate them all, every last one,' she wrote with uncharacteristic bluntness.

By nineteen her heart was set on moving on. She scoured the newspapers for job advertisements, wrote many letters of application, mostly to the biscuit, cardboard-box and glasswork factories in her home borough. But biscuit factories didn't need women with perfect handwriting and scholarly punctuation. She suffered dozens of rejections. Finally, Boots the Chemist announced that it was extending its branches into many East End districts. They did need women clever enough to decipher the illegible scribbles made by doctors on their prescriptions, and fastidious enough to measure and mix small quantities of medicinal substances. Frances wrote off and secured a position.

For the last eight years she'd worked hard to establish herself as an indispensable employee of the pharmacy. The work was repetitive and tiring, but it wasn't demeaning. To have broken out of the degrading cycle imposed on most

East End girls in service was a matter of pride to her. She even went on with her learning, through Workers' Education classes in literature and politics. It set her further apart.

At twenty-eight she had become this serious, subdued woman in grey, sitting beneath the gaudy advertisements in the underground train, staunch in her family loyalty, respected but not popular. Frances would nevertheless rescue Jess from the Holdens and keep the family together. She steeled herself to the task, left the train and emerged up the steps into the cold grey light.

Getting Jess out of the house in Hackney proved straightforward enough. Frances arrived on the Holdens' front doorstep and announced that she'd come to take her sister home.

Mrs Holden, a whalebone-plated woman with a wistful and rather helpless air despite her ample proportions, looked puzzled. She'd just returned from church, and called to her husband for help with this strange request. He came down the stairs past the gilt-framed pictures, across the Turkish rug. Mr Holden was prepared to stand no nonsense.

Before he could say, 'Now look here!' between clenched teeth, Frances stepped in with, 'Your son, Gilbert, has misbehaved towards my sister, Mr Holden, and we want her home to look after her.' She looked him straight in the eye.

The head of the household blustered, the wife looked shocked and faint. But it turned out, when Jess was summoned and the final confrontation took place in the housekeeper's room, that Mr Holden was forced to admit that his wayward son was already a father twice over, in similar circumstances. That Jess was merely an unfortunate third couldn't be denied. Still she had to suffer Mr Holden's unreasonable indignation at her for 'putting herself in Gilbert's way, don't you know!' and tempting him once again off the straight and narrow.

'Hush,' Frances warned Jess, who struggled through her tears to defend her bludgeoned reputation. 'My sister will take her wages and we'll leave without fuss, Mr Holden. We wouldn't want to cause your family any distress just before Christmas, you see. And you can tell your wife that I'm very sorry indeed for her son's behaviour. I trust she'll soon recover her spirits.' Mrs Holden had already been led away upstairs in a state of shock.

Mr Holden, rendered powerless by Frances's cool tactics, handed Jess eight pounds ten shillings; half her annual wage. She went up and packed her small canvas bag while Frances was sent to wait in the back scullery. No one spoke as they took their leave of the house by the servants' door; not the housekeeper who'd seen it coming a mile off, not the cook who'd befriended Jess for a time, and certainly not Gilbert Holden, conspicuous by his absence during the row, but who stood now in his shirt-sleeves looking down on them from an upstairs window. The glass reflected light from the cloud-laden sky as Jess glanced back up.

'Good riddance,' Frances said, hurrying Jess down the path on to the street. 'Now, Jess, you got to know Pa ain't exactly waiting to welcome you with open arms when we get back.' Her voice had relaxed into the East End twang.

Jess nodded. 'What about the rest?'

'Let's wait and see, shall we?' She hurried away, the nasty taste of hypocrisy still in her mouth. 'Oh, it's very nice being shocked and throwing a faint all over the place!' she exclaimed. 'But what's the betting she's back at church with that son of hers, for the nativity service, loving her neighbour and angling for a respectable girl for him to marry!'

'Poor cow, whoever she is,' Jess agreed. 'But don't let's talk about it no more.' She looked straight ahead, shoulders back, walking firmly alongside her eldest sister. 'And there's one more thing, Frances. I don't want to explain nothing about what happened back there, and that's that!'

It hurt too much to remember Gilbert's endless dirty remarks, his hands pawing her at every end and turn, the disgusting behaviour that had led to this disgrace. There was one dark and violent moment that Jess would lock away for ever and never talk about. In those unspeakable seconds, a woman was helpless, friendless and alone. Then she had to carry her own pain and humiliation as best she could. Jess clutched her bag and marched along.

'I don't think Pa could believe it at first.' Frances felt deeply for Duke in all this. They'd descended into the underground on to an almost empty platform.

'Me neither. I sometimes think maybe I'll wake up tomorrow and find the whole thing's been a bad dream.' She grinned at Frances in a brave attempt to lighten the mood.

Frances smiled back. 'Ready?' she asked when they'd negotiated the tram journey and the light traffic of Duke Street.

Jess pulled at the skirt of her dark-blue coat and checked her reflection in the windows of the Duke. 'Ready as I'll ever be,' she announced, stepping upstairs into the lion's den.

'She's here!' Hettie called back into the living room. She'd peeped over the banisters and seen the top of Jess's head coming upstairs. Then she fled into the kitchen.

Sadie sat as instructed at the table with Ernie, stiff and awkward as if they expected visitors she hardly knew. She pulled her long plait in front of one shoulder, then tossed it back again. She bit her lip. 'Sit still, Ern!' she told him. She could hear Jess and Frances pause on the landing before they came in.

Ernie glanced at Robert for his lead. Rob leaned against the mantelpiece smoking a cigarette. Everything was all right then, Ernie thought. He smiled back at Sadie.

So when Jess finally came in, Ernie jumped up as he always did when she came home to visit on her half day off. He went right up to her and hugged her, knocking her hat off. 'Make the tea!' he shouted through to Hettie. 'Jess is here!'

'Watch it, Ern!' Robert jumped nimbly forward to rescue the hat.

'Leave him be, I won't break, you know,' Jess said. 'I'm only having a kid.' She put one arm around Ernie's waist and gave him a cuddle.

'Blimey.' Even Robert had to admire her coolness. 'I thought I was the one who knew my way around the place!' He felt he was seeing a new Jess here. He had expected her to creep back home like a mouse, yet here she was making jokes about the worst thing that could happen to a girl. 'Good for you.' He winked. 'I'll go down and tell Pa you're here.'

Then Hettie came in with a full pot of tea, tears in her eyes, hardly knowing where to look. Jess was the last one she'd expected to be in this mess. It was one thing when a girl at the Palace got into trouble. There was a network, people to tell them what to do next. But not your sister. She thought Jess looked pinched and peaky. They'd worn her out at that horrible place and sent her home in this condition, fit for nothing.

Jess let go of Ernie and went up to Hettie. 'That's a nice blouse you got on, Ett.' She took the pot from her and set it on the hob. 'I like the trimming.'

'I got it from Annie. It's a bit she had left over on the roll,' Hettie said. 'I'll try and get you some next time I'm down the market.' She plumped up a cushion in the easy chair, inviting Jess to sit in it. The 'trouble' was vanishing like Rob's cigarette smoke.

And soon they were having their Sunday afternoon chat; Sadie complaining to Jess that Charlie Ogden was made of stone, despite all her efforts. 'I want him to ask me to walk out with him,' she protested. 'But he's always got his nose stuck in some flamin' book!'

'He must be blind then,' Jess commiserated. Sadie had come to sit at her feet on the hearthrug. 'You getting to look so pretty and all.'

Sadie beamed up at her. 'Do you think so? Here, how do you like *my* new blouse? It's only an old one of Ett's, but we put a bit of extra lace round the neck. What d'you think?'

Without them knowing it, Duke had sidled into the room and taken a cup of tea from Frances. He stood by the door listening to the female chit-chat, watching his grown-up children gathered together; the contented smiles, the pleasant laughter.

His gaze fell on Jess and his mind flew back down the years. A third daughter, the midwife had told him. 'But there, never mind, we can't choose these things.'

When Robert followed on a couple of years after, it was almost as if Duke completely forgot about Jess. With her father's mind absorbed by his son, little Jess missed the fussing and petting he'd lavished on the older girls, and she seemed easy to overlook. He recalled her as a quiet child, without Frances's strong will or Hettie's sparkle. The only clear memory he had of Jess from her early years was that she ran like the wind. She carried home prizes from the running races at school, having beaten all the boys. 'Look, Pa!' She would hold up her spinning-top for him to see.

'Ern, go and give Robert a hand downstairs,' he said gruffly.

Jess started at the sound of his deep voice. The blood rushed to her face as she stood up to face him. Frances edged her forward. 'Go on!'

Jess recalled all the times in her childhood when she'd looked up to her father and tried to please him; how she'd often failed. Then she would hide her hurt by withdrawing into a corner, and he would call that sulking. Well, she'd displeased him now, and no mistake. 'Hello, Pa,' she said quietly, hanging her head.

'Pa?' Sadie jumped in, anxious to fill the gap.

He looked Jess up and down. 'If I could get my hands on him!' he threatened.

'Now, Pa.' Frances laid a hand on his arm. Jess finally met his gaze.

He sighed. 'Well, we'll have to make the best of it,' he said. 'Since it's the season of goodwill.'

They all nodded and smiled.

'Let's make it a Christmas to remember,' Frances suggested. 'A real family gathering.' She and Hettie had been busy baking, and ordering, a turkey, beef and ham. They'd kept their fingers crossed.

'A celebration,' Duke conceded. 'Why not?' He still studied Jess, trying to judge how she would manage the shame of the baby's birth.

Then Daisy came running upstairs, bursting in without knocking to tell them that little Jimmy had been sick again. 'He had a dreadful night, coughing and coughing, and all the little 'uns were whimpering and whining about it. But this time we had the money to help him straight off, thank God. So Ma goes up for Dr Fry and that medicine he gave him did the trick like before. Magic it was!' Her lovely face was all smiles. She'd only just popped in to tell them the news, she said. 'And hello and Happy Christmas, Jess!' She winked and sped off, while they stayed and caught Jess up on all the street news, and the comings and goings down Paradise Court.

Chapter Seven

Amy Ogden sat behind a row of wooden heads stuck on poles arranged along a narrow table. The heads were of various sizes, shiny and featureless, and marked with figures showing measurements for the top hats which the workshop produced. She was one of six women and two men, excluding the supervisor Bert Buggles. As the youngest there, she was the recipient of many of the worst jobs in the lengthy hatting process. Sometimes she moulded the stubborn leather band around the crown of the wooden model, or else she ironed the swansdown forehead pad firmly in position before the lining was attached. Her hands were always chapped, her breathing hindered by the ceaseless steam from the irons.

Strips of russia leather and gauze lay lengthways down the table, while the precious moire silk for the linings was carefully stacked in bolts on a shelf behind.

Despite the luxurious quality of the finished article, conditions in Coopers' sweatshop were grim. The low room with its sloping ceilings and tiny skylights was poorly lit and ventilated, but it was cold none the less. Damp plaster fell away to expose bare brick wall and was never repaired. The place stank of leather and glue.

Only the determined cheerfulness of the women made the place bearable, with the unfortunate Bert providing the main butt of their humour. Today, for instance, in the run-up to Christmas, one of the women had been forced to bring in her youngest infant who was sick with croup. Still under three and hardly able to speak in sentences, the child was dressed up in the supervisor's apron, with a measuring tape around his neck. 'We got ourselves a new gaffer. Let's all take orders from Donald!' they proclaimed. 'We'll get more sense out of 'im, any rate!'

Bert slouched off unmoved by the *coup*, and poor Donald was soon responding to the women's calls; 'Please, Bert, can you 'elp with this gauze vent!' and, 'Look 'ere, Bert, I asked two days back for you to soften up this leather for me!' He would clamber on their knees in his big leather apron, barking his hard, dry cough all over the half-made hats.

In the early afternoon Teddy Cooper paid his routine visit. As usual, he looked as if he had very little to do with the place. His grey Homburg hat was perched on the back of his head, and his immaculate striped bow-tie, his collar and natty tweed suit suggested a day at the races rather than any serious function in office or shop.

Amy glanced up as he came in, and a smile brightened her small, blunt features. In the dull stretch of the day, when her back had begun to ache and her fingers to rub into blisters, a visit from Teddy was a breath of fresh air. Today he brought oranges and a news story from the papers about a famous music-hall star, George Robey, who'd earned one thousand pounds in just one week.

'What'd you do with a thousand a week, Emmy?' he asked the mother of the sick boy.

'I should think I'd died and gone to heaven,' came the caustic reply. Emmy was impervious to his charms.

'Watch this.' Undeterred, Teddy winked and invited Donald to come up close. 'I'm Extraordinary Edward, the famous juggler. Watch!' And he set up a rapid display with the three oranges, flipping them between his hands, behind his back with surprising dexterity. 'Dazzling! Delightful! Delictitious!. . . But chiefly your own!' he declaimed. Everyone shrieked, whistled and clapped. Sam, the leather worker, and Dora the chief moulder each caught an orange from him and whisked them off.

Amy laughed. 'You been practising. I can tell.'

When she looked up at him, her eyes were shining white orbs with blue centres. 'Now that's very observant of you, Amy.' Teddy gave Donald the last orange and came to perch at her section of the table. 'As a matter of fact, I have!'

As he leaned sideways across her station and screened her from view, the others took it as a signal that the show was over. They bowed their heads to their work and Emmy came to draw Donald further off.

Teddy studied Amy's face from close quarters. Her skin was milky white and smooth. The upper lip arched in a full curve, the blue eyes conveyed guilelessness. 'What's a nice girl like you . . .' he began.

'Doin' in a place like this?' she giggled. 'Don't ask me, ask your pa!'

'Hm. What if I ask the governor to look out for a place for you in the shop?' he asked, looping his fingers through a pair of scissors and threatening to snip at one of Amy's blonde curls.

She gasped. 'Would you?'

'Course I would. I can just picture you behind the counter in your little white collar and cuffs; a good-looking girl like you.' The scissors snipped close to Amy's earlobe. She didn't flinch. '"Yes, madam, no, madam, three bags full, madam!"' He replaced the scissors with a flourish. 'I'll ask him straight after Christmas if you like.'

'Really and truly?' Teddy was offering her a dream come true; a move out of this overcrowded, tawdry sweat-shop into the world of mahogany counters and glass display cases where she felt she belonged. 'Will you really?' She stared up at Teddy. He was part of that world in his expensive suit and tie, with his nice voice and manners. He called the severe Mr Cooper 'the governor' and made it seem as if he could do anything. After all, he was the boss's son.

Teddy bent low over Amy to whisper in her ear. 'For you, my dear, anything!' He grinned and sat upright. 'And let's start with that jaunt I promised.'

'What jaunt?' She felt flushed by his boldness in front of the other women, yet at the same time determined not to care. She wanted to lead him on to the point where the job in the shop was a reality. That was all that mattered.

'Our trip to the Empire,' he reminded her. 'How about tonight? Meet me downstairs outside the back entrance, half seven sharp.' He swung his legs off the table and stood up, hands in pockets.

All she had time to do was to nod her head once, then he was off, ruffling Donald's hair, winking at Emmy, humming a tune. He went out of the workshop in fine fettle, down into Hosiery in the basement, to fill up his social diary into the New Year. If only all the girls were as easy to seduce as Amy Ogden, he thought. Unluckily, most of them had their eyes a bit more wide open and they played harder to get; though get them he did in the end.

Amy sat and held her breath. She finished here at half six. She'd have to be off like a shot to get changed and be back for half seven, looking her very best. There wasn't much time. Maybe Bert would let her clock off ten minutes early today. These thoughts swam through her head.

'Where is it this time?' Dora broke into her plans. 'The

Jewel, the Gem or the Empire?' Dora was a tall, masculine-looking woman, very blunt. She knew how the boss's son operated. He only ever took a girl out once, got as far as he could with her, then dropped her. They all knew about it. The only wonder was why his old man never tried to put a stop to it.

Amy stiffened. 'None of your business.'

'"Let me take you away from this horrible place, my darlin'!"' Dora mocked. 'Oh my gawd, Amy, you ain't fell for that line, have you? It's old as the hills!'

'Just watch it,' Emmy advised more kindly. 'Dora's right; don't be a ninny and go falling for it.'

'I won't.' Amy nodded and put on a firmer expression.

'That's right, don't believe a word he says and you'll be fine.' Emmy shifted a bolt of grey silk from the shelf to the table and picked up her scissors. 'It don't stop you from going out and having a good time, just as long as you keep your head screwed on.'

'Just don't say we didn't warn you,' Dora insisted darkly. 'Ask Louise Makins in House'old Appliances. He took her to the Empire last week, I think it was. Ask Louise Makins about his nibs!'

Amy frowned. 'No need. I can look after myself, don't you worry.'

The women gossiped on, growing more ribald about Teddy Cooper's style of courtship. 'He looks a proper gent at first, don't he?' Dora said. 'He talks like a toff and he always gives the girls a bit of a treat first off; a night out at the local fleapit, or a slap-up meal. But they soon find out he's no gent after all.'

'How would you know, Dora Kennedy? He asked you out, has he?' Amy was nettled. She knew for a fact that Teddy would never ask the angular, tall moulder. She was only speaking out of pique, Amy told herself.

'Ask anyone. Ask Louise.' Dora turned to Emmy, hands on hips, determined to undermine Amy's silly vanity. 'You hear what she told me? She says he don't mind where he does it, or who he does it with. And when he does do it, it's over so quick you'd wonder what all the fuss was about.' Dora grinned. 'She says it's about as exciting as posting a letter!'

'She never!' Emmy guffawed. Then she reflected a moment. 'Yes, that'd be right. He's a boss, ain't he? It's always like that with the bosses.'

Amy refused to join in. Teddy Cooper was the only purveyor of bright dreams in her dim, twilit world. The others could say what they liked. She'd hang on to him, come what may.

Ernie Parsons sat beside Robert in the red velvet seats at the Southwark Palace. He was in his own seventh heaven.

Every time the crimson curtains swept down across the stage, he roared himself hoarse and clapped until the last echo had died in the vast, domed auditorium. When they opened again on to the golden stage, he laughed till he cried at the little man with heavy eyebrows who flip-flapped across the boards in his giant boots, performing all manner of acrobatic stilt walks on the tips of their wooden soles. He laughed when Robert laughed at the jokes about mothers-in-law and unpaid rent. But it was Ernie who led the singing when it came to Gilbert the Filbert and Daisy.

This last he sung until his lungs nearly burst. 'Steady on, Ern,' Robert said. He pulled him back in his seat. 'Daisy's coming back on in a bit.' He gave the couple sitting next to him an embarrassed smile, then hid behind a cloud of cigarette smoke tinged pink by the lights that blazed down on to the stage.

Ernie sat back entranced as the creamy-limbed chorus girls finally returned. Here he sat in the midst of thousands of people; the balconies were crammed full, there were men standing shoulder to shoulder at the back, and he alone seemed to have a special link with the girls onstage. One was his sister, one was his friend. It was as if Daisy and Hettie sang specially for him. To him they blew their kisses across their white-gloved palms, to him they curtseyed. The orchestra played, the audience joined in the songs. Ernie couldn't imagine anything better.

'C'mon, Ern,' Robert said when the curtain fell for the last time. 'Let's get round to the stage door and join the queue for the postcard queens.' If he was giving Ernie a treat, he had to do the thing right. They had to end up crowding the stage door, waiting for the chorus girls to emerge. He dragged Ernie up the gangway, nodding hello to a few mates, but not stopping to chat.

Ernie, overwhelmed by the squeaks and thuds of the hinged seats as hundreds of people stood up and stretched their legs, grabbed Robert's coat-tails. His face twitched with alarm.

'Don't do that. You're not a little kid any more!' Robert said sharply. He snatched his jacket free. 'C'mon, you want to see Daisy, don't you?'

Ernie took his courage in both hands and nodded. He put one elbow up as a shield, ducked his head and followed on through the crowd.

At the stage door, Robert thrust his way past a group of twenty or so young men towards a high, narrow window further down the alley; the same window young Tommy had used to signal to Daisy. Seconds later, Hettie came to the door, opened it a crack and let Robert and Ernie in. Then she shut it fast on the noisy gang outside.

'Lucky for you Mr Mills went off early,' she explained.

'So you can come in and wait for us in the warm tonight.' She hurried ahead of them down the corridor into the dressing room. 'Everybody decent?' she sang out. Those who weren't would have time to nip behind the screens.

'More's the pity,' Robert said with a wink. 'Come on, Ern, don't be shy.' He played the man about town with bravado, though on a docker's pay his cheap worsted jacket and clumsily cut waistcoat weren't up to the role. Still, he made up for it with his confident manner and sturdy good looks. All the girls sang out cheerful hellos and smiled kindly at Ernie.

'Hello, Ern. You come to walk us home?' Daisy's muffled voice asked. Her back was to them and her arms raised to fix her hair in the mirror. Then she twisted to look at him, two hairpins clenched between her white teeth.

Ernie nodded hard. 'Yes, please.'

'That's good. You can be my new beau,' she teased. She finished her hair and swept towards Ernie.

'Leave off, Daisy,' Hettie muttered. 'He'll think you mean it.' But she didn't want to spoil Ernie's big night out, so she held her tongue as Daisy ignored her advice and asked Ernie to help her on with her coat and hat. The thrill he felt was spread all over his broad, open face. Who could want to spoil that?

Fully dressed now, Daisy held up her arm, face to face with Ernie. 'C'mon,' she insisted, 'you gotta hook your arm like this, Ern, and I gotta slip mine through the hook, like this, see. That's if we're walking out together!'

Mechanically Ernie did as he was told. Disbelief spread across his face and he turned to Robert.

'You sure Chalky White don't mind?' Robert asked, half serious. He wasn't one to spare her blushes. 'We don't want Ern messing with the likes of Chalky and his gang.'

Daisy coloured up. 'That was ages ago. Anyhow, it ain't none of your business,' she said, with a deft little push against his chest. 'Ready, Ern? Let's go.' She sailed down the corridor with him, out into the cold alley and up past the gaggle of men at the door.

Hettie and Robert followed on. 'That the truth?' he asked. 'She got rid of Chalky?' He watched Daisy carefully from behind.

Hettie sighed. 'That's what she reckons. Says she told him she didn't like the look of him thank you very much.' They reached the main street, still humming with traffic and people.

'They looked pretty flaming friendly down our place that Saturday night.' Robert was taken aback. He knew it was usually Chalky who gave the girls their marching orders.

'You don't know Daisy,' Hettie said with a small frown.

'What you on about? She's only lived down the court ever since I can remember!'

'No. I mean she takes it into her head that she likes some bloke or other, or else she doesn't, and either way she goes at it like a steam engine. I can just picture her telling Chalky to get lost. And look at her now with poor Ern. See what I mean?'

Daisy was showing Ernie how to walk in step, arms entwined around each other's waists.

'Poor Ern, nothing!' Robert said. 'He's enjoying every second of it!'

'But she's putting it on,' Hettie told him. 'She's like that with all the men; it's all an act with Daisy. Show her a man, and she'll make up to him no matter what. Next day it's all over. She blows hot and cold; it'll get her into deep trouble one of these days.'

Robert shrugged. 'Leave off, Ett, she's a big girl now.

What's her game, though? She after someone with plenty of cash, then? Some rich charlie to get her out of that lousy tenement?'

Hettie shook her head. 'Gawd knows. I don't think *she* does.' They walked together in silence. 'I tell you one thing, Rob; she ain't after poor Ern!'

The foursome walked through pools of light past dingy, windswept alleys, and underneath a railway arch as a train thundered overhead.

Amy's rendezvous with the boss's son took place as planned. The fact that she'd never been to the cinema before heightened the thrill of meeting up with Teddy Cooper, who looked dashing as usual.

He was a loose-limbed man, slight but well proportioned, with a small head and fine, almost straw-coloured hair parted neatly to one side. He had his mother's straight, slim features from the Kearney side. The Coopers were smaller, squatter, more pugnacious. Teddy had early learned the value of a smile to bridge those awkward family moments of disapproval. A smile had always melted his mother's soft heart and disarmed even his short-tempered father. Now he used it to good effect with the girls.

'My, you're a bobby dazzler!' he told Amy, linking arms and rushing her up the street to find a taxi.

Amy was gratified. It had been worth the effort of dashing into the Duke on her way home to borrow one of Hettie's best blouses. At seventeen, Amy's own wardrobe was practically non-existent. What she had, her mother pawned anyway. As she sat beside Teddy in the taxi, smelling the brown leather seats, she saw the familiar streets whirl by and almost pinched herself to believe her luck.

The unreality of her evening was reinforced by the incredible magic of the moving picture show. If Teddy was bored by this part of the outing, he managed not to show it, sitting at ease with his arm draped around Amy's soft, round shoulder. The flickering light fell on her upturned face and across the creamy lace on her breasts. She held his hand tight as a train appeared to rush straight at them on the screen, and she marvelled at the actualities that showed the suffragettes rallying at Hyde Park and going on to attack the Houses of Parliament. 'What's it say, Teddy?' she leaned over and whispered. The screen writing was moving on too quickly for her to follow.

'It says, "The fooligans were repulsed by the police with heavy loss of dignity, drapery and millinery!"' he read out in a voice loud enough for others to overhear.

They laughed out loud at the pictures of small, well-dressed women being picked up lock, stock and barrel by burly policemen and carted off to prison. Then the piano struck up the first dramatic chords for the main feature. It began with a flying machine accident and a thrilling rescue from the spars of its flimsy wings. Amy held her breath. Sometimes she had to close her eyes and let Teddy hug her close. These were the thrills of a lifetime, sitting there watching the flickering black and white pictures, casting off dull care.

'Oh, Teddy, that was wonderful!' Amy sat glued to her seat until the last piano chord had died away. She sighed happily and let him raise her and lead her into the aisle. On his arm, being led out of the cinema, she felt very grand to be introduced to a friend of Teddy's as 'Miss Amy Ogden'. Teddy said the man's name was Maurice Leigh.

The man nodded. 'Did you enjoy the picture, Miss Ogden?'

'Oh yes!' She cast an animated glance at Teddy.

'Enjoy it? She missed half of it!' Teddy laughed. 'Half the time she had her head buried inside my jacket!'

'Oh, Teddy, I never!'

'Oh, Teddy, she did! You'd better tell your manager this picture's too strong for the weaker sex, Maurice. It'll have them fainting in the aisles in the more thrilling bits if he's not careful!'

The man grinned back without much amusement. He'd recently transferred to working at the Empire from being deputy manager at the Southwark Palace under Fred Mills. That was where he'd regularly come across Teddy Cooper before; it was one of his man-about-town haunts. Maurice saw moving pictures as the new thing, bound to supersede the old music halls before the decade was out. He first fell under their spell during the short bioscope sequences grudgingly added to the bill by Mr Mills, to follow the novelty acts he booked each week. Wanting to keep up with the times, Maurice moved on to the Balham Empire. 'I'll tell Mr Phillips what you say,' he told Teddy. 'Too much excitement isn't good for the ladies, eh?'

'That's the ticket.' Teddy drew Amy quickly on, out through the glittering foyer. In the street he hailed another taxi. 'Time for a little drink,' he said.

Amy was surprised when he stopped the taxi outside Coopers'. 'I thought you said we was going for a drink?' she queried. A few hundred yards up the street the Duke's bright lights beckoned.

Teddy paid the driver and the cab drove off. He pulled Amy along by the side of the store, past windows full of tan shoes, kid gloves, walking canes with silver handles. 'So I did. A quiet little drink, not a nasty noisy one up at the pub.' He took a key from his pocket and unlocked a tradesmen's door at the back of the shop. 'Courtesy of my old man. He keeps a good drinks cabinet in the office.' He grinned.

Amy grinned back. Teddy had a cheek, taking her up to his old man's office on the first floor, getting out his whisky. She followed, dragging at his coat sleeve as they passed through the department which sold women's costumes. He stopped and let her finger the trimmings on a black velvet costume which would cost weeks of wages to Amy. He fiddled with the change machines as she went and touched costume after costume with her fingertips, sending the small canisters flying along the overhead system of pulleys and fine, taut steel wires. Amy heard their ghostly whir and ping in the dark, empty store.

'C'mon.' Teddy went and pulled her along. 'I need a drink.' He pointed through an archway into the next department. 'See, that's ladies' millinery.'

She had a glimpse of magnificent hats the size of large dinner plates, swathed in net, edged with lace, resplendent with feathers and bows. 'Is that where I'll work, after Christmas, Teddy?' She went close to him and nestled inside his arm against his chest. 'After you've asked your old man?'

He wouldn't have believed her simplicity if he hadn't seen it so often before. He nodded, made more promises and drew her on.

Teddy Cooper didn't expect to expend much more energy on words at this stage of the seduction. He'd offer the girl a strong drink. She'd take it. There'd be surrender in her eyes as he backed her up against the big, flat expanse of his father's desk.

At the last minute Amy struggled, being young and ignorant. It wasn't out of self-respect that she tried to push him off, nor any vestige of honour, but out of sheer panic. She felt Teddy's strong body close against her. It pressed her down and back. There was some fumbling and breathlessness. She tried to scream, but he put one hand over her mouth. Afterwards, she opened her eyes in time to see his face backing off into the dim room, hard and expressionless.

'Get dressed quickly,' he said. He went and wiped the two whisky glasses and placed them back in the cupboard along with the bottle, which he put to the back of the shelf.

Dazed and confused, Amy did as she was told. Sobs rose and racked her throat as she struggled to fasten her blouse. She felt him take her roughly by the arm and send her out of the office. She heard doors lock as they passed from department to department and down the stairs. The magnificent hats taunted her from their stands. Even she now knew they mocked her with Teddy's empty promises.

Only once she dared to glance up at him as he locked the last door and they stood out on the dark, cold street. His face showed nothing at all. Next day in the workshop he wouldn't even bother to acknowledge her.

Chapter Eight

The next day came without blurring Amy's razor-sharp awareness of the horrible scene in Mr Cooper's office. But her sleepless night did allow her to make private adjustments to her hopes and dreams. When Teddy cut her dead at work, she knew for a certainty that she'd never set foot in the hatshop again. Still shocked, she felt a hot surge of anger. Bleeding idiot! she told herself. Bleeding little fool! But Dora's told-you-so looks gradually eased and the women grew kinder as they saw how far she'd fallen off her little pedestal of vanity. They promised not to breathe a word of the affair to Amy's mother, Dolly, when they spotted her trudging up out of the depths of the basement after a hard day's work, and Amy herself decided that her family would never know. If they all kept quiet, at least she would be able to hang on to her job. But if a breath of it got through to old man Cooper, Amy would be out on the street and begging Annie Wiggin for her old job back, for it would be Amy not Teddy who got the blame.

There was one blessing, she told herself; at least she could be sure she hadn't gone and got herself pregnant like Jess Parsons. Everyone knew Jess had been forced to leave her place in Hackney and was hanging around waiting for the nine months to be up. Dress it up how you like, Jess had landed herself in more of a mess than Amy. Frances

Parsons might be forbidding anyone in the family to talk about it, but the gossip was up and down the court, and all along the neighbouring streets.

Christmas came and went at the Duke with plenty of eating and drinking upstairs, and the usual neighbourhood gatherings in the bar below. Jess settled well into the family routine. Her greatest surprise in coming home under these circumstances was her sister Frances's reaction to it all. Frances, whom she considered so proper, talked most matter-of-factly about the possibilities concerning the baby. Would Jess want to go through with the pregnancy, or did she want Frances to talk to the women she knew at the Workers' Education Institute who would have respectable connections in the medical profession? If Jess wanted to go ahead and have the baby, would she then put it up for adoption? There were many middle-class women, childless and pining for a baby, who would give it a good home. All this Frances considered over her pile of mending, or sitting in rare moments with her feet up after a long day in the pharmacy. 'Let's do what we think is best, Jess,' she insisted. 'Let's not get bogged down by all that nonsense about who's to blame and your life being ruined. It's so old hat.'

'Does Pa think I'm ruined, then?' Jess had taken over the cooking since she came back. She was busy peeling enough potatoes to feed a battalion, sleeves rolled back, sharp knife in hand.

Frances put her head to one side. 'Most likely. He was brought up strict, remember, and he's seen some terrible things. Girls being driven out on to the street, men setting out to get drunk and go and ruin a girl's good name. He's lived too long round here to take it well.'

'If it's that bad for him having me round, I can pack my things and go, y'know.' Jess's condition still made her hypersensitive as far as Duke was concerned.

'Don't be soft. We managed to have a good Christmas together, didn't we? Does it look as if he's dying to get rid of you? No, you've got to stay and see it through, whatever you decide.'

'I've already decided.' Jess came in from the kitchen, drying her hands on the apron. She knelt beside the fire and leaned back against her sister's lap. 'I want to keep this baby, Frances.' She said it quietly, with complete conviction.

Frances listened to the tick of the clock and watched the flames flicker in the background.

'I've thought it through a thousand times. I never wanted this baby, and I'd give hundreds of pounds for it never to have happened in the first place.' She paused. When she continued, her rich voice was deliberately flattened out and quiet. 'And before you ask, Frances, I ain't never going to talk about exactly how it happened. Only to say I never did nothing to make it happen, and when it did I fought it like mad, only it didn't make no difference.' She looked up quickly. 'Don't you tell Pa! It wouldn't do any good telling him. That's that. That's all there is to it.'

Frances kept quiet about having told Duke as much, right at the start. 'Why? Why is that all, Jess? There should be a price for him to pay, that's what I think. As it is, he gets away scot-free.'

'Oh yes.' Jess's voice rose a little in scorn. 'Maybe he does. But what do I do about it? Where do I turn? To his ma and pa? You seen them, Frances. All the years I worked for them in that big house, scrubbing and polishing, fetching and carrying. Well, it counted for nothing when it came to protecting their precious little boy!'

Frances had to concede the point. 'It's a crying shame,' she said softly.

Jess took her hand. 'You're right there. Any rate, I'll keep the child, but I still ain't happy about what Pa thinks.' She could take the blame, deal with gossip from people on the fringes of her life, the neighbours up and down Duke Street, but she didn't know if she could stand Duke's anger and hurt. And she was past being able to sit in a corner to sulk.

Frances stroked Jess's bowed head. Her hair curled softly; the only one of the sisters whose hair lifted from her forehead in dark waves. Otherwise she was plainer; less pleasing at first glance according to general opinion. Her cheeks were thinner, her mouth less curved. Her straight brows tapered over deep-set, dark eyes which gave her the look of someone in retreat from the world. Jess's natural look was one of suspicion and withdrawal. In figure she was too spare about the shoulders, and she never allowed her dress to emphasize her natural curves. 'You don't make the best of yourself,' Hettie used to natter. 'Anyone would think you was a proper ugly duckling!' Jess would laugh self-consciously and go on to praise the copper highlights in Hettie's luxurious hair.

The day after their talk, Frances came back from work with some new information for Jess. She knew of a place out in the Kent countryside where Jess could go while her baby was born. Jess heard her race upstairs in unaccustomed haste. 'Oh, Jess!' she cried, flinging her hat down on the chair. 'I got some good news for you. There's a woman I know from night class. She came in the shop today, and guess what! Her sister lives out in the country in a small place, and she says she'd be glad to have you stay with them. They're nice people. And the best of it is, Jess, this woman's been a midwife all these years. Delivering babies is nothing to her!'

Jess stood by the kitchen range, hands covered in flour. She was in the midst of an evening bread-baking session, with Ernie moulding scoops of dough into round shapes on a floured board. The room smelt of fermenting yeast and sugar.

'D'you hear, Jess? I found a place for you to have the baby!'

'Thanks but no thanks,' Jess replied. She ducked her head and carried on kneading dough.

'What do you mean? Think about it. It'll be the middle of summer, it'd be like a holiday for you. Fresh air and sunshine. Jess, think about it, please!' If she stayed here for the birth, if there were complications, Duke wouldn't cope so easily. Besides the benefit of the baby being given a healthy start, there was her father to consider. Going away was easily the best plan, if only stubborn Jess would listen. 'There'd be the hop picking, if you felt up to it. Remember what good fun that was when you was a little tiny kid, Jess, sitting high up on them carts down the narrow lanes.'

'Stop going on about it, Frances, will you. I said thanks but no thanks.' Clouds of flour rose from the board as Ernie passed her the soft round shapes and she kneaded them a second time. 'And while we're at it, Frances, you can stop looking around for work for me an' all. I can do that myself when the time comes.'

Frances stood stock-still in the middle of the room as if Jess had struck her across the face. A look of pain filled her eyes. She'd been making plans for all their sakes, determined to make the best of it. As the oldest sister, that was her responsibility. Besides, she had the right connections.

As soon as Jess saw the impact of her words, she wiped

her hands and went across. 'Don't take on. Look here, Frances, God knows what I'd've done without you, the way you stood up to the Holdens and made everything straight with Pa so I could come back home.' Jess's own dark eyes filled with tears. She put one arm round Frances's shoulder. 'But now I got to start thinking for myself. When the birth comes near, that'll be time enough to think about midwives. Maybe then I'll want to get away from it all for a bit, I don't know.'

Frances, drying her eyes on a handkerchief, glanced up with a glimmer of hope.

'But maybe not. Like I say, Frances, I just don't know yet. And maybe I *will* feel like working in the Post Office, or maybe I'll take in work here and look after the baby all by myself.'

'Take in work? You mean washing?' Frances thought of Mary O'Hagan slaving away over her tub and board, day in, day out.

'No need to look like you swallowed a lemon!' Jess laughed. 'I ain't proud, Frances. I can't afford to be now, can I?' She went and resumed her work on the loaves of bread.

'Well, that sort of talk makes me mad, I can tell you!' At last Frances unbuttoned her coat and began to bustle about as normal. 'It's not the fact of having a baby or a sister who's a fallen woman that matters!'

'Frances!' Jess protested with a half laugh.

'No, I said it's not that. I bet I'll love this little baby nearly as much as you, Jess. And in my opinion, it's him who's fallen from grace, as you very well know.'

'So?' Jess pummelled away, handing finished loaves to Ernie to put them into the tins.

'So it's where it leaves you, having to take in washing, working like a skivvy for the rest of your born days!'

Frances sounded really angry as she went and hung her coat on the peg.

Jess went up to her again and hugged her. The flour came off her apron on to Frances's tailored grey skirt. 'Don't worry, we'll manage,' she promised. 'Just you wait and see. When the time comes, we'll manage.'

As Jess's pregnancy continued, Frances learned to step aside and let her make her own plans. March came, and the short winter days began to lengthen, so she could walk up to work in the half-light and begin each long day in better spirits.

Her life at the chemist's shop was one round of filling shelves and making up prescriptions, in which she took great pride. In the shop with the brightly coloured carboys arranged along the high shelf in the front window, she began the day by replenishing empty sections in the great bank of tiny drawers behind the counter. Their contents were indicated by strange, abbreviated Latin labels. Then, as customers came in with prescriptions, it was Frances's job to make up the pills, ointments, capsules and suppositories.

All day she worked with mortar and pestle, mixing powders from the drawers with solidifying agents such as syrup of glucose or gum tragacanth. She would work the carefully measured ingredients into a smooth paste then roll this out on to a board with a hinged, ridged cutter attached. This divided the paste into semicircular scallops. These were further rounded by hand, pressed, pulled and pushed again on the cutting block, and finished off in a rounding machine which she had to work in a small figure-of-eight motion until each pill emerged. Then she varnished or silvered them with silver leaf, ready for the customer to come back and collect. As far as she knew, she had never made a mistake in the intricate process, and her pills were commended for their perfect roundness.

Between times, she sold pick-me-ups such as Seidlitz Powders or Andrews Liver Salts, and Williams Pink Pills for anaemia. Her customers relied on her knowledge of the proprietary brands and often trusted her advice over any doctor's.

So her daily life went on, full and entirely predictable. One change came about in the evenings, though. She began to take an interest through friends at the Workers' Education Institute in Mrs Pankhurst's campaign to get women the vote. She went to a meeting and heard one of the Pankhurst daughters speak. She liked her ringing tones and call to action. But coming away, outside the hall, she felt it was for other women to act; women with money and good speaking voices and influence with politicians, not for working women like her. Besides, the direct action alarmed her. Frances wasn't one for setting fire to post-boxes or smashing shop windows. Only, she went home and looked at pregnant Jess, and thought how unfair it was for women living in this man's world. It made her feel helpless, watching Jess struggle.

At home, Robert joked his way through chores in the bar, pitting his strength against the thirty-six-gallon barrels as he rolled, tipped and heaved them on to their wooden gantry, alongside Joxer. Fixing them in place with wooden chocks and tapping the bung holes for Duke was his daily task, done in the early hours before he ventured down to the dockside. He held a blue ticket, second in line to the red-ticket men, but ahead of the casuals who turned up on these raw mornings with little hope of work.

The dockers' living was always precarious, but Robert was healthy and often favoured because of his strength and good nature. Only, Chalky White seemed to have developed a grudge against him after the minor row in the pub, and he often put in a bad word with the gaffers, who themselves had to keep Chalky sweet. He knew all the angles and could exert a certain influence over who got work, so Robert's heart would sink whenever he saw Chalky's tall, pale figure in the queue. It was often a sign that he'd be turned away, back to hanging about at home or down at the boxing club.

At twenty-two, and with too much time on his hands, he would drift into pubs further afield, knowing Duke would disapprove of any serious drinking bout on home territory. He'd heard what his pa said about the men who came in at Christmas, slammed their guinea on the bar and ordered drink for as long as the money lasted. This would send them home dead-drunk after five or six separate sessions, while their wives and kids went without. 'A man who can't hold his drink ain't a proper man,' Duke said. 'And that includes knowing when to stop.'

Once or twice during the spring Robert took Ernie back to the Palace to watch Daisy and Hettie do their stage routines. The boy treated it like magic still, but it was beginning to bore Robert. He liked to spend more and more time with the ladies, and though Daisy would flirt gamely with both him and Ernie after the show, she'd begun to lose some of her sparkle. Anyway, they'd known each other for donkey's years. He wanted grown-up, worldly women who knew their way around. Frances could sniff and make comments about that 'type' of woman all she liked; it wouldn't stop him from going out with them and having a good time.

*

Hettie confided her own worries about Daisy to Jess, who kept indoors most of the time these days.

'There's something up with her, and I can't put my finger on it.' She shrugged. 'Why should I worry, that's what I'd like to know?'

'I seen her the other day when you brought her up here. She looks all right to me.' Jess had hold of one end of a sheet, Hettie the other. They were folding laundry.

'No, she's getting thin, losing her looks. And you seen how Robert was acting up to her, same as he always does. She hardly took no notice.'

'Good thing, too. Rotten little flirt.'

'Who, Robert?' Hettie took the folded sheet and smoothed it flat on top of the pile on the table.

Jess laughed. 'Yes, Robert! No, it's Daisy I'm on about, ain't it? It's time she started to behave.'

Hettie had to admit it was true. 'Only I still feel sorry for her, giving over most of her money to keep them kids fed. And she has to keep herself looking decent, too. You have to in our line of work. And she ain't even twenty yet. It ain't much of a life.'

'Better than being in service,' Jess reminded her.

'Sorry, Jess, I never thought.' Hettie took another sheet from the basket and tossed one end to Jess. 'It ain't all a bed of roses up at the Palace, you know.'

'I never said it was.'

'No, but I know that's what people think. Anyway, I seen poor Daisy having a ding-dong battle with Archie Small when I came away last night. They was in the girls' dressing room after the show. Archie was trying it on with Daisy as per usual, and she was pushing him off as quick as ever he came at her. You should've seen his chins wobble whenever she pushed him, never mind his horrible fat belly!'

'Ugh!' Jess shrieked and shook out the sheet with a sharp snap.

Hettie laughed. 'See! And I'd 've done the same if he came pestering me. Only, you can't afford to go making enemies in that place. That's why Daisy had to get in with Chalky White that time.'

'Why?' Placidly Jess folded the last sheet and glanced at her sister.

'Because Freddie wanted her to.'

Jess tutted. 'That ain't right.'

'No, it ain't. And Daisy still gets the silly bleeders round the stage door bringing her chocolates all the time. She's still as popular as ever, but there's something going on with her. Like I said, I can't put my finger on it.'

'She out of her depth? I mean to say, one sweetheart bringing chocolates is nice for a girl. Three or four with chocolates is a headache.' Jess lifted the pile of laundry and made off to the bedrooms. 'Tell her to give one of them to me if he's halfway decent!'

Hettie stifled her laugh as Duke's footsteps came upstairs. At the same time, Sadie shot in from the kitchen. 'Here, you wasn't listening, was you?' Hettie made a grab for her youngest sister.

'No. Listen, he's coming now, Ett! Can you hear? Will you ask him now? You promised!' Sadie tugged at Hettie's arm.

'I never. Any rate, why don't you ask him yourself?'

'Oh, Ett, please! He'll say yes if you ask him!' The undreamt of had happened to Sadie two days before. After school, Charlie Ogden had come up and asked her to go cycling that weekend. Now she needed her pa's permission.

'Pipe down!' Hettie warned.

Duke opened the door. 'Here, what you two up to?' he

asked. Sadie had scrambled to the table to sit, but he'd heard her squeaking on to Hettie about something.

Hettie made a great show of clearing her throat. 'Sadie's got a young man!' She came out with it, plain as a pike-staff.

Sadie yelped. 'Oh, Ett, I haven't!'

'Well, then, you won't want to go cycling with him if he don't exist!' She stood, hands on hips, a smile playing round her pretty mouth.

'I do.' Sadie gasped and darted at her. 'Oh, Ett, how could you!' She stopped, pulled her skirt straight and faced her father. 'Pa, can I go cycling on Sunday with Charlie Ogden?' Her face flamed red with embarrassment. She'd kill Hettie after.

Duke brushed the ends of his grey moustache. Hettie could see his own eyes light up in a hidden grin. 'Well, my pet, there's just one thing about that when you stop to think.'

'What, Pa? Charlie's a nice boy. He reads books!' Sadie pleaded.

Duke nodded. 'I dare say he does. But does he own a bicycle?'

She stared hard. 'He'll borrow one!'

'Do *you* own a bicycle?'

'I'll borrow one an' all!'

Duke checked the venue, grumbled about women on bicycles, but he was visibly weakening. Finally, despite his resolution to be strict with Sadie, he agreed. He remembered his own young days, before the army, when he and a gang of pals used to go cycling into the countryside. His youngest daughter was growing up, he realized. They had their share of troubles, but the family was sticking together. That was what mattered to him most of all.

Frances came home as Hettie got ready to go out to

work. She gathered them round the supper table, with Ernie sitting opposite. 'I've got a piece of really good news,' she said, laying her gloves across her lap and leaning forward towards him.

Chapter Nine

At eighteen Ernie had never held down a job. He was willing and strong, but employers would look him up and down and decide against him. They set him against skinnier but brighter lads and weren't to know that Ernie's goodwill was worth more than sharp wit in the fetching and carrying kind of job Ernie wanted to do. So the family had to put up over the years with the general opinion that he was useless in the work sense. Duke could keep him busy in the pub and Ernie seemed happy helping Robert or Joxer to take delivery from the draymen, or to roll the empty barrels up the slope into their carts. But now things were about to change.

'Henshaw's want an errand boy,' Frances announced. 'The last one's gone off hop picking for the summer and they need someone else.'

Henshaw's was a thriving corner shop and eating-house on the edge of the market area up Duke Street. They did good business in the café selling hot pea soup and tea to the traders. The shop had also built up its own profits by running a good delivery service on orders for eggs and bread. Their errand boys were usually much younger than Ernie, Mr Henshaw told Frances, but he knew him as a steady, strong lad and he might be willing to give him a go.

'This last lad has left me in the lurch. You can't get a

steady delivery boy for love nor money,' he said. He'd caught Frances in passing on her way back from work.

'Ernie's steady,' she promised. Mr Henshaw was offering the chance of a lifetime.

'And can he ride a bike?'

'Yes, Robert taught him. He's really very willing, Mr Henshaw. You won't find a more willing lad than Ernie, and he won't let you down like some.'

The shopkeeper, an upstanding Methodist, nodded. 'Can he read the names on the orders, though? We never considered that, did we?'

Frances frowned. 'Ernie can't read, it's true. But his memory's good. You just have to tell him the name and he'll remember it. He knows his numbers. You just show him the house number on the order and he'll remember the rest.'

In the end Henshaw agreed. He and his wife, Bea, were childless after an early tragedy with their only son. The boy had died of scarlet fever and the couple had lost heart. But Henshaw had a soft spot for Ernie Parsons, who was known up and down the street as a gentle giant. Though he was often on the receiving end of the street boys' name-calling and tricks, he was never seen to use his strength to retaliate. He would just stick his fists in his pockets and whistle, cap tilted back, looking straight ahead. And he knew these streets inside out, going up and down to the public baths, the football park, the market stalls.

'Mr Henshaw will set you to work tomorrow morning, Ern, and he'll see how you do. You'll have to be up early and you'll have to look smart. They'll give you an apron at the shop, and they'll show you what to do when you get there.'

Slowly Ernie took it all in. He was going to join the great London workforce. He'd be trusted to run errands and then he'd be paid for doing them. Mr Henshaw would give him a wage at the end of each week.

'Oh, Ern, you'll ride that nice bike with Henshaw's name printed on, and you'll carry all the stuff in that great basket on the front. It'll be smashing.' Hettie was delighted for him.

'Pa?' Ernie turned for advice. If his pa said yes, he'd love to try. But he was afraid that Duke would miss him too much in the pub. What would he do without him? That's what his pa always said.

'I don't know, son. It's a big step.' Duke was worried. He wasn't sure that Frances hadn't overestimated Ernie. If he were to bite off more than he could chew, it could do real damage to the boy. Duke didn't know if even Frances realized how much Ernie relied on slow, clear orders given to him step by step by someone who understood the way his mind worked. 'He's used to me telling him what to do,' he explained.

'But it'd do him good to learn something different, Pa. He can't rely on you for ever!' Frances glanced at Hettie and Jess for support. This was a sore subject for Duke. 'The job will give him a whole new life. It's time he had a go.'

'Frank Henshaw will keep an eye on him, Pa,' Hettie added. 'If you ask me, it's a good idea.' She went up and kissed Ernie on the cheek. 'I gotta go now, Ern. I hope it all works out. See you tomorrow.' She breezed out with a wink at Robert. 'See if you can talk the old man round,' she whispered.

'I don't know.' Duke sat stubbornly at the table, heavy forearms resting on the cloth. 'I don't want Ern to take a knock over it. What if Henshaw decides it ain't working out?'

Solemnly Ernie looked from face to face as the family conference was played out. Sometimes he felt as if he wanted the chance to prove himself like Frances, Jess and Robert said. But other times he just wanted to stay in the bar and help his pa. 'No, I'll stay here!' He put in a comment of his own at last. 'Pa needs me.'

It brought Frances to a full stop. She turned to Duke in mute appeal.

The old man grinned then sighed. 'No, Ern, I reckon you'd best give it a go. I can't keep you here with me for ever, like Frances says.' He stood up and put a hand on his son's shoulder. 'I couldn't sleep for thinking I'd ditched your chances over this. Go ahead, son, do it!'

Ernie sat opposite, looking suddenly down in the mouth.

'No need to take on. I'm not saying I don't need you no more! You can do this little job for Henshaw and you can still come home and help me and Robert with the barrels.' Duke went and gave his shoulder a friendly slap when he saw the boy's face light up again. 'I only hope it's the right thing, son, and I wish you luck.'

Frances was satisfied. Duke would always have to have the last word, of course, and she had to admit he was getting a bit contrary in his old age. He was set in his ways, but not too set to give way over the thorny problem with Jess, or to see reason over Ernie's future now. She smiled at having performed the usual balancing trick, sizing people up and sorting out their problems. She was good at that; in a way it was like mixing minute quantities of medicine at work and weighing them on the little brass scales.

'Well done, Frances,' Jess said later. 'Ern's thrilled to bits.'

'Yes. I'm sure it'll help make him more responsible.' Frances struggled for the right word. Even so, she went to bed that night with her fingers crossed, hoping to goodness that she was right.

*

So, during April, Duke Street got used to Ernie in his long white apron making his wobbly way between the stalls, his basket loaded with fresh bread and eggs. It was a wonder to see him keep his precarious balance on his sit-up-and-beg, his long legs pedalling, his elbows stuck out wide. But the noises of the street didn't distract him; not the roar of the taxi-cabs, nor the rattle of the tram-cars. He swerved round horses and carts, and barrows piled high with fruit. With total dedication he would steer his way to number 11 Meredith Close down the side of Coopers', to the black door with the lion knocker; or to number 32 Oliver Street, past the Board School to the house with the broken basement window. He would deliver his goods and wobble back to Henshaw's with his empty basket, perhaps stopping for a word with Nora Brady at her fish stall, or more likely Annie Wiggin, whose own stall stood right outside his corner shop.

'Blimey, that was quick, Ern,' Annie would call. Spring had arrived, so she'd switched her black shiny hat for a pale straw one, decked out with red ribbon from her range of haberdashery.

Ernie grinned. 'Mr Henshaw says we got a busy day ahead of us.'

'Oh well, better not hold you up, then.' Annie could talk and serve at the same time, measuring lace along the length of her arm from shoulder to wrist, and throwing in an extra few inches for good measure. She would wrap it in a cone of white tissue paper, exchange it for money and give the right change without even pausing. 'How's that sister of yours getting on, Ern? The one with the baby. Is it born yet? Can't be, else we'd all get an earful of its yelling through the window of a night. Jess, ain't it? Tell her I was asking after her.' Annie's one-way conversation rattled on as Ernie propped his bike on its metal stand. 'And tell your pa I was asking after him an' all, miserable old bleeder!'

Mrs Henshaw was on the doorstep for a breath of air and her eyebrows shot up at Annie's bad language. 'Come along inside, Ernie. There's another order ready here.' Her primly curled head turned away.

Ernie followed her into the Aladdin's cave of soup-tin pyramids and stacks of silver-wrapped chocolate bars while Annie grumbled on. 'Bleeding slave-drivers. Call themselves Christians, they won't even give the poor blighter five minutes' peace. I know what I'd do with their bleeding orders if I was him!' She jammed pins into a pincushion, voodoo style.

Late spring and early summer also brought perfect days for Sadie. Her bike rides with Charlie Ogden had become a regular thing since Duke's first reluctant consent. Escaping from grimy Southwark on a Sunday morning, through Rotherhithe and the newer suburbs further east, they might stop off by the river at Thamesmead. Their more adventurous rides took them far afield along quiet country roads full of the scent of flowers, the woods and hedgerows. They would pile their bicycles alongside dozens of others at a country inn and step inside for ginger-beers out of stone bottles. Once, Sadie had ridden back home with a sheaf of bluebells tied across her handlebars, and their perfume had filled the living room.

Still Duke complained that women couldn't ride bicycles to save their lives. 'When a motor comes up behind, why they gives a scream and falls off,' he teased. 'I seen it.'

'Pa!' Sadie protested with a flounce out of the room. But she didn't worry; her cycling trips with Charlie were too well established for her to mind much.

Charlie came to the tiny backyard of the Duke every fine Sunday. He now had a cycle on permanent loan from the lamed brother of one of the women who worked with his mother in the hosiery department at Coopers'. Sadie's family had clubbed together to buy her a shiny new one of her own. Her heart skipped a beat as she heard his bell ring below, and she would be downstairs in a flash, not bothered about coat or hat.

Once on the road, she felt exhilarated and free, despite her cumbersome skirts, her good mood heightened by the knowledge that Charlie would glimpse her slim ankles and calves. He would show off in turn, riding ahead with a dare-devil call of, 'Look, no hands!' They'd sit to rest on the high grassy banks and Charlie would confide his dreams; how he'd leave the East End behind him for good once he'd passed his scholarship to go to college in Birmingham or Manchester.

'Is that what you want, Charlie?' Sadie lay back in the grass on one of these days out, staring into blue nothing. It all seemed so far ahead. 'What about your ma and pa?'

'What about them? I want to be an engineer. I'll make machines that change the world, like flying machines. I'll be part of something wonderful like that, Sadie, to make my life really mean something! I won't rot away in Paradise Court!'

Hesitantly she said she understood.

'I got a friend at school living out in Putney now. Posh house, a garden even. I wouldn't want to bring him down the court if I could help it, would I?'

Sadie bit back a sharp reply. Paradise Court was good enough for her; she didn't always want something better, like Charlie did. But then maybe he was right; there was a whole big world out there. 'C'mon, let's go.' She sat up and brushed the palms of her hands, unsettled by the turn of conversation.

That was the time when he caught her wrist and stared at her. They knelt face to face, and Charlie tilted his body towards her and kissed her on the lips. 'Don't take on,' he whispered. 'There's all kinds of things I want in this life!'

'Not just books, Charlie Ogden?'

He kissed her again. 'Not just books, Sadie Parsons. And not just a house with a garden.'

That night she had a scolding from Frances for being late and giddy with it. 'Out till all hours, God knows where. Honestly, Sadie, it's not as if you ain't been brought up to know better.'

Sadie went out mouthing Frances's words, mimicking her. She banged the door of the room she shared with Jess. Jess sat at the open window, a shawl thrown loosely over her night-dress. She started as Sadie came in, then went back to staring over the rooftops up into the star-filled sky.

Jess's baby was due in July. In June she finally agreed with Frances's plan for her to go out into Kent, to spare Duke the details of childbirth which held bad memories for him since Pattie's death. A letter from his sister Florrie had finally made up her mind on this.

Florrie was living with a married son in Brighton. She heard the family news on the grapevine, and saw fit to write and tell Jess what a silly girl she'd been, but there, least said about that soonest mended. Only she'd better not cause her poor pa any more trouble, what with business going downhill all the time amidst all this talk of war. Before they knew it, they'd have lost Robert to the army and all the pubs would be empty of custom, and then where would they be? 'Your pa's had enough trouble for one life,' Florrie wrote. 'It's my place as your godmother to tell you this for your own good, Jess. Be a good girl and don't cause no more. Go away somewhere nice and quiet until the worst is over, and be glad if you've still got a home to go back to. I'll close now, wishing you health and happiness, your loving Aunt Flo. PS: My rheumatics is better, thanks to the sea air, Tom says.'

The letter stormed Jess's sensitive heart. She was a burden, a disgrace. If not only Frances but others saw it that way, it must be true. She would go into Kent soon and lie low. Everything was arranged through the friend of Frances. In the meantime, Jess kept to her room, except to cook and clean.

Florrie in Brighton wasn't the only one to be troubled by prospects of war. If it wasn't bleeding Ireland, it was that demon Kaiser, the bar-stool politicians in the Duke muttered darkly. Joe O'Hagan shuffled in one evening, furnished with a sixpence from his daughter Daisy's purse. He was a depressing enough sight in himself, pale and drawn, with a listless eye. Daisy had given him the money to spare her mother the sight of him for an hour or two. 'Go drown your sorrows, Pa!' she cried.

Mary sighed after his retreating footsteps. 'Go ditch them on some other poor fool, you mean.'

Arthur Ogden saw Joe enter the bar. He was at a terrible loose end himself, having read through the *Daily Express* headlines. His glass was empty, as was his pocket, so he hailed the newcomer with a faint hope of some improvement there. 'Hello, Joe. Some bleeding bertie's got himself shot, it says here,' he said as he thrust the newspaper under the illiterate newcomer's nose. 'And it says the whole of Europe's turned upside down over it.'

'That beats me,' Joe said in his nasal drawl. He ordered two pints of half and half; one for Arthur. 'All I know for sure with this shambles you call a government is that they can't even sort out the mess in their own backyard.' He sat by Arthur to make up a gloomy pair. The cellarman Joxer was there to serve them their drinks, and he scowled from under dark brows. Joxer had nothing particular against them. He never smiled and he never spoke to the customers at the bar, preferring a shadowy existence in the cellar. No one knew where he slept or how he lived. He was a drifter who'd found an unexpected soft spot in Duke's heart, and was accepted as such.

'By "backyard" I take it you mean Dublin?' Arthur took up the conversation with a self-important air. 'You mean your home turf?'

'Certainly I do. It's in a state of chaos, I'm telling you here and now. And we've no need of any Kaiser to go complicating things.' Joe spoke bitterly and brought the short conversation to an abrupt end.

'Drink up,' Robert encouraged. 'And cheer up, for gawd's sake.' He was taking over from Joxer and found himself rattled by the dreary talk. An army career didn't appeal, not when there was a good chance of being shot at into the bargain. He'd disagreed with Duke about it recently, resenting his father's patriotic talk. He certainly wasn't as keen as his father's generation had been to fight for king and country. 'It's the twentieth century, Pa. We do things in a different way now,' he insisted.

'Tell me that when the fighting starts,' Duke replied. 'And if you do I'll say you're no son of mine!'

'Anyone'd think you'd just got your call-up papers,' Robert told Arthur and Joe. 'You two are out of it whatever happens, ain't you? So bleeding well cheer up!'

Joxer's mouth bent in a sarcastic grin as he passed by. His night's work done, he was drifting off to wherever he spent his lonely nights. But instead of heading off down Duke Street, he turned and swung open the door again. 'Trouble!' he announced. 'Up the street!'

As word went round, people crowded out of the pubs and houses into the street. It was a clear June night when curiosity could be satisfied without the dampening effect of cold, wind or rain.

'What's happening?' Annie asked, darting quick as a flash up the court to the pub corner. 'What's all that bleeding noise?'

Dolly and Amy Ogden rushed up the street after her. Whatever it was, it came from up near Coopers'. They could hear shouts organized into a kind of high chant, then the crash of splintering glass. Amy broke into a run; more than her mother could manage. Ahead of her she saw Robert Parsons with Frances at his side. Even Duke had come downstairs and strode along, leaving Jess and Sadie with Ernie to look down from the window. He strode along, right up the middle of the street past a stationary hansom, the horses champing at the bit.

'Window-smashers!' someone gasped. 'It's them suffragettists!' A mob had gathered on the corner of Duke Street and Meredith Close. Now everyone converged on that focal point.

Frances heard the word spread like wildfire. 'Window-smashers!' The sound of splintering glass grew louder. Soon it was plain that the mob was made up entirely of women.

Some of the men in the crowd of onlookers pushed their hats to the back of their heads and whistled in amazement at the sight.

Terrified by the violence, but thrilled by their daring, Frances drew level with Coopers' shop front. She held her breath. She'd never seen a sight like this in all her life. Twenty or thirty women pelted stones and rained hammer blows against the plate glass. They'd broken through in several places, so the windows were crazed in giant spider's web patterns all along the length of the department store, which was twenty yards or so fronting on to Duke Street. Now they'd run down the side into Meredith Close. As one woman succeeded with her hammer blow, another would dart forward and add her own force. Glass caved in on the expensive goods on display, glinting like dangerous jewels under the street-lights. The women cheered, their faces savage with delight as they surged down the close together. Then the police arrived, whistles blowing, truncheons at the ready.

'Police!' women's voices cried, sharp and hysterical.

The onlookers stood back to let the men in uniform through. 'You need bleeding strait-jackets, not truncheons,' Arthur Ogden warned. Amy and Dolly stood speechless at his side, joining in the crowd's lust for action. It looked like none of the women would go quietly. Trapped down the close, they fought tooth and nail.

Then there was a hush in the crowd as Jack Cooper and his son rolled up in their big black motor car. They both jumped out and pushed roughly through. Faced with a devastated shop front, the older man stopped dead in his tracks as if the life-blood had suddenly drained from him. He stared in disbelief at the expanses of shattered glass. But Teddy strode angrily over the shards and turned the corner into the close.

The women outnumbered policemen by about three to one, and although one or two had been manhandled off up the street into waiting vans, the gathered crowd hadn't lifted a finger to help. They stood passively, waiting to see the police get the better of the law-breakers, but by no means determined to see it over quickly. So the women were able to fight back by kicking and scratching, shouting all the while at the tops of their enraged voices.

Frances found herself at first roused and then moved to tears. She stood back from the main crowd, watching the struggles of the ones who were roughly taken off to prison.

But Teddy Cooper, beside himself, began lashing out at the women still at large. He lunged at one whose face was already bleeding from flying glass and caught her off balance. Down she went on to the pavement amongst the scuffling, stamping feet. Frances heard her scream. She saw Teddy Cooper poised to smash his boot down on her. Two policemen turned and moved to restrain him. Then Amy Ogden rushed forward.

The woman screamed again. For Amy, the sound brought back a terrible memory. She flung herself at Teddy, yelling his name and sobbing at him to stop. He had time to wrench himself free, there was time to recognize dawning contempt on his face as he made out his assailant, before the policemen took hold of him and dragged him clear of the two women; one knocked full length on the pavement, one desperately calling his name.

It was only a matter of time now before reinforcements arrived and the mob of women was subdued. More uniforms swept up Duke Street and into the close. The crowd saw it was all over and broke up. The last women were carried off. Still Jack Cooper stood there staring at the ruins of his shop, while the police took details from Teddy. Amy was led quietly away by a puzzled Dolly.

Duke and Robert stood their ground as the crowd melted. Regardless of his like or dislike of the local employers, Duke's sense of fair play was upset. He was against the mayhem caused by these women and had to feel sorry for a man whose livelihood stood in ruins before his eyes. So he went up to Cooper. 'You'll need a hand to clear this lot up,' he said. Robert was sent to round up a few fit and sober helpers, along with brooms to sweep up the mess.

Cooper nodded slowly, emerging from his daze. Teddy had gone inside to assess the damage. Unnoticed, Frances stood and watched as the men set to. She felt nothing now after the shock of events; just a coldness round her heart towards these men.

There was a story her mother told her when she was very young about a girl whose heart was pierced by a fragment of glass, and the glass froze her heart so she could no longer love and no longer cry. She became the Ice Queen's child.

The story settled in Frances's mind again now. Robert and her father had no right to help Frank Cooper. She saw it clearly as she turned and walked home. It was the women, driven to desperate action, who needed help. Who cared about the state of a few broken windows when women had to fight these mighty injustices? Frances's rebellious thoughts took shape from this one violent episode. She went slowly back to the Duke, but she felt the ties with her home, her family, her whole history break with each step she took.

Chapter Ten

'Them women need a good hiding,' Duke grumbled when he got back from sweeping up the glass. 'That's what they need.'

Frances couldn't bear to hear him lay down the law. Her hair came loose as she swung round to confront him. 'How can you say that? Do you know what they do when they get them to Holloway? They stick a tube down their throats to feed them! Think of that. It's downright disgusting!'

But his own code was violated. 'Women who go about smashing windows need the feel of the birch on their backs!' he shouted. 'Teach 'em their proper place.' Duke roused was a terrifying spectacle.

Frances sobbed. 'It ain't right. They're sticking up for all us women, not just themselves. And look what happens.'

'You ain't telling me that what they did was sticking up for other women?' He stared at her in disbelief.

'I am! That's just it, Pa. We need to be treated equal; that's what all this is about!'

A look of scorn slowly crept on to his face. He refused to follow her wild reasoning. 'It ain't no wonder you're on the shelf, girl,' he said quietly.

'What!' she screeched in disbelief. She was the one out of control now.

'You heard. I said it ain't no wonder you can't find yourself a decent man like all the other girls.'

He regretted the words even as he spoke them. Frances looked as if she'd been stabbed in the chest. Jess ran in from the bedroom to stop her from falling in a dead faint. He could hear Sadie sobbing. But a stubborn voice reminded him that women would always try to gain the upper hand, either by worming their way in or by outright defiance. You had to fight it for all you were worth. 'I'm off downstairs to finish up,' he told Jess gruffly. 'You sort her out and get her off to bed. She'll come to her senses tomorrow.'

Jess took Frances's full weight as she half fell against her. She called out for Sadie to stop crying. 'Lend a hand. Help me get her to our room.' She struggled, but Frances pushed her off.

'You heard him!' she gasped. 'How can I stay here now? You heard what he said about me!'

'He don't mean it, Frances. Just give him a chance to calm down. Everything will look different tomorrow.' Jess put one hand to her belly as she felt the baby twist and kick. There was a sharp stab of pain low in her abdomen. She sat down and gripped the edge of the table.

'Frances, it's Jess!' Sadie rushed forward to drag her oldest sister away from the dark window. 'She's gone white as a sheet, look!'

Frances was still gripped by a blind determination to cut loose, to live her own life and begin to fight for the cause she believed in. Her lips were set in a straight line as she stared at her own reflection.

'Frances!' Sadie let out another terrified cry. Jess had used both hands to push herself upright. She began to stumble towards the bedroom door.

111

'Get help,' she gasped. 'It's the baby. Go on, fetch someone, quick!'

Frances spun round and ran towards her. 'Oh, Jess, no! Not yet! For God's sake, Sadie, do as she says! No, help me get her into bed!' The sight of Jess doubled up in pain pierced her heart. Selfish, selfish! she told herself. My fault, my fault! 'Oh God, no, Jess. Just hang on. Sadie, run for Dr Fry. Knock until you get an answer. Tell him what's happened.'

Sadie ran wild-eyed down the stairs, out into the street, while Frances used all her strength to lift the fainting Jess safely on to her own bed. She loosened her clothes, then ran to the airing-cupboard for towels. 'It's all right, Jess. Everything's fine. Sadie's gone to fetch Dr Fry.' She stroked her sister's forehead, cold and wet with sweat. 'Is it bad? Is it, my dear?'

Jess turned her head. 'Make this baby live, Frances. Make her live!'

'Oh!' Frances moaned. She could hardly meet Jess's pleading gaze.

'Not your fault,' Jess whispered. Then she turned to grip the bedstead as the spasm of pain came strong and sharp.

Frances felt another hammer blow to her heart. She called out for more help. Robert came running and was sent to boil up water in the kitchen. Duke came up in alarm. He rested a forearm against the door jamb, then retreated. He'd seen it before; a woman struggling in childbirth, fear in the air, the doctor arriving brisk and businesslike because things were not as they should be. The closed door. The cries.

Long into the night Jess struggled. Weakened by loss of blood, faint with pain, she gave birth to a daughter.

Dr Fry cut the cord. Frances gave him a clean square of

linen in which he wrapped the baby tight. 'Here's your little girl, Jess,' he said as he handed her over. Frances wept. She leaned over the bed.

Jess's hands shook. She saw the face of her daughter, her own child. She held her close. Dark eyes opened towards her. She looked up at Frances and smiled.

'Now we've work to do,' Dr Fry said, his voice low and kind. 'Let your sister take the child, Jess. She'll take good care.' He took the baby away from her.

Jess's world was empty. Her head swam with pain.

'We have to stop the bleeding,' the doctor told Frances.

'She will be all right, won't she?' Frances felt the light weight in her arms.

Dr Fry grunted. 'Go through and show Duke his new granddaughter,' he advised. 'I'll do what I can here.'

Duke sat with bowed head by the fire. Robert stood, elbow against the mantelpiece, keeping Ernie calm. Sadie hovered with Hettie by the kitchen door.

Frances stepped forward. 'It's a girl,' she announced.

'Thank God!' Hettie breathed. She'd come in from work, full of news about the window-smashing, only to be greeted by this crisis. Jess's time wasn't up for another month yet. But she found Sadie at the top of the stairs, her hands covering her ears.

Duke looked up.

'A granddaughter for you, Pa.' She spoke softly, held out the child towards him; her own peace offering. The family would need her now, more than ever.

'What about Jess?' Duke's face was drained, his voice cracked. 'I've been praying for her, Frances. She's still with us, ain't she?'

'She is, Pa, and she's putting up a fight.'

113

'Has she seen the child?'

'She has.'

He nodded. 'Then she'll live. She's got everything to live for now, ain't she?' He stood gazing down into the infant's sleeping face. 'My Pattie never saw Sadie when she was born. Never ever saw her face.'

Sadie ran up and put both arms around him. Frances cried on Hettie's shoulder. Robert frowned to stop his own eyes from filling up. Ernie hung his head. They waited.

At three in the morning Dr Fry emerged from the bedroom. He rolled down his shirtsleeves. 'Awake,' he reported. 'And asking for her daughter.'

There was a cry of relief.

'She's weak. There's a danger of infection. You must take good care.' The doctor's gaze took in each of them in turn. 'I know she's in good hands,' he told Frances. 'Your work at the chemists has taught you about hygiene during a recovery such as this?'

Frances nodded. Tears streamed down her face.

'Good. In that case . . .' Dr Fry snapped his black leather bag shut and reached for his jacket, which Ernie handed to him. 'Congratulations, Duke.' He came and shook him by the hand.

'The child?' Duke wouldn't let go until he answered.

'Small.'

'Ailing?'

'No. Only weak with the difficult birth. We'll need to get her weight up.'

Duke considered. 'Thank you, Doctor.'

'Keep an eye on them both, and send for me again if you think I'm needed.' He buttoned up his jacket.

Hettie saw him out. Dawn streaked the sky above the grey roofs as she watched the small, dark figure down the street. Upstairs, they moved quietly, careful of each other, fearful for Jess and her newborn baby.

At seven o'clock, Frances made breakfast. She was pale but calm. The others watched her for their lead. They sat down to an edgy affair of boiled bacon, hot tea, whispers and worried looks. Sadie had filled Hettie in on the row between Duke and Frances, and they all waited nervously for some solution to this problem. Frances had never in her life before lost control like that, and no one had shown Duke such open defiance.

But that had been before the emergency over Jess. Now Duke seemed determined to let the other matter drop. He listened quietly at the breakfast table as Rob discussed with Hettie the damage done to Coopers' windows in terms of cost and loss of trade. Rob didn't think any of the workers would be laid off; quite the opposite. It seemed to him they'd have to put in extra hours in the sweatshops to replace damaged stock. 'Everything'll be back to normal in a couple of days,' he said.

Frances sat and listened without reacting. During a long, brilliant dawn, measured by silence, the baby's cries, and then the early noises of carts rattling down the cobbled street, she'd decided there was no point arguing further with Duke. She would stay on at home and try to live peacefully with him. Her loyalty was to Jess now.

Like all the other men round here, her father regarded the women's demonstration as a sideshow at the fair, performed by freaks of nature. But Frances knew different. She had the ability to think things through. There was justice in the women's cause; they should be treated equally in this day and age. She used logic to soothe away the hurt Duke had inflicted; if she'd been a man of twenty-eight and still single, people would say she was a good catch, with her respectable job and good prospects. Just because she was a woman they said she was on the shelf. And old maids like her were regarded with mixed scorn and pity. When day broke Frances was ready to meet it, for Jess's sake. But things would never be quite the same in the family. They would have to get used to a new edge to her, even more remote and determined.

'It's eating her up inside,' Annie Wiggin confided to Dolly Ogden. 'She's turned into one of them man-haters, and it ain't doing her no good.'

The two women stood gossiping in the street outside Henshaw's on a sultry August day. Their subject was the Parsons family and Frances in particular. Her long-standing row with Duke was by now common knowledge. She went openly to the suffragists' meetings and wore their purple and green sash.

'He don't like it,' Annie reported. She said 'he' in an awed tone. Duke was looked up to by many of the older women and Dolly caught Annie's meaning right away. 'He ain't got no time for it and it's causing bad feeling in the house, believe me.'

'D'you think it's brought on all this trouble young Jess had with that baby?' Dolly didn't really want Annie's opinion. With her expert knowledge of the complexities of childbirth, she'd already made up her mind. 'I mean to say, the poor girl started that very night. She didn't have no chance to get away like she planned. Poor little blighter was born there and then, right above the pub. Sadie had to run for Dr Fry. Everyone down the court heard the rumpus.'

Annie nodded. 'Weeks early. By all accounts, the poor

little mite was no bigger than a wax doll. Jess was in a pretty bad way herself and all. It can't have been easy.'

Dolly seized the opportunity to confide the secrets of her own difficult labours. 'Take Charlie. Arse about face he was. Dr Phillips has a feel and tells me he's lying the wrong way "hentirely". That's what he says. It was two whole days before Charlie finally consents to put in his appearance, all nine pounds eight ounces. He was just about the death of me, I can tell you!' The stout woman reminisced with pride. 'He always was an awkward little bugger!'

Annie nodded her way through Dolly's fascinating account, but was anxious to steer things back on course. 'They thought they was going to lose her,' she said.

'Who, the baby?'

'No, Jess. Everything went black for Duke. Course he was remembering his old lady and how he lost her over young Sadie. He heard the state Jess was in and everything went black all over again. He just put his head in his hands and sat there still as a statue, with the poor girl clinging to life by a thread in the very next room!'

Even Dolly was impressed. She stared at Annie. 'How come you know all this?'

'Hettie told me. She came down the stall the other day and we had a little chat. Poor old man, he was in a state for days till he knew Jess was on the mend. Just sat there without moving for days!'

'He never! Who looked after things downstairs then?'

'Robert, of course. He ran the whole place. I'm surprised your Arthur never told you that. No one expected the old man to take it so bad.' Annie shook her head. 'The whole family was gutted, mind you.'

'And what's she decided to call the baby, then?' Dolly needed to be on her way back to work. 'Supposing the poor little bleeder decides to make it through to her christening.'

Annie had begun serving mother-of-pearl buttons to a woman from the pawn shop. She counted them on to her palm. 'Seven, eight, nine. Grace. That's threepence to you, ta very much. Hettie says they're calling her Grace. And she's a pretty, dark-haired thing, but still sickly.' Annie pocketed the money and watched Dolly on her way.

Dolly too had much on her mind. The chat with Annie had cheered her up, as other people's troubles often did, but she had several of her own, over and above the usual. For one thing, it was getting too much to put up with, these constant rows with Amy over something and nothing, with Arthur putting in his own two penn'orth. Ever since the window-smashing episode Amy had been behaving like a little fool. She claimed to hate the boss's son, but there was more to it than that. She would be always bursting into tears, turning her nose up at the food on her plate. She was getting thin; most unlike her. What's more, she looked for arguments with Charlie all the time. It was time to put her foot down, Dolly decided.

'If there's one thing I can't stand, it's a person who goes looking for a quarrel,' she told herself, descending out of the sunlight into the depths of Hosiery. Cooper had long since had his windows repaired and they were good as new. The workers had put in overtime and business was back to normal, as Duke Parsons had predicted. 'I'm going to have to have a talk with that girl when we get home tonight!'

That morning Amy had smashed her cup into the sink and stormed off. Dolly had only mentioned in passing that the case against Teddy Cooper was coming up before the beak. One of the women in the mob had done him for assault. 'Don't mention his name to me!' Amy screamed.

Her face went all twisted and she dashed her cup down. Dolly had been able to glue it back together, but it'd never be the same. 'Don't ask me what's up with her, but I'm going to put my foot down,' she said again, sitting down at the long table behind her machine for knitting the hose.

In the early afternoon, cocooned by the network of muffled sounds that comprised her working day – the hum of the machinery, the distant yell for orders, the low chat of the women – Dolly was roused by an unexpected event. She looked up in the dim light, surprised to see Bert Buggles sneak into the workshop. He headed straight for her, a look of spiteful glee in his weasel eyes. Sticking his pointed nose right up to her face, he whispered a message.

Dolly's machine clattered to a halt. She launched herself off her bench, scattering bobbins of beige silk thread.

'Hang on, Dolly, where you off to?' one of the women called. Bert had already darted away up the back stairs.

'Hats!' Dolly replied, with a face like thunder.

'Here, you can't do that,' her supervisor warned. 'You ain't asked permission!'

'Stuff your permission!' Dolly's sturdy figure never hesitated. 'My Amy's in trouble. I got to sort her out.'

They could tell by her tone of voice that the situation was serious. The women looked at each other, shrugged and ducked their heads to carry on with their work. What one had actually overheard Bert say was that Amy Ogden had laid into Teddy Cooper with a pair of scissors. Trouble that shape and size was best avoided.

Dolly took the four flights of narrow back stairs two at a time in a rush of skirts and a creak of stays. Her breath came short and there was a sharp pain in her chest. By the time she reached Amy's workshop she was clutching at her blouse and gasping. If Teddy Cooper had laid a finger on her to provoke her into having a go at him, her mother's wrath would know no bounds. She barged into the low attic room ready for anything.

The boss's son was there all right. He must have grabbed the scissors from Amy, but not before she'd nicked him on the left cheek. Dolly saw the bright-red cut and the thin trickle of blood. Teddy had backed Amy away into a corner, where she cowered in a crumpled heap. She snivelled something that Dolly couldn't make out.

Just then Teddy made a grab for her, scissors still in one hand. Out of control himself, he jerked her to her feet. 'Shut your face, you hear!' The scissors were at her throat, and Amy's head forced back against the wall.

'Stay clear,' Dora warned. The tall woman moved to restrain Dolly. They'd seen it coming for weeks, if Dolly did but know it; the barbed comments, the filthy looks from Amy whenever Teddy Cooper showed his face. 'Let them sort it out.'

But Dolly was a lioness protecting her cub. She roared across the room. Startled, Teddy lost his hold and the girl pulled free. He felt the full force of Dolly's weight against him. His head cracked sideways on to the yellowed plaster, but he swung out wildly and managed to keep Dolly at bay as she moved in a second time. 'Get these bitches off me!' he snarled at Dora, Emmy and the rest. 'And for God's sake keep them quiet!' He stood upright, trying to regain his self-control, as several women moved in to restrain the mother and daughter.

'A nice bastard you are!' Amy's hysterical voice rose, even as Dora tried to lead her off. 'He attacks women, he does!' she cried to her mother.

Dolly looked from Amy to Teddy and back again.

'Shut your face!' he threatened. His face was smeared with blood, he took deep breaths to pull himself together.

'He does, he attacks women, Ma!'

'I know. I was there, I seen him.' Dolly moved in to take Amy away from Dora.

'No, you never saw what he did to me!' Amy's body was wracked with sobs and gasps.

Dolly's arm was halfway round her shoulder. It froze in mid-air. Everyone else drew back. Even Teddy stopped cursing and fuming. 'What you on about?' Dolly asked slowly.

'He don't deserve to live, that's what! I seen him putting the boot in on that poor girl and I thinks of what he done to me, every little thing. It all comes flashing back!'

'What you saying, Amy?' Dolly stared at Teddy. 'Are you saying what I think you're saying?' She saw his head go down, the back of one hand against his mouth as he failed to meet her outraged stare.

But Bert Buggles had acted as messenger again. His route took him from Hosiery to Jack Cooper's office, where he passed on the news of trouble in his attic workshop. 'Will you come, Mr Cooper? Only, one of the girls is a bit upset,' he said in his oily way. Then he sneaked off ahead.

Jack Cooper strode upstairs, coat-tails flying. Girls didn't get upset in his workshops, or if they did he soon sent them packing. It was bad for routine, bad for discipline. The heavy man came upstairs preparing a self-important lecture on the high standards expected of those who worked for Coopers' Drapery Stores.

He opened the door on chaos. Not a single woman was at her workplace. The Ogden woman had stormed up from the basement. He saw her sturdy back view and someone else cowering in a corner. There was a lot of noise. Materials had been swept from a work top on to the floor. A girl was sobbing and swearing by turns. Mr Cooper advanced into the room.

'What's going on here?' He stood legs apart, thumbs hooked into his waistcoat pockets.

Dolly turned. The figure in the corner stepped forward.

'Teddy!' Jack Cooper's fine speech deserted him.

'It's all right, Father, I can manage here.' Teddy attempted to defuse the situation before it got any further out of hand.

'What do you mean, it's all right?' Furious, Cooper strode over to Amy and pulled her upright, for the girl had slumped against her mother, half-fainting. 'Stand up straight, for God's sake!' He turned to his son. 'I'll take over here. Let me just deal with these Ogden women.' For the first time he saw the open cut on his son's face. He frowned. 'You'd better go home and tend to that,' he said, very formal and unsympathetic.

It gave Dolly time to gather herself. Jack Cooper meant to sack them both on the spot, it was clear. But he'd hear the full story before he chucked her out, and she wouldn't mince words. She pulled Amy to her side. 'You ought to be ashamed,' she challenged. Suddenly Cooper's flabby chin and plump, gold-ringed fingers offended her. He'd begun like all the rest down Duke Street in the battle to survive, trundling barrows. He'd done well on cheap labour and high prices, working his women like slaves in the sweat-shops he set up in flea-ridden cellars, before he moved up to owning his own shop. Now he thought himself high and mighty. 'I'll deal with these Ogden women,' he sneered. Dolly launched into him. 'You and that son! Call himself a man! And listen, you can stick your job up your arse! I wouldn't work for you, not now!'

'What are you talking about, woman?' He could see she was incoherent with rage.

Dolly took a deep breath. She saw the son take another

step forward, and out of the corner of her eye the look of amazement on Dora's long face. 'Your precious son's had his wicked way with nearly every girl in this bleeding place, as if you didn't know. And now he's tried it on with my girl!' For a second her voice broke down. She took Amy by the hand. 'Look here, Mr Cooper, you go ahead and give us the push, but you'll hear me out. Your boy's done my girl serious harm and he has to pay for it. Me and Amy's going straight out of here up to the coppers!'

They sailed out of Coopers' for the very last time to a long, stunned silence.

At home down Paradise Court Arthur fumed over the loss of two whole wages coming into the house. 'What you bleeding well have to lay into the boss's son for?' he ranted. 'Silly cows, what d'you expect me to do about it now, go back down the bleeding glass factory with my lungs in this state?' He coughed raucously.

'What's wrong with your lungs, Arthur Ogden?' Dolly said evenly. 'Look, we all know we cooked our goose with Cooper good and proper, so there's no point going on about it.' She sat heavily in a chair at the kitchen table. 'Make us a cup of tea, Charlie, there's a good lad.'

Amy hung about miserably by the door leading upstairs. 'What about me, Pa? Ain't you going to do nothing for me?'

He turned on her. 'No, I ain't. How could you be so bleeding silly to think a toff like Cooper would want to walk out with a girl like you? Did you think he just wanted to hold your hand then? 'Struth, girl, you wasn't born yesterday.' He ran his hand through his thinning hair. 'If you ask me you brought it on yourself.'

Amy wailed and turned back to her mother.

'And don't go thinking your ma's taking you up to the peelers, neither. We'd be a laughing stock.'

Amy flew at him in angry despair. 'You heard what that Teddy Cooper done to me, and you ain't going to do nothing about it! But you can't stop Ma and me, can he, Ma?'

Dolly sat and sipped her tea, deep in thought. She'd already sent Charlie packing. 'Get upstairs, it ain't nice for you to hear,' she told him. Charlie had been glad to escape. Now Dolly stared cold reality in the face. Arthur was right; the family had lost the only money coming in, and there was nothing left to pawn. She stared round at the empty shelves and the one crooked picture on the wall; a cross-stitch sampler done by Amy at school. 'Bless this house,' it said. What's more he was probably right about the police. She looked up at Amy. 'Calm down, girl. Your pa's right. We done as much as we can do.'

'But I thought you said we was going to the station?'

'I did. But think about it. We've left it too long for them to believe us. Who'd take our word against Cooper's?'

'We're not going then?' Amy was stunned into silence. She sat on the doorstep, suddenly limp.

'No. But we'll let the Coopers think we are.' Dolly arched her eyebrows. 'Leastways they'll have to sweat it out for a bit.'

Arthur nodded, glad she'd seen sense.

'And I got another plan.' Dolly stood up, ready to tackle the sinkful of dirty pots and pans. 'We'll move Charlie out of his room at the top of the house again and we'll take a lodger. That'll keep the money coming in!'

*

Back at the workshop Jack Cooper re-established order and got the women settled back to work once more. He promised them a shilling each if they made up for lost time, but they'd have to take on the Ogden girl's work until he filled her position. He bullied and bribed them back into place, his sagging, mottled face betraying the strain of the recent scene. The women resented every inch of the pompous little man, every whiff of his hair oil and every stab of his stubby finger on the table in front of them. But they needed the shilling. They bowed their heads and the waters closed without trace over the scandal of Amy Ogden.

At home in Richmond, Edith Cooper bathed the cut on her son's face. After twenty-five years of marriage to Jack, she'd trained herself never to ask questions. She'd slid into place alongside him on all his upward moves from tenement to rooms above the first shop and eventually out to the leafy suburb. Her clothes and her accent improved along with her surroundings. She was by now a tall, slight, sandy-haired woman of good taste and manners, with a fondness for cameo brooches and amber necklaces, and an outstanding lack of curiosity about the business which paid for them.

She finished dabbing at Teddy's wound as Jack's car drove up the drive, and she quietly crept out of the room with her basinful of disinfected water.

Jack lectured his son. What he did with his women was his own affair, but never again would he put up with a situation where Teddy's fooling got in the way of profits at work. There were girls on every street-corner; why did Teddy have to pick them up in the workplace? From now on he strictly forbade that. He'd noted what the Ogden woman had said; there was every chance she'd lay charges against him and it would serve him right. 'Does your mother know?' he asked. He fumbled in a silver cigar box, his hand shaking.

Teddy shook his head. 'I haven't told her. Listen, Pa, how will this affect things? Will they really lay this second charge, do you think?' He was in trouble up to his neck, what with the mad suffragette and now that little fool, Amy Ogden. His self-confidence was visibly dented and he presented a pathetic figure; pale, cut and bruised, with a wheedling tone. 'You'll back me up, won't you, Pa?'

Jack treated him to a contemptuous glare. He thought of all the years bartering on the docks and barrows, the fights he'd had for the best market pitches in the early days, his first shop with his name in gold letters above the door. He pictured what he had now; the acres of floor space, the precious plate-glass expanse on Duke Street, newly restored. He'd built Coopers' Drapery Stores from nothing, and this young fool sitting before him was the son he must hand it on to. 'You don't deserve it, Teddy,' he said with grim resignation. 'The best you can do is hope the Ogden woman keeps quiet.' He lit his cigar and felt the smoke ease down the back of his throat. 'Or if you're very clever and think about it long enough, maybe you can work out a way of making her!'

Chapter Eleven

Daisy O'Hagan called up to see Hettie in the middle of one Saturday morning in August, not long after Dolly Ogden's notorious row with her employer.

'Good for her,' Daisy said to Robert, who was sweeping out in the pub before the day's trade began. It had been the talk of the street for days. 'It's high time someone took that Teddy Cooper down a peg or two.'

Robert leaned against his broom handle, keeping it propped at an angle so that Daisy couldn't get upstairs. He wore his usual teasing smile. 'You could've fooled me. Last time I seen you, you was with Teddy Cooper and you couldn't get so much as this broomstick between the pair of you. Very friendly, you was.'

Daisy flared up. 'Where was that, I'd like to know?'

'After the show last Tuesday or Wednesday, I think it was. He dropped you off down the court in a taxi; either him or his double.' Robert shook his head. 'You got a nerve, Daisy my girl.'

Daisy tossed her own head backwards and brazened it out. 'It ain't none of your business, Robert Parsons.'

'But you're breaking my heart, Miss O'Hagan, pushing me over for the likes of him!'

'Teddy Cooper's a gent, not a scuttler like you!' Daisy attempted to barge past Robert.

'Tell that to Amy Ogden,' he said quietly. 'Or Chalky White for that matter. I'm sure he'd be interested in your high opinion of Mr Cooper.' Robert had heard rumours that Daisy was still involved with the shady docker, despite her denials.

Daisy felt Robert had gone too far this time. Her temper snapped, and she raised a hand to give his cheek a smart slap, but Robert moved quickly and caught her wrist. He grinned condescendingly. 'That Irish temper of yours ain't going to get you nowhere with me, Daisy.'

'It ain't meant to, you bleeding idiot! Now let go of me.' She struggled to prise his fingers from her wrist. 'I gotta go upstairs!'

Robert, at such close quarters with Daisy, could see why she was the most popular of all the girls at the Palace. A spirited mixture of jokiness and independence overlaid a real passion. Her eyes said everything. Wide and expressive, they flashed with anger, but they conveyed vulnerability beneath. And she was so pretty and wild. He stood, unwilling to let her go.

'Look, just let me be,' Daisy pleaded. She glanced swiftly up the stairs and back into the empty bar, then stamped hard on Robert's foot with the thin heel of her boot. He yelped and let go. Daisy hurried upstairs, hot and flustered. 'Serve you right!' she called down.

'Our Rob been having a go at you, has he?' Hettie greeted her friend with a shrewd look. She worried about her a good deal these days. 'You want me to have a word with him for you?'

Daisy sank gratefully into a fireside chair. 'No need, thanks. I can look after myself.'

'So what's up then?' Hettie had spent the morning washing her hair and looking after baby Grace while Jess went out shopping. Her hair hung free almost to the waist.

128

She stood by the mirror over the mantelpiece, brush in hand.

Daisy sighed. 'If it ain't one bleeding thing it's another.' The grind of poverty at home was having its effect on her for a start; the lack of privacy and her father's constant grumbling. Her mother would turn to her for both money and a sympathetic ear.

Being Irish, the O'Hagans were cut off from most of the other families down the court. They were regarded as outsiders and drifters, likely to flit whenever they fell too far short with their rent. Their children tumbled up and down the stairways and hovered in alleys, got ill, picked at the gutters for scraps, crawled under the market stalls and generally went to the bad. So Mary had no one except Daisy to share her troubles with, except for occasional lifts from good-hearted neighbours like Frances Parsons. 'Ma's worried sick about Tommy,' Daisy told Hettie. 'We ain't seen hide nor hair of him since Wednesday. The little sod's gone and vanished on us again!'

'He'll turn up, won't he?' Hettie knew that Tommy often took off for a day or two, perhaps teaming up with one of the local rag-and-bone men to go picking iron off the rubbish tips. Or else he'd be cab-ducking up at Waterloo. Tommy turned his hand to anything that would earn him a copper or two.

'He mostly leaves us word though. Last time he was cutting up hay at the carter's place down Angel Yard. He got a bed in the hayloft and never come back home for a week. But he sent Ma word where he was and we never lost no sleep.' Daisy came close to the mirror to push stray hairs into the framework of pins that held her elaborate style in place. 'Any rate, I told her I'd ask around. You ain't seen him, have you, Ett?'

'Wait here, I'll ask Sadie.' Hettie went off, while Daisy

stooped to look at Jess's baby, sleeping peacefully in its crib in the corner. The tiny, unmarked face made her sigh again.

'Sadie says she ain't seen him since midweek, but she remembers him going on about them cage birds he keeps in the cellar. Said he was feeding them up so he could go up the West End and get good money for them. She ain't seen him since.' She looked at Daisy and squeezed her arm. 'Don't take on. Tom's the same as you; he can look after himself.'

'We have to in our family,' Daisy agreed. 'But I think you're right. Just pass the word will you, Ett? If anyone catches sight of him, let me know. Then Ma can stop worrying herself.' She made as if to go. 'See you later up at the stop?'

Hettie smiled and nodded. 'Six o'clock on the dot.' The baby showed signs of waking, so she went and gingerly lifted her from the crib.

'Suits you, I'm sure!' Daisy said with one of her old, lively grins.

'Cheeky sod!' Hettie cradled Grace in the crook of her arm as Daisy went on her way to look for Tommy.

To Hettie's relief, Jess soon returned to look after the baby.

'Here, give her to me,' she offered, putting her basket down on the table. She smiled at Grace and grasped hold of her tiny fist. The baby gurgled and puckered her wet lips. 'How's she been?' Jess asked.

'Fine. Sleeping mostly.' Hettie came up to look, her hair swinging free. 'Ain't it time you started to breathe more easy over her, Jess? She's eight weeks now, and Dr Fry says she's coming on in leaps and bounds.'

'I ain't worried no more,' Jess lied. 'Leastways, not like at first.'

'Me neither.' Hettie gave her a hug. She began to tie back her hair in a loose plait. 'You didn't half give us a fright,' she confessed. 'Both of you. Pa never knew what to do with himself, all that time you was sick.'

'I know that.' Jess held Grace close to her cheek. She felt the little fists uncurl, the sharp little nails catch at her lips. She pressed them together and kissed the baby's fingers.

Her confidence had grown day by day since the difficult birth. If the pregnancy had been unwanted and fraught with anxieties, and the birth itself a time of searing pain for which no one, not even her own mother, could have prepared her; the weeks since then had been ones of extraordinary fulfilment. Once she came round and held the fragile scrap in her arms, tiny but tenacious, all Jess's fears and pent-up shame dissolved into nothing. Her strong life force passed into the little mite and she willed it out of its sickly beginnings into contented babyhood. She would never hear a word of doubt about its survival.

With Frances's help in keeping things scrubbed and spotless, Grace soon gained physical strength and was now considered out of danger, a healthy baby. She was still slightly underweight, but gaining fast. And Jess had taken on every aspect of her care with complete dedication, rising in the night, cleaning, washing, feeding with infinite patience and care. The family had soon stopped moving from room to room in a stilted, hushed way, as if present at a death, with Duke's huge figure sitting bowed by the fireside. He did blame himself for the premature birth; or rather, it was the row he'd had with Frances over the suffragettes that had brought it on.

He sat and remembered loyal, long-suffering Pattie, her pale face surprisingly sharp in his mind's eye again after all these years. But the first sight of the baby in Frances's arms had brought him back to the present. He went in to see

Jess, propped up on pillows, ghostly white, too weak to do more than smile as he patted her hand. Illness, so rare in his life, unbalanced him further. Tears came to his eyes.

'Have you taken a look at your granddaughter, Pa?' Jess whispered.

Duke nodded without speaking. 'You hurry up and get well, now,' he said at last.

From that moment he doted on Jess and his grandchild. He would want to know when the baby woke, when she slept and fed. He would shut windows against draughts, open them for fresh air, talk of days in the countryside once Jess and Grace were fit to travel. If anyone had even mentioned the circumstances of the baby's begetting, the family felt he would have killed in Jess's defence.

He came upstairs after Jess now for a glimpse of his grandchild and a short break from duty behind the bar, settling at the table with a contented smile. 'Has she been out for her walk yet?' he enquired. There was a smell of linen and soap in the room; Jess kept the baby scrupulously clean.

'Not yet, Pa,' she answered evenly.

'Don't leave it too late. Get out there in the sunshine and fresh air. Take Sadie with you for company.'

'Sadie's at Maudie's.' Jess wrapped Grace in a fine white shawl and put her back in her crib. 'Frances and Ern are both at work, Ett's busy, and I don't think walking babies is Rob's cup of tea exactly. Why don't you come and walk her with me instead?' This was a daring request, asking for Duke to put the public seal of approval on his illegitimate granddaughter.

He jumped at it without a second thought, and soon they threaded their way up Duke Street, Jess pushing the high-handled pram, Duke strutting alongside. He took all compliments as his very own, accepting good wishes from neighbours and friends.

'About time, too!' Annie Wiggin exclaimed. She leaned into the pram, then stood up wreathed in smiles. 'Ain't she a picture! I ain't never hardly seen such a pretty little thing!'

'Oh, Annie,' Jess demurred.

'Why thank you, Annie!' Duke beamed back, chest out, head up.

'There's a couple of yards of spare lace at the back of my stall here. I want you to have it for any little dress or smock you make up for her.' Annie handed a small packet of tissue paper and lace to a surprised Jess. She held up her hand to wave off protest. 'I been keeping it handy, hoping I'd catch you. It ain't nothing much, but I hope it comes in.'

'That's very kind of you, I'm sure.' Duke took the packet from Jess and put it in his pocket. He smiled again and strolled on, steering them through the crowded market.

Jess raised her eyebrows at him. 'Who'd have thought old Annie Wiggin would go all soft over little Grace!'

'Course she would,' Duke remonstrated. 'Anyone would. And less of the old. Annie's a spring chicken.'

'Leave off, Pa. She's fifty if she's a day.' Jess paused, and seeing Ernie pedal by on the far side of the street, raised her hand and gave him a big wave. Ernie wobbled and waved back.

'She's not. And besides, I'm nearly sixty,' he reminded her. 'Old Duke Parsons with a brand new granddaughter.' They walked on in the sunshine, proud as peacocks.

He was in a good mood back behind the bar when a new customer came in. Since most of the men had gone to watch the Crystal Palace versus Bury match, business was slack and the newcomer stood out all the more. Smartly dressed in a dark suit and bowler hat, he approached the bar and gave his order. Duke took in his clean-shaven, sallow skin, his confident air. 'Are you just passing through?' he enquired, pushing the glass towards him. 'Or visiting down the court?'

'To tell the truth, I'm looking for a room,' the young man said pleasantly. 'I thought the local pub was as good a place as any to start.' He took a long draught of the cool beer, glad to be out of the hot sun.

'That's true,' Duke said. 'We get to hear most things.'

'I don't want nothing flash to start with, just a respectable room till I get set up proper. You heard of anything?'

Maurice Leigh was moving on from the Balham Empire. He'd been offered the manager's job at a new picture palace on St Thomas Street at a starting salary of two pounds ten shillings per week. Convinced as he was that moving pictures was the entertainment form of the future, he'd seized the chance to get a new establishment underway. He was full of plans and bursting with enthusiasm. Lodgings were a minor detail which he hoped to sort out without too much bother.

Duke studied the stranger. He wouldn't recommend lodgings unless he approved of the enquirer. By his voice he was East End born and bred, but not from this neck of the woods exactly; more Bethnal Green. By his looks, his background was Jewish; second, maybe third generation of emigrants from Eastern Europe. Duke was practised in the art of pinning down newcomers. 'You found work round here?' he asked with some scepticism. Jobs were still like gold dust, though that might change again as men enlisted and went off to the war. The rumblings had turned into certainty, with the declaration on the 4th of August. Even now posters were going up on street-corners calling the young men to arms.

Maurice nodded and confirmed Duke's theory. 'I'm the new manager at the Gem Picture Palace. This area's nice and handy for my work, see, if I can find a place.' He drank up, took a watch from his waistcoat pocket and looked about.

'Well, maybe I can help.' Duke came to the conclusion that the man was a good prospect. 'It just so happens there's a room going down Paradise Court.' He leaned over and gave details of Dolly Ogden's place. 'Not grand, of course, but she keeps her place clean. I know for a fact she's looking for someone. I'd try there if I was you.'

Maurice thanked him and went quickly out. He smiled and lifted his hat to Jess in the hallway, ready to hold the door for her to slip out on her last errand of the day.

She dipped her head and thanked him before picking up her skirts and sailing off. Maurice watched her go, half absent, half appreciative. Then he went straight off down the court to knock at Dolly Ogden's door.

It was a godsend. He was a clean young man with a proper job. His manners were perfect. Dolly went into raptures over her new lodger. He'd gone up and looked the room over, and decided there and then that he'd take it. Charlie would have to move his things out double quick to make room for Mr Leigh, and never mind pulling a face about it. Needs must. She bustled about in high excitement, threatening to dust and polish Arthur unless he moved himself out of the way. 'His rent's set at seven and sixpence and he seems quite happy,' she told him. She knew how persuasive the sound of money coming in was to her husband. 'Amy's out looking for work this minute, poor girl, and Charlie boy himself should be earning before the next twelve months is up. By then I'll have got myself another job and all.' Her calculations put her into good heart. 'So just you behave yourself, Arthur. With a bit of luck we'll pull through this bad patch.'

Charlie cleared the set of drawers in his attic room, and swept his school books from the little work-table into an orange-box. He was furious. The indignity of sleeping in Amy's room, with an old curtain slung across the middle for privacy caused a burning sensation in his throat, but he bit back the words of angry protest and followed his mother's instructions. What could he do? At least until he finished school, he must live here under her terms and conditions. As he stacked his books on the window ledge in Amy's room, he stored up the confidences he would share with Sadie during their precious bike ride next day; his feelings of being born in the wrong place at the wrong time, prince by nature, pauper by birth. It didn't make him feel any better when Maurice Leigh returned with his two suitcases, dumped them in Charlie's room, took his hat off to Amy and started to flatter her shallow vanity with his polite attention.

'Ain't I seen you before?' Maurice asked, curiosity roused. He recognized her soft features and fair colouring, probably on the arm of someone he knew. He racked his brains.

Amy blushed. 'I don't think so, Mr Leigh.'

'Yes, I've got it. At the Empire, a few weeks back!' Maurice saw being polite to the landlady's daughter as a price he had to pay for cheap lodging near to his place of work.

By now Amy was brick red and beginning to chew the corner of her lip. 'No, I don't think so.'

136

'With Teddy Cooper, wasn't it?' His memory for faces was sharp. He rarely got it wrong.

'No!' Amy couldn't bear to be reminded of the worst mistake in her life. Neither did she want her mother to know that Teddy Cooper had since been in touch with a mixture of threats and promises. 'If you keep quiet,' he said, 'I'll help you find a new job. If you go gabbing to the police, I'll tell them you made it all up and demand your proof.' Unwisely, she'd accepted a present of ten shillings to tide her over. She regretted it at the time, but told herself that Teddy could be very persuasive when he wanted to be. And in a way she was pulling one over on him, she thought, since he'd absolutely no idea that her ma now had no intention of going to the police. Perhaps she could string him along for a few more weeks and make something out of the whole sorry business. Amy was a dangerous mixture of naïvety and manipulativeness, bound together by the glue of dishonesty. So, 'No!' she said to Maurice Leigh, recognizing him at once as the young under manager at the Balham Empire. 'We never met!'

Maurice merely nodded, and after a little more small-talk he went up to his new room. The sun had gone down over the slate roofs of Paradise Court, and deep shadows filled the alleyways. A narrow dormer window gave a bird's eye view of the place. From here you could squint down and see the kids playing at pitch and toss, hear the clang and clatter of their metal horseshoes. The women stood at their doors and gossiped as their men came home from the match. A street like any other.

Part Two

LONG
SHADOWS

Chapter Twelve

Robert had given the first match of the season a miss that afternoon for the sake of a good work-out with Walter down at Milo's gym. It was September. News of the brave boys out in France filtered through, but, for Rob, life went on much as before.

Football was only the second love in his life to boxing, a sport in which his sturdy physique gave him a good advantage over many of the scrawnier, less athletic East-Enders. Whether it was taking swings at the huge leather punch-bags, lifting weights, or sparring in the ring, Robert seemed to excel. His balance was good, the co-ordination between eye, hand and feet very precise. He took pride in his reputation as one of the best young boxers in the neighbourhood. So far, none of his opponents had been able to mark or mar his handsome dark features.

He stood now at the ringside, towel slung around his neck, watching Walter train against one of the merchant seamen who came off the docks to lodgings in Southwark; a Norwegian, with limbs as strong and solid as the pine trees of his native country. Walter stood up to him though, and the thud of padded leather against muscle went on apace. Robert observed the technique of the two men, looking for pointers to pass on to Walter when the bout was over.

He felt rather than saw a presence behind him. Something warned him not to look round; this wasn't a friendly arrival. It was only when the sneering remarks began, under the breath and hostile, that he gave way to provocation and looked round.

'Bleeding cart-horses, both of them. Too slow to catch cold,' came the first comment.

In the ring, Walter hesitated mid-stride, while the Norwegian, oblivious to the insult, swung a hefty right to his head. Sweat sprayed over the canvas, the hostile onlookers guffawed.

Robert, who'd felt the sweat cool on his own skin after his training bout, now felt himself heat up again. He'd recognized Chalky White's scoffing tone. His jaw muscles jumped. Chalky was difficult to ignore, but retaliation was unwise. The pair in the ring side-stepped and swiped at one another, evenly matched.

'You put my old lady up in there and she'd knock 'em both dead in ten seconds flat,' Chalky pressed on.

Against his better judgement, Robert spun round. 'Know what,' he said to Chalky loud and clear, 'you got a mouth on you as big as a bleeding railway tunnel, you have, and I'm gonna close it for you if you don't watch out!'

The punch-bags all around the gym fell silent, weights sagged to the floor. Men stopped their training to listen. Only the ones in the ring continued their bout, Walter still having to defend himself hotly against the foreigner.

The smile never wavered on Chalky's mouth. He felt big and confident in front of his mates. Robert Parsons was a cocky lad with a pea-sized brain and a bad temper to match; just the sort he liked to wind up. 'You and whose army?' He grinned. Syd and Whitey Lewis were there to back him up if necessary.

'Me and nobody's army!' Robert turned and motioned to Walter and the big Norwegian to stop their bout. 'But we'll have this out here and now,' he challenged. 'You been wanting to have a go at me, Chalky, and now's your chance.' He hopped into the ring while Walter explained the tense situation to the sailor. They withdrew to the floor, breathing hard. 'C'mon, what you waiting for?' Robert insisted. 'Let's see you put your money where your mouth is.'

Chalky White had a code of his own, as Robert well knew, and it was a point of honour not to lose face in front of his mates. He was taller than Robert, with a longer reach. Though he'd not expected the hot-headed publican's son to jump the gun like this, and if anything had planned a dark meeting with him down a side alley late at night, he calculated he could probably step into the ring with him and settle things now. The kid was getting on his nerves, the way he bristled up and stared in undisguised loathing. Well, Chalky would teach him a public lesson. Slowly, and with great bravado, he climbed into the ring.

They began circling each other with raised fists. Daylight poured into the gym through long windows, casting dramatic strips of light and shade across the room. Dust motes whirled in upward blasts of air as each man danced and began to place his shot. All was silent, except for their hard breathing and the scuff of their shoes on the sprung boards.

Even to the hard-bitten men and boys of Milo's gym, there was tension in the air. With their short-cropped hair, bull necks and calloused hands, they gathered to watch Robert Parsons spar with Chalky White. As they saw it, there wasn't much in it for the victor; no glory or reward, but there was a lot to lose. This was a needle match and respect was at stake. Whoever ended up on the canvas was a man without his reputation. The spectators looked on with sharpened appetite, as Robert moved in under Chalky's guard and landed two or three heavy blows.

Chalky staggered as he took the punches to his ribcage, and saw the look of concentrated anger in Robert's eyes. He pushed him off and recovered his guard; upright, backing off, ready to side-step.

From Robert's angle Chalky didn't look so clever now. His reach meant nothing if the punch behind it lacked force, and Robert's own well-coordinated movement was backed by real muscle. He wouldn't jab to the face, but he would swing more upper-cuts to the body and jaw. That way he was sure he had his man. His eyes levelled on the target and he moved in, ducking, weaving to the left and right, displaying his skill.

In the end they had to pull him off. He'd backed his opponent into a corner and hammered blows on him until he slumped, a dead weight at his feet. Milo moved in swiftly with a bucket of cold water and sharp orders to Robert to back off. Walter Davidson rushed into the ring and seized him under the arms from behind, while Syd and Whitey moved in to rescue their leader. For several seconds Chalky was dead to the world, then the icy rush of water revived him. His head jerked, his eyes opened in time to see the back-slapping crowd follow Robert towards the changing room.

'What got into you?' Walter urged, as they stripped, towelled and climbed into their clothes. 'Ain't you got eyes in your head? Your man was already down, for gawd's sake! Why go that far?'

Robert nodded, only now returning fully to his senses. 'He had it coming to him,' he said, buckling his belt and reaching for his cap.

'That's all well and good, but Chalky White ain't the

right man to pick a quarrel with.' Walter had to run alongside Robert to keep up as he swung through the door out into the street.

'I didn't; he did.'

'But did you have to beat his brains out?' Walter caught his friend by the arm. 'This ain't the end of it, you know. From now on, Chalky's got you down as a marked man. Ain't no way he'll live down a thrashing like that without getting his own back, and some more!'

Robert pulled himself free. He walked on savagely into the subsiding evening traffic. 'Think I don't know that?' Without waiting at the kerb, he nipped smartly between cabs and trams, caught up in their roar. 'Anyhow, it don't make no difference to me now.'

'How's that?'

Robert glanced sideways. He'd got himself into a tight corner over Chalky, all right. The man's pride had taken a bad battering. 'I ain't planning on hanging around waiting for Chalky to get even,' he said.

They entered the railway arch at the top of Duke Street, their footsteps echoing, its damp stench filling their nostrils. They emerged into the setting sun. 'I'm thinking of joining up, Walt,' he said in casual, throwaway style.

Walter stopped short in sudden, stunned silence.

'What you looking at me like that for?'

'This is the first I ever heard of it, Rob!'

'So? I don't have to tell you every bleeding thing, do I?' He bridled at the shock which registered on his friend's face. 'There's a war on, Walt, in case you hadn't heard!' He reached into his jacket pocket for a pack of cigarettes, pulled it out and lit one in the shelter of the railway arch. Flicking the spent match into the gutter, he hunched his shoulders and strode off.

This was the first time Robert had broken the news to

anyone. The war was less than a month old, but already the post-boxes sported posters inviting men to enlist. Queues were a familiar sight around the Town Hall; hundreds of smiling faces clutched papers and crowded in on the impromptu recruiting office. Hope was high that the Schlieffen Plan would be defeated by Christmas and the enemy attack on Paris would be over. Robert himself was sick of queuing for work or hanging around the pub until something better came along. Though he'd warned his father he wouldn't be rushing to risk his neck for king and country if the war broke out, he didn't see any real danger in joining up now and being treated as a war hero when he came back. At least it would get him off Chalky White's turf for a time. That was it; if there was a deciding factor, it was the need to take the heat out of the rash row with Chalky and his gang.

In the meantime, he'd jolly them up at home by taking Ernie off on one last trip to the Palace. That should be harmless enough, as long as he kept a weather eye out. He was pretty certain Chalky's cuts and bruises wouldn't allow him to venture far that evening. With a bit of luck, Robert would have himself enlisted, assigned to a regiment and be gone within the week.

'What if Joxer don't turn up?' Duke grumbled his objection to Robert's plan to take Ernie to the Palace. Rob had put in time setting full barrels on the gantry and adjusting half-empty ones on their wooden chocks, but the old man didn't like being left without extra pairs of hands on a Saturday night. He wasn't sure he approved of Ernie's more frequent nights out to the music hall either. He twitched his moustache and scowled at Robert.

'Get one of the girls to lend a hand,' came the flippant

reply. Robert knew Duke didn't like to get them involved in the serious Saturday night drinking. 'Get Frances. She won't mind.' He winked, but the joke went down badly. His father and his strait-laced sister were still at odds, with Frances often on her high horse and Duke sulking. 'Anyhow, Joxer'll be here, you wait.'

Good-hearted Jess came down when she realized, and gave the bar top a quick polish, while Sadie sorted out a clean collar for Ernie and spruced him up for his night out. Jess was still in the bar when the Ogdens' new lodger called in on his way to work, smart and clean-cut as before. He was grateful to Duke for the recommendation, he said. Things had worked out well.

He stayed to chat for a little longer than he'd intended, drawn by Jess's quiet ease. He learned some details of his new neighbourhood from her and explained his job. She listened carefully and asked how they made the voices fit the pictures on screen in the new talkies. 'I read about them, but I ain't seen them yet.' It seemed miraculous to her.

Maurice caught her genuine interest and waxed enthusiastic about the new Chronophone method. It was early days and not much in demand yet, but he was sure it was the up-and-coming thing to have sound in the cinema. 'I want the Gem to be the first picture house round here to have it. They'd queue up by the hundred and pay to see that,' he said. 'It looks really and truly like the words are coming from their mouths, only it's a gramophone record played through loudspeakers. They synchronize it with the faces. Clever, ain't it?' He was proud of the word, 'synchronize', and told Jess she should come along to his new cinema. He'd look after her, see to it she got good seats and everything. 'Bring a girl friend with you,' he said. 'Tell them at the desk that you know the manager.'

Jess blushed. 'I don't know. I got a lot on here.' Duke

had come up from the cellar with Joxer, who'd recently arrived.

So Maurice was put off his stride and backed off. He downed his pint and left the pub. She thought he was too brash and pushy, he reflected as he swung out through the decorated doors. Pity; there was something about her that caught his eye. Something different to the flighty, flirty shop and factory girls like Amy Ogden, he thought with a grimace. The woman behind the bar was an ocean to Amy's paddling pool when it came to depth of character.

Being a determined sort, he planned his next move as he strode up Duke Street, crossed into St Thomas Street and between the mock-classical pillars of the Southwark Gem.

With Joxer installed behind the bar like some monumental carved beast, his features set in habitual glum expression, Jess went upstairs, the rhythm of her own evening fixed around her baby's pattern of sleeping and waking. She saw Robert and Ernie off and gathered with her sisters by the open window to watch them down the street. Frances had one of her meetings and left soon after. Then Sadie vanished off to Maudie's house. The room settled into its evening calm.

The hum of noise from the pub below kept Jess company in her dainty stitching as she sewed Annie Wiggin's lace into the smock she was making for Grace. At the back of her mind she planned how she might bring in some money to support herself and her baby by advertising on the board in the Henshaws' shop as a seamstress and invisible mender. She could do alterations to women's costumes, let out growing boys' jackets. Better than taking in washing, she thought, and it was a solid notion based on the fact that so many women were now out at work themselves. They had no time for complicated sewing work when they got home at night. Excited by her idea, she sat through the evening in peace and quiet.

Raucous shouts and thunderous applause echoed through the ornate balconies at the Palace. It was a full house, as if war talk, which depressed people in their workaday world, sent them scurrying all the faster to the easy glamour and excitement of the music hall, set on enjoyment and forgetfulness. Despite their confidence in victory and the wave of patriotic fervour that had greeted the declaration, it was a sobering experience to see sons and husbands trickle off from Victoria Station, hanging out of the carriage windows in their khaki uniforms, waving their caps. Laughter, song and dance was a refuge from that, so the audience roared at Archie Small's broad humour and they ogled the white limbs and bosoms of the chorus girls under the artificial glare.

Ernie thrilled to it all. He joined in the words of the songs which he could sing under his breath as he pedalled his bike for Mr Henshaw, belting them out now to the swelling sounds of the orchestra. After the show, he and Rob would swagger off to the stage door and join the swells. He was picking up the routine, learning the jargon. Best of all, he would meet up with Daisy and walk her home.

'C'mon, Ern!' Robert sprang to his feet as the final curtain fell. He was eager to beat the crowds. Hettie and Daisy didn't know they were here tonight, so it might prove more of a problem to get backstage. He'd have to signal through the window before anyone else arrived. Hurrying up the aisle, he expected Ernie to be hard on his heels.

But Ernie had difficulty with huddles and knots of people. They put him off his stride, standing there blocking his way. He hesitated, felt confused then flustered, then lost sight of his brother up ahead. Still, he knew where to go, he told himself. He knew to head for the stage door down that dark alley, where he'd find Robert ready to tell him off for getting lost. He nodded his head to a series of simple instructions which he gave himself as he headed out of the hall.

Robert slid easily past the groups of unhurried spectators gathered under the stone portico in feathered finery and Sunday jackets, unwilling to spill out on to the streets. Only one or two bunches of people had beaten him to it and were hanging about on the corner, or setting off in cheerful twos and threes on their long walks home. He glanced back, annoyed with Ernie, who'd been swallowed up back there. Bleeding idiot, he thought. Slowly he drifted to the corner, ready to light up a cigarette and hang about until the kid showed up.

But things didn't work out. A group of shadowy figures in a side doorway attracted his attention. He recognized Syd Swan's tough-looking outline lounging against the wall, chin jutting out, eyeing him up and down. He saw Whitey Lewis and a couple of other thugs, all obviously on the prowl tonight minus their injured leader. They'd spotted Robert too. It was time to make himself scarce.

Robert spun on his toes, hitched his collar and darted into the traffic. A passing omnibus made things easy for him; he nipped on to the open platform, swung round on the pole and waved a cheery goodbye to his pursuers. But his luck wasn't in after all. A snarl-up of traffic at the next junction brought the bus to a halt, and Syd and company had by no means given up. He could see them belting down the pavement towards him, jackets flying open, arms working like pistons. They meant business. Robert swung down from the platform with a shrug of apology at the approaching conductor. He had to beat it on foot if he was to come out of it clean. Lucky for him, he knew his way around, down to every last nook and cranny.

Ernie struggled on alone. The women's long skirts got in his way, the men would tell jokes standing bang in the middle of the aisle. No one seemed to care that he'd lost sight of Robert. When finally he broke through the foyer out into the street, his brother had disappeared. But Ernie clung to the idea of going to meet Daisy. That's what they did after a show; he didn't need anyone to remind him of that. He even knew the way.

Slowly, long after the main crowd had drifted off, he finally reached the familiar corner. Down this alley, at the far, dark end away from the lights, he would meet up with Robert, Robert would tell him off and then they would go inside and see Daisy.

Hettie was out of sorts as she made her way home after the show. She'd had to cold shoulder lecherous Archie Small, all because Daisy wasn't around to divert his attention. He was a slug in a cellar, slimy little man. Even the manager, Mr Mills, came looking for Daisy to give her her wages. And when it came time to link up with her for the walk back to Duke Street, could she be found? 'Silly cow's gone walking home with some new beau, most like,' one of the other girls offered. 'Let's hope he's a gent.'

'Fat chance,' Hettie said. Daisy might have thought to let her know. She was practically the last to leave the place, losing all this time looking for her, asking everyone where she was. Hettie banged the door and hurried off up the empty alley. Even the stage-door johnnies had given up and gone home, it was so late.

She met Robert coming towards her, going at a steady trot, head back, elbows out.

'What the bleeding hell you doing here?' she barked.

He stopped and doubled over to regain his breath. Behind him the street was empty. 'We seen the show,' he gasped. 'But then I ran into a spot of bother back there. Nothing serious.' He stood up, hands on hips.

'"We?" Who's we?'

'Me and Ern.' Robert's face, which had been relaxing into a grin, narrowed again. 'Why? Ain't you seen him?'

Hettie shook her head. 'No. He ain't waiting by the door neither, if that's what you think. I just come from there.'

Robert frowned. 'Bleeding idiot.'

'It ain't his fault,' Hettie said hotly. 'And I keep telling you, don't call him names!' Then she thought, standing out on the street. 'Listen, I bet that's where Daisy got to. Wouldn't you just know!'

'What?'

'She's met up with Ern and walked him home. I been looking everywhere for her.'

Brother and sister turned and began to walk the route home. Hettie was tired after her second performance of the day, and Robert still looked warily about. 'You sure about this?' he asked. 'What if Ern got himself well and truly lost back there. What'll Pa say?'

Hettie stopped and sighed. Come to think of it, she couldn't see Daisy playing nursemaid to Ernie if there was anything else in the offing. 'Let's go back and check,' she agreed. It would only take ten minutes and then at least they'd be sure. They began to retrace their steps.

The alley was deserted, dry and dusty in the September night. Never silent, it rustled with small, unexplained noises behind drainpipes, along the gutter. Hettie picked up her skirts and trod gingerly. 'I hate it down here when it's all gone quiet,' she said.

'C'mon,' Robert urged. He wished he'd never had the stupid idea of bringing Ernie along in the first place.

'He ain't here.' Hettie pursed her lips. Robert had gone to check in the deepest shadows down by the high window and he'd come back none the wiser.

'He ain't gone inside, has he?' Robert pushed at the door, which stood off the latch.

'Here, you can't go in there!' Hettie pulled him to one side and sailed in. 'Wait here. I'll go.' She negotiated the familiar obstacles of ladders, ropes and cables cluttering the long corridor, and smelt the old stale smells of cheap perfume, dust and sweat.

'He ain't here!' She sent a loud whisper back to Robert.

'Try the dressing room!' With growing irritation Robert stood hunched by the door. 'And bleeding well be quick about it, will you!'

'If he ain't in here, I'm off home. You can tell Pa anything you like, it ain't nothing to do with me,' Hettie moaned. The girls' stage dresses looked drab and creased in the low light which fell from the corridor into the room; purple, crimson and emerald all merging into shadowy grey. 'Ain't no one here!' she called back.

But something made her check again. Things weren't quite right. A rail of dresses was swung out from the wall, and a screen which the girls used to change behind had tipped forward against it. Hettie went to investigate, fumbling to set the screen upright. But she came across a large object stopping her. She pulled the whole thing free and began to scream.

Robert ran. He used the doorpost to brake and swung himself into the dressing room. Hettie was stumbling towards him, hands to her face. In the far corner of the room, clear of the rail and screen, she'd exposed the object and dropped to her knees over it. She'd touched the blood on the white face, she'd knelt in a pool of it and drenched her skirts before she jerked on to her feet and staggered back screaming.

Robert caught hold of her. He stared at the body. Blood poured from the neck and chest, the face stared up at the ceiling. 'Oh my gawd!' he moaned. Hettie had buried her head against him. He clung to her. 'It's Daisy, ain't it?'

The light from the corridor caught the corpse in its full glare. The mouth hung open, the blank eyes stared. One arm was flung wide across the floor.

More footsteps ran down from the direction of the stage. Fred Mills had been on the point of locking up when the screaming started. Now he came running. He saw the body. He'd telephone the police, get help. This didn't happen, it was something you read about in the newspapers, Jack the Ripper stuff, really nasty.

'She was a lovely girl,' he told the sergeant. 'One of my best lookers, a good dancer. She had a voice like a bird.'

Chapter Thirteen

At the end of her meeting Frances said goodbye to friends on Union Street. She walked through the back closes off Blackfriars Road with Billy Wray, a newspaper vendor in the market with an ailing wife; one of the organizers of the lecture she'd attended that evening. As they came through on to Duke Street, they too parted company and went their separate ways.

It was then that she met Ernie. Astonished to see his tall, ungainly figure half-stumbling up the road, she ran to catch him up. 'Ern, what you doing out this time of night? Where's your hat? What happened?'

Ernie plodded on, as if dazed. 'I lost Rob,' he told her. He sounded dull and miserable. 'I never saw where he went.'

'The nuisance!' Frances said under her breath, determined to give Robert a piece of her mind. 'You mean to say he dumped you and never came back to find you?' she cried, seizing Ernie by the elbow and heading firmly for home. That was the sort of thing Robert would do; dump poor Ernie if he bumped into a few friends and got tempted by the promise of drink and girls.

'I lost him. I never saw where he went,' Ernie repeated. He was looking into the distance, straight ahead.

'Well, never mind now. We're here.' Frances ushered him through the door of the Duke and straight upstairs.

Midnight had chimed on the church clock as they walked the final stretch. The last drinkers had already left the pub.

Upstairs, Frances was glad to find that Jess was still up, greeting them with a smile and the offer of a cup of tea. 'Thanks!' Her hat and jacket were already off and hung on the peg. She turned and smoothed Ernie's dishevelled hair. 'Ern here could do with one, couldn't you, Ern?'

'What happened to you?' Jess stared at his pale, blank face. 'You look like you seen a ghost, Ern! For God's sake get him sat down nice and comfy, Frances. No, on second thoughts, you fetch that tea. I'll sort Ern out.' She bustled to help him out of his jacket and unbutton his waistcoat. Then she gently stroked his cheek. 'C'mon, Ern, it ain't that bad, surely.'

Frances soon came back from the kitchen. She still felt livid with their feckless brother. 'That Robert went and dumped him. Took him out for a treat up the Palace and left him. I just found him wandering back all by himself. It ain't right!'

'No.' Jess wanted to soothe away Ernie's hurt. 'But don't tell Pa,' she said to Frances. 'There'd only be a row.'

'Hm.' Once they'd straightened Ernie out with a hot cup of tea, Frances began to calm down. 'Did Ett get back home yet?'

'No. Sadie came in and went off to bed like a good girl, but that's all.' The sisters looked at one another, puzzled frowns on both their faces, but the ticking clock, the sound of Duke locking doors below lulled them into security.

'We'd best get you off to bed then, Ern.' Jess rose and pulled him to his feet. 'No point hoping he'll manage by himself tonight,' she told Frances. Sometimes he went all quiet and helpless, and you had to treat him like a little kid.

'Just wait till he comes home.' Frances gazed at the back of Ernie's stooped head as Jess took him gently off to the bedroom shared by the two brothers. 'He ain't never learned to use his head, that Robert.' She settled with her feet up, nursing her cup of tea. The lecture had contained lantern slides of the Seven Wonders of the World. Billy Wray had given a good talk, considering. Frances drifted off into her own world.

Jess sat Ernie down on the edge of his bed. 'C'mon, Ern, let's take your boots off.' He sat passively while she unlaced them. 'Give us a hand,' she urged. But he stared straight ahead, sitting in his shirt-sleeves, his collar unbuttoned and loose around his neck. So Jess struggled and finally held both boots in one hand, ready to take them away. 'Wait here while I go and put these down on a bit of clean newspaper, Ern.' She was surprised by the nasty, greasy feel of the uppers. They would need a good clean.

In the bright kitchen light Jess set the boots down on paper and went to wipe her hands at the sink. Her fingers were stained a sticky red. For a moment she spread her palms and stared in disbelief. Then she went straight back to Ernie's boots to scrape and scrub at them with the paper, anxious now to wipe them clean. She screwed the paper into a tight ball, went to the kitchen range, which they always kept lit for cooking, and thrust it far into the back of the fire, holding it there with the poker. She took the boot polish from the cupboard, blacked Ernie's boots and polished them until they shone. Finally, she washed her hands at the sink.

Ernie still sat in the very same place when she got back to him, but it was less than a minute more before she'd eased him between the sheets and drawn his eiderdown up to his chin. He stared at the ceiling, numb and silent. 'G'night, Ern,' she whispered. 'I got to go check on Grace now. You get off to sleep and we'll sort things out in the morning, eh?'

'What d'you suppose Ern was up to?' Frances asked when Jess returned. In a roundabout way her daydreams had brought her back to the subject. She remembered breaking off from her lively conversation with Billy and seeing poor, lonely Ernie up ahead. 'When you think about it, there's a whole hour missing between him losing Robert and ending up back here. It don't take an hour to walk that little stretch!'

Jess shook her head. 'Don't ask me.'

'No need to bite my head off.'

'Sorry.' Jess found it hard to get rid of the sick feeling in the pit of her stomach. The boots bothered her. She was sure it was blood on them.

Duke came up and told the girls to get off to bed. It was his habit of a lifetime never to retire until all the family were in and accounted for, so he sat in his shirt-sleeves, poring over the latest reports of the war in France. At two in the morning Robert and Hettie walked in looking as if the world had come to an end.

A solitary policeman came down the court still later into the night to give the O'Hagans news of their daughter's death. 'I drew the short straw there,' he told them back at the station. 'This scraggy woman comes to the door, which anyhow don't shut tight on account of its hinges. She opens it a crack and I says, "I'm very sorry to have to tell you this, Mrs O'Hagan, but your daughter Daisy has been murdered." There ain't no nice way to put it. The woman looks at me like she ain't heard. I can see through the door that the whole place is a tip. I tells her she can go along to the mortuary in the morning and see the body, and we'll do our best to find out who did it. I still ain't sure she's heard. But then she nods and closes the door on me, and I can hear my own footsteps going back down them stairs, knock-knock against the bare boards and out into the street.'

His sergeant nodded. 'Good lad. Needle in a bleeding haystack this is, though.' There was paperwork to do. He opened the black ledger and chose a pen.

'What is?'

'Finding the bloke what done it. It could be any one of them hooligans done her in, the way them girls carry on after a show. I know, I seen 'em often enough.' Dutifully he wrote down the details: 9 September 1914. A quarter to twelve. Summoned to the Southwark Palace Music Hall by the manager, Mr Frederick Mills. Body on the premises. Female. Nineteen years. Stab wounds to throat and chest area. Identity: Daisy O'Hagan of Paradise Court, music-hall dancer and singer. Time of death, half-past eleven approximately.

'Ain't you got no one particular in mind?' The young police constable was recovering from his experience as the bearer of bad tidings. He supposed it was something else you got used to in this job.

The sergeant sucked in air loudly and shook his head. 'Well, I never took to the manager, Mills, for a start.' He finished writing, blotted the page and closed the book. 'All that stuff about what a lovely girl she was. Who's he trying to kid?'

'I can see you don't reckon much to her, Serg?'

'They're all the same, them showgirls.'

'What about the witness?' The young man's imagination was more fired up by the murder than his more experienced boss's. 'You reckon he had anything to do with it?'

'Parsons? Ain't come across him before. He was pretty worked up all right. Dunno. The sister was in a proper state and all.'

'It couldn't be a woman what done it, could it?'

'Don't see why not. Like I said, it could be any bleeding one!'

159

Their work finished for the night, they buttoned their capes and left the sombre brick building with its barred windows and iron railings. At least they could get away to their Sunday roasts and walks in the park. Not like the poor O'Hagans, they said, walking in step away from it all.

Hettie sat up all night. The rising tide of hysteria she'd felt as she knelt by Daisy's body soon passed. Afterwards she was acutely aware of every detail; every word Fred Mills gabbled to the sergeant, the phosphoric flash of the police photographer's camera, the rubber gloves of the surgeon as he inspected the corpse, until she'd been bundled out into the corridor, baldly questioned and packed off home.

Now it seemed she was floating free in her mind, telling her own body to stop shaking, ordering her hand to raise the glass to her mouth. You know it's true, she told herself. You saw poor Daisy lying there in a pool of her own blood. She never went on home like you thought.

Robert whispered the full story to Duke. The shock had given even him a bad knock.

'How come you was there, you and Ett?' Duke asked. There were misgivings in the old man's mind. He didn't like Robert being mixed up in this.

Robert had to confess how they went back looking for Ernie. 'He got home all right in the end, didn't he?' he asked suddenly.

'Ssh! Yes, no thanks to you. I seen him coming up with Frances about midnight. Keep your voice down.' Duke didn't want to wake the others. He shook his head and glanced across at Hettie. 'What we going to do with her?' She was sitting across the room from them, upright and quiet, but seemingly out of touch with her surroundings.

'Leave her be.' Robert knocked whisky to the back of his throat, felt it burn. 'She'll soon come round.'

Next morning, shock waves rippled up and down the court. No one could believe it. Poor Daisy O'Hagan was dead, stabbed through the heart by some unknown villain, her young life ebbing away in the dingy back rooms of the dark, deserted Palace. That bright, fresh young girl done away with in some dark corner; it was a cruel thing for everyone who knew her.

Hettie had sat through the night. 'I ain't going back to the Palace,' she told Frances. 'I decided I don't want to work there no more.' Her hands were folded in her lap. Frances, seeing her shiver, had thought to put a shawl around her shoulders. Now they'd all heard the horrible story and were letting the news sink in.

'Oh, Ett, that's a shame.' Frances had always recognized that her sister had talent, right from being a small child. The music hall was her life. 'I don't see why you should give it all up just because of this.'

Hettie never blinked.

'Ett? Listen, the life suits you, don't it? You like being up on that stage with the other girls. Wait a bit. Don't make no rash moves.'

'It ain't the same after what's happened.'

'Not now it ain't, course not. But just wait a bit.'

'I thought you never liked the place?' Hettie turned towards Frances. 'It weren't never good enough for you. You never liked Daisy much neither, did you?'

'Oh, Ett, how could you think that?' Frances's arms went around her sister and she hugged her close. 'I thought Daisy was a lovely girl, only just a bit lively sometimes. I never said nothing against her!'

'You never had to. She was scared stiff of you, Frances. She said you always made her feel like she had to sit up straight and talk proper.' Hettie recalled all the laughing remarks. Tears rolled down her cheeks.

'I know. I can't help it, Ett,' Frances said humbly. She cried too. 'I'm so sorry for what's happened!'

'And you'll go up today and tell Mr Mills for me? I ain't never going back, Fran.'

Frances nodded and blew her nose. 'No more singing and dancing,' she agreed.

'I thought you'd be over the moon.'

'Well, I ain't, Ett, believe me.'

But she went up that afternoon and gave the news to Fred Mills. He was sorry, he said, but he couldn't really blame Hettie. A lot of the girls were very scared by the murder and worried it would be their turn next. 'And they ain't even seen it, not like your sister, Miss Parsons.' He frowned. 'I had to clear up a lot of the mess myself. Very upsetting. I'm telling them to take more care who they hang round with from now on. You never know.'

Frances spoke to him in his small, dingy room behind the box-office. His face was grey as he stood and shook her hand; a little man whose confidence was demolished. She received an extra week's wages on Hettie's behalf. 'Hettie seems to think it's her fault, Mr Mills,' she confided. 'She thinks if she'd tried a bit harder to track Daisy down last night and walk home with her like normal, this would never have happened.'

'We could all think that about ourselves,' the manager confessed, his features blank and unreadable, his voice flat. 'Tell her not to think it though. It don't do no good, and it weren't her fault. Tell her that.'

Frances nodded once and went on her way. She walked out through the foyer, under glass chandeliers, between rows of laughing faces. Glossy, smiling photographs of the stars beamed down; the comedians, singers and showgirls seemed to follow her with their eyes.

No one had been able to prevent Hettie from going to see the O'Hagans. Jess was busy with Ernie, who still hadn't recovered his bearings from the night before and was going around in a dream. She'd pushed the business about the boots firmly to the back of her mind and locked it away. Now she tried in vain to get him to eat toast and drink tea. The poor boy seemed lost in a mental maze and refused everything.

Sadie had cancelled her bike ride with Charlie Ogden to sit with poor Hettie, but she'd given in without protest when her sister insisted there was something she must do. Frances returned from the Palace to find Sadie sitting miserably in her own room. She scolded her for not looking after Hettie better, then immediately hugged her. 'It's not your fault, I just hope Hettie don't find it all too upsetting. It takes a lot to go and see the O'Hagans after what's just happened. Now dry them eyes, come with me and we'll make some scones,' she suggested impulsively. Sooner or later they would all have to pull themselves together and go down the court to number 48.

Father O'Rourke came down the tenement stairs as Hettie went up. He bowed silently. His rosary swung forward towards her. Then he went on his way. She found Mary sitting stranded in a sea of miserable children, half-finished laundry, broken furniture; the flotsam of her poverty-stricken life. Her eyes were sunken, her blouse unbuttoned at the top and torn at the sleeve. She sat on the one chair, shoulders slumped, staring with unseeing eyes.

Hettie bent over and took her hand. Beside the worn-out woman she looked proud and supple. Try as she might, she couldn't avert her eyes from the squalor of the room. This is how Daisy had to live, she thought.

An older child struggled to manage the needs of the little ones, but the dirty, ill-fed infants wailed on. There was no sign of Joe O'Hagan, who, unable to bear any more, had slunk off to roam the streets at daybreak. So Mary's bleak figure formed the focus of the children's movements. They crawled around her, dragged at her skirt and climbed on to her unresponsive lap.

Hettie felt her heart break. Robbed of words, she began to look around for practical ways of lifting the woman out of her misery. 'Go down the backyard and fetch clean water in this bucket,' she told the oldest child; a girl of about ten. 'Bring it back up here quick.' She wanted to wash the little ones' faces, and the water in the tap at the sink had dried up. She found a brush for their hair, sent the girl, Cathleen, on a second errand up the court to the Duke for milk and bread. 'Tell them Hettie says to send as much as they can spare,' she ordered. Quickly she began to make improvements to the state of the two rooms, working around the silent mother. Frances sent fresh scones along with the bread and milk, and the children set about them ravenously. It was the first food to pass their lips since Friday, Cathleen said.

At last Mary roused herself to ask Hettie tearful questions. How could such a thing have happened? Why didn't anyone try to save her poor girl?

'We wasn't there. We'd all packed up and gone home,' Hettie answered. 'It happened when the whole place was empty.'

'And how did she die?' Mary looked Hettie in the eyes for the first time.

Hettie drew a sharp breath. 'Didn't the policeman tell you that?'

'Most likely. I don't remember,' came the dull reply.

The words shaped themselves out of the images in Hettie's mind; a pool of blood, staring eyes, an outstretched hand. 'She was stabbed, Mary.'

'What with?'

'They don't know that yet.'

'Who done it to her, Hettie?' The look she gave the young woman still shook her to the core.

'They don't know that neither.'

'And did you see her?' The tortured inquisition continued. 'Did she suffer?' Mary's sobs came thick and fast. 'Did my poor girl suffer long?'

Hettie breathed in deeply. She was regaining control. Once the words were out, you had to accept them. 'They think it was pretty quick. I heard the police doctor say there weren't much sign of a struggle. Whoever it was must've sprung it on her out of the blue.'

Mary nodded, satisfied. 'She was a good girl.'

'She was, Mrs O'Hagan. Daisy was one of the best.'

People could raise their eyebrows at Daisy's goings-on, and Hettie herself used to scoff at her naïve belief that one day the right man would be standing at the stage door with a bunch of flowers and true romance. She warned her to be more careful. 'Just because they're giving you presents, it don't mean they want your hand in marriage,' she said right from the start. But Daisy had found it hard to rein back her high spirits.

As for the presents, she always brought them straight back home to this place of neglect and despair. She gave the chocolates to her brothers and sisters, her wages to Mary, and she brought them their only ray of light with her bright, loving smiles.

'She was a beauty though.' Pride shone through Mary's tears. She pulled a small object from her shabby skirt pocket and laid it in the palm of her hand to show Hettie. 'It's her birthday next Thursday. I was saving this for her.' The object was a shiny tortoiseshell comb for Daisy's hair. 'I ain't got much to give, but I was saving this for her.' Her fingers closed over it. 'She'll have to wear it for her funeral now.'

Chapter Fourteen

Hettie went back home and organized more supplies of food for the struggling family. Frances, Jess and Sadie joined in with a will. 'We got to help them get back on their feet,' Frances agreed. 'This is a bad blow for them and we all got to rally round.'

'I told young Cathleen to call here at six to see what we've managed to rustle up. Her ma ain't fit to do it. We'll ask around the other women in the court too; see what they can spare. Mary needs clothes for them kids as well as food. There's a lot to do.' Since recounting events to poor Mary, Hettie had broken out of her own lethargy. Now she was intent on doing good.

Sadie listened and slipped off to her room. She came back with two items of clothing, a skirt that had been lengthened to its limit but was now too small, and a pair of boots. 'Tell Cathleen she can have these when she comes,' she offered. 'The boots is too small for me, but there's plenty of wear left in them.' In fact, they were her favourite Sunday boots, fastened with buttons. She would have continued to squeeze her feet into them for months to come if not for this sudden emergency. Until now she'd known Cathleen O'Hagan only as the wild-haired child who ran barefoot up the street.

Hettie hugged her and began to make up a box of things

that Cathleen could take. 'Go down and pass the word around,' she told Jess. 'Pa's already opened up. They was all stood on the doorstep gossiping about poor Daisy.'

Jess went down into the pub's smoky atmosphere to talk to Duke about it. There was a lot of sympathy for the O'Hagans, he told her, especially since their boy Tommy had gone missing too. He hadn't been seen for weeks. All in all, things looked pretty bleak for them.

Maurice Leigh couldn't help overhearing. He leaned at the bar, intrigued by the buzz of scandal, but vague about the details. As a stranger, he'd been excluded from the gossip, though he gathered something pretty bad had occurred. 'What's going on?' He collared Jess, choosing her to set him straight. 'I come in for a quiet pint and the whole place is up in arms.'

Jess was struck by his direct, energetic manner. He didn't beat about the bush. His gaze unsettled her because she felt it sought her out without knowing her circumstances. At the same time, she felt she wanted to talk to him. The confusion brought colour to her cheeks. 'Something happened last night. A friend of ours got herself killed. Ain't Dolly told you?'

'I ain't seen Mrs Ogden this morning. She shot out early and I ain't seen her since.'

'Well, poor Daisy O'Hagan got stabbed to death, and now we got to round up some stuff to help the family. Daisy was the only one bringing in any money to speak of.' Jess raised her head to look him in the eye. 'That's what this is all about.'

He nodded, wanting to know more about the victim. 'Here's me thinking I moved into a respectable street!' he challenged.

'You have.' She missed the amused light in his eyes and

hotly defended Paradise Court. 'We never normally go round killing people. It's a terrible shock!'

Maurice smiled. His face, which was angular and a bit tense, relaxed. Still he stared at Jess. 'Any idea who done the girl in?' He pulled up a stool and sat facing her across the bar, more interested in engaging Jess in conversation than the murder itself.

'Well, first off, I just heard my brother Robert sounding off about the manager of the place where she worked, saying he wouldn't trust him as far as he could throw him. He was on the premises when it happened. Fred Mills, the manager, that is. But my sister Ett reckons there's a bloke there called Archie Small and he was always bothering Daisy.' Jess listed them on her fingers. 'But we think the police have got their work cut out. It could just be any Tom, Dick or Harry for all we know.'

Maurice nodded. Despite his comment about a respectable street, he was himself no stranger to the seamier side of life. A boyhood in Bethnal Green as the middle son of parents working in the book binding business hadn't shielded him from the ragged men and women who tramped the streets all night, unable to find a bed. He'd played in those streets with boys who died of fever, and knew the hollow feeling of a stomach that had gone forty-eight hours without food. His father had died when Maurice was just twelve, and the family, made homeless by the dead man's employers, had moved through a succession of ever seedier boarding-houses.

With a keen eye on self-improvement, however, Maurice had made himself useful to a landlord in one of these places, a pawnbroker who eventually set him behind the counter to conduct business whenever he was called away. Maurice was a lad he could trust. That was how he'd first become one of the flashiest and best-groomed boys in the area, showing off on a Saturday night in other men's pawned Sunday best. By slow and gradual stages, he'd moved into manning the box-office at an old music hall in Stepney, and from there to the Palace, and then into cinema management.

There was no doubt that the moves had been helped by his appearance. He was a dapper young man, tall and upright, and his dark colouring gave him a sophisticated air. His features were even, his jawline strong. Perhaps he was able to find work in the cinemas because he represented in the flesh an echo of the romantic actors who glamorized life on screen. Now, at twenty-seven, he was seen as well set up, ambitious and eligible. But Maurice himself acknowledged his own single-minded streak and up till now had used it as an excuse to avoid entanglements. Life was hard enough, he thought, as a single man trying to make his way. 'No complications' was his motto, and it seemed to work.

In the bar, Dolly Ogden vied with Annie Wiggin to solve the mystery of Daisy's murder.

'It ain't what you think, Annie,' she announced. 'To my way of thinking, this bloke what done her in is someone she knew!'

'No, a complete stranger, more like.' Annie felt irritated by the impression Dolly gave that she knew all the answers. 'There was hundreds of blokes in that audience. Thousands gawping at her all evening. Any one of them could've nipped back and done it easy as anything.' Annie planted her feet firmly under the table and took a long drink. Seeing Duke with his eye on her, she resisted the impulse to wipe her mouth on her sleeve.

'That's right, Annie,' Duke called across. He returned

the kindness she'd shown to baby Grace by backing her now.

Annie clutched the edge of the table in surprise. 'See!' she said, recovering enough to put Dolly in her place.

'See, nothing!' Dolly shook her head slowly, gathering herself to present her case. 'Now, look, who'd murder the girl just for the fun of it? No, this bloke must've known her, else how did he get backstage in the first place? Say, for instance, he arranged to meet up with her and she invited him in, not suspecting a thing of course. What then? Easy as pie to hang around till everyone's gone off home, and then stab her to death, see.' She appealed to her listeners, hands outspread.

Robert's ears pricked up. The murder had left him gloomy. On top of his little difficulty with Chalky White and the general feeling that life was going to the dogs, Daisy's death, lonely and brutal, had set the seal on his ambition to move away and make a complete break. He'd meant what he said to Walter about joining up. He'd thought about it long enough and planned to break the news to Duke that night. But natural curiosity diverted his thoughts and drew him into the women's orbit. 'You lot think it's a boyfriend what done this to Daisy?' he repeated.

Dolly looked up at him and nodded. She enjoyed lording it with her opinions. 'Ain't no doubt in my mind. Why, did you know her latest beau?' she quizzed.

'It were *him!*' Liz Sargent said. 'You was sweet on Daisy, wasn't you?' Unlike most of the local women, she thought Robert Parsons was too big for his boots, and enjoyed getting in this sly dig.

Robert bristled. He set a tray of full glasses down on the women's table. 'We was all sweet on Daisy, Liz. She was a real postcard queen.' He regarded her through narrowed eyes; her thin, grim mouth, her prominent nose. 'I just wish there was more like Daisy around.'

'Lay off him, Liz. He's been through a lot,' Annie said. 'Him and Ett found the corpse.'

'I'm asking you, who's her young man then?' Dolly took on the role of chief investigator. She sensed Robert had a juicy detail to give them.

'I can tell you of one that'll interest you, Dolly, at any rate.' He pulled up a chair and straddled it. 'Of course, this is between you and me and the gatepost.'

'Cut it out, Robert, just get on with it. Tell us what you know,' she grumbled. But she warmed to the flattery implied by Robert's special attention; even many of the older women found his looks and manner irresistible.

'Well,' he said in a low voice, 'the one I have in mind is the one your Amy had that bother with.'

'Teddy Cooper!' Dolly gripped his arm. 'You ain't stringing me along, Robert Parsons?'

'Cross my heart and hope to die, Dolly. Daisy told me about it herself. And anyhow I seen it with my own eyes; Teddy Cooper in a taxi with her, Wednesday of last week I think it was.'

For a second Dolly sat there stunned. The others considered it, willing to give it a hearing. Teddy Cooper's reputation was very poor, spreading beyond the sweat-shops, amongst all the factory and shop-girls. He was after anyone he could lay his hands on, the younger the better.

''Struth! Where was he last night, does anyone know?' Liz Sargent asked.

'He was at the Gem,' a cool voice said. Maurice Leigh felt all the women's eyes swivel and fall on him. 'He came to see the new Karno picture. I remember seeing him there, clear as day.' His comment was greeted with hostile silence.

Jess quickly rescued him from their disappointment.

172

They could turn ugly if he went and ruined their nice theory. Maurice hadn't got their measure yet, otherwise he would have spoken more tactfully. 'About what time did the picture finish?' she asked, knowing that cinema shows often turned out early.

'Ten o'clock,' he confirmed. 'There was a couple of shorts on first, and then the Karno. That lasts forty-five minutes, so I can get them all out by ten. I turned off the lights at a quarter past.'

'See!' Dolly recharged her battery. 'Plenty of time for him to gallop up to the Palace. Who was he with, do you know?'

'Not with a woman, if that's what you're getting at,' Maurice said. 'I had a word with him and a bunch of his mates. Said they'd come into town to give my new place a try out. We been open a week, that's all. They seemed pleased as punch with it.'

The women nodded, warming to the well-informed newcomer. 'Thanks, Mr Leigh. So, we know for a fact he's got in with Daisy. We know he had time to go over and meet up with her.' Dolly paraded the evidence. 'And of course we all know what he's bleeding well like!' By now she was willing to swear on the Bible that Teddy Cooper was the one. Her hatred of him ran deep. 'There's nothing'll stop him and his filthy tricks!'

The others sat silent and sympathetic. In their minds too Teddy Cooper, the boss's son, leapt from womanizer to murderer in one easy bound. 'And of course Daisy was a lively girl with a bit of a temper herself. It ain't as if she'd take it from him if it didn't suit her,' Annie chipped in. 'What I mean to say is, the girl could put up a fight.'

'She could,' Robert agreed. 'Poor cow.' With his forearms folded along the hooped back of the wooden chair, he rested his chin and fell silent.

'So!' Dolly took it up again. 'She puts up a scrap and it turns nasty. Only he's not like other blokes. He's a devil when his temper goes. He snaps and comes at her with a knife. It's all over in seconds.' She led them through the scene. By the end, the jury didn't even need to go out. 'He's guilty as sin, I'm telling you!' Dolly declared.

'Don't tell us, tell the coppers!' Liz suggested. 'They ought to know about this.'

'They been round?' Dolly asked.

'Only to the O'Hagans' place,' Annie reported.

'They talk to you at the Palace last night?' Dolly asked Robert directly. 'Did you think to mention Cooper's name?'

'The state Hettie and me was in, we never even thought to mention our own bleeding names!' He got up to go. 'I wouldn't pin too many hopes on the coppers, though. Not if I was you.'

'How come?' Dolly was all for marching up to the station and laying a charge.

Robert shrugged. 'I dunno. I just got the feeling they wasn't that interested.'

'The poor girl's lying there dead!' Annie protested. 'What d'you mean, not interested?'

'But they never knew her. To them Daisy's just another chorus girl up the Palace, a girl who made a careless slip, worse luck. It ain't nothing to them. They seen it all before.' He went off to help Joxer shift some barrels.

The women looked downcast. 'She weren't just another chorus girl to me,' Annie remarked. 'She was a beauty, was Daisy.'

'And what about her poor bleeding mother?' Dolly added. 'It's broke her poor heart!'

'Ssh!' Jess warned from the bar. She'd heard Ernie's footsteps coming down, unmistakably jerky and heavy. 'Ern feels real bad about Daisy,' she explained to Maurice. 'He worshipped her, poor lamb.'

Maurice watched as Ernie came into the bar, head down, avoiding people's eyes. He realized at once that the kid was slow; you could read it in the angle of his body, with its slight forwards tilt, and the way his face looked somehow open and unguarded. He was tall and well built, not gawky like so many of the other simple-minded kids round the streets, and he kept himself clean and tidy. His thick, dark hair was well cut, his white shirt starched, his boots polished. The family evidently did a good job of keeping him in trim and looking after him.

'Ern, this is Mr Leigh,' Jess said gently as he came and waited at her side. 'Mr Leigh's just moved in with the Ogdens.'

Maurice shook the boy's hand. 'Nice to meet you.'

Ernie nodded and looked back at Jess.

'I better see what Pa's got lined up for him to do,' she said. 'He ain't feeling himself today. None of us is.'

She linked up with her brother and took him down to the far end of the bar where the old man showed him the tray of dirty glasses to wash.

Maurice sat and studied the family group; the grey-haired landlord once probably strong as an ox, now in decline, but still upright and smart, the salt of the earth. There was the boy, led by the hand, made in the same mould as the father and older brother, but raw and unfinished. And the daughter. Maurice stared for a long time at Jess; not flashy, not even aware of how nice looking she was. She was patience itself with the boy, and gentle. She wore her brown hair high on her head, but little wavy strands escaped and curled against the nape of her neck. She wore a dark-blue blouse, high-necked, with a cream flowered pattern, nipped in at the waist. Finding him watching her, she smiled self-consciously and put a hand to the stray strands of hair. Maurice looked away. If he wasn't careful, she'd get through to him in a serious way and undermine his motto. No complications, he reminded himself. New job; plenty to do, places to go.

Little Katie O'Hagan came up to the corner of the court at six as arranged. Hettie was waiting with a cardboard box full of smocks, trousers, socks and boots; all the assorted belongings that the women of the street had been able to muster. 'We ain't having them going up before the Officer at a time like this,' Hettie insisted. The Relief Board was notoriously unsympathetic towards people like the O'Hagans, who couldn't join in the panel schemes for those who paid out national insurance contributions and who weren't eligible for any of the benefits so far introduced by liberal governments. So Hettie even persuaded some of the men to dip into their pockets to help save Daisy from a pauper's grave. She appealed shamelessly to their guilt. 'C'mon, Walt,' she cajoled Robert's friend. 'Things ain't as bad as all that if you can pay good money to go down Milo's every other day and beat each other's brains out!' She collected the money, together with the clothes, and brought them down to the waiting girl.

'Tell your ma I'll be down with a bit of something extra in the morning,' she told her. She planned to go round the market stalls for damaged fruit and veg. 'And you be a good girl, Katie, and help her all you can.'

The girl nodded, wide-eyed. Daisy used to come home and tell them all about Hettie; how kind she was, and what a nice house she lived in. Cathleen walked off a few steps with the huge box in her arms, turned round and smiled.

Hettie stood on the corner, watching her down the narrow court. Women stood or sat at their doorsteps in the evening sun, following the girl with their eyes. Children stopped playing as she passed. The bright light cast long shadows until, at the bottom of the court, the two black, towering tenement buildings swallowed the sun, and Cathleen stepped into their gloom, her grubby smock ghostly. Then she vanished up the narrow stairs.

Hettie went slowly up to their own comfortable living room, where the sun shone and life followed its natural rhythm. The window was raised for Jess to stand and give Grace a few minutes' fresh air, cradled in her arms.

'I been thinking, Ett,' she said. She looked out across Duke Street at the row of small shops; Edgars' Tobacconist's advertising Navy Cut and Flaked Virginia, Powells' ironmonger's, Henshaw's eating-house and grocer's shop. 'Nice as it is, I can't go on like this.'

Hettie looked alarmed. 'You ain't thinking of leaving us again, are you, Jess?' She was closest to her in age; there was only a year between them, and though their personalities were opposites, a strong bond held them close. Ever since Jess had come home, Hettie had looked to her for company and advice. Besides, there was little Grace to fuss over and adore. 'What's wrong? Ain't you settled here?' She went across and stood by the open window.

'That's just it, I'm more than settled.' Jess sighed. 'Pa's been better with Grace than I ever dreamt. He won't hear a word against her.'

'And no wonder,' Hettie put in. 'She's an angel.'

'And the rest of you, you've been grand too. No, I ain't gonna leave again.' She smiled at Hettie's relieved face. 'But I gotta do something to get a bit of money coming in. I tried talking to Pa about it, but he don't want to know. I mean it though, Ett, and last night, before this terrible

177

thing with Daisy came along and hit us like a steam engine, I sat here and had an idea.'

Hettie heard the excitement in Jess's voice. Everything was changing for the sisters; Frances seemed to be backing out of the heart of family life after all these years in charge. Jess had mellowed into motherhood overnight. Sadie was all talk of Charlie Ogden, and was growing up fast. And now Hettie herself had chucked her job and stood at a crossroads. 'Go on then, I can see you bursting to tell me,' she said, breathing in the warm air. 'How you gonna earn your pot of gold, Jess?'

'It ain't worth a fortune, don't get me wrong. But it's a start. I want to take in a bit of sewing work; alterations and mending. I'll advertise in Henshaw's window and get people to bring their stuff along here. That way there's no trouble getting Grace seen to. What d'you think?' Jess looked nervously at Hettie. 'It ain't a stupid idea, is it?'

'It ain't stupid,' Hettie said slowly. 'But it ain't exactly the Post Office telephonist or the typewriter Frances had in mind.'

'Frances is Frances,' Jess said firmly, 'and I'm me. It's good-hearted of her to look out all these job advertisements for me, but honest to goodness, Ett, I don't feel like going out all day and leaving Grace with someone else. No, I know what I want, and that's to be a proper mother to my baby. She ain't got no father, and that's a fact. All the more reason for me to stay home, I say. So you see, the sewing work suits me down to the ground. I can hand over what I earn to Pa, and I'll feel we can stay here long as we want, Grace and me!'

By the end of the long, heartfelt speech, Hettie found herself smiling broadly. 'Good for you, girl,' she said, turning with a swing of her skirt and striding to the middle of the room. 'Tell you what, Jess, let's be partners, you and me. Business partners. I can come in with you if you like. If two of us take in work, we can get through twice as much and make a name for ourselves twice as quick. "Them Parsons girls do a good, quick piece of work, very neat and tidy!" That's what they'll say. We'll be snowed under with work before we know where we are!'

Jess beamed back at her. 'You sure, Ett? It's a bleeding big jump from the bright lights to this.'

'Good thing too,' Hettie said. 'I'd had enough prancing about up there. What happened to Daisy was the last straw, but how much longer can a girl go on kicking her legs about every night, without landing on the scrap heap?' She stood looking at Jess, challenging her to contradict.

'Ett, you're not even twenty-six till next birthday! You're in your prime!' Jess laughed.

'Says you.' Hettie's light-hearted manner subsided again. 'But honest, what happened to Daisy made me think. It ain't a proper life, Jess. There's gotta be more to it than that, ain't there? As a matter of fact, I think I know what it is!'

'What?' Jess lay the sleeping baby in her crib and came back.

'I ain't saying. You'll think it's daft.'

'No I won't, Ett. Go on, I'm listening.'

'No, honest. I got something in mind, but I want to keep it to myself. Sorry for dragging it up.' Hettie struggled to change the subject. 'Listen here, am I in with you on this sewing lark or not? You can be the boss, since it's your idea. I'll be the skivvy. How's that?'

'Oh no, equal partners!'

'Right you are!' They shook hands and straight away set about drafting a card to put in Henshaw's window. 'Ern

179

can take it across for us tomorrow morning,' Hettie suggested. 'You write it out neat, Jess, with all the charges made up in a proper list.'

They only stopped work when Duke rushed upstairs late in the evening. They raised their heads in surprise at the sound of his steps.

He came into the room, arms raised wide, his face delighted. 'Girls,' he said, 'I've got a bit of good news!' Propped against the mantelpiece, he could hardly contain himself. For months he'd been worried about Robert; not enough work down the docks, too many scraps and bits of bother. Now the problem was solved in the best way he could imagine. Duke's heart swelled with pride. 'I just been talking to Robert,' he told them. 'The boy's been keeping something from me, but he just give me the news and it couldn't be better. Tomorrow morning he's going for his papers. You know what that means, don't you, girls? It means he's enlisting. He's going to join in the war effort and fight for the King!'

Chapter Fifteen

Later that week, as September rolled steadily on, Charlie Ogden stood staring long and hard at the poster roughly pasted on to the red pillar-box at the top of the court. The initials 'G.R.' sat either side of the King's coat of arms, above the giant black lettering. 'Your King and Country Need You!' He read that 100,000 men were needed in the present grave emergency. 'Lord Kitchener is confident that this appeal will be at once responded to by all those who have the safety of our Empire at heart.' They wanted only men at least five foot three inches tall, with a chest measurement of at least thirty-four inches, both of which qualifications Charlie proudly met. But you had to be nineteen. He was just sixteen. Charlie's heart fell. It would be all over before he got the chance to serve. The army offered him no escape from the present misery at home. Even lying about his age wouldn't work; Charlie had one of those fair, smooth-skinned faces with small features, and his physique, though tall, was slender. The army would have to be desperate before they overlooked his birth certificate and accepted him for duty on the Western Front.

'Hello there, Charlie!' Sadie threw open the window and leaned out. Downstairs, everyone was hard at work preparing to give Rob a grand send-off. Even Frances had left work early to come and lend a hand. 'Wait there a sec.' She disappeared from view and soon joined him on the street-corner.

'You're not thinking of enlisting, are you, Charlie?' she said breezily. 'Ain't one soldier in the street enough for you, then?' She linked arms and kept him company to his front door.

'I'd go like a shot if they'd take me.' Moodily he kicked the bottom doorstep. 'Fighting in France is better than living in this dump.' Maurice Leigh might suit his mother, with his polite ways and his rent paid in advance, but sleeping in a room with Amy was a terrible indignity for Charlie.

Sadie sighed. 'And here's me thinking you was studying hard so you could leave home and go to college.' His bad moods unsettled her. For her part, just seeing him pass by or walking with him up to school was enough to lift her spirits for the day, while their Sunday bike rides made the whole of life worthwhile. She never fell into these gloomy spells, and wondered why Charlie couldn't just sail along on her cloud with her.

'I am,' he said, head down, scuffing the step.

'Well, then, ain't no point going off to France and getting yourself shot at, is there?'

Charlie looked up with a patient but stern expression. 'Answering the call to arms is a very fine thing,' he pointed out.

'I know it, Charlie.'

'It's terrible being too young to serve.' He sat on the step, hands clasped and resting on his knees. 'All our best men are going out there, Sadie. And you know what, Mr Donaldson told us at school today that they've shipped more than fifty thousand horses across the English Channel to France. It'll be all over by Christmas.'

She nodded, secretly glad that Robert wouldn't have to see much fighting by the sound of it. He'd signed up and got his uniform, but there were a few weeks' training at his barracks near the south coast before he went off to save Paris for the French. 'Would you like to come to our Robert's send-off?' she asked. 'It starts at six tonight.'

'Maybe.' He shrugged.

Feeling snubbed, Sadie backed off. 'Well, then, I gotta go.'

No answer from Charlie, who'd resorted to notions of following Tommy O'Hagan's lead and simply vanishing as an answer to domestic problems.

Then Sadie made the common woman's mistake of pressing harder for a small commitment from him when the best tactic was to withdraw. 'But you'll still come on our bike ride this Sunday, won't you, Charlie?' There was an edge of panic in her voice. What had happened to him, and all his kisses and promises?

He shook his head, staring down at his hands. 'Is that all you think of, Sadie Parsons? Cycling out into the country-side when we're at war with Germany, and to cap it all there's been a terrible murder of someone we've both known ever since we can remember? Is that all you think about?' He got up quickly and flung open the door.

'No it ain't!' Her retaliation was too slow. Charlie was already halfway down the gloomy corridor. 'Who d'you think has been taking stuff up to the O'Hagans all week? I been up and down them stairs like a jack-in-the-box, and I tell you something, Charlie Ogden, I ain't never seen you up there offering no help!'

Hot tears sprang to her eyes as she stormed off up the court. For all his reading and studying, Charlie missed the obvious things. It was true, Sadie never saw him reach out to help others. He grumbled and dreamt a lot, but he never put himself out. But neither could she bear to argue and think badly of him. It was like making cuts into her own flesh; painful and disfiguring. Sadly she went back to help her sisters.

'Cheer up, Sadie!' Jess cried. The bar shone from top to bottom. She put the finishing touches to the bread and butter and pastries that lined the bar top. 'Put a good face on it for Pa's sake. Don't let him think you're sad to see Rob go. We gotta be happy for him!'

Sadie nodded and pulled herself together. 'What d'you want me to do, Jess?'

'Go over to Henshaw's and fetch Ernie, will you. I said I wanted him home early, but it seems like he forgot. And when you find him you can help him spruce himself up a bit for the party.'

Sadie went off to look for her brother while preparations continued. The sisters brought down huge plates of cold pressed beef, veal and ham pie and fruit tarts. Duke fussed with the bungs and chocks under the barrels in the cellar, and even Joxer showed up in collar and tie instead of his usual bare neck and scarf. At six o'clock, people began to stroll in off the street to a liquid welcome and tables heaped with food.

'Just like good old Teddy's Coronation feast, ain't it?' Annie Wiggin declared. She was first over the threshold in a new hat and her old boots. As far as Annie was concerned, a party was an invitation to reminisce. She went up to Duke and settled herself at the bar. 'You remember that, don't you? We had steak and kidney pie and boiled beef, as much as we could stuff. And we had Bass beer, gallons of it, all paid for by the King himself. I went down the chapel for my dinner that day, and then across to Stepney to see Dan Leno and good old Vesta Tilley. Was you there, Duke?'

He leaned on the bar; the ice with Annie well and truly broken. 'Not me. I was up to me ears here, serving drinks to the whole of bleeding Southwark it seemed like.'

'Them was the good old days, wasn't they, Duke?'

'What was good about them? Your old man had just buggered off and left you, I seem to recall. We was all struggling in them dark days.'

Annie nodded. 'Well, fancy you remembering that.'

'What's that?'

She smiled, weighing her words well. 'The time when my better half departed this life.'

'Course I remember. He owed me half a crown,' Duke said.

'Your Pattie had just passed on and all, and that sister of yours, Florrie Searles, was living here. She came to lend a hand in your hour of need, according to her.' Annie took a long draught from her own special pint pot.

Duke smiled at Annie. 'Florrie ain't that bad, believe me. A bit loud for some people's liking, but her heart's in the right place.'

Annie grunted. 'A voice like a bleeding foghorn. And she treated them poor kids like they was in the bleeding army and all!'

'She never meant no harm.'

'Do this, do that, bleeding parade ground . . .'

The pub was filling up and Duke went off to serve his customers, leaving Annie to bad-mouth his sister to her heart's content. Another strong-minded woman in the street had been one too many for the likes of Annie and Dolly Ogden. 'Arthur, come over here!' Annie called. 'I ain't seen nothing of your Charlie lately.'

Arthur shuffled across, one fist grasping a huge slice of veal and ham pie. 'Why, what you want him for?'

'To catch some rats for me. They're all over the bleeding place again, since young Tommy O'Hagan hopped it. As if they didn't have enough on their plates. He ain't been seen for weeks, not since that poor girl was murdered. He was a dab hand at rat-catching, he was.'

Arthur considered the job in terms of family income before he dismissed it out of hand. 'He's too busy studying,' he replied.

'La-di-da!' She looked around for someone else to take up her offer, and spotted Ernie, head and shoulders above the rest of the crowd. Say what you liked about Ernie, he was twice as reliable as all the other little ikeys put together. There he was, still looking down-in-the-mouth about Daisy, sitting by Walter Davidson. Annie hopped off her stool and went to proposition him for the rat-catching job.

Soon the pub thronged with neighbours and friends, all come to give Robert a good send-off. At last he made his grand entrance, coming downstairs in full uniform, shining from head to foot. Every button sparkled, every lapel and epaulette sat pressed and straight on the khaki jacket. His shiny boots clicked on the stone floor, his flat army cap sat fair and square across his forehead. Duke grinned at him across the room, then carried on serving pints.

Surrounded by friends from the dock, attracting the attention of the girls, Robert was in his element. The uniform made him seem special in his own eyes too, as if he'd been training his body for years to fit its rugged lines like a glove. Less than a week ago joining up had seemed like the best of a bad job; an idea that caught him at a low ebb. Now it began to offer adventure and excitement, and to invest him with a clean-cut courage over and above the tough image he'd adopted on the streets and in the gym.

He glanced with contempt at Chalky, Syd and Whitey, who had drifted in for the free drink, and made a disparaging remark about them to Walter Davidson.

Whitey Lewis sat with his arm around Amy Ogden. He'd got well in with her and a couple of her old friends from Coopers'. Chalkey, on the other hand, ignored them. It was the first time he'd been seen out and about since his defeat down at the gym. He sat slumped forward over his beer, collar up, cigarette hanging from his mouth. He'd seen but ignored Robert's entrance. Memory of his disgrace in the boxing ring still seemed to weigh heavy. His stooping look was a new thing, although the bruising Robert had inflicted had almost faded.

'Bleeding cheek, showing his face round here,' Walter said to Robert. 'You want me to go over and tell him to push off?'

'Leave him be. It ain't no skin off my nose.' Robert had risen above Chalky White and his gang. He circulated, glass in hand, enjoying his last hour of freedom.

Charlie Ogden came, and Sadie was happy. Even Frances sat in a corner with some friends from her classes, though she'd been tactful enough not to invite the women from the suffragette meetings. Their table was quiet and respectable, the least rowdy of the lot, discussing the successful case brought against Teddy Cooper by Miss Amelia Jones. Frances herself had stood up in court as a witness and described the accused's actions on the night of the window-smashing. Her evidence had helped bring about a conviction. 'It ain't right though,' Frances complained. 'They find him guilty of assault and let him off with a footling little fine. They take Amelia herself to court for smashing a window and they give her six months in Holloway. Call that justice!'

The others agreed. 'Lucky little swine,' Rosie Cornwell

said. She'd just given up her good job as a typewriter in Swan and Edgar's office to train as a nurse for the war effort; a pretty, round-faced girl with light brown hair braided into a coronet around her brow.

'Hers was a crime against property,' Billy Wray pointed out. 'His was a crime against the person. It's obvious which one they think is more serious, ain't it? Besides, he's a boss.' He spoke quietly, stating the obvious with deadly effect. 'They could get away with murder without too much trouble, believe you me.'

Frances shuddered. 'Don't say that.' She'd heard the rumours, spreading like wildfire around the streets, fanned by Dolly Ogden. No one had seen much sign of Teddy Cooper since the murder, even at Coopers' Drapery Stores. People there said the police had paid him a visit and questioned him. It was only a matter of time before the arrest.

'Why not? What did I say?' Billy didn't live locally enough to have heard the rumours. His interests were political, not personal, with his long history in the hunger marches of 1908 and 1911. 'Starved to Death in a Land of Plenty' was his banner. Tittle-tattle wasn't up his street, but he noticed Frances shake her head and go pale.

'Nothing. The girl who got murdered up at the Palace lived down our street, that's all. They say Teddy Cooper's a suspect.'

'Him and five hundred others,' Rosie reminded her, and steered the talk in another direction.

Robert stood at the bar now, grasping his father's hand. 'Time I was off, Pa.'

Duke gave his son's hand one firm shake. He felt choked with pride. In his uniform, Robert looked the perfect son, the conquering hero. 'The girls will go and see you off,

Rob. Me and Ernie will say goodbye here.' He wouldn't trust his voice to say more.

Robert nodded.

Hettie came downstairs with his trenchcoat over her arm, while Jess went out to hail a cab. She too said goodbye on the doorstep. 'There's Grace to see to,' she said quietly. 'The little beggar's hungry again. Look after yourself, Rob. We're proud of you.' She looked up into his face and squeezed his arm.

So Robert set off for Victoria with Hettie, Frances and Sadie, waving farewell to the old life.

'G'bye, Ern! Look after things here while I'm gone!' he yelled. The horses clipped smartly up the street, the old cab swayed along. Crossing the main thoroughfares in the early autumn evening, they came to the sluggish grey river. They passed high over the water along London Bridge, over the slow barges. Victoria's mighty façade, with its great ribbed awning of iron and glass, greeted them as they spilled from the cab. The station platforms thronged with uniforms; soldiers with rifles slung across their shoulders, sailors with their kitbags. All the faces looked brisk and hopeful, of young men embarking for battle, making good farewells.

Robert slung his own bag down on a bench and turned to the women. 'That one's mine.' He pointed to the mighty engine, its funnel gently hissing steam.

Hettie ignored a small convoy of wounded men crossing a faraway platform, some on crutches, some carried on stretchers. She smiled bravely. 'Write and tell us how you're getting along,' she reminded him. 'And there's no need to tell you again to make sure and look after yourself, is there?'

'You too, Ett.' Robert gave her a quick hug. 'And keep an eye on the O'Hagans.'

'Try and stop me.'

'She's a one-woman Sally Army,' Frances put in. She took Robert's hand, clasping it in her own small, gloved ones.

'Well, say a prayer for old Daisy then,' Robert said to Hettie, one foot on the carriage step.

She nodded. 'I already did.' The train door slammed, Robert leaned out of the window.

'Go give him a kiss, quick!' Frances said to Sadie, who ran and reached up to his cheek. She clung on to his coat for a second, before the great iron wheels began to turn. Robert's face drew away into the distance. He raised his cap and waved, then went and sat in his carriage, with its smell of musty heat. The train left the station, shuttling between the backs of tall houses, through black tunnels, out into the open countryside, where shadows fell deep and the place names were hazy with steam and yellow flowering shrubs.

Annie Wiggin lingered until after most guests had left. The food was picked over, all the free beer drunk. Robert's departure had signalled the end of the party, of course. 'Like *Hamlet* without the bleeding prince,' she said to Dolly. 'Ain't you lucky your Charlie's too young for this lark?'

She ambled out on to the pavement in time to see a flat-topped police car drive up. She noticed its soft rubber tyres with their smart white rims, its dicky-seat at the back crammed with three coppers in full uniform, besides the sergeant and his mate sitting comfortably inside. They all climbed out and looked up and down Duke Street. Trouble, she thought, and nipped back inside the pub for a ringside view.

To her surprise, the coppers actually followed her into

the bar in single file, then fanned out across the room. Everyone stood stock-still, as if posing for a photograph. Joxer and Duke looked out from behind the bar.

'Wilf Parsons?' the sergeant asked. 'We want to talk to your boy.'

'He just left.' Duke's voice was strained, but he returned the policeman's stare. 'He enlisted for France. You won't find him here.' Whatever Robert had been up to would pale into insignificance beside that.

'Your boy, Ernest,' the man continued.

Duke breathed out, almost scornful. 'Well, there's been some mistake there. Ernie's . . .'

'No mistake,' the officer barked. He took a creased cloth cap from a pocket and held it up for inspection. Jess gasped and took a step towards it. 'This belongs to him, don't it?' He stuffed it back into his pocket without waiting for a reply. 'We already identified it through witnesses. He was seen, you understand. This is his cap, all right. We found it at the scene of the crime.'

Jess backed off, feeling herself go faint. The sticky sensation of blood on her fingers came back to her with redoubled force. She looked round wildly to see where Ernie was. The policemen watched her like hawks.

'Where? What crime?' Duke stared around the room.

'He ain't exactly hard to spot by all accounts. Several witnesses seen him hanging about the place just before the murder.'

'Murder? What you on about?' Duke lifted the bar hinge and stepped forward. 'What the bleeding hell you trying to say?'

The policemen stiffened, but didn't move in on Duke. They waited while the sergeant explained.

'We need to talk to Ernie.' He motioned two of the men to barge past Joxer down into the cellar. 'It's in connection with the murder at the Palace. Bad news, I'm afraid. We got to arrest your boy.'

Jess cried out loud and went to cling on to Annie. Annie screeched at the nearest copper; a young man with a thin moustache. Duke lunged at the sergeant, but Joxer managed to restrain him as the two policemen emerged from the cellar on either side of a bewildered Ernie.

'You can't arrest him, you bleeding idiot!' Annie yelled. 'The poor boy wouldn't harm a fly!'

'We got to take him down the station and ask him a few questions.' The sergeant turned to speak to Jess, who seemed to be the only one to have come to her senses. She was stunned but quiet. 'I've got to warn you though that we'll most likely charge him and keep him in the cells. After that, you can go and visit him in the Scrubs. Got it?'

Ernie stared at the chaos around him. Two policemen held him by the arms. In confusion, he began to struggle. One arm was wrenched up his back, the other shackled by handcuffs. He felt the cold metal click around his wrist. 'Pa?' he pleaded.

Duke pushed Joxer off and stood up straight. His head was up, though his hands trembled. 'Go with them, there's a good boy, Ern.'

Ernie nodded and let himself be led off.

Duke's head dropped to his chest. He turned away.

'Ern don't understand,' Jess told the sergeant. 'You got to explain things to him clear and simple. You get him down the station and explain the charge, right? You tell him he's supposed to have stabbed Daisy to death. Then you listen to him. He'll tell you the truth.' She held on to the policeman's braided cuff. 'You hear me? Ernie can't lie, he don't know how. You listen to him well and good, you hear?'

The man nodded, glad the boy was going quietly. 'He was up the Palace that night, weren't he?'

Slowly Jess admitted it.

'Shh, Jess,' Annie warned. 'Don't tell them nothing.'

Duke watched the doors swing to after the men. Only the sergeant remained. 'There's been a mistake,' he whispered.

Jess made one final appeal. 'Ernie wouldn't kill Daisy!' Tears poured down her face. 'He worshipped the girl!'

The sergeant sighed. 'I've seen everything in this job,' he said. 'Most of it you wouldn't believe unless you'd seen it with your own eyes.' He looked almost sorry for them as he fixed his hat on his head and pulled the strap under his chin. 'Look after your old man,' he advised. 'He looks like he could do with a stiff drink.'

Annie followed him to the door, in time to see him clamber into the car, and to catch a glimpse of Ernie's pale, bewildered face staring out from between the blue uniforms as they drove him off up the street.

Chapter Sixteen

Ernie understood that they thought he'd done something very bad. He knew they could give him the cat or put him in prison, and he was very afraid. But his father had told him to go along quietly, and it surely wouldn't be long before they came from home and fetched him. Probably Frances would come, when she got back from sending Robert off to war, and she would sort things out. This went through his head as the policemen manhandled him from the car into the station. The handcuffs locked both arms tight in front of him. They chafed his skin as he was wrenched this way and that down the bare corridor into a room with a table and two chairs. One high, barred window provided daylight, and an electric light shone under a green metal shade. The door banged shut. He was alone.

Then a man he'd never seen before came in. He wore a long, pale coat and a brown bowler hat. A dark moustache hid his mouth. His cheeks were thin, his eyes set close together. He never smiled or said hello; just threw his coat across the back of one of the chairs and slammed some papers down on the table. He looked at Ernie. 'Sit,' he said. He turned to the policeman in uniform who'd followed him in and puffed air into his thin cheeks. Then he blew it out in a loud sigh. 'Best get cracking on this one, Sergeant. What's he said so far?'

'Not a dicky bird, sir.' The sergeant stared at the blank wall above Ernie's head. 'He's all yours.'

The inspector took a mottled blue fountain pen from his top pocket, preparing to make notes for the duration of the interview. 'Does he know the charge?'

The sergeant blinked. 'No, sir. His sister says you have to take it slow. He ain't all that bright.'

'Oh my gawd.' The inspector stared narrowly at Ernie. 'He don't look that bad to me. Come quietly, did he?' The youth looked strong enough to cause trouble if so inclined. They were charging him with a nasty business; stabbing the girl at least ten or a dozen times and leaving her to bleed to death.

'Like a lamb, sir. Better tell him the charge and get it over with.'

'Easy does it. Now listen, son, you know why we brought you down here?'

Ernie stared back. He shook his head. 'I ain't done nothing wrong.'

'That's for us to say. But you know about the girl what got killed at the music hall, don't you? Daisy O'Hagan; she lived down your street.'

Slowly Ernie nodded. Pain at the memory of Daisy creased his forehead into a frown.

'And you was at the music hall yourself that night, wasn't you?' The inspector leaned across the table towards him. 'You was seen, mate, so you gotta tell us exactly what happened. Take your time, no rush.' He eased back in his seat and held his pen poised over the paper.

The man's voice sounded gentle. Ernie looked at him in surprise. 'Rob took me to see Ett and Daisy again,' he explained. 'We went to meet up with them after the show, but I lost Rob. I never saw where he went.'

The inspector glanced at the sergeant. 'Robert Parsons,

older brother, just gone and joined up,' the uniformed man informed him.

'Oh, very handy!' The inspector raised his close-knit eyebrows. 'Maybe we'd have got more sense out of him. Never mind. And what happened to you after you lost Rob, Ernie?' he asked. 'You're on your way backstage to see Ett and Daisy, remember?'

Ernie nodded. 'Ett's my sister,' he offered obligingly.

'Good, we're getting somewhere, then. But I want you to tell me what happened next. You lose your big brother. Now what?'

Ernie had begun to tremble. 'I never saw him out in the street neither. There was people all around, but I never let them put me off. I just had to go and meet Ett and Daisy like we always do. That's what Rob says, and then we walk home with them!' For a moment his face cleared.

The inspector sighed. 'Very nice, son. But it ain't like that on this particular night, is it? What happens when you finally get to the stage door? That's the bit we're interested in.'

Drawn back to that moment, Ernie's hands shook more violently against the bare table top. 'I'm too late. They all gone home. Rob ain't there. It's dark and empty.'

'What is?'

'The alley. I got held up by all those crowds, see. I was late.'

'Steady on, don't panic. What d'you do then, Ern?'

'I don't know. I can't remember.' Ernie's voice fell to a low whisper. 'Rob won't go home without me, I know that. He's gotta be somewhere.' He swallowed hard. 'Rob gets mad with me when I get lost.' He stopped, suddenly unable to go on.

'So what did you do next, Ernie?' The inspector concentrated on the boy's face. The confession had hit a brick wall.

Their suspect had gone blank on the crucial part. He glanced down to bring his notes up to date. 'Go ahead, son, tell us.'

'I don't remember.' Ernie's blank face searched the room for clues.

The inspector frowned. 'You don't expect us to buy that, do you, son?'

Ernie raised his tethered hands to his forehead. 'I know I'm in the right place to wait for Rob. But something's not right. I don't know. I'm looking everywhere, but Rob ain't there. What am I gonna do now?' He stood up, reliving the incident. 'Then I don't know what happens. Everything's gone wrong. I don't know!'

'Easy, son, easy. What happened after you'd waited for a bit? Did you go inside? Who did you see?'

'No! I don't know!'

'Did you go inside and find Rob? Or Daisy? Did you find her?'

Ernie stood up and came to appeal to the inspector. 'It ain't right. Rob shouldn't 've gone off, should he?'

'Hang on a bit.' The inspector's voice hardened and he motioned the sergeant to come forward with a brown envelope. The sergeant tipped it and emptied a kitchen knife on to the table, then stood back. 'Try thinking about this instead. Did you have this in your pocket that night, Ernie?' He looked keenly at the suspect, devoid of sympathy. They'd reached the crux of the matter.

Ernie shook his head.

'I want you to think this through carefully, Ernie.'

He nodded, anxious to play the scene through to its conclusion and get it off his chest. 'It ain't my fault, is it? Rob should never 've gone off. I was waiting for him, like he said.' He paused. When he took up again, his voice was strangled and faint. He shook his head. 'I never meant to do it!' Ernie caught hold of the policeman. 'Tell Rob I never meant to!'

'All right, all right, ease off!' The inspector pulled away as Ernie seized his jacket sleeve. 'That'll do for now. Have him taken down, Sergeant,' he said abruptly. He pulled his cuff straight and stood up as the constables came in to lead Ernie off to the cells. The heavy door shut behind them on to a long silence.

'What d'you reckon?' the sergeant asked at last.

The inspector looked up at the ceiling and scratched his neck. 'I think it's in the bag. He's got a touch of convenient amnesia around the actual stabbing, but I don't think the jury will wear that one. Maybe we'll never get it all out of him. He'll stay clammed up in court, if you want my opinion, but it won't make no difference. The rest is staring them in the face; he was there, his cap was there. This knife here is the murder weapon, and you can buy it from the ironmonger's opposite his house. Powells', ain't it?' He flicked the blade with his fingernail and made the knife spin under the glare of the electric light. 'Very neat.'

'No blood on him?' the sergeant asked.

'Too late to find out. Maybe he had someone who cleaned him up? That'd be worth checking. You can trot back to the pub and ferret around,' he suggested. Then he shrugged, picked up the knife and put it back in the envelope. 'You happy with what we got so far, Sergeant?'

The other man nodded. 'He ain't put up much of a defence, has he? Losing your memory don't convince no one that you're innocent.'

'What above a motive? That's what the jury will be asking.'

'Maybe he found her with another bloke,' the sergeant surmised. 'The sister back at the pub reckons he worshipped the girl. The way he sees things in black and white I reckon

198

he'd go barmy if he caught her with someone else, which she was more than likely to do by all accounts.'

The inspector nodded. 'How about the older brother? That would account for him making himself scarce with a sudden attack of patriotism. Joining up is a surefire way of staying out of bother; he must know that. Anyhow, it looks to me like it'll hang together in front of a jury. Better get him properly charged. Ain't much more we can do now.' He sat to do the paperwork; suspect arrested at half-past seven on the 14th of September 1914. Ernest Parsons, aged eighteen, of the Duke of Wellington public house, Duke Street, Southwark.

Ernie's arrest shattered Duke. Men had died at his side in the army, and he'd watched his poor wife fade away under his own eyes. In the early days at the Duke, an unemployed scaffolder from one of the tenements had collapsed on his doorstep. They'd found the wife and three-year-old daughter dead of starvation at home. Horror stories of rats gnawing babies to death in Riddington's Yard, and anarchists shot dead by police in the Sydney Street siege were part and parcel of life in the East End, and now the war against Germany brought news of families who'd lost sons or fathers, or had them sent home wounded and broken. But nothing had robbed Duke of his will to battle on like this latest blow. They'd taken Ernie off in a police car, and life hollowed out to blank horizons, a slow stumble towards nothing.

'Don't take on,' Annie patted his hand. 'They got the wrong man, we know that. Soon as they ask him a few questions, they'll see they got it wrong.' She couldn't bear to see the strong man reduced to this empty shell. She looked up at Jess, tears in her eyes. 'Tell him not to take on,

Jess. We need him to be thinking straight when the others get back home.'

But Jess's own thoughts ran riot. She'd wiped blood off Ernie's boots and burnt the evidence. She'd washed her hands clean and asked no questions. Even when news of the murder ran through the streets, she'd kept quiet. What a fool she'd been, thinking that by cleaning the boots she could keep Ernie out of trouble. 'I done wrong,' she wept on Annie's shoulder. 'I never asked Ernie about his boots. I could've got the truth out of him, but I never. I left it! I done wrong over it. Poor Ern!'

'Don't you take on neither.' Annie put her arms round Jess. 'You got enough on your plate looking after little Grace. Now you go up and pull yourself together, girl. I'll look after your old man, and Joxer here will get the place straight.'

The wreckage of Robert's send-off celebrations still littered the bar, only bringing home to Duke the fact that he'd lost both his sons at one stroke. He sat in a daze as Joxer cleared off the glasses and swept the floors. Annie sat quiet and held his hand, watching the minutes tick by. She stared at his face; saw the lined cheeks, the jutting forehead and hooked nose, watching for signs of revival. But Duke sat on, scarcely blinking, trying to imagine what was happening to Ernie right that minute up at Union Street station. 'He ain't never been away from home before,' he told Annie. 'He ain't never slept in no other bed.'

Frances, Sadie and Hettie came back from Victoria by underground train and tram. Their effort to stay cheerful for Rob's send-off had worn them into a subdued silence on their return journey, and their memories of the uniformed hordes all making their farewells held an uneasy sadness. How many of those bright young men would return on stretchers like the ones carried along the side platform? How many would never come back at all?

'Chin up,' Frances said as they stood on the tram platform, ready to alight. 'Robert made his own choice. No need to ruin Pa's day by looking so down in the mouth about it now.' The tram rattled on while the sisters turned into Duke Street and walked the final stretch.

They wondered at everyone standing, arms folded and staring, as they drew near home. The pub doors were shut. Hettie grasped Sadie's hand and followed Frances along the pavement, then across the street. She noticed people withdraw inside their open doors to avoid them as they passed close by. 'Oh gawd, I hope Pa's not been took ill by it all!' she gasped. Frances pushed the ornate brass door handle, familiar to her as the back of her own hand.

Jess stood at the top of the stairs holding Grace in her arms. The bar-room door stood wedged open. Joxer was there, leaning on his broom, staring at them. Duke sat at a table, unmarked by illness or accident, and only the mystery of the staring neighbours, the closed pub doors remained. Their father was well, at any rate.

'What is it? What's wrong, Pa?' Frances hurried ahead again, picking at the fingers of her gloves, bag tucked under her arm. Sadie raised her arms to remove her hat. Hettie smiled up at Jess.

'It's Ernie,' Annie Wiggin rushed forward to intercept them. 'Your pa's had a shock, that's all. You'd best sit down.'

Hettie's smile turned to a look of alarm. She went and grabbed Annie by the arm. 'What's up with Ernie? Is that why we're all closed up here? Oh gawd, he's had an accident, ain't he? Is it bad?'

'Sit down, Ett.' Frances drew her on to a chair. 'And you

201

too, Sadie. Come and sit close by me.' She stared at the bowed figure of her father. 'Go ahead, Annie, you tell us what happened.' She felt sure Ernie must be dead; she just wanted someone to tell them the news.

'The coppers came.' Annie wrung her hands. She stood beside Duke. 'They think Ernie killed Daisy O'Hagan. They took him away.'

Sadie cried out loud; the long, protesting cry of a young child, her mouth hanging wide. Frances stood up and walked to the window to stare out. Hettie hung her head. 'It ain't possible,' she whispered. 'Don't they know he couldn't hurt a fly?'

'They wouldn't listen. It's hit your pa very hard, Ett. We can't get a word out of him hardly!' Annie gabbled. Now that the news was broken, she darted round the room from one to another. 'We gotta think straight, Frances. You got your head screwed on, girl. Think what we gotta do next!'

'Why on earth would they want to charge Ernie?' Frances asked. Across the street she saw the net curtains twitch. A group of women stood out on the street by the post-box, heads tilted into the middle of their circle, glancing every now and then towards the Duke. 'What evidence did they have?'

Annie shook her head. 'His cap. They say they found Ernie's cap by Daisy's body. But that don't prove nothing!'

'Where is he?'

'Union Street station.'

'Then that's where I have to go.' Frances flinched at the idea of facing the gossips again, but she had to try and see Ernie, and the sooner the better. God only knew what words the police would put into his mouth. They could get someone like Ernie to put his name to anything they wanted. 'He can't even read his statement!' she realized.

'He'll be confessing to everything up there, just to get back home. Ett, Sadie, you two stay and help look after things here. We gotta pull round. Try and rouse Pa. Tell him we'll put up a fight for Ernie. Ain't no way the police can get away with this!'

Dusk fell down Paradise Court, and not one inhabitant remained ignorant of Ernie Parsons's arrest. The murder had been bad enough. It was a terrible thing when a girl's life was snuffed out and her family left wondering why in God's name it had to happen to them. The neighbours had rallied round. This last week the little O'Hagan kids had actually looked better and been better fed than in their whole lives before, thanks mainly to Hettie Parsons. Joe O'Hagan had turned up for the girl's funeral in a halfway decent suit. There was talk of him getting work in a Tooley Street factory making cardboard boxes, to help the family back on its feet. Mary O'Hagan looked beaten by it all, but that was only to be expected.

Now they'd caught poor Daisy's killer, and it turned out to be someone else living right under their noses; none other than Ernie Parsons. He had a thing about Daisy, anyone could see that. He was always making up to her in his own, simple way. And Daisy was none too careful about leading him on. Everyone had seen problems there; at the very least, heartbreak for Ernie. You just had to think how she'd been seen carrying on with that weasel, Chalky White, to know she'd not got the sense she was born with. Now if it had been that young man who'd gone and got himself arrested, that would have been no surprise. But Chalky had been laid low by Robert Parsons that very afternoon. He'd kept to his bed to lick his wounds. No, all the best bets had been on Teddy Cooper, the boss's son. But Ernie Parsons had been thought of as harmless. It just went to show, you never could tell.

The mild evening kept folk out on their doorsteps until long after the moon rose over the dull slate roofs. By the time Annie Wiggin made her sorrowful way out of the Duke down to the end of the court, Ernie was established as a deep one, a youth with thwarted dreams who'd turned to violence when his love was spurned. It was a crime of passion, a tragedy for all concerned. Imagination came colourful in the drab East End.

Annie trudged on down the street. 'How's he taking it?' Nora Brady called from her doorstep. 'How's Duke?'

'Bad.'

'Have they sent Robert the news yet?' someone asked.

Annie shook her head, too weary to look round. But something about the situation roused her. By the time she reached the Ogden place her mettle was up. She looked Dolly straight in the eye. 'He ain't guilty, y'know!'

'I never said he was.' Dolly backed off. Annie's vehemence surprised her. Anyway, she'd been no great subscriber to the Ernie Parsons theory, preferring her own old judgement against the boss's son. 'As a matter of fact, didn't I just say the poor boy was innocent as the day?' she claimed.

In the background, Amy nodded.

'Yes, and don't no one go round saying nothing different, you hear!' Annie's voice rose like a soap-box orator's. She shook her fist at them all. 'We lived alongside that boy for nearly twenty years, some of us. We watched him grow up, we looked out for him up and down this street. Ernie ain't the brightest of lads, we all know that. But he ain't no murderer neither. Anyone who says different will have me to answer to!'

She stormed on her way, a small, slight figure, very

ferocious. Her speech had turned the whole thing round. Opinion swayed after her; 'Fancy carting poor Ernie Parsons off. They must be barmy. What the bleeding hell they up to over at that police station?' And so on, from doorstep to doorstep.

Annie closed her own door tight shut and sank into a chair. Only then did she give way to her feelings. In the privacy of her own front room, behind the aspidistra, she began to cry her eyes out for Duke and his family, and for the poor boy locked up in a cold prison cell.

Late that night Mary O'Hagan came up the court. She waited until lights were beginning to go out in upstairs rooms before she reached for her shawl and told Cathleen to mind the little ones. It was a quiet, pale figure that trod the pavement to see Hettie. 'I must speak to her,' she told the rough cellarman. 'Will you please go and fetch her?'

Joxer told her to wait in the corridor leading to the slope down into the cellar, but Hettie soon appeared on the stairs and said she must come up. Mary had never ventured inside the pub before. She trembled as Hettie came and grasped her hand and drew her upstairs. On the landing Mary resisted. 'It's you I must speak with,' she whispered. The attractive Irish brogue belied her haggard face and the clothes hanging almost in rags from her thin frame.

Hettie looked deep into her eyes. 'You heard the news?'

Mary nodded. 'That's why I came.'

'Poor Ernie!' Hettie broke down in tears. 'This is a terrible thing, Mary. I don't know what to say.'

'Then say nothing,' came the kind reply. 'Only I came to tell you not to worry. That boy never killed my Daisy, and the sooner they find that out the better.'

Hettie looked up again through tear-filled eyes. 'It's very good of you to come here,' she told her. Lost for words, the women fell into each other's arms.

'I never wanted my trouble to land in your lap, Hettie, believe me. You been good to Daisy, and you been good to us. We have to pray to God that they'll set the boy free soon. I don't like to think of him locked away for something he never did.' Mary held both of Hettie's hands and spoke rapidly, earnestly.

'Or worse,' Hettie agreed. 'They'll hang him if they find him guilty, Mary. That's the worst of it!'

'Oh never!' Mary gasped. 'It'll never come to that. What can we do to stop it? Oh, Hettie, they can't do that to the boy. Where's the justice? Where's the sense? Oh, your poor Pa!'

Jess came out, found them sobbing anew, and took them inside. The family blessed Mary for coming; it was a great comfort. Even Duke moved out of his profound hopelessness to offer her words of thanks. 'It ain't over yet,' Jess promised. 'We got a long way to go in this family before we're through!'

Chapter Seventeen

After softening the desk sergeant's heart at Union Street and gaining just five minutes with Ernie to try and reassure him that all would be well, Frances decided to set about using her contacts to get him good expert advice. He seemed to understand that he must stay in custody until they'd sorted things out for him, but he was worried about what Mr Henshaw would say if he failed to turn up for work next day. Frances promised to explain. 'Don't you worry, Ern, Mr Henshaw will understand.'

'Will he get another boy?' Ernie asked. He pictured someone else riding the shiny black bike up and down Duke Street.

'I hope not, Ern. I'll talk to him for you.' Frances and Sadie rose to go. 'You gotta stay here and be patient, and try not to worry too much. Do as they tell you and you'll be fine.' She bent and kissed his cheek. 'Cheer up, Ern, we'll do everything we can to get you out of here.'

She and Sadie sailed out of the police station, heads high. But they carried with them the memory of Ernie's stricken face as the coppers came in to lead him back to his lonely cell.

'He loves this job, Mr Henshaw,' Frances told the shopkeeper next day. 'He's afraid you'll think badly of him for letting you down.' She was on her way to work at

Boots, calling at Henshaw's, then planning to stop at Billy Wray's newspaper stand to ask about a solicitor.

Henshaw tied the strings around the waist of his long calico apron. 'Tell him from me his job will be here waiting for him when he gets out, Miss Parsons. I ain't found a boy as steady as Ernie for donkey's years.' He looked her straight in the eye. 'And tell your Pa that Mrs Henshaw and me are sorry for his trouble. You be sure and tell him that.'

Frances nodded. 'Thanks, Mr Henshaw.'

He stood at the shop door; apron tied, sleeves rolled up, dark hair parted down the middle. He could see the effort Frances had to put into making her way to work as usual, threading through the handcarts and the men loading up their stalls with the day's produce, a neat figure in her grey costume, stepping smartly over puddles, past street-sweepers and boys scavenging for fruit.

When she reached Meredith Close, the scene of the arrests during Coopers' window-smashing incident, she found Billy Wray already at his news-stand, surrounded by billboards proclaiming wonderful advances against the Germans, and the enemy's imminent collapse. Billy greeted her with a quick handshake. He'd heard the bad news about Ernie, who hadn't? Was there anything he could do? Frances discussed the sort of legal help they needed; she was afraid the duty solicitor wouldn't take much interest in a case like Ernie's. It turned out Billy had contacts at the Workers' Education Institute on St Thomas Street. He promised to nip along there today and do his best to help. Moved by his and the Henshaws' generosity, Frances felt her nerve begin to give way. She was prepared for battle, but not for kindness. Quietly she took a handkerchief from her pocket and blew her nose.

Billy too watched her on her way, oblivious to her surroundings, walking automatically amongst the heavy morning traffic, until she was swallowed by the trams and omnibuses, emerging briefly on the far side of the street, only to disappear again amidst the sea of cloth caps and boaters jostling to work.

A telephone message made its way to Florrie Searles in Brighton. A well-meaning neighbour in Paradise Court took it upon herself to go to the Post Office to ring and tell Florrie's son, Tom, that the Parsons had landed in terrible trouble. By noon that day, the indomitable Florrie had packed her bag and boarded the express train into Waterloo.

'Wilf will go to pieces about this if I'm not there to back him up,' she told Tom. 'I know him; never says nothing, but it's all going on inside his head. And there's that pub to run. It don't run itself. Wilf needs me there!'

'Now, Ma, go easy,' the thin, middle-aged man warned. He looked up from the platform at her determined expression. 'Don't go rampaging.'

Florrie's look switched to one of prim outrage. 'Me? Rampage? What you on about? I have to go when my one and only brother lands in trouble, don't I? We make these sacrifices in our family, always have. Why, I'm practically a mother to them poor girls!' She sniffed and glanced sharply up and down the platform. 'Now listen, Thomas, no need for you to fret while I'm away. It ain't as if I never taught you how to cook and do for yourself, is it?' She cast him a worried, protective look.

Tom, afraid that she was going to make a scene, gave a quick shake of his head. 'No, Ma!'

'And it ain't as if you won't have Lizzie coming in to clean for you, Monday to Friday. She'll lay the fires of a night, and leave plenty in the pantry. All you have to do is heat it up.'

'Yes, Ma.'

'Lizzie's a decent sort.'

'Yes, Ma.' Lizzie Makins was a scrawny old skinflint whose gravy didn't stand up to scrutiny. Tom curled his thin top lip over his bottom one. The guard waved his flag and blew his whistle. Steam gushed from the engine.

Florrie thrust her son back from the side of the train. 'Stand clear, Thomas, we're moving off!' Her waving handkerchief and brave farewell echoed the scenes in romantic novels where noble heroines gave their all.

Standing on the platform in a cloud of steam, Tom felt a great weight lift from his shoulders. His mother was a large woman and a great gossip, convinced of her own indispensability in every area of life. He'd carried her, slung around his neck like an albatross, for some crime he was unaware of having committed; for being born most likely. He waved the stout figure off, and she waved back under her mountainous cream-coloured hat. He heaved a huge sigh of relief.

She arrived in Duke Street in style, throwing a penny at the boy who bobbed up beside the taxi to carry her bag. She stood for a minute in the street, gazing up at the Duke's golden lettering, inspecting the windows for signs of the least neglect, glancing down the court. 'Dreadful thing to have happened, ain't it?' she confided to the taxi-driver as she paid her fare. She rolled her eyes sideways towards the pub.

The man nodded, nonplussed.

'A terrible thing for a respectable family, but I ain't ashamed to own up to him as my brother. Oh no, we Parsons gotta hold our heads up, make no mistake!' She grasped the man's hand as she slipped the two silver coins into it.

'Good for you, missus.' He tried to snatch his hand away.

'It's at times like this you know who your real friends are.' Florrie let the man go at last, stood up straight and braced herself. She pulled her brown jacket straight across her bosom, then adjusted her giant hat. The taxi-driver sped off like a greyhound from the trap. Her bag carrier stood and staggered under the weight.

'What you got in here, missus, a bleeding iron mangle?'

Florrie tapped him on the backside with her umbrella. 'Cheek. Watch it, sonny, there's a step up here. Don't knock the paintwork. Turn right through here. Watch them edges. Here, now you can put it down. Careful!' She stood in the middle of the empty bar, surrounded by gleaming mirrors, fancy plaster cornices, dark wood panelling. The old place hadn't changed a bit. 'Wilf!' She spread her arms wide and advanced like the *Titanic*. She plunged towards him. 'Ain't no need to say nothing. Your boy's innocent, we know that. Just stop worrying. Everything's gonna be all right, I'm here to help!'

Florrie's tidal-wave effect threw up survivors. She was something to stand up to, after all, and a reminder that they'd weathered bad times before. When Hettie and Jess surfaced after the shock of her arrival, they rearranged beds, emptied drawers and resigned themselves to being buffeted by her loud opinions and enormous personality. If anything, she was larger than before; stouter around the middle, her shoulders and bosom puffed out with yards of gathered white cotton. And the hats had certainly increased in size along with the rest of her. This cream one sat like an upturned shopping basket, loaded with violent red silk poppies all around the brim. She kept it on as she distributed her possessions around the house, keeping it pinioned to her jet-black hair by half a dozen vicious hatpins.

When a sergeant called in the late afternoon to follow up the arrest by interviewing members of the suspect's family, Florrie had to be restrained. 'You stay here, Auntie,' Jess protested. 'Joxer says it's me he wants to see first.'

She let this information penetrate. 'You? What's he want with you?'

'I don't know, do I?' Jess went to make sure that Grace was sound asleep before she made for the landing.

'Leave her be,' Florrie said, waving her off. 'I looked after more babies than you've had hot dinners, girl. Better go and make sure you give that copper a piece of your mind. Ask him when they gonna let that poor boy out. Tell him it'll be the death of his old man down there if they don't!'

Florrie's voice gushed downstairs after her. Jess pushed open the bar-room door, afraid of the line the police questioning might take. Was there anything unusual about Ernie when he came home on the night of the murder? the sergeant would ask. He'd be gathering evidence and writing down what she said. She looked at him in cold fear, knowing that Duke stood in the background listening.

The sergeant pressed hard. 'Did you think to ask him where he'd been?' He sat, pencil poised.

Jess tried to hold her voice steady. 'I knew where he'd been. He was up at the Palace with Robert.'

'But he came back by himself, did he?'

She nodded. 'He got lost.'

'And would you say he was in a bit of a state? Out of breath? Upset?'

'He was very quiet. He never said nothing.' Jess glanced at Duke. She was unwilling to admit the state Ernie had been in, but she felt like a lamb being led to the slaughter. Soon the policeman would be sure to pin her down.

'Just normal?'

'Yes. He don't say much.'

The sergeant began to feel irritated by her stonewalling. 'But did you notice anything different? Was his clothes messed about, for instanc? Had he been in a fight?'

'No.'

'What about his boots?' The sergeant remembered a trail of bloody footprints leading out of the murdered girl's dressing room.

She wasn't quick enough with the direct lie. 'No,' she faltered. She met his stern gaze, then cast her eyes down, unable to hold it.

'Hm, fair enough,' the sergeant said. He was no court prosecutor, but anyone with experience could break this story. He bet his life that Jess could be brought up as an accessory after the fact. Closing his notebook, he thanked her for her time with a touch of sarcasm in his voice, then he turned to Duke.

Jess rose quickly. 'How's Ern? Is he all right?'

'He's due in court tomorrow to face charges. Then they'll move him on to a remand cell in the Scrubs.' He spoke evasively, being the one to avoid her eyes now.

'But how is he in himself? He ain't gone to pieces, has he?' Jess begged.

'He's taking it quietly, I'd say. He ain't no trouble.' The policeman nodded at Duke, asked him for a few minutes of his time, and told Jess to leave them alone together.

If there was anyone he felt sorry for in all this mess, it was the old man. When they had the room to themselves, he questioned him more gently and soon decided to call it a day. His inspector had ordered him to head back to Union Street by half four. They were due to take detailed statements from some of the eyewitnesses, having hauled in some of the low life from down Duke Street. He expected to interview Syd Swan, Chalky White and Whitey Lewis, among others, and they were there when the sergeant got back to base. In fact, Chalky White was already slinging his hook.

'Hey!' He put himself between the petty crook and the exit.

'It's all right, Sergeant, let him go.' The inspector looked up from his desk and sniffed. 'He's got an alibi to say he was nowhere around.'

Chalky grinned into the sergeant's face. 'And there ain't a thing you can do about it!' he sneered. 'Ask them!' He jerked his thumb towards Syd and the others.

'That's right, he weren't well, Sergeant. He had a bit of a headache,' Syd confirmed.

The sergeant sneered back. 'Too much to drink, Chalky?'

'A crack on the head, as a matter of fact,' Whitey put in.

'All right, all right!' Chalky's pasty face shadowed over. 'Let's just say I was below par, safely tucked up in my own little bed!' He pushed roughly past.

The sergeant shrugged then let him by. 'Mind how you go,' he mocked. Then he went to join the bunch of seedy-looking hooligans, headed by a cocky Syd Swan.

'Don't worry,' the inspector said. 'There's plenty more fish in the sea. And Syd here tells me he's got some valuable information to impart.' Pen poised, he got ready to write down the eyewitness account.

Duke had seen the sergeant out of the pub, more worried than ever. Jess protested that she'd done nothing wrong, but she had to confess about Ernie's boots when he pushed her to give him the truth. 'But, Pa, it don't prove nothing! All right, so we know what Ernie walked in on! He blundered into the middle of a murder, that's what, and he came home too upset to talk about it. He literally walked into it and he never even noticed the blood. Honest, if it'd been him what done it, the blood would've got everywhere. All over his hands, his clothes, everywhere. But he'd only got it on his boots, I swear to God! Just think about it; it can't be Ernie. Why can't they see that?'

Duke's head had sunk to his chest. 'They see what they want to see. As long as they can lock up some poor sod for doing Daisy in, they're happy.' He sighed. 'We ain't doing Ernie no favours, Jess, by not telling them the whole truth.'

She was stunned, but at last she saw he was right. 'All right then, we better get started.' Pulling herself together, she sprang into action. 'If Ernie ain't the one they want, who've we got left?' She counted people off on her fingers. 'There's the manager, that other bloke who works there, and Teddy bleeding Cooper. It's gotta be someone, Pa!' Distraught at the notion that she'd made things worse for her brother, she pushed herself on. 'What's the time? I'm off up to Coopers' before they close. You wait here, Pa, and ask Auntie Florrie to keep an eye on Grace for me, will you?'

Without bothering with hat or coat, Jess flew out of the door and up the street to the drapery store.

Teddy Cooper sat back in his father's office chair, his feet up on the desk. The old man had gone off on the train to the woollen mill in Bradford where they bought most of the worsted cloth for the men's suits. He'd be away for at least three days. Meanwhile, Teddy enjoyed the luxury of driving the motor car and draining his father's drinks cupboard. With experienced foremen, the place more or less ran itself, leaving him free to flirt with the shop-girls and put in a token appearance every now and then in the workshops. Thick-skinned as he was, his unpopularity didn't dent his confidence; he strutted about the place in Mr Cooper's absence, from electrical goods into menswear, and up into household linens.

But when Jess burst into the office to confront him, even his self-satisfied smile faded. He was presented with a breathless, half-demented woman demanding to know what he'd done to Daisy O'Hagan; how she'd go to the police station and tell them all about his affair with poor Daisy if he didn't go himself. 'How can you sit there and let someone else get the blame?' she shouted, beside herself. 'The whole street knows about you! Ain't it about time you owned up, you bleeding bastard!'

Teddy stood up and motioned one of the shopwomen who'd pursued Jess through the store out of the room. He advanced and kicked the door shut. 'Don't let my father hear you chucking insults like that around,' he said coolly. 'Good job he ain't here.'

'I don't care if he *is* here! If you ain't got the decency to own up when they nab the wrong person, I can call you any names I like!' She stood, gasping and dishevelled. 'Go on then, tell me where you was when it happened!'

'Ah!' Teddy rested on the edge of the big mahogany desk and fiddled with a glass paperweight. 'So you think I'm Jack the Ripper, do you?'

His flippant crudeness shocked her into silence. She was suddenly aware of onlookers crowding round for a better view outside the glass partition.

'Well, I'm sorry to disappoint you.' He put the cut-glass sphere on the palm of his hand and balanced it.

'You would say that,' she faltered. As the heat of her anger began to cool, she grew aware of the futility of the confrontation.

'I would, wouldn't I? Even if it was true, I wouldn't be on my knees confessing to you, would I? I'd be denying it even if you had *six* brothers locked up in Union Street.' He grinned at her surprise. 'How do I know who you are? That's what you're thinking. You're the Parsons sister who went wrong, the black sheep. I know all about you, see. You push your pram along here on the way to the park. The girls here gossip about it, naturally.' He paused, circling behind her as he talked.

Jess drew herself together. She stared straight ahead. 'I can still go to the coppers and tell them about you and Daisy. You'll have to tell them where you was that night, and you ain't exactly no angel as far as they're concerned neither.'

'A nice speech, I'm sure.' Teddy drew up alongside her. His top lip curled into a sneer. One lock of fair hair had fallen over his forehead. 'Again, I'm sorry to disappoint you.'

'What d'you mean?'

'The police have already paid me a visit. I had to give them an alibi, and that meant having to drop someone you know into a nasty hole.'

Jess took a deep breath. 'Why? What alibi? You mean to say you was with someone when it happened?'

'Certainly.' Teddy went back and settled on the desk. He tossed the paperweight and caught it with a small, slapping noise. 'I met someone after I left the picture house. I've done my best to protect her of course, but the police insisted on knowing my whereabouts. I was obliged to give them her name.'

'Who then?' Jess felt herself begin to shake, afraid of his answer.

Teddy enjoyed the cat-and-mouse game. He paused. Jess was one girl in the street he'd never had much to do with. She'd been away in service, but as he stood and looked at her now he saw her as an experienced, strong-minded woman, a cut above the ones he often went with. She had wonderful wavy hair and deep, dark eyes. Her skin was dark too, almost Italian-looking. 'Are you sure you want me to tell you?'

'Just say it!' Jess fended off his nasty look.

'Well, as a matter of fact, it was Amy Ogden who I met up with.' He stared right into her eyes to study the effect of his words.

'Liar!'

He laughed. 'More insults. Why not go and ask her? Poor Amy will have to admit it, but she'll be in deep trouble with her ma. Her ma don't like me, you see.'

'I will!' Jess turned and wrenched open the door. 'I'll go and get the truth out of her, just you wait!'

Teddy watched her go. The little interlude had brightened up a dull day. Now he'd best get the women packed off home and begin to shut up shop. He went about it with a smile. Amy Ogden was his precious alibi. He enjoyed all the little ironies of that situation. It was a pity about Jess Parsons though. There was a good woman going to waste.

With a sinking heart, Jess went down the court to Amy Ogden's house and knocked on the door. Possibly Teddy Cooper was lying. She could cling on to that hope and have a word with Amy. Come to think of it, surely Amy would have had to mention this before now, especially with Dolly Ogden going on and on about Teddy Cooper being the killer. She knocked again. Amy had better not try any silly games over this; Jess was determined to get at the truth.

Maurice Leigh took his time to answer the door. He had no friends in the area who would come visiting him here; the caller was bound to be for the Ogdens, but he didn't mind coming down to take a message. He opened the door to Jess Parsons.

'Is Amy here, please?' Jess was thrown off her stride and backed off.

'No, they're all out. Come in a minute.' Maurice had just finished shaving. He rolled his shirt-sleeves down his forearms. 'Would you like to leave a message with me?'

Jess stepped over the threshold, looking suddenly dejected. 'I don't know. If Amy ain't here, perhaps I'd best be off.'

'Why, what's the trouble? Can I help?' The narrow corridor made it difficult to carry on a relaxed conversation. Maurice led the way to the kitchen, turning and holding out one arm in welcome.

Jess laughed self-consciously. 'Ain't nobody can help if what I just heard is true.'

'That right?' He stopped and waited for her to catch up, feeling her skirt brush against one leg. On impulse, he took her gently by the elbow. 'Tell me about it.'

As if the effort of standing upright had suddenly overwhelmed her, Jess sank against him. She shook her head. 'Ain't nothing I can do.'

Maurice folded both arms around her shoulders and stood there holding on to her. He realized she was in deep trouble, and he wanted to shield her from it if he could. Being near to her, feeling the soft hair at the nape of her neck, smelling the soap on her skin gave him pleasure. He kissed her cheek, then her mouth.

Jess returned his kiss, then drew back. His arms were locked around her so she turned her head sideways in confusion. As a girl she'd received boys' inexperienced kisses, and as a woman she'd borne a child. But she'd never clung to a kiss and desired it as she had this one.

'What's wrong?' he murmured. 'Don't you like me?'

She nodded, unable to trust her voice.

'Well, then.' He stroked her hair, her smooth, slim back.

'You don't know nothing about me,' she said plaintively. 'It ain't right.'

'What's to know?' He let her pull away; he knew not to rush her. His smile broke the mood. 'Shall I tell Amy you called?'

'Yes please.'

'I will then.'

They stood facing each other in the run-down kitchen, until Jess finally turned away. 'Thanks,' she said quietly.

'My pleasure.' Maurice meant it. From the moment he set eyes on her, he knew Jess was special. Now he knew she liked him too. That was progress, he thought, as he went upstairs to get ready for work. Tomorrow, or the day after, he'd take things further; one step at a time.

Chapter Eighteen

Maurice's kiss had unsettled Jess more than she could say. In a flurry of confusion, she locked the episode away and tried to fix her mind back on her vow to help Ernie.

Later that evening, she decided to send Hettie down to the Ogdens' place to discover the truth of what Teddy Cooper had to say.

'Get down there yourself, why don't you?' Florrie urged. 'You started this thing, girl. You'd better finish it.'

Hettie hesitated by the door.

'I'm tired, Auntie.' Jess bent her head over her sewing. 'Hettie don't mind.'

'I dare say she don't.' Florrie eyed her knowingly. 'But it looks fishy to me. Who's down there that you don't want to bump into?'

'No one!' Jess coloured up. She knew Maurice would be out at work by this time, but she was still keen to steer clear of the Ogden house for a bit. Memories of Maurice's embrace came crowding in on her again. She needed time to think. Not much chance of that with Florrie around, she thought.

'Let's both go,' Hettie suggested. 'Get a breath of fresh air. I can back you if Amy plays up. Come on.'

So they stepped downstairs together and went along the court arm in arm. Little Katie O'Hagan waved at them from the far end. Three men came out of her tenement doorway and staggered up to the pub; one of them Chalky White.

The women gave the men a curt hello. 'Blimey, if he didn't have his mates to prop him up, he'd fall flat on his face, he would,' Hettie commented about Chalky.

'Why, what's up?' Jess glanced back at the trio.

'Drunk as a lord.'

'He ain't!'

'He is too. I don't like the look of him, Jess. I ain't seen him sober for weeks,' Hettie declared. 'He ain't never out of our place these days.'

Jess too turned up her nose. 'He's another one I ain't keen on. I don't know which one I hate the most; him or Teddy Cooper!' White's slouching walk got on her nerves, and she knew Robert and he had never seen eye to eye.

Hettie grinned and told her to hush before she knocked on Amy's door. 'Mind you, what we've come here to say won't go down too well as it is!'

'Are they in?'

'They are. I can hear Dolly coming now. Hold on to your hat, girl.'

Jess stood, working out exactly what she wanted to say.

Dolly opened the door with a warm welcome. 'Don't stand out there. It's drawing in cold of a night. Now, girls, sit and have a cup of tea with us.' Her sympathy for the family's plight was genuine. 'Amy, put the kettle on. Let me get rid of these things.' She began to clear a space on the table, where piles of fawn stockings lay waiting to be finished off. She'd taken in more outwork since her dismissal from Coopers' and had to work every waking hour to make ends meet.

'It's Amy we come to see,' Jess said quietly. She blushed and looked across at Hettie.

'Best make short work of this,' Hettie went on. 'Can you cope with a bit of a shock, Dolly?'

The stout woman stood uneasily in the middle of the bare room. 'You know me,' she said, trying to smile. 'I take it this ain't a social call, then?'

Amy, sensing that she would have some awkward explaining to do, bent over the hob, her face averted.

'Look here, Amy,' Jess began again. 'I been talking to Teddy Cooper this afternoon, and he told me where he was when Daisy went and got herself bumped off.' She looked up anxiously at Dolly, who'd bridled.

'So?' Amy made a feeble attempt to brazen it out. 'What's it to do with me?'

'Everything, according to him. He says we can count him out of it, Dolly. He can't have killed Daisy.' Jess hoped Amy would come clean. Things were getting very strained. But there was silence from her corner.

'Why's that, then?' Dolly had trumpeted the theory about the detested boss's son far and wide. But her skin began to crawl with a dreadful realization. 'Amy, come over here, will you. Leave that bleeding kettle alone and come and do like I tell you!'

'Hang on, just hear what Jess wants to say,' Hettie interrupted.

'Teddy Cooper told me he was with you that night, Amy. He says you're his alibi.' Jess wished herself anywhere else in the world, rather than have to look Dolly in the face right now. She saw Amy go sullen.

'Is he right?' Dolly asked.

Amy would have lied if she thought she could pull it off. But she was trapped. If she denied it, she could keep her mother off her back, but the Parsons sisters would go and land Teddy right in it, and she was back to the old bind. Who would the police believe; her or Teddy Cooper? If she confessed, on the other hand, Dolly would kill her. So she stood in silence, waiting for the storm to break.

Dolly made a lunge for her. 'I'll get this out of you if I have to shake it out!' she cried. Humiliation came with a sharp sting. She'd be a laughing stock when this got out. She seized Amy by both elbows and shook her hard. 'Was you with him, or not? Yes or no? Yes or no?'

'Yes!'

'Hold on, Dolly!' Hettie rushed forward to restrain her. The older woman took some pulling off. Amy crashed back against a chair and sat on it, sobbing.

But her mother darted forward again and slapped her cheek. 'Bloody little fool!' she cried. 'Dirty, disgusting, bloody little fool! How could you?'

Amy whimpered. 'Look what you done!' she hissed at Jess.

'Jess ain't done nothing.' Dolly pulled herself up, her fingers still tingling. But she was back in control. 'It's you, girl! I lost my bleeding job over you! We walked out of Coopers' with our heads up after what he done to you. Stuff their bleeding jobs! And what do you do? You let him get back in with you. First you yell and scream at me and your pa for not going up to the coppers with it, then you sneak off behind our backs and get back in with him again! Tell me why, girl, 'cos I don't understand you. The man's a monster, ain't he?' She breathed heavily, appealing to Jess and Hettie in her last remark.

Hettie bent over Amy's chair. The girl had slumped forward, head on her knees, arms over her head. 'Tell your ma why you went off with him, and why you never said nothing,' she whispered.

'I just went up to the shop 'cos I wanted to try and put a bit of pressure on him.' Through her tears, Amy thought she could make them understand. The fight had brought her hair down and pulled her blouse loose at the back. 'I went to tell him I could still go to the coppers if I liked!'

'What for?' Hettie was horrified. You couldn't go messing Teddy Cooper around like that.

Amy sat up straight. 'I thought I could get some cash out of him.'

'Bleeding blackmail!' Dolly's mouth hung open in disbelief.

'And did he give you any?' Hettie handed Amy a handkerchief.

'He gave me ten shillings. He weren't nasty to me neither. He said not to worry, he'd get me another job before too long, if I was nice to him and never went up to the police.'

'Oh, Amy!' Jess stood, holding on to Dolly, who still quivered from head to foot. 'You never believed him?'

Amy gave a miserable shrug. 'He was nice to me, like he was at first. I said I'd meet up with him again that night, that's all. It didn't mean nothing, and I thought he'd be different with me this time.'

'And was he?' Jess kept a firm hold of Dolly.

Amy's full tragedy came tumbling out. 'No, he weren't! I didn't even get to go to the picture house with him this time. He met up with me outside Coopers', and we went up to the office like before.' She sobbed into the handkerchief.

'*Everything* just like before?' Dolly asked.

Amy nodded. She looked up through bleary eyes. 'But I couldn't tell no one about it, could I? Especially when Daisy went and got herself killed, and, Ma, you went on and on about it being Teddy! What was I meant to say?'

'And have you seen him since?' Hettie asked. She put her arm around Amy's shoulder, thinking how young she looked for her seventeen or eighteen years.

Amy sniffed. 'He don't want to know me. He sent me packing and he was laughing at me, saying I might cry rape once but not twice, and anyway they'd soon see what sort of a slut I was. He warned me to stay away or he'd have me thrown in gaol as a common prostitute. That's what he said.' The memory sent her off into fresh wails of misery.

Dolly stood there stunned. 'I ain't dragged you up to go off and do this kind of thing,' she whispered. 'I lost my bleeding job over you!'

Amy sobbed harder. 'Oh, Ma, why didn't we go up to the police first off?'

Dolly steadied herself against Jess. 'Your Pa said why not. They'd never have believed us.'

Jess and Hettie worked hard to pull them round after the first shock had worn off. They talked about Florrie arriving out of the blue to lend a hand, and Frances getting hold of the very best advice for Ernie through a friend of hers. If they all pulled together they were sure they could get him out. 'But we gotta admit Teddy Cooper's out of the picture now,' Jess said to Dolly out on her front doorstep again. 'Try not to be too hard on the girl, if you can help it.'

The sisters walked back up the court. They felt down, in spite of their efforts to look on the bright side. The next day, the second of Ernie's imprisonment, Frances had arranged a visiting order to go and see their brother. They'd keep themselves busy by making up a food parcel and helping Duke in the bar. The old man was determined to carry on business as usual, but he moved like an automaton, drifting from dawn to dusk.

Wormwood Scrubs was a loathsome place. The warders made visitors queue up and answer to the number belonging to the inmate they had come to see. 'Janeki 743, Madigan 621, Parsons 684.'

Terrified, Frances walked in single file along the inside of the perimeter wall, which rose twenty feet high to their left. Built like a fortress, black with age and soot, the prison must deaden the spirit of whoever set foot inside its iron doors and metal landings. She was angry and astonished that men lived here like caged beasts. Looking out of a window, she saw prisoners shuffling the narrow triangular path in the exercise yard, heads bowed and shaven. She saw their faces at the door hatches, gaunt and brutal. Doors clanged, footsteps echoed, the stench of boiled food sickened.

All eyes followed the female visitors along the landings, drilling holes into their backs, resentful of their freedom. Frances felt faint, but she clutched Ernie's food parcel and marched on behind the warder. At last he stopped and turned the key of cell number 684.

'This your first visit?' he asked, holding the door ajar.

She nodded.

'It ain't that bad,' he reassured her. 'Not when you get used to it.'

Then he locked her in with Ernie, telling her they had half an hour. Ernie rose from his iron bed and came blindly towards her, reaching out his arms. She cried as she hugged him, then broke into questions: did he have enough to eat? Was he warm enough? Had they treated him well? She opened up the food parcel, happy to see him tuck into some left-over veal pie. She told him to expect to see a Mr Sewell, a good man who would help explain things to the judge in court. Ernie must tell Mr Sewell everything he could recall about that night. 'Think long and hard before you answer him, Ern. A lot will depend on exactly what you remember.'

He nodded faithfully.

'Try to think who you saw, and where and when. Or think, did you hear any noises from inside? How long did you stand waiting outside the stage door? Mr Sewell will ask you them sort of questions, Ern, so you gotta be clear in your own mind.'

But Ernie was so pleased to see her, he just sat and smiled and nodded, and he cried silently when it was time for her to go. She got up and leaned over the table to kiss him.

'We'll look after you, Ern,' she promised. 'But it's gonna take a bit of time, so you just got to hang on here.'

'Don't have much choice, do he?' the warder said as he beckoned her out of the cell. He eased the giant key in the lock.

Shocked to the core, Frances followed him down the metal staircases, under brick arches, out through the fortress-like gate. By the time she'd travelled the streets back to Southwark, she'd come to, but when Billy Wray intercepted her on Duke Street with the offer of a cup of coffee in Henshaw's, she was glad to accept. 'You look done in,' he told her. They settled in a dark corner of the eating-house, away from the window, while Bea Henshaw went for their order.

'I got to write to Robert tonight and tell him about Ernie,' she said faintly. 'I put it off yesterday, and I still ain't looking forward to doing it.'

'No, and there ain't nothing he can do about it in his position. Has he been shipped out to France yet?'

Frances shook her head. 'No. He ought to be told what's going on back here though, don't you think?'

Billy nodded. 'Even if it is a bit hard on him. But I should think the police will be in touch with him pretty soon. I'd get a move on and write that letter if I was you. It's better if he hears the news from family in my opinion.'

'Only, I think if Robert was here Ernie would have a better chance, and I'm afraid Rob might think so too. I just hope he don't go and do nothing stupid.'

'Go AWOL? No, you gotta write and explain we're doing everything we can.' He settled back in his seat, watching with concern as Frances sipped her coffee. 'How do you feel now? You didn't half give me a fright when I saw you step off that tram. You nearly went straight under the wheels of a car, not looking where you was going.'

'That prison's a terrible place, Billy.' Frances stared down at the linen tablecloth. 'I never expected it to be that bad.'

'I fixed up for Mr Sewell to visit him tomorrow morning. That'll help keep his chin up.' If Billy Wray could have moved a mountain for Frances Parsons, he would have done. He admired her determined way. His own wife, Ada, had always been a passive sort, content to stay at home. Now, with her illness, she leaned on him a lot. Billy was a devoted husband, but he felt as he sat watching Frances that marriage was his own sort of prison. Then he regretted thinking it. If Frances had been less good-looking, he'd have things more under control. The truth was, he liked her precise, neat movements, and the graceful turn of her dark head.

'What does Mr Sewell think of Ernie's chances?' Frances asked. She knew through Billy that Sewell was regarded as a supporter of good causes such as women's rights and Fabianism. But was he any good at fighting individual cases? She had to put her trust in Billy's judgement. Knowing from their meetings and lectures how well informed he was, she turned to him in this time of crisis.

'I managed to have a few words with him about it. He says the police have built their case on what he calls circumstantial evidence, but he admits there's a combination of things that will make it hard for a jury. He says to wait till he's seen Ernie before he jumps to any conclusions.'

Frances nodded. 'Thanks, Billy.'

'Try not to worry.' He put his hand over hers. 'No, I don't mean that. You're bound to worry, it's only natural. I just wish I could be more help.'

She smiled. 'You've been very good to us, Billy. I don't know what we'd do without you.'

Frances's gratitude was cold comfort when he found himself wanting more. But she was eaten up by her family problem, and he was tied to Ada. Come to that, she probably never looked at him as woman to man. She was a spinster born and bred, they said up at Union Street. And he was married.

When Maurice Leigh heard the news about Amy's feather-brained entanglement with Teddy Cooper, he decided to steer clear of the women in his household until the upset had died down. He had a serious aversion to female hysterics, and in this sense his relationship with his landlady and her daughter was bound to be problematic. He was a poor shoulder to cry on, he told himself, so keeping out of the way seemed his best tactic.

Still, he couldn't help feeling sorry for the one who seemed overlooked in all this; and that was Charlie. The poor boy wandered in from school and could hardly find a seat to park himself on. Once, while there was some bother rumbling on down in the kitchen and Maurice was just slipping out to work, he found Charlie sitting on the stairs, chin in hands. 'How do you fancy coming up to the Gem with me tonight?' he offered. 'You can sit in with the projectionist and see how things work.'

Charlie stared back, his face suddenly alive with excitement. 'You're not kidding?'

Maurice stood in the stairwell, hands in pockets. 'I take it that means yes? Right, get your jacket on and hurry up. If you like what you see, I might even find you a little job one or two evenings a week. Keep you out of trouble!'

The two were already out on the street. Charlie walked jauntily along, cap tilted to the back of his head. 'I ain't *in* trouble.'

'Well, a boy of your age ought to be,' Maurice replied. They swung diagonally across Duke Street, getting into their stride. 'If I was you going bike-riding with a pretty girl like Sadie Parsons of a Sunday, I'd make bleeding sure I was in trouble!'

Charlie grunted. 'I don't think you should be encouraging me that way.' Privately, he realized that those bike rides, so precious at first, were beginning to lose their charm, now that the novelty had worn off.

Maurice laughed. 'No? You most likely don't need no encouraging neither.'

'That'd be telling.' Charlie followed on Maurice's tail into the plush picture house. This was it; he'd arrived! This was the future, these were the machines he wanted to learn about. Magic flickered up there on the screen. He fell in love with the giant reels of celluloid, the whir of the projector, the hot dust rising in the tiny projection room. Their lodger had offered him a gateway to heaven, and Charlie was about to dash headlong through it.

Maurice offered Jess a gateway of a different kind, which she approached timidly and full of doubt. For a start, it didn't seem right to her to be having thoughts about anything except Ernie's trial. She saw Frances moving heaven and earth to get him the best solicitor in the East End, delving into her own savings and working long hours at the chemist's shop to pay for it. She watched Hettie transformed from a music-hall girl with a spring in her step to a quiet, nunlike figure, grieving for Daisy. Duke was a shell, an empty husk; even Florrie had given up trying to jolly him along and had to leave him alone.

And Jess already felt guilty for the comfort she found in nursing little Grace and in watching her baby develop her first smiles. Sewing work had come in from the advert, and this too brought satisfaction. Jess, who less than a year ago expected to be the most miserable of women, feared she was blossoming in spite of her family's troubles. She racked her brains to see what more she could do to help, and constantly asked herself how could she rein back her hopes for the future.

'Jess?' Hettie said tentatively, in the middle of one long afternoon's sewing. She was altering the sleeves in a ladies' jacket to bring it back into fashion. Jess sat at their new sewing-machine, running up girls' petticoats for Mrs Henshaw's nieces. 'You remember me mentioning I wanted to put something better into my life than working the halls?'

Jess glanced up from the yards of fine white cotton, but she kept the treadle moving. The machine whirred on. 'You said to mind my own business if I remember right.'

'I never did. Or if I did, it was because I hadn't made up my mind then. I have now.' Hettie was moving on from helping Mary O'Hagan out of her terrible hole. Now she felt that she'd like to help others too. It grew harder to walk by the huddled shapes under the railway arches, and she began to loathe the effects of the demon drink as she watched the men stagger from the pub at night. Then one day, when she'd been lending Mary a hand by asking after

Tommy O'Hagan up at Waterloo Station, she fell in with a Salvation Army woman called Freda Barnes, who described the work done for the poor at her industrial home in Lambeth. 'We provide food, shelter and honest work,' she said. She told Hettie that she was going to man a stall of goods made by the inebriates in a special home set up by the Army, then back to the industrial home for an evening meeting. 'Why not come along?' she said.

Hettie went and joined in their rousing choruses to the accompaniment of a brass band. She was singing again, but this time she was singing for Jesus.

'I signed the pledge,' she told Jess. 'I took the plunge the other day. Look!'

Jess stopped treadling in surprise. She read the richly decorated card which Hettie handed to her: 'I Promise by Divine Assistance to Abstain from all Beverages that Contain Alcohol. Also from Opium and Tobacco in Every Form; and that I will not Gamble or use Profane Language, but will Strive to be Loving, Pure, and True in Thought, Word, and Deed.' Signed Hesther Parsons, 20 September 1914. 'Blimey, Ett!' Jess sat staring at the picture of cherubs against a twinkling night sky. 'What you gonna tell Pa?'

Hettie laughed. 'I ain't gone and done nothing terrible, you know.'

'Ain't you? Talk about cat among the pigeons,' she grumbled. She needed to think more carefully about Hettie's new fad.

'No, I only signed the pledge. I think it's common sense when you watch what drink does to a man. As a matter of fact, it wouldn't surprise me if drink played a part in poor Daisy's death.'

Jess nodded. She began to see the train of Hettie's thoughts.

'Pa won't mind,' Hettie cajoled. 'He likes to have the

Army come round collecting. He always dips his hand in his pocket.'

'If you're sure, Ett.' Jess couldn't picture pretty Hettie in a drab blue uniform and homely bonnet, all buttons and old-fashioned maroon bows. 'You ain't acting a bit sudden, are you?'

'"They that be wise shall shine as the brightness of the firmament,"' Hettie read out from her pledge card. 'Well, I don't know if I can be wise, Jess, but I should like to do a little bit of good!'

'Oh, Ett!' Jess stood up and embraced her. 'You've got a heart of gold, you have. Don't tell me I gotta get used to another angel in the family! Ain't Frances enough?'

'Listen, Jess, it don't mean we can't carry on being partners in the business, you know.'

'Good!' Jess smiled and went back to her work. 'These petticoats won't make themselves.' She'd been on the point of confiding to Hettie over Maurice Leigh, but the subject sounded trivial somehow alongside Hettie's momentous decision.

On the last Sunday of September, Charlie came calling for Sadie as usual, eager to show off about his new job at the cinema. He waited in the yard for her to finish tying up her hair, or whatever it was that took a girl so long to achieve between his ring on the bell and her coming down to unlock her bike from the shed, ready to set off. Sadie sent Jess to keep him company, and she was still standing in the side alley waving them off when Maurice came running up the court. She turned to go in, almost bumping into him.

'Damn!' He watched Charlie disappear up the street. 'I meant to ask him to work a couple of extra hours for me tomorrow night.' He didn't seem unduly upset about missing him, however, and turned instead into the alley with Jess. 'Are you busy today?' he asked.

She felt the same confusion; a mixture of liking, longing, fear, doubt. It twisted around her chest like a tight band whenever Maurice came near. 'I don't know yet. Why?'

'I thought we might walk out this afternoon?'

'Oh, I don't know,' she demurred.

'Why not? Don't you want to?' He put one hand over her shoulder against the high wall, leaning in, confident that she wouldn't move away. 'We got to stop meeting in these narrow places,' he joked. 'It ain't dignified. How about meeting up with me at the park gates at half two?'

Jess looked up at him, took a deep breath and nodded. 'Half two, then.' She was committed. Quickly she went up by the metal fire escape, and Maurice swung out into the street back home to his attic room.

'Nice to clap eyes on a cheerful face,' Arthur Ogden grumbled, as they crossed paths on the doorstep. 'Like a bleeding morgue in there these days if it wasn't for you.'

Maurice nodded and whistled up the stairs. He planned to polish his shoes, find a clean collar, have a shave.

Back at the Duke, Jess had to ask Florrie a favour. To her surprise, her aunt practically whirled her out of the place. 'Mind? Why should I mind? I been saying you should get out more! Of course, the others don't notice, but I do, girl! Blinded by their troubles, they are, but I seen you was looking peaky the minute I walked in. I says to myself, "That girl needs to get out!" It ain't no fun looking after a baby all by yourself, but no one knows that better than me!'

Jess smiled gratefully at her larger-than-life aunt, gearing herself up for the usual reminiscences.

'My Tom was always a sickly child, coughing and

wheezing. And there I was stuck with him after his poor father passed on. Day in, day out without a break. Oh, there's no need to tell me what it means for a mother to have to manage by herself.' She swept up and down the living-room carpet, baby Grace settled on one broad hip, little legs dangling. 'So you go and have a break, girl. Go out and enjoy yourself.'

Jess had put on her best hat; a dark-blue velvet one, and a new soft-collared white blouse. She liked the fashion of wearing a strip of dark silk around her neck like a loose man's tie; she thought it looked jaunty and modern. Her even features smiled back at her in the mirror.

Florrie came up close for a confidential whisper, though there was no one else in the room. 'You go and find yourself a nice young man. You got my blessing, and never mind about young Grace here. It don't mean you got to lock yourself away like a nun for the rest of your life!'

Jess turned to her. 'You sure, Auntie?' Florrie's early letter about the baby had sounded stiff and stern. But since her arrival on the scene, little Grace's soft dark curls, her rosebud mouth and huge dark eyes seemed to have melted the old lady's heart. 'Do you think I'm doing right?'

Florrie answered the appeal warmly. 'I know you are. You're a lovely girl, even if Wilf ain't never seen it in you. And you're only young once. So just leave me to get on with things here and you take as long as you like.' She gave Jess a wink. 'What's he like? I bet he's a bobby dazzler.'

Jess laughed and blushed. 'He is, Auntie. Well, I think so at any rate!'

Chapter Nineteen

Maurice decided that a walk in the local park wouldn't do for the type of treat he had in mind for Jess. He was ambitious for this courtship from the beginning, seeing it as something different. So he hopped her up on to one of the new 'B' type buses when it stopped at the crossroads, and they sat on the open upper deck in the rich autumn sunlight, all along the Embankment, up to the great green space of Hyde Park.

Jess felt the bus roll smoothly past splendid shops under mellow golden trees. She saw ladies walking white lap-dogs past the hotels on Park Lane, heard the rant of orators on Speakers' Corner. During all her years in service she'd had little free time for Sunday afternoon jaunts. Her time off had been spent visiting family and helping in the pub. Now she and Maurice alighted arm in arm from the bus and joined the people strolling through the iron gates.

'Oh, look!' She pointed to a corner of the park where a collection of giant hot-air balloons hovered at rest. A crowd of women in white skirts, carrying pale parasols, and men in long jackets and trilbies had gathered round. Children stood in small knots, heads craned back to study the tethered monsters. Then a gasp escaped as one took off. It rose slowly, silently over their heads into the perfect blue sky. Jess heard the 'oh!' and clutched Maurice's hand. 'Look, there's people in them things! How are they supposed to get down?'

He laughed and looped her hand through his arm. 'They just have to let some of the hot air out and down they come.'

'What if they want to go higher?'

'They chuck a couple of passengers overboard.'

They walked on happily together. 'Ever been to the seaside?' he asked, as they passed colourful posters on Magical Margate. When she shook her head his plans grew extravagant; he'd borrow a motor car if she liked, and take her on an outing to the sea. Jess was impressed that he had friends with cars. 'Talbot Invincible, that's the best one out,' he recommended. 'Say you'll come.'

But Jess made no promises. 'Ain't you got too much on with your new job?' she asked. They'd walked away from the crowd down an avenue of beech trees. Sunlight cast a dappled pattern over his face as she glanced sideways at him. 'From what I hear, your place is bursting at the seams most nights.'

'That's why I deserve a day off every so often.' His success in drawing audiences to the Gem away from the halls, with his clever mix of comedies, romances and the latest foreign epics had set him in good stead. He stopped and turned to face her. 'I ain't larking about with you, Jess. You know that?'

She nodded and received his kiss. Her arms went up round his neck, he pulled her close. There was an intense look in his dark eyes when she tried to pull away. Instead, he offered more close kisses which made her melt against him once again.

'I'm serious,' he whispered, his mouth against her neck. 'I ain't never been this serious with any girl.'

Suddenly she drew away. This was a temptation almost

too much to resist; to swoon in his arms and let herself be kissed into unconsciousness. But she had to get straight with him. The misery of getting involved and then having him break it off later when he discovered the truth would be too much to bear. She was pretty sure Maurice wasn't the type to have got involved in any of the street gossip since he came to live at the Ogdens. Yet telling him about Grace must surely finish things off before they'd truly begun. Jess struggled with her conscience. At last, self-denial, always a strong force in her, won through.

'What?' Maurice pulled at her wrist. 'Don't walk off. I said too much, I'm sorry.' He thought he'd scared her.

She hung her head. 'It ain't that.'

'What then?' He caught her round the waist and made her walk along the path with him again. 'Look, Jess, I ain't sure what's going on here.'

She saw it wasn't fair; that he might think she was teasing and leading him on. So she forced herself to try and explain. 'It's me. I told you, you don't know nothing about me.'

'And?' He watched her struggling to confess, felt certain there was nothing she could say which would alter this build up of feeling towards her. He held her close around the waist.

'You sure you ain't heard?' She looked fearfully into his eyes. 'Ain't Dolly said nothing?'

'No. Why should she?'

The corners of her mouth went down. 'It's to do with why I had to come back home to the Duke in the first place. I ain't always lived there, you know. Before you came to live in the court, I was in service.'

'Don't cry.' He offered to wipe the tears from her cheeks with the flat of his thumbs. His voice was soft and gentle.

'You know what I'm gonna say, don't you?'

He nodded. 'I think I can guess what's coming. But you gotta say it, Jess. Don't be scared.'

'All right then. I came home because of the son in that family I worked for. Gilbert Holden. He got me into trouble.' She paused, unable to go on. Then she gathered herself together. 'Pa took pity on me and took me back, thanks to Frances. You see, Maurice, it ain't just me. I got a baby to think about.'

His forehead went down on to her shoulder and he closed his eyes. 'It's all right, I ain't shocked,' he murmured.

'Ain't you? I am. I can hear myself telling you these things and I can't hardly believe it myself. I'm sorry, Maurice. I ain't never been more sorry in my life!' She tried to draw away, struggling for some scraps of dignity.

'It don't make no difference.' She was still the woman he desired. The old 'no complications' motto was good enough when you only felt things on the surface; easy come, easy go. But it didn't seem to operate now that he'd met Jess.

In some way which he couldn't put into words, the fact that she had this baby made him want her more. It moved her further away from the child-women he came across in gaggles on park benches and on the front row at the picture house, putting her into new realms of experience for him. 'Just tell me you like me, and you want to be with me,' he said, gathering her to him.

'Do you still want me?' Relief flooded through her as she stroked the short hair at the back of his head. 'I thought no one would want me now.'

He kissed her wet cheeks, her open mouth, her long neck as she raised her head. She felt the branches of the trees shift and whirl overhead. Then a sense of being out in the open, in public, brought her back to herself. She put her fingertips over his mouth. 'No, stop. Let's walk on. We gotta think,' she insisted. 'We gotta wait a couple of days for things to settle down, see how we feel.'

They walked on together, hands firmly clasped. In the distance, a silent, white hot-air balloon coasted gently to the ground.

By late autumn of 1914, war talk had taken over from the Irish problem and threats of strikes in all the East End bar rooms. Their British lads had joined the French and the Belgians to become an army of moles, tunnelling into the muddy fields around Ypres, Vimy and Neuve Chapelle. The Germans had been halted short of Paris, but only just. Now the two sides fought across barren wastes of barbed wire, and the faces of recruits lining up outside Southwark Town Hall looked less than exuberant, more resigned to a hard slog in the trenches.

Robert Parsons sent letters home, full of concern and advice over Ernie. When he addressed his letters to the whole family, he would tell of the crossing to Calais and the huge operation to shift men, horses and machines to the front. He told them to keep their chins up over Ernie; they'd have him home by Christmas once the lawyers had done their work. To himself, he hoped the promise didn't sound as hollow as the one about the war being soon over now looked from this side of the Channel. As for the war, he said, morale was good. He wouldn't have his pa thinking any different and anyway it'd never get past the censor. So he chatted on about meeting up with an old pal from the docks; George Mann. They were in the same regiment. George was strong as an ox; single-handedly he'd dragged a water cart out of the axle-deep mud, making him the sergeant-major's blue-eyed boy. They hoped to get leave together eventually, and Robert would bring George back to meet the family.

His letters to Duke alone were less gung-ho. He told him how hard it was to get a night's rest, sharing board and lodgings with rats. A recent infestation of lice also kept them awake. They were stationed half a mile west of the front in the Somme valley. You heard the big guns go off and longed to get at the Hun. But for the time being they were stalled, waiting for action.

'I got a lot of time on my hands,' he wrote. 'And I get to brooding about poor Ern. If I never took him up to the Palace that night, he'd never be in the Scrubs now. And if I'd not been in that scrap with Chalky White earlier in the day, I wouldn't have had to make myself scarce and drop Ernie right in it. That's a fact. It preys on my mind, day in, day out.'

Duke wrote back words of consolation. What was done was done. Ernie understood Robert hadn't dropped him in it on purpose. Now they'd have to rely on British justice to get him out. Meanwhile Robert must concentrate on the army and keep himself safe. He told him Hettie had taken the pledge and joined the Sally Army, and he sent his regards to George Mann. Frances believed she knew his sister, Susan, who came in for prescriptions for their mother.

Everyone brought stories of the Western Front into the bar at the Duke; of cousins killed or sent home wounded. Convalescent homes were set up in great houses in the Kent and Essex countryside, where the injured men lived the life of Riley.

'I ain't so sure.' Annie Wiggin delivered her opinion over a glass of porter. She'd taken to coming in of a tea-time, instead of scuttling off back down the court with her jug.

Her ties with Duke had strengthened over Ernie's arrest; she felt he'd appreciated her being there to lend a hand and would pick her out to confide in when the time was right. But Florrie's arrival had put her nose out of joint. The daft ha'p'orth fancied herself as her namesake, Florence Nightingale. She treated Duke as if he was sick instead of boosting him up. Annie thought Florrie was going about it the wrong way, sighing and dabbing her eyes at every mention of the court case. So she stayed put on her bar stool, following Florrie's every move behind the bar, looking out for Duke. 'It ain't no picnic over in them trenches,' she pointed out. 'And it ain't a nice thing to be sitting in them hospitals with your legs blown off, even if there is roses climbing up the bleeding walls!'

'That ain't very nice,' Florrie sniffed. 'Them boys is heroes in my eyes. I bet they feel proud, no matter what. I'd feel proud if my Tom joined up, then came home wounded, I can tell you.'

Annie looked sceptical. She glanced round to check that Duke was at the far end of the bar out of earshot. 'Your Tom's way too old even to enlist,' she reminded her. 'So there ain't no danger to his limbs exactly. Easy to say you'd be proud when he's just about ready to go down the Post Office and draw the pension what nice Mr Asquith's handing out.'

Florrie took the bait. Her expression flashed outrage at Annie. 'My Tom's fit as a fiddle!'

'And not a day under forty.'

'That's a lie!'

'Forty if he's a day. And what does that make you, Florrie Searles? You're pushing seventy for all your fancy blouses.'

Florrie leaned over the bar towards her skinny opponent.

Her bosom settled on its mahogany surface, squat and steady behind its whalebone plating. 'Say that once more, Annie Wiggin, and I'll throttle you!'

'You and whose army? We all know you, Florrie. We remember you from the old days, poking your nose in where it's not wanted. And just look at you now, girl. Who you trying to kid with all them beads and bits and pieces? Come down my stall and I'll deck you out with something more suited to your situation!' She was scornful of Florrie's attempts to dress like a woman half her age, and snorted whenever she saw her begin to flirt with Duke's customers. When you were over the hill, you ought to have the guts to recognize it, Annie reckoned. As for herself, she still had a bit of life in her. Florrie Searles was a good fifteen years older than her.

'Look at you!' Florrie's foghorn voice floated over Arthur Ogden's head. Duke glanced around. 'Them boots you wear is a disgrace for a start. Can't you take no better care of yourself, Annie, and show a bit of self-respect?'

'Them's my old man's boots!' Annie stood up, face to face. 'As if you didn't know. They're a keepsake, so you keep your nose out!'

Florrie had hit a raw nerve, and she knew it. 'Keepsake? What the bleeding hell do you want to remember him for? Useless article, he was, going off and leaving you in the lurch!' Florrie's throat and chest were flushed red with the effort of hurling insults. She'd never liked Annie's snappy, whippet-like ways, and she liked her even less now that she'd obviously set her sights on Duke. The poor bloke needed protecting, especially since he was so down over Ernie. Annie might catch him at a low point and he'd find himself doing and saying things he'd regret.

'My old man was lost at sea,' Annie said with fierce dignity. She held her head high and her shoulders back.

244

'Lost at bleeding sea, nothing! Lost in the arms of another woman, more like!'

Annie saw red. But she wouldn't descend to fisticuffs. She'd stick the knife in where it hurt instead. 'Them who lives in glass houses,' she began. She rolled her eyes and stuck her tongue in her cheek.

Florrie choked. 'You go and wash your mouth out,' she threatened. 'Thomas was a good husband to me before the consumption came and took him after we moved to Brighton for the sea air and all.'

'Consumption!' It was Annie's turn to gloat. 'Thomas Searles was a weedy little bloke all right, but it weren't the consumption what took him off, believe you me.' She winked at Arthur, who enjoyed this from a ringside seat. 'Her problem is she's got all twisted up in her mind about what's true and what ain't. She thinks her old man popped his clogs from consumption, she really does. She thinks she's a widow woman of thirty, when she's sixty-five if she's a day. She even thinks she's worth turning round in the street for a second look, but just have a gander at her close up!'

'Oh!' Florrie had gone purple with helpless rage. Small, strangled noises were emitted from her throat, the scarlet silk flowers in her hair trembled uncontrollably. 'Oh, I ain't feeling well,' she whispered to Arthur, clutching at her bodice. And she retired upstairs hurt.

Annie looked down her nose after her. 'Serve her right.'

'But it ain't true, is it?' Arthur wanted to know. He'd never fancied Florrie Searles as deserted wife material.

'Every word is God's honest truth,' Annie insisted with utter sincerity.

Arthur took his half-empty glass and went off to chat with Duke. 'All over a pair of boots,' he ruminated, eyeing the shapeless offending articles on Annie's feet. 'I dunno,

245

women fall out over some bleeding stupid things once their dander's up.'

Arthur spoke from bitter experience. His house echoed with the small artillery fire between mother and daughter ever since Dolly had found out how badly Amy had let her down. She picked fault with the way the girl sat, ate and breathed. She criticized her dress, her manner, her laziness in not finding work. The more she went on, the more Amy dug in her stubborn heels. She didn't get out of bed until eleven, then spent an hour or more at her bedroom mirror. Perhaps she'd meet up with her old mates from Coopers' at dinner time, then she'd walk on alone up to other department stores to study the goods which she had no means of affording. Evenings were spent joining up with her pals again, to hang around street-corners or outside the picture houses where they hoped for someone in the money to come along and stand them a treat.

Amy's reputation had nosedived indeed when the truth emerged about her involvement with Teddy Cooper. He bragged about his clever way of compromising her for good on that second night, feeling that it showed his clear-headedness as well as his way with women. His own friends smirked and congratulated him, while the girls Amy hung around with turned up their noses. 'Oh, Amy, how could you?' Emmy protested. 'Ain't once on the big office desk enough for you, girl?'

But Amy found she could ride out this level of disapproval, and even began to turn the episode to her advantage amongst girls younger than Emmy and Dora. She gave out the story that Teddy had found her irresistible, and that she'd used her charms to screw some money out of the poor sod. This hard veneer gave her a certain status with little Lettie Harris who'd taken over Amy's job in hats, and with other girls still at school or just on the very bottom rung of the work ladder. 'He ain't such a catch, I can tell you,' she intimated. 'He thinks he's big with all the girls, but he don't know they only put up with him 'cos he's the boss's son and they have to.'

Outside work, the girls were bolder, especially in their street-corner gangs. Led by Amy, they stood outside the Southwark Gem one night in mid-October, dropping snide, giggling remarks as Teddy and two or three cronies swaggered down the pavement into the cinema. Their brash, broad smiles antagonized the girls. 'Who do they think they are?' they muttered, watching the men's backs as they paid at the box-office window. 'Bleeding Prince Charming?' Amy had already caught Teddy's eye and brazened it out. He wasn't so high and mighty that she couldn't try and get her own back, after all. 'Come here, Lettie,' she whispered. All the girls huddled round. Before long, they'd despatched pretty Lettie to worm her way into the picture house along with Teddy and the boys. 'Ten o'clock, round the back,' they reminded her. 'Make sure you bring him all on his ownio!'

At ten, they waited quietly down the alley, tight in against the blank, high wall. Amy had managed to whip up feeling against the boss's son almost to fever pitch. Every girl had recounted a story about his ugly behaviour. Most had come out of it better than Amy, but more by luck than judgement. All detested his groping, hot-breathed presence. Amy was good at stoking up their guilty disgust. 'Might as well be pieces of meat on a slab for all he cares,' she said.

So they braved the cold autumn night, prepared to stick it out and help take him down a peg or two. They weren't sure how things would work out, but they longed to turn Teddy Cooper into a figure of fun, if only for one night, down here in the dark alley.

'What if he recognizes us?' Olwyn Williams wanted to

know. She worked in a department at Cooper's which made men's shirts. She was plump and homely, but this hadn't disqualified her from attracting Teddy's unwelcome attentions. 'Will he get us the sack?'

Amy laughed, then shivered. Vanity had kept her in her figure-hugging summer jacket long after the season was past. 'He won't dare say nothing, or he'd never live it down!' She longed to get her own back for one brief moment.

The others laughed too, making an echo down the hollow passage between two high walls. Then someone said, 'Hush!' as footsteps approached.

They made out Teddy's tall, slim figure in silhouette, backed by street-lights up on St Thomas Street. He had draped himself all over Lettie, whose head scarcely came up to his shoulder. Giggling and leaning her body towards him, she led him out of the yellow pool of light into deep shadow.

Teddy was intent on the task. Lettie was so small and slight she wouldn't put up much of a fight. He'd sent on the friends he'd arrived with, intending to catch up with them in a pub after an hour or so. She was a bit skinny and underdeveloped, but she seemed willing, so he'd come for swift satisfaction. He pressed himself against her, scarcely bothered with preliminaries such as talking and kissing.

He had Lettie backed up against the blank wall and she was beginning to struggle, just as a fierce finger poked him in the back. He grunted and swung round, expecting a drunken onlooker come to share the fun. Instead, he was confronted by five or six grinning, jeering girls.

'Charming, I'm sure,' one of them said, staring down at his state of undress.

Teddy fumbled with the buttoms at the waistband of his trousers as Lettie slipped sideways to join the row. They all stood, hands on hips or arms linked, summing him up. He recognized Amy Ogden as the ringleader. 'Oh, very funny, Amy. I expect this is your idea.' He was so livid he didn't see the danger, only the ridicule. He moved forward to shove through their rank and head off up the alley.

But Amy stood her ground and thrust him back by the shoulder. With her other hand she snatched at his shirt and dragged it free of the loosened waistband. Then she shoved him again. He felt the cold wall with the flat of both hands. He lunged forward once more.

This time, Lettie and Olwyn stood in his way. The Welsh girl stared him in the face, eyes glinting, a sarcastic smile twisting her mouth. She reached her fingers inside his collar, wrenched it and tore it free. He heard the studs snap the collar and hit the ground in the shocked silence that followed. Olwyn glanced round at Amy, who nodded approval.

The group moved in closer. 'Ain't so cocky now, is he?' a voice jeered, high and excited. 'He won't go round bragging after we finished with him.'

'Not if we show him we mean business,' Amy said. She stepped to the front of the semi-circle. 'Let's see how big and strong you are now, Mister Teddy Cooper!' Standing there with her full lips parted, her eyes gleaming with hatred, she defied him to strike out at her.

When he did, with a savage, slicing blow at waist height, she was ready. She plunged sideways, twisted and caught him round the middle to drag him off balance. His legs shot from under him, grabbed by other hands which began to tear at his clothes. He felt his shirt ripped open. The women's hands clutched and pulled at him, then one dug in her nails. He kicked and punched back, face upwards on the ground under the flailing arms and flying hair.

Soon they had the clothes from his back. He rolled on

to his side, trying to curl and cling on to his trousers which were halfway down his buttocks. Fists pounded his ribs, nails snatched at him as each girl fought to aim her blow. They shrieked with savage energy, fuelled by the unique satisfaction of having him at their mercy. 'Get them off me!' he cried at Amy. 'Do you want them to kill me?'

She stood back to look at the writhing heap of bodies; arms pummelling at Teddy's naked white flesh. His face and chest were scored red. He'd had enough, she decided. Coolly she went and hammered on the fire-exit door, and as help came she cleared her friends off. They ran wildly up the alley, screaming with victory. Olwyn clutched Teddy's collar like a trophy. They ran laughing and gasping on to the tram that rattled its way towards them down the street.

In response to the violent hammering on the door at the back of the cinema, Maurice Leigh wrenched open the iron bolts which he'd just locked. He darted into the alley in time to see silhouetted figures of laughing girls, and on the ground the groaning, nearly naked figure of a man.

He picked him up, recognized him at once, offered his own coat and took him inside. Teddy Cooper was a mess; severely bruised and scratched. Maurice suggested calling the police, but Cooper refused. 'It's nothing. Just telephone this number and get my father to send the car for me.' He wrote down a number for Maurice on a piece of office paper. The pain of the scratches was nothing compared with the blow to his pride, and he wouldn't forget the hyena faces of those women as they laid into him. He shivered inside another man's coat, clutching his torn clothes, covered in claw marks.

Maurice quietly made the necessary arrangements. He was alarmed by what had happened. Skirmishes like this could give the Gem a bad reputation, so he didn't push to involve the police. He knew enough about Cooper to guess that he probably deserved what had happened. Still, Maurice didn't like it when women turned nasty. His sympathy for Cooper's ex-girlfriends didn't extend to condoning what they'd done; as a man he had to back male vanity by giving it a stiff drink and hustling it half-naked into the car sent over from Richmond.

He stood on the pavement watching Teddy being driven off with his jacket round his shoulders. I expect that's the last I'll see of that, he reflected. Back to the pawn shop for a decent replacement. The man had had his come-uppance and no doubt his family would patch him up. It was time they sorted him out and put a stop to his antics with women, though. Maurice went and locked up the cinema, arriving back at his lodgings at the same time as Amy Ogden returned home after an innocent evening out with the girls.

Chapter Twenty

Next day, Edith Cooper was closeted with her husband, Jack, in the office of their department store. She sat opposite him at the great desk, determined to stay put until he gave her an answer. It wasn't her habit to make confrontations, but she'd considered things long and hard, and knew something must be done about Teddy.

'Why can't you leave him to me?' Jack asked. He drummed the desk with his fingers. 'You'll only get out of your depth, Edith, I'm warning you. This business is better dealt with by me.'

She sighed. 'I've left it to you for twenty-three years, Jack, ever since Teddy was born. But now I feel I have to put my foot down.'

Jack Cooper glared at his wife. Their relationship, stormy in the beginning, had levelled out over the years to one of mutual non-interference. As prosperity increased, so did the veneer of politeness, in direct inverse proportion to the passion they'd once felt. Jack might bully his work-force, fleece his suppliers and browbeat his rivals, but he would go home each night and listen attentively to Edith's tribulations over the upstairs maid. He dressed for dinner, complimented her housekeeping and learned not to swear in front of her ladies' sewing circle.

For her part, Edith willingly paid the price for going up

in the world. She didn't expect to play a part in the core of her husband's life, his drapery store, as long as she was left to her own devices of spending money on clothes and house. She had quiet, refined tastes and a placid temperament which had let certain things slide, she now realized. But when Teddy had come home last night with most of his clothes gone and his face scratched red raw by a gang of vengeful shop-girls, her tolerance reached its limit. 'It's a terrible thing to be ashamed of your own son,' she told Jack. 'I asked myself what Teddy could possibly have done to deserve what they did to him, but I can't bear to think about it.' Her eyes began to water and she reached in her bag for a handkerchief.

'See, you should leave it to me and not bother your head over it. Don't worry, I'll have a heart to heart with him when I get the chance.' Jack chewed the end of an unlit cigar. His own view was that Teddy just wasn't careful enough, even after the warning he'd received over the Ogden girl. What he got up to was his own business, but he was a fool for being indiscreet.

'What good will it do this time or any other time?' Edith had taken the plunge by coming into the store especially to discuss this. At home, surrounded by fire-screens and occasional tables and all the gadgetry which was the fruit of Jack's labours, she could never pluck up the courage. The more impersonal atmosphere of the office gave her the necessary determination. 'No, Jack, I want you to do something about his behaviour. I want to be able to hold my head up when I come through the store, knowing that he's behaving himself like a gentleman.'

'How's that?' Jack snorted. He might aspire to the status himself, at least in outward show, but he also scorned many of the gentlemanly attributes, such as fair play and openness.

'You know very well what I'm talking about.' Edith wouldn't let herself be thrown off course. 'I want you to *do* something, Jack!'

The stout shop-owner's patience, fragile at best, began to give way. He stood and leaned forward, resting his knuckles on the desk. 'For God's sake, woman, what do you mean, "do something"? He's a grown man, in case you'd forgotten. He goes his own way. Do you think I want him bringing down the family name and trampling it in the mud down all these filthy back courts and yards? Course not. I brought him up better, and God knows it cost me plenty. But I don't see what I'm supposed to "do" about it, as you put it. It's his choice, ain't it?'

'But listen to me, Jack.' She got up and walked agitatedly back and forth between the desk and the door. 'I'm not just speaking out of turn here. I've an idea that there is something we can do to rescue Teddy from himself.'

Her husband snorted again. 'You've been reading too many novels,' he declared. '"Rescue Teddy from himself"!'

Edith was stung. 'If they're not the right words, it's only because what your son gets up to is too filthy to describe! If you want me to be plain, I'll ask you a question. Do you want him to go on dragging girls down the back of cinemas or using his key to bring them up here for his pleasure? One night he'll go too far and the police will arrest him and put him in prison. Is that what you want?'

'Using his key?' Cooper had begun to parrot his wife's words, this time in disbelief.

'Yes. Don't you bother to keep your ears open at all? It's what the girls say when they whisper in corners; that he uses your whisky from that cupboard there to get them drunk, and then he uses this very desk to . . .!' She broke down. 'I can't say it. I didn't believe it when I first heard the rumour, so I asked directly; three or four of the women who work here for you. Then I had to believe it.' She hid her face in her hands and gave a shudder.

Jack Cooper slammed his cigar into the ashtray, making the glass paperweight bounce and rock. 'I'll horsewhip him! I will, I'll flog him!' He went and looked wildly along the shelves of the cupboard where he kept his drink, then turned with a look of violent disgust. 'Where is he? Still licking his wounds at home, I expect.' He wrenched the telephone off the hook, ready to yell his home number through to the telephonist.

'No, Jack, I want to explain my idea.' Edith's self-control was restored. She thought she could use his outrage to force a decision, so she made him replace the telephone and listen. 'I want Teddy to join the war effort. It's a good, decent thing for him to do. The army will give him some discipline for a start, and that will be something he'll never lose. Besides, Lord Kitchener tells us all young men should serve. That's true, isn't it? It's their duty. Teddy's fit and able-bodied.' She spoke quietly and firmly, ignoring Jack's sarcastic grunt. 'I've thought it all through. You could get him a commission, then he won't have to go into the ranks. I wouldn't want that. Conditions would be better for him, he'd earn the men's respect, it would change his whole life. Listen, Jack, I don't think we'd ever need worry about him again!'

Rattled more by the fact that Teddy continued to risk the firm's reputation than by the red-blooded activities themselves, Jack Cooper listened and brooded. 'How are we going to get him into uniform if he don't want to?' He was beginning to see the good side of the plan, and if he was honest with himself, he knew he could easily do without his son's so-called help around here. But he didn't see how you could force someone to join a war, commission or not.

Edith had thought of that too. 'You hold the purse strings, don't you? If you cut off his allowance, he'll go to France soon enough.' She spoke steadily, coolly.

Jack thrust his head back and stared at the wood panelling on the ceiling. His eyes darted from side to side. Edith had sewn this up nicely; he wouldn't have believed she had it in her. At last he nodded. 'Right then, I'll put it to him.'

'When?'

'When I get the chance.' He began to shuffle papers into order on the desk.

'If I know you, the war will be over and done with before you get the chance, Jack Cooper. I want you to talk to Teddy tonight.' She stuck fast until he agreed. Then she gathered her bag and gloves.

'It's a hard mother who sends her only son off to war, you know that?' Jack got in a sour dig in retaliation for the way he'd been so successfully manoeuvred.

Edith looked him in the eye. 'And it's a soft father who turns a blind eye to all his shenanigans.'

They stared at each other, then called a truce. Edith went down through the store dignified as usual, pausing for a word with the supervisors in various departments, stopping again on the pavement outside the main entrance to drop coppers from her purse into Hettie's Salvation Army collection box.

Hettie recognized the store-owner's wife and immediately drew her into conversation. There was a family down Paradise Court, she said, who'd suffered a lot of bad luck. 'You heard the business about Daisy's murder, I expect?' She approached the subject frankly, not meaning to disconcert Mrs Cooper.

The fair woman's complexion flushed bright red. 'The music-hall girl?' Uneasily she put her purse back in her bag, fearful that Teddy could be dragged into yet another scandal over a girl.

'Yes, Daisy O'Hagan. Well, her family ain't taking it too well. They live down my street and they're pretty much cut up about it.'

Edith Cooper overcame her discomfiture and nodded. 'How do you want me to help?'

'There's a lot of mouths to feed, and Mary ain't up to it all by herself. Joe, her husband, would take work if he could get it, but they already turned him down at Tooley Street. I wondered if there was anything he could turn his hand to here?' Hettie glanced back at the shiny, fatly stocked windows. 'Just a little job would do for a start.'

Edith promised to try, though she didn't normally interfere with her husband's workforce. Hettie's sincerity had affected her. Hepton drove off through the dingy, cold street while she sat on the leather upholstery, looking to right and left at the stall-holders, flower and newspaper sellers, crossing sweepers and children picking at gutters. Helping one family wasn't much, she reflected. Still, she would try, if only to resist Jack's accusation that her heart had frazzled up and died during these years of plenty.

She went home to prepare the way with Teddy. He was in a weak position, and even his confidence was knocked by the livid scars and humiliation at the hands of Amy Ogden. Edith thought she could manage to carry the day. Teddy would look good in uniform and she would be able to speak of him with pride.

All through October, Hettie was the one in the Parsons family who most often braved the bleak walls and metal gangways of the prison. She went two or three times a week to the remand wing, sometimes taking Duke to see

Ernie, sometimes going with Jess. But Jess had taken on the task of visiting people round about to see what she could dig up about the murder. Though she'd drawn a blank with Teddy Cooper, she still had names on her list, and planned to see Fred Mills, the manager at the Palace. 'The coppers don't care,' she told Hettie in a bitter voice. 'They interviewed a few witnesses and they think it's cut and dried. As far as they're concerned, Ernie did it and that's that.'

As Hettie sat across the table from Ernie in her navy-blue Army uniform, she held his hand tight. 'We're gonna pray to Jesus, Ern,' she said fervently. 'He's the one what watches over us, even in the bad times. You gotta believe that. We're gonna march under the banner of Jesus, you and me, and He ain't gonna let us down!'

Ernie nodded. He'd remembered to pray, like Hettie taught him on her last visit. It was someone to talk to in his lonely cell late at night, and Hettie promised that He heard and would answer his prayers. The warders would look in on him through the grille and shake their hard heads. The lad mouthed his prayers audibly. 'Lord, keep me safe and send me home to my pa.'

In the earnestness of her new-found religion, Hettie taught him the psalm which brought her most comfort in her hour of need. 'The Lord is my shepherd,' she began. Ernie repeated after her, phrase by phrase. 'I shall not want.'

'I shall not want.'

'He maketh me to lie down in green pastures.'

'He maketh me . . .'

'To lie down.'

'To lie down.'

'In green pastures.'

Ernie nodded again and completed the line. He liked to

think of green fields and still waters. He wanted to dwell in the house of the Lord for ever.

Their dream was interrupted on one occasion in early November by the arrival of the solicitor, Mr Sewell. He was a short, balding man, decisive in his movements, with a confident, cheerful voice. He introduced himself to Hettie, then told Ernie some news. 'We have a date set for the trial at last.' He drew up another chair and sat at the table. 'It's going to be the tenth of December, so that gives us more than another month to prepare.'

Hettie heard the date and felt it etch itself painfully in her mind. She smiled to reassure Ernie. 'See, it'll soon be over. Don't you worry.'

Mr Sewell was brisk. 'I've received a letter this morning from your brother Robert in France. He tells me that the prosecution counsel doesn't plan to drag him away from the front line to stand as a witness for them. So I'm going to ask for his written testimony to use in your defence, Ernie. I'm sure it will corroborate – back up – your own account of your movements that night. I'll also ask him to provide a character reference, which should help us a great deal.' He gave the sister a quick glance. 'Does he understand what I say?'

Hettie shook her head. 'I doubt it. Still, you go ahead, I'll explain it to Ern later. What about Rob's letter. *Will* it help?'

'The jury will have to take it into account. It looks very good, coming from a member of our armed forces, patriotism being what it is now there's a war on. Our job is to build up a picture of a respectable family background, you see, to impress members of the jury.'

Hettie nodded. Sewell's talk made the trial all too real. Though she was cheerful for Ernie's sake, she went home full of fear. Ernie's life lay in the hands of twelve strangers. What would they see when they came into court? Who would they believe?

The setting of a date for the trial for the 10th sent Jess straight away up to Hettie's old haunt, the Southwark Palace. She left Duke to keep an eye on Grace, since Florrie was out at the market. Joxer could easily manage the trickle of early afternoon custom. It was Saturday; a match day. Jess could be over there and home again before the football crowd filtered back through the streets into the pubs. Grace sat, plump and content, on her grandfather's knee. 'If she cries, you can give her a spoonful of that mashed veg.' Jess buttoned her emerald-blue coat and put on her velvet hat. 'Auntie Florrie won't be long down the market. Do you think you can manage here?'

Duke rallied to something like his old self. 'I ain't completely useless yet, you know.' He jiggled Grace up and down, making her smile and gurgle. 'Her and me get on like a house on fire, don't we, girl?'

'She can go down for a nap if she looks sleepy,' Jess advised, hovering by the door.

Duke growled at her to get going. Baby Grace reminded him of Sadie as a child, dark and definite. She'd soon let him know if she was unhappy. 'I'll manage here. You run along on your errand, girl; quick before I change my mind.'

Jess's arrival at the music hall coincided with the end of a matinée performance. The cheerful crowd spilled on to the street; mainly family groups all dressed up for the occasion. They bantered and inexpertly repeated jokes they'd heard onstage. Jess shuddered to think this must have been the scene on the night of the murder, with Ernie lost in just such a crowd.

She waited until it dispersed. She'd picked this time to talk to Fred Mills because she knew from Hettie that the manager never went home between the afternoon and evening shows. He took tea in his office, brought in from a pie stall, and ate it tucked away behind the main foyer, counting the afternoon takings and dividing up the wages. Jess was bound to find him there.

As she walked in under the giant circular chandelier, she crossed paths with a fat, dapper man in spats, who raised his trilby hat and asked if she needed any help. She asked the way to the manager's office. 'Certainly, this way please.' The man grinned and turned on his shiny heel. She followed him across the crimson carpet. 'Who shall I say wants him?'

Jess held her little leather bag neatly in front of her. 'Jess Parsons, Hettie Parsons's sister.'

Archie Small stopped dead in his tracks. He raised his eyebrows and studied the visitor. 'You're not looking for employment, I take it?' She lacked the sister's style. Though she was good-looking in a striking, sultry sort of way, he couldn't imagine her treading the boards for a living like Hettie.

'No, I came on a personal matter.' Jess coloured up with suppressed irritation. 'If you'd just let Mr Mills know I'm here.'

But Archie thrust both hands deep in his pockets and began to circle round her. 'Personal matter? Connected with Daisy O'Hagan, by any chance?' He knew they'd arrested Hettie's simpleton of a brother for the murder. A visit from another sister could only upset the applecart and bring the police poking their noses back in.

Things had died down nicely, as far as Archie was concerned. He didn't want questions asked about his relationships with the ladies of the chorus line. They were murky to say the least. Archie exchanged promises of work

261

for favours from the girls; they all lived in the knowledge that he was well in with the manager and could get them kicked out at a moment's notice. Everyone knew how the system worked, except for Archie's wife, Clemmie. He didn't much want to have to face her if the truth came out. Clemmie had a bruising side to her nature. Besides, if the police realized he'd been pestering Daisy, they might drag him in as a fresh suspect. 'I should let sleeping dogs lie if I was you,' he advised Jess. 'Instead of barging in here demanding to see Mr Mills.'

'I ain't barging in.' Jess stood her ground. She looked around to see if she could spot a sign on the manager's door. She set off towards it. 'I just want to speak to him.'

Archie stepped smartly in front of her. 'I don't really think you do.' He was wondering what to say to get rid of her when Mr Mills's door opened and the manager himself came out. Jess tried to side-step. 'I'm telling you you can't go in there without an appointment,' he blustered, catching at her arm.

'Losing your touch, Archie?' Fred Mills asked with a cool smile. His unbuttoned jacket showed an expanse of starched white shirt and braces. He wore his dark wavy hair slicked back and he ducked his head forward in an insinuating way. Nothing he had to say seemed sincere. 'How can I help?' He gestured Jess out of the way into the office, allowing Archie to slip in and close the door after her.

Inside Mills's cluttered, poky office, Jess explained her mission. There was a heavy iron safe in one corner, and a stack of light bulbs in cardboard boxes against the wall. A metal shade on the desk lamp cast a small pool of light, leaving much of the room in semi-darkness, since there was no window. More of a cupboard than an office, it was Mills's domain, reflecting much about his slapdash, penny-pinching way. 'You know they arrested our brother, Ernie, for Daisy's murder, Mr Mills. The trial comes up next month, and we all have to do what we can to help get him off.'

Mills let her speak, but he was already discounting her. No need for Archie to get hot under the collar; he could deal with the girl easily enough. She lacked guile, she just came out with things straight. But if she wanted someone at the Palace to give her another little fact, a tiny piece of evidence to get her brother off, she must look elsewhere. Like Archie, he preferred things the way they were. 'What can I do, Miss Parsons?' He expressed concern, but he was half turned away, riffling through papers on his desk.

Jess heard the other man light up a cigar, and felt its pungent smoke prick her nostrils. The room was tiny and claustrophobic. 'I want to know more about that night, Mr Mills; what you found when you checked things through with the police, anything unusual that you couldn't quite place, either before or after Daisy got killed.'

Mills glanced up. 'A proper little Sherlock Holmes, ain't you? You ain't thinking of interfering with a prosecution witness, are you, Miss Parsons?'

Hastily Jess shook her head. 'Course not. Only I thought, since you was the one here inside the place when Ett discovered poor Daisy lying there, that you'd want to help. I ain't asking you to do nothing wrong, am I?' She was shocked at the idea. 'If you was me, you'd want to do your best for Ern, wouldn't you?'

Archie came up from behind. 'Listen, girl, you can't go asking Mr Mills to tell you more than he already told the coppers. What he told them's gonna come out at the trial, clear as daylight. If I was you, I'd go on home and talk things through with Ett.' He paused, drew deep on his cigar and exhaled. 'Lovely girl, that. What's she doing with herself these days?'

Jess's heart sank. She ignored the lecherous comedian as best she could. 'For Ernie's sake, Mr Mills, ain't there nothing at all that'd help? Who was Daisy hanging round with that week? Who'd want to meet up with her after the show?'

Mills looked Archie in the eye and grinned. 'A whole football team, I shouldn't wonder, Miss Parsons. She was a popular girl. Like I said, I think you should ask your sister. She knew Daisy better than most.'

'I already done that! What do you think, that I'd come over here without talking to Ett?' Jess's indignation rose to the surface. In her innocence she'd believed that people at the Palace would want to help them. Now she saw they had reasons for wanting to hide things. She turned on Archie Small. 'You was one of them!' she accused. 'According to Ett, you was one what fancied having a fling with Daisy!'

The man backed off, then he wheeled. 'Other way round as a matter of fact. Daisy O'Hagan went after anything wearing trousers, if you want to know. I had to tell her to keep her hands off me; I'm a married man.' Beads of sweat glistened on his forehead. His cigar glowed, then he was masked again by a cloud of blue-grey smoke.

Jess struggled to choke back her anger. She swung round to face Mills, finding herself sandwiched between them in this muggy, confined space.

'I'd be more careful what I said if I was you,' Mills said smoothly. 'It might just backfire in front of a jury, and the family of the dear departed might have to listen to some awkward facts about their darling girl.' He buttoned his jacket. 'Now then, if you'll excuse me, I've got a show to put on.' He pressed by her with an empty smile, then hung on a moment longer by the door. 'We know how you feel, believe me. I don't even blame you for having a go. I wish you luck on the day. But if your brother did go all haywire and do the poor girl in, like the coppers say, you ain't doing no good going round putting people's backs up, are you?'

'Leave it to the lawyers,' Archie cut in. 'They can talk the hind leg off a bleeding donkey and bore everyone to death. With a bit of luck they'll get a not-guilty verdict for him just so we can all go home!'

His false cheerfulness disgusted her. 'We need more than luck!' She stalked out into the foyer. 'What we need is the truth!' Her cheeks burned as she glared at them both. 'And it seems to me that it's in short supply around here!'

Her anger only died away in the cold evening air. When she finally got rid of their grinning, furtive faces from her mind's eye, she shook with fresh doubt. She feared that she'd done more harm than good again as she went home to confess to Frances that her search for new evidence had led to a dead end, or worse.

Ever since Ernie's arrest, Frances had kept herself in touch with the outside world through her meetings and her work. Her nerves were strung out, but she kept up the front of continuing to cope because giving in was not an idea that ever crossed her mind. She wasn't a crier or a shouter, except over her big split with Duke, when they'd leapt to opposite sides of a giant chasm over the window-smashing at Coopers'. She was a doer. If anything, she worked harder now in the pharmacy, kept herself abreast of preparations for the trial, and attended more meetings.

Her friend, Rosie, kept a watchful eye on her. 'Don't wear yourself out,' she advised. It was the evening of Jess's failed mission to the Palace. 'You have to take care of yourself, Frances, whatever happens.'

'Oh, I'm never ill, I'm not the type.' Frances sat in the coffee room at the lecture hall after a talk by the brilliant

Elizabeth Garrett Anderson on the need for better health care for women. Rosie had encouraged her to attend. 'I got the constitution of an ox.'

Rosie looked doubtful. She was a cheerful, practical woman, perversely enjoying the war effort because her training as a nurse was proving immediately useful. She felt herself moving for ever out of the trap of factory work and marriage. 'I ain't never seen an ox look this pale and thin,' she said. 'In fact, I got patients with shell-shock at the hospital looking healthier than you.'

'Thanks!' Frances stirred her coffee.

'Don't mention it.' Rosie laughed and got up from the table. 'Speaking of which, I gotta go to work on the night shift. Are you walking that way?'

Frances looked up at the wall clock. 'No, I'll hang on here. I want to speak to Billy about defence witnesses for Ernie. He's seeing Mr Sewell after a class upstairs.'

Her companion nodded. 'Don't wait too long. It's late already. And get him to walk you home. It ain't safe if you leave it too late.'

'Says who?' Frances appreciated her concern. She smiled warmly.

'Says me. Here's Billy now. I'll leave you in his tender care. Look after her, Billy. She's worn herself out as usual.' Rosie sailed out, the picture of health.

Billy took her place at the bare table with a look of concern. 'You sure you're all right?' His heart went out to her. 'She's right, you look done in.'

'The next person to tell me that had better watch out,' she warned. 'Now, what did Mr Sewell say?'

Billy discussed the latest tactics; Hettie must be prepared to be called as chief witness for the defence, since they only had Robert's written statement.

'Will Ern be called to give evidence?' Frances tried to consider how he would cope.

'It ain't been decided yet. Mr Sewell ain't sure about the prosecution line. They could chew Ernie up good and proper. On the other hand, he's working hard at getting him to remember more about what went on at the stage door. If he can do that, it could help the defence case to hear Ernie give his version. Sewell says we'll wait and see. He says he'll discuss it with you if you call into his office.' Billy delivered all the information without once taking his eyes off her face.

Frances put on her gloves and got up to go. The wall behind her was lined with red and blue books, a gaslight on the side wall shone its soft light on her face and made a halo of her hair. People passed downstairs and through the entrance hall, hidden from view. Suddenly Billy seized her hand and came to stand close by her. She didn't react.

'I ain't got no right,' he began. One arm was around her shoulder. 'Tell me I ain't!'

'That's right, Billy, you ain't.' Gently she tried to extricate herself. She felt a fool. How had she missed the signs of his interest, to be taken so much by surprise now? Was it that she'd given up thinking of herself as a desirable woman? She had one hand against his chest, the other clasped in his at waist level, forming a barrier between them. 'We mustn't mix things up. It'll ruin us!'

But he felt he'd stepped off the edge of a cliff. He'd trodden this path for a long time; studying Frances, watching her, helping her. He could have gone on for a lifetime; only, as she slid her slim white hand into her glove, his heart had missed its footing and gone tumbling down. He kissed her long and hard.

Their simplicity went smash. She found she liked his

kiss, and he knew she liked it. She couldn't say it was a mistake and go back to how they were. New knowledge got in the way. Slowly she drew away, searching in his face for what they should do next.

Billy put his hand to her face and held his palm against it. Not for the first time he told himself that he was forty-three years old; a newspaper vendor with a sick wife, a mother-in-law and a discontented outlook. No catch for someone like Frances. He wanted to turn back the clock ticking overhead, not five minutes, but twenty years. He wanted his time over again.

Frances reached up and held the hand that stroked her face.

'Would you have me?' he whispered.

She nodded. 'If things were different, yes.' Her voice was full of longing.

'Will you have me as it is?'

Her heart jumped at the directness of the question. How many women said 'yes' on the spur of despair? 'No, Billy, how can I?'

He let his hand drop to his side. 'Like I said, I ain't got no right.'

The caretaker trawled the building for people left gossiping in classrooms. His footsteps approached the coffee room.

'But we'll be friends,' Frances said hurriedly, with no experience of the torment involved.

He nodded. 'We'll try.' He had a better idea of the misery in store behind that harmless phrase.

She gathered herself and went out into the hallway before him. The caretaker shuffled towards them, ushered them out and locked the door against them.

Billy walked Frances to the corner of Duke Street as usual. When they parted, exhaustion overtook her. She arrived home at last and met Duke toiling his way up from the cellar, preparing to close down the empty bar. Her father looked at her strained, tragic face and held his arms wide. She sobbed silently against his chest, before they went upstairs to join the others. They sat together until long after midnight, missing Ernie and Robert, dreading the start of the trial.

Part Three

SHOULDER
TO
SHOULDER

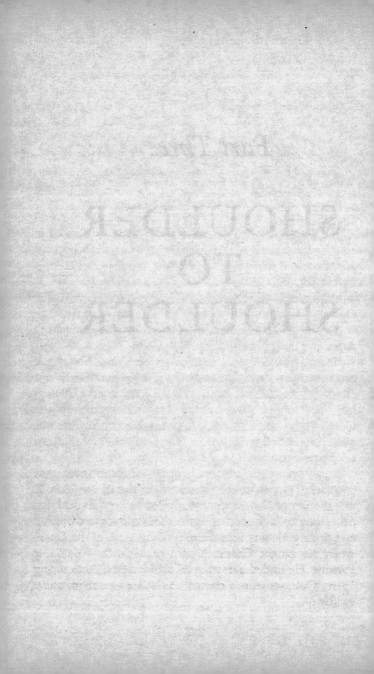

Chapter Twenty-One

As the winds blew through the trees in Hyde Park and tore off their golden leaves, the Parsons family hoped and prayed for a new lead that would clear Ernie. October turned into November.

'A miracle's what we need,' Florrie confided to Dolly Ogden.

'Or for Ernie to remember what did happen that night,' Annie put in.

'Exactly, a bleeding miracle,' Florrie insisted. She shook her head and went on wiping glasses at the bar. 'He always clams up when he gets into a state about something. Always has. You can't get a word out of him. Duke reckons he just blocks things out, as if they ain't never happened.' She was 'worrying herself to a shadow over him', as she told Tom on the telephone.

But Paradise Court as a whole had other events to consider. Tommy turned up one night out of the blue. It was the 5th of November. He strolled down the court, his new jacket collar turned up against the cold wind, whistling and poking his way into the alley at the back of the Duke, where he caught Charlie Ogden in a clinch with Sadie Parsons. He rattled a dustbin lid and watched them spring apart. 'Ooh, someone's clicked!' he crowed, ready to move swiftly on.

Charlie had been busily impressing his girlfriend with his mastery of the screen kiss. He'd studied it in detail from the projection room at the Gem; you had to draw the girl towards you by the waist, so she leaned her face back, then you craned towards her with heavy-lidded eyes and put your mouth firmly against hers, gently forcing her lips apart. It worked like a dream until Tommy O'Hagan came and interrupted them. 'Bleeding hell, Tommy!' he called out, dragging Sadie with him out into the court.

Tommy turned with a cheeky grin, relaxed and unconcerned, as if he'd just taken a stroll down the park before tea. He had more flesh on his bones and shoes on his feet, besides the new jacket. This one didn't skim his backside and fail to fasten across the chest like the other. An optimistic streak must have told him that he'd grow into this one eventually, since he was filling out nicely and losing the peaky look of the Barnardo's posters. 'Now then, Charlie, is that what they teach you at school nowadays? "Bleeding this and bleeding that"!'

Charlie approached him warily. 'Where you been, Tommy?'

'Here and there. Why, did you miss me, then?' Tommy glanced ahead towards the grim tenements. 'Blimey, the old place still looks horrible as ever, don't it?'

Sadie clutched Charlie's hand. 'Ain't you heard, Tommy?'

'Where I been I ain't heard nothing, believe me.' Tommy had taken it into his head to go downriver and look for a ship. It was a spur-of-the-moment decision; things couldn't be worse at sea than they were at home, he reckoned. He met up with a Norwegian captain and persuaded him to take him on as dogsbody on his fishing boat. They set sail straight away. After five days of throwing up and staggering about the place like a lunatic, he'd found his sea legs. In no time, the oily smell of fish had crept into every pore. All day he cleaned each cog and wheel of the old boat's engine with filthy rags, and all night they would chug and grind in his dreams. But the food made up for the grimy work, even though everything tasted of engine oil. There was plenty of it at any rate. One short voyage was enough, however, so Tommy inherited the first mate's jacket during a drunken brawl on their first night ashore, then he hightailed it back upriver.

With money in his pocket and a determination to make a success of himself before he headed home to Paradise Court, he turned his hand to wheeling and dealing on dry land. He set his sights on a barrow and a pitch outside Waterloo, his old hunting ground. So he befriended a feeble old-timer who had a fruit stall and persuaded him he'd be better off with his feet up by the fire as winter drew on. He offered him cash, of course. The old codger snatched his hand off.

Now Tommy was part of the early morning scene at Covent Garden, and all day you could hear his raucous shout between the great main archway of Waterloo Station. This evening he'd come home to show off.

He turned to Charlie. 'Why's she got a face on her? Ain't she pleased to see me?'

'Pleased as punch, Tommy,' Charlie faltered. He and Sadie fell into step beside him. 'You going straight on home?'

'Looks like it.'

Sadie tugged at Charlie's sleeve. 'Leave him be, Charlie!'

They halted, and Tommy headed on without breaking his stride. They heard him whistle a romantic tune and saw the derision of the unattached and fancy free in his swaggering walk. 'Blimey!' Charlie shook his head. 'He ain't half in for a shock.'

It made Sadie cry all over again, to imagine Mary's

haggard face as she told Tommy the news about Daisy. Charlie's hug contained nothing of the screen hero this time; he was finding it hard to hold back tears himself.

Maurice Leigh had also done some hard thinking since his golden walk in Hyde Park with Jess. In the cool light of day, the problems of being involved with a woman who had a kid in tow shone clear and sharp. He summed them up in the dreaded word, 'ties'.

For Maurice this wasn't the callow reaction of irresponsible youth. At eighteen or nineteen, perhaps, being tied down went against a natural spirit of fun and denied the opportunity all young men needed to play the field. But he was now in his late twenties, smart and successful, and outwardly in a position where a man might want to settle down with wife and family. However, life had made him wary of such a move. His Jewish background, strict and claustrophobic when his father was alive, had invited bad name-calling at school and turned him into a poor attender. There was a particular hatred of Eastern European immigrant Jews, to which group Maurice's family belonged. They survived in small, isolated pockets in areas like Bethnal Green, and he recalled all too well the heavy sentimentality of family ties and the strict moralizing which held him almost in chains and apart from other boys.

Since the work in the book-binding shop kept the family hovering only just above the desperate poverty of the homeless and jobless who roamed the East End streets at the turn of the century, Maurice quickly learned to suspect the value of his closed community. His father worked for an uncle who ran the small business; his mother's brother. He paid the men a pittance to make them stoop all week over glue and leather, doling out gold leaf for the page edging with miserly caution. His meanness eventually cast the fatherless family on to the street; he needed the garret to provide lodgings for his new employee, he said. Maurice's mother begged for Marcus, Maurice's oldest brother, to be taken on in his dead father's place, but the uncle refused to consider it. So much for family loyalty. The brothers lived on their wits to support themselves and their mother in a series of run-down rooms until she too died of tuberculosis when Maurice was just fourteen. Then he was alone and free.

Working to survive, he primed street-lamps, got birched so regularly at his industrial school for hopping the wag that he soon gave up going altogether, and eventually fell in with Monty Phillips, the pawnbroker who also ran a stall selling secondhand clothes on the railings down the rag fair. From here life took off. Decently dressed in other boys' clothes, he used his spare time to gamble over cigarette cards or to pinch a bicycle for a day to ride out into the countryside, when he showed off his athleticism by storming ahead up the hills and freewheeling down the other side, hands in pockets. Ditching the bike back with its owner, he would buy a fish supper and retire to bed under the counter at Monty's. No complications. No ties.

From this start, he'd moved on through a mixture of opportunism and hard work into his present respectable job. He was still convinced that his motto held good. What did he want with a woman and a child? The difficulty was, this wasn't just any woman. This was Jess.

He was annoyed with himself for prolonging the unfamiliar state of indecision, which had now lasted more than a month. He and Jess danced around each other whenever they met, half longing, half afraid. He took her out once or twice a week, and at times the passion was intense. But the relationship seemed to have stalled. She felt she didn't want

Maurice to see Grace; the commitment would be too great. And she worried about Ernie. For his part, Maurice worked hard at the picture palace and bided his time.

On the day after Tommy O'Hagan turned up in the court, he decided to shelve these things and go to join a session at Milo's gym. It was the nearest place to Paradise Court for a good, strenuous training bout. He was as quick with his fists as with his brain, and straight away impressed regulars, including Walter Davidson, with his clean punching and neat footwork. Maurice had finished his work-out and stood chatting with Walter and Milo himself, when Chalky White approached to introduce himself.

They shook hands. 'Nice piece of work,' Chalky said. He stood, arms akimbo, clutching the ends of a towel which was slung like a scarf around his neck. His own singlet was damp from a work-out on the weights.

Maurice immediately resented the condescending tone. In the code he had been attuned to all his life, 'Nice piece of work' signalled, 'This is my turf'. It was an unasked for seal of approval from the gangland boss. Maurice felt he didn't need it, so he nodded once and kept quiet.

Chalky pumped him for information on where he lived, where he'd come from, what he did. It didn't take him long to work out the Jewish connection, and this put an extra edge of superiority into his conversation. 'Maybe I'll bring my girl down your place this Saturday,' he told him, as if bestowing a favour. He'd found a replacement for Daisy in yet another girl from the chorus line at the Palace, but he didn't usually meet up with her until late at night. So he also went out to pick up a casual girl earlier in the evening, in a pub or at a dance, and he and his mates would parade the streets, girls in tow. Meeting up with Maurice gave him the chance to angle for free tickets to the Gem; one of the up-and-coming places to be seen.

'It'd be nice to see you there,' was Maurice's non-committal reply. He kept his eyes on the pair who'd just stepped into the ring and begun to spar.

'Reckon I might put a bit of business your way,' Chalky boasted. He'd already taken against Maurice as a tight-arse.

'Fine.'

'Me and my mates, Syd and Whitey up there.' He pointed to the two boxers.

Not so tough, Maurice thought, casting a critical eye. Neither would last two minutes in the ring with him. If Chalky was only as good as these two at handling himself, there was not much to worry about. 'Best come early and miss the queues,' he advised. 'The place gets packed out and I have to turn people away these days.'

Chalky rubbed the towel across his face. Jumped up tight-arse, he repeated to himself. Leigh had just made a bad move, treating him like a nobody. Chalky would show him different as soon as he got the chance. He spat a ball of phlegm on to the floor and strode off.

Milo, still standing nearby, pulled a face at Maurice and went about his business. 'Bad move,' Walter said later when Maurice went to the changing room to put on his outdoor clothes.

'I ain't bothered.' Maurice combed his hair in the speckled, steamy mirror. 'I can deal with his type no trouble.'

In this reckless mood he went straight up to the Duke to invite Jess to a dance that Friday night at the Town Hall. 'I'll get time off,' he told her. She looked doubtful, glass and tea-towel in hand. Duke kept an eye on her from the cellar steps.

'Oh, I don't know. I ain't been to a dance in ages. I've forgotten how.'

'All the better. That means I can teach you; the Tango, the Turkey Trot!' He looked animated. 'Go on, Jess, say you'll come!'

In the end she nodded. 'I'll see if I can.'

'This Friday, eight on the dot. Make a date!' He drank up, chatted amiably with Arthur and Dolly at a table by the door, then went on his way in high spirits. 'Babe! Come along! O, kid! O, kid!' He hummed the latest American dance. 'Hug 'em. Hug 'em. Put your arms around me, Babe!'

In the bar, Florrie warned Duke not to be a misery. 'The girl needs some fun, just like everyone else.'

Duke concentrated on tapping the new barrel. 'I ain't said nothing.'

'You don't have to, your face says it all. You'll put her off going if you go round looking like that.'

He sighed. 'I ain't exactly feeling on top of the world, Flo.'

'Same as the rest of us, Wilf. It ain't no better for Jess. And she's doing her best for Ern. In fact, she's more than pulling her weight if you ask me, getting the sewing off the ground with Ett. She's a good girl if you did but know it.'

Duke grunted. 'But do you think he knows about . . . you know?' He tilted his head sideways, glancing up through the cellar ceiling. 'He ain't in for a shock when he finds out, is he?'

Florrie tutted and shoved him to one side while she turned on the tap and let beer froth into her jug. 'No, she told him about Grace weeks since. He took it well, she says.'

'It makes me mad!' He went behind the gantry and put his shoulder to a second barrel, wedging the chock up a notch with angry force.

Florrie stepped back in surprise. 'Steady on. What got into you?'

'I'm just thinking of him what done this to her. I tell you, if I could get my hands on him, I'd throttle him!'

'Yes, and you won't even let on to your one and only sister who it was, and that's a fact!' Florrie stood, arms crossed.

He shook his head. 'No. Frances said not to. They don't want no one poking their noses in.'

'Including me.' Florrie sniffed and folded her arms, doing her best to assume a wounded look. 'It ain't for want of asking, Duke Parsons!' In fact, she'd nagged them to death to get at the truth.

'Jess says it ain't important no more.' He clenched his teeth and hammered at the chock with the edge of his massive fist.

Florrie regained her momentum and began to badger him once more. 'Well, he ain't gonna be a father to the kid, is he? So in a way she's right. And the sooner Jess gets out and about and finds herself someone else who will be, the better. Tell her she can go to this dance, Wilf. She needs your blessing.'

'First time for years,' he grumbled. Then he straightened up and shrugged. 'He seems a decent sort at any rate.'

'Go tell her!'

Florrie stood and watched her brother's broad back, stooping a little as he eased his stiff legs up the steep cellar steps. He carried his troubles well, considering. Sewell had recently warned Frances not to hold out too many hopes for the trial, just in case. She'd come home white as a sheet and passed the message on to Duke. 'Don't tell the others,' he said to Florrie. 'There's no point dragging them down no more.'

She knew he nattered and worried about Robert too. It was a couple of weeks since they'd had a letter from him. Two sons in the firing line, if you looked on the black side. Poor old man, he needed all the help he could get.

Chapter Twenty-Two

Annie Wiggin did brisk business on her haberdashery stall during the week leading up to the dance at the Town Hall. She sold silk flowers for head-dresses and corsages, all shades of ribbon to thread through lace collars and cuffs, tiny buttons of pearl and glass, filigree buckles and the inevitable yards of delicate lace.

Late on the Friday, Jess sent Hettie down the market. The mission was to, 'buy something to brighten up this bodice when I've finished running it up on the machine'. Her feet treadled hard and her hands steered the silky jade-coloured fabric through the swiftly stabbing needle. She held a clutch of pins in the corner of her mouth, and mumbled that it would never be finished in time. She would have to go to the dance in her ordinary day wear of white blouse and blue skirt.

'Calm down, Jess.' Hettie had finished her day's task of altering waistbands on three pairs of trousers. She clattered her scissors down on the table and stood up. 'There's heaps of time. And it's gonna look lovely on you.'

Jess came to the end of a seam. She took the pins from her mouth and put them in a shallow tin. 'It ain't had no proper tacking. I just slung it together in a big rush.' She held up the nearly complete garment for inspection.

'It looks fine to me.'

'It ain't too low-cut?' Jess asked. 'You don't think it needs a bit more lace round the neckline to raise it?' The bodice was shaped and cut to show off both bust and arms.

Hettie laughed. 'I told you, it looks fine to me. I'll nip down to Annie's for matching ribbon, so we can ruche it up here around the shoulders. With my black skirt and belt to finish things off, you'll be the best-dressed girl there!'

Hettie rushed off to consult with Annie, who showed her which ribbon would best do the job. Jess's dark hair, with its fashionable wave, needed a pale cream flower or two to set it off. 'What about you, Ett? Ain't you going dancing with your sister?'

Hettie blushed. 'No. Sadie's going along early with young Charlie Ogden, but I'm staying home to help with the baby. Dancing ain't for me these days, Annie.' She paid for the ribbon and flowers.

'Why not? It was, not so long since.' Annie gave her a reproachful look. 'Life and soul of the party, you was, Hettie Parsons.' She launched into a well-meaning speech. 'No need to chuck out your dancing shoes for good, is there, girl? We all know it was a terrible thing what happened to Daisy, and you had a nasty shock yourself, finding her like that. But it don't mean you have to go overboard on the tambourine bashing and hymn singing, do it? Why not have a bit of fun as well?'

Taken aback, Hettie defended herself hotly. 'I signed the pledge, Annie. I'm not going near if there's alcohol on sale, I promised.' She regarded the oath seriously, taking it to earnest extremes.

'That's rich, with you living right over the Duke!' Annie scoffed. 'What's your pa say about you saving poor sinners and helping to empty his till while you're about it?'

'He ain't said much,' Hettie replied quietly.

'I bet he ain't. I expect he's waiting for you to grow out

of it, girl. Honest to God, Ett, it breaks my heart to see you decked out in that bleeding horrible uniform, when I think of how you used to be.'

'It's vanity that lands us in trouble in the first place,' Hettie insisted. 'Anyhow, I made up my mind.'

'Pity. It used to brighten my day, seeing your hats all trimmed up with the bits and pieces I sold you off this stall. Pretty as a picture!'

'Well, I am sorry about that, Annie.' Hettie smiled self-consciously and squeezed Annie's hand.

'Not half so sorry as the scuttlers round here. They miss you and Daisy something rotten.' She looked wistfully at Hettie's pale, serious face. 'No hard feelings?' she checked.

'No hard feelings. I'm happy the way I am now. I feel I can be a bit of use.' She set off home with Jess's carefully wrapped trimmings, glad she'd stood her ground. They'd have to get used to her and her new mission; her Quakerish uniform and tambourine bashing, as Annie called it.

Frances came in from work just as Jess was trying on her finished outfit. She took off her hat and coat and hung them in significant silence, avoiding looking directly at Jess.

Already in a bad state of nerves over the whole business of accepting Maurice's invitation, Jess's confidence collapsed. 'Oh, Frances, you don't think I should go, do you?' She came up close to her unresponsive sister, while Hettie and Sadie hung back frowning.

'I never said that,' Frances replied, sinking into a chair. 'I'm all in. Sadie, make me a cup of tea, there's a good girl.'

'You don't have to say nothing,' Jess went on. 'I can tell by your face you think it ain't right.'

Sadie had already jumped a few steps ahead. 'Does that mean I can't go neither?' she wailed at Hettie. She knew

Duke would only let her go to the early part of the dance if Jess was there to supervise things. She stood in her best blouse, hair swept up for the very first time, close to tears.

Frances intervened with a weary shake of her head. 'Don't take on, Sadie. Just make me that cuppa, will you?'

Miserably hanging her head, Sadie went off into the kitchen.

There was an uneasy silence as Jess considered sending back word to Maurice. Frances's disapproval would hurt her badly and bring a poor atmosphere into the house when they least needed it. 'It ain't right, is that what you think?' she persisted.

The phrase struck a chord in Frances's memory. It was Billy's phrase before he kissed her. Suddenly her rigid distinction between right and wrong began to crumble. It was true, she'd thought Jess's affair with Maurice, coming close on the heels of the baby and in the very midst of their worries over Ernie, was ill advised. Better to wait at least until after the trial, she thought. As she stood all day and weighed, rolled and cut paste for pills, she divided moral issues into neat and tidy boxes, and thought life could follow prescribed patterns. Jess shouldn't enjoy herself with a new boyfriend. Ernie should be at home, not in prison. Everyone should do what was right.

But her memory played this sudden trick. She pictured herself in Billy's arms responding to his kiss, not fending him off as she should have done. Love, longing, loneliness were enormous forces pushing people into one another's arms. Who was she to judge? Humbly, Frances took hold of Jess's hand. 'Don't mind me,' she sighed. 'I'm just tired out. Why don't you go off and have a good time? You and Sadie with your Cake Walk and your Dandy Dance!'

Sadie came in with the tea to hear the last part of this speech. Her face lit up, then she teased her oldest sister.

'Frances, it ain't the Cake Walk no more. That's old hat. No, these days it's the Turkey Trot. I been practising with Charlie!' She went and dragged Hettie across the floor with her arms slung around her shoulders, walking with wriggling sideways steps.

'Oh my Lord!' Jess looked at Frances in wild-eyed alarm.

'Go on, get out of here quick before I change my mind,' Frances moaned. She put one hand over her eyes and squinted through her fingers as Sadie rushed for her jacket. 'And mind you're back by ten!' she called.

Sadie and Jess grinned, and sailed downstairs together.

Maurice and Charlie met up with Jess and Sadie in the fuzzy halo of the street-lamp outside the pub. They walked four abreast up the greasy pavement, hopped on to a tram and joined the steady stream of young people heading for the Town Hall.

The dance was held in a huge central room bedecked with strings of coloured electric lights. It buzzed with expectation as the band arrived on the raised platform to strike up the first tune. One novelty of the occasion was the array of uniforms on show. Recent recruits to the army and navy, or veterans sent home on leave strutted through the hall. Khaki mingled with navy-blue under giant coloured posters which displayed men at arms, women in nurses' uniform or busy in munitions factories. 'Are YOU in this?' read the challenge below. It was the first time the war had seemed real to many of the young civilians gathered there, but the uniforms seemed to inspire rather than depress them. Many minds were made up as they talked, wide-eyed and eager, to the battle-scarrred heroes of the day.

Teddy Cooper turned up in the grey-blue uniform of a pilot in the Royal Flying Corps; the most glamorous outfit of all with its belted jacket and breeches. After nearly a month of haggling at home, he'd conceded defeat and agreed to serve the war effort, but on his own terms. Not for him the mud and sweat of a Flanders field. He preferred the soaring blue reaches and a mission to bring back information on enemy positions. His mother complained of the danger involved in piloting the flimsy bi-planes, but Teddy declared they were safe as houses. He'd fight a clean war of darting raids across the Channel. A rumour that the Flying Corps was preparing to drop bombs on the enemy sounded to him an exciting but unlikely development.

So he stepped into the dashing uniform and role in adventurous spirits. The Town Hall dance would be a good send-off; a chance to be admired and envied.

Ugly duckling civilians like Walter Davidson and the Chalky White gang hung back in the shadows while the boys in uniform glided on to the dance floor with the best-looking girls. Chalky, adrift again from his latest girlfriend, eventually picked up Olwyn Williams, who'd recently ditched her job in the shirt sweatshop at Coopers' and taken work as a bus conductress. The war had opened many jobs to women, and Olwyn was one of the first to seize the new opportunity. She liked the uniform: a military-style jacket, a shorter than usual plaid skirt and jaunty brimmed hat with its company badge. And she liked the independence. As she swung by on Chalky's arm, she winked at Amy Ogden. Amy had picked up Syd Swan, regarded as a slimy customer by most of the girls. 'That's the ticket, clippie!' Syd grinned inanely at Olwyn. Amy pulled him back on course to instruct him in elementary tango. He enjoyed the sweaty, grappling aspect, but the nifty footwork was beyond him.

Soon the music and heat generated by hundreds of dancing couples set the evening in swing. Charlie danced energetically with Sadie, having picked up more handy tips from the American bioscopes, where women with crimped hair and pouting dark lipstick swooned in the arms of broad-shouldered, square-jawed heroes. Jess stood at the side with her arm linked through Maurice's. She smiled at the new style of dancing. 'I hope you don't expect me to try nothing like that,' she said, looking prim.

Maurice was flattered by the effort Jess had put into her appearance this evening. There were complicated swirls in her thick hair, and tiny pearl-drop earrings in perpetual motion as she turned her head this way and that. Her sloping shoulders and full breasts showed to advantage in her new, tight-fitting bodice. Her arms were long and slender. 'What, ain't you never done the tango?' he asked, taking her by the waist and leading her on to the dance floor. 'It's easy. You just slide around a bit. Let yourself go, trust me!'

Jess laughed. 'If you let go of me, Maurice Leigh, I'll crown you!' She felt herself tipped backwards in a dangerous, plunging motion, then pulled upright by the strength of his arm around her waist.

He held her, his cheek against hers, feeling her soft, smooth skin against him. He felt her mouth smile. 'Oh, I won't let go of you, Jess, don't worry,' he whispered. He pulled her close, to breathe in the clean, perfumed smell of her hair.

The strutting music of the tango merged seamlessly into a more sedate waltz, leaving only the romantically inclined couples on the floor. Sadie and Charlie went off hand in hand to the refreshment bar. Amy Ogden struggled into a more upright position with Syd Swan, whose arm still snaked around her, too close for comfort. Chalky threaded through the couples in the opposite direction to his ex-partner, Olwyn. He paused to wink at Syd and then considered Jess as she danced with Maurice. He knew enough street gossip to register surprise that she was out on the town. Slowly he lit up a cigarette, flicked the match to the floor and circled in their direction, preparing a cutting remark. He fancied somehow hitting the newcomer, Maurice Leigh, with the bombshell about Jess's baby. With narrowed eyes he halted again and exhaled smoke by jutting out his bottom lip and directing it straight up in front of him.

Maurice spotted Chalky's intention to come over and upset things. He could see the sneering face draw near. Jess was oblivious, her head against his shoulder. This was awkward timing; Maurice could hardly snap Jess out of the slow, smooth movement of the waltz without alerting her to Chalky's sly approach.

Jess felt Maurice stiffen, and glanced up to see the cause. Chalky White stood close by, in the middle of the revolving pairs, his snake eyes fixed on them.

'What's he think he's staring at?' Maurice muttered, now that Jess had seen.

'Take no notice,' she pleaded. She wanted the music to stop so they could walk swiftly away.

But then luckily Chalky's attention was diverted. Amy had spotted Teddy Cooper in his smart uniform and whispered something to her new boyfriend, Syd Swan, which made him swear loudly, then round up a couple of mates. They soon started to square up to Teddy and his officer-type pals, facing each other in a corner of the hall. A space had cleared and a ripple of excitement spread through the room. The band wavered, then played on, now almost ignored. Chalky responded quickly, dropping his vendetta against Maurice and roughly pushing through the middle of the dance floor to side with Syd. Jess breathed a sigh of relief. 'Time I went and rounded up young Sadie,' she told Maurice. 'I promised Pa I'd send her home safe and sound.'

Maurice kept one eye on the trouble brewing in the corner; shirt-sleeves were already rolled up, each side taunted and mocked the other. He went with Jess to the refreshment table. 'Let's walk with them,' he suggested. 'There's a bit of a scrap on the cards over there. They can sort it out while we take Sadie home, then we can come back and pick up where we left off.'

Jess smiled and nodded. Charlie, who thought it was a bad idea, was soon overruled. Sadie left with a long face, pleading for half an hour more, but soon they were out in the cold, windy street, huddling together and half running for warmth, until they came under the railway arch on to Duke Street, when Maurice and Jess chose to walk diplomatically ahead, leaving the young couple to their midnight kiss.

'Don't she look lovely tonight?' Jess glanced back, then slid her arm close inside Maurice's. 'Ain't no wonder he's smitten, poor boy.'

Maurice glanced back. 'Hm. He's more smitten with himself than anyone else, if you ask me.' He smiled at her. 'Do you think we're past standing in an alley like them?' He turned her towards him in the full glow of the street-lamp and took a bold kiss.

'Just like a couple of kids,' Jess protested. She steered him on down the street past Henshaw's frosty window, past the unlit courts. 'Come on, Sadie. It's too cold to hang about,' she called.

Sadie grumbled and called them spoil-sports, but they got home just fifteen minutes late and delivered her into the anxious care of a tired-looking Frances, who stood wrapped in a shawl at the head of the stairs.

Charlie watched her go with a lingering look, then trudged into the bar to meet up with his ma and pa.

'Do you reckon it's safe to go back to the Town Hall now?' Jess asked. Her feet felt like blocks of ice and her cheeks tingled, but she wanted to avoid any chance of Maurice getting involved in a brawl. If Chalky had it in for him in some way, they'd best steer clear.

'Storm in a bleeding teacup,' he told her. 'But come down to my place to keep warm, if you like. Ain't no rush, is there?'

Jess let herself be guided down Paradise Court, and over Dolly Ogden's whitened step. Caution went flying on the wind and she let her feelings surface. Soon she was clinging to Maurice in the safety of his room.

He felt her willingness, and every fibre in his body wanted to take advantage of it. Her body seemed part of him already, open and defenceless. He held her close and ran the flat of his hand up and down her back. For a second his mind raced ahead; what if she regretted this later? She might be angry at being rushed into the situation and blame him for it. It might raise a terrible memory. So he pulled back a fraction and stared into her face. 'Are you sure?' he murmured.

Jess stroked his forehead. 'Don't frown.' Then she kissed his face. The voices of her upbringing had fled; the elderly chorus of Sunday schoolteachers and maiden aunts who stood in line down the years, shaking their heads and speaking of respect, decency, reputation. All she saw was Maurice's face, his deep brown eyes and the desire there. 'Kiss me again,' she whispered, drowning in the warm moment.

He unhooked the small fastening of the blue-green silk bodice. There was a layer of thin white silk beneath, held in place by a tie on each shoulder, which easily slid away.

Then he ran his fingertips over her breasts, felt her shiver as he bent to kiss them, felt himself driven on beyond thought by a desperate need to have her.

Jess felt him lift her and gently lay her on the bed. Her eyes were closed. She heard the small snap of his collar studs, the rustle of his shirt lifted over his head. She opened her eyes as she felt the side of the bed dip, and reached out to touch the smoothness of his shoulder and chest. She rested her forefinger in the shallow dish beneath the Adam's apple, then she raised her finger and brushed it across his mouth. He bent with an urgent groan to smother her neck and breasts with kisses, before he pressed her back with the full weight of his long, strong body and kissed her mouth until her lips ached.

Now he roused her with his hands, caressing her in open celebration of her beauty as she consented to more and more intimate moments. He stroked the sleek line from hip to thigh, resting his head against her belly. For the first time in her life she felt delight pass from a man's touch into her own body, and she responded with unselfconscious pleasure. They taught that you gave away something precious to the man you loved, but they had it the wrong way round. She felt Maurice offered her the gift of himself, unguarded, utterly whole. That men could be like this stunned her mind and roused her body. She thrilled and held him to her.

Their love-making over at last, they lay intertwined, falling from breathlessness into gentle contentment and then the strange, redundant moments of shyness, when she gathered the sheets around her and wondered what was the next move. Her clothes lay scattered on the floor. She gazed at him, not knowing what to do or say.

Raised on one elbow, he smudged away signs of her tears, as he had done once before. 'Don't go and cry on me,' he whispered. 'I ain't no good with a handkerchief!' He seemed to read her mind, for, without rushing, he went and gathered her things and put them on the end of the bed within reach. 'You've got lovely hair,' he murmured, running one hand back from her brow across the shining dark mass on the pillow. 'Listen, you get your things on while I go down and make us a cup of tea.'

She laughed. 'You'll give Dolly the fright of her life if they've just got back and you go down like that!'

'The thrill of her life, you mean.' He grabbed some clothes. 'Anyhow, Dolly's up at the Duke, well away by now, I shouldn't wonder.' He went off down the dark stairs.

Jess lay flat on her back for a few moments, staring at the shapes made on the sloping ceiling by cracks in the plaster; a human profile, a starfish. Then she roused herself and got dressed, glad when she went down of the low fire in Dolly's kitchen grate. Maurice kissed her and they hugged close together while they sipped the tea. It was midnight when he took her back up the court. The last drinkers spilled out of the pub. Charlie, Dolly, and Arthur met them fair and square on the doorstep.

Dolly, her free and easy tongue loosened by an evening's sociable drinking, hollered blessings at them. 'That's a girl, you enjoy yourself. You only live once and that's a fact!' She winked at her lodger. 'Mind you treat Jess right, Mr Leigh. She needs someone to look out for her. Don't we all?' She gave Arthur, as inert as his wife was lively, a hefty nudge which unbalanced him on top of Maurice. Maurice set him straight with a good-natured smile.

By this time, Jess could feel herself blushing from head to toe, so she gave Maurice a hasty kiss on the cheek and fled upstairs.

*

Hettie had spent part of the evening with Mary O'Hagan, and become a willing helper in the crowded bed-time routine of the three older children, who washed in cold water at the restored kitchen tap, scraped a comb through their hair and climbed into one big bed, at the end opposite to the three younger ones, already sound asleep.

She noticed signs of improvement. Besides the running water, there was a white cloth on the kitchen table and a piece of net curtain draped across rough twine to block out the worst of the grimy outlook down on to the back court. Mary herself had tidied her hair and made sure her blouse was clean and decent. The washing she'd taken in that day was already laundered. It awaited the iron in neat piles. She welcomed Hettie with a calm smile and offered tea, making only half-hearted attempts to keep the children from clinging to the visitor's skirt.

During the evening, Mary pieced together the family's latest news; Tommy was still on the scene, putting his mind to earning good money in place of poor Daisy. 'Poor boy, he never believed she'd been done in first off. I had to hang on to him to stop him racing straight over the Palace to bring her home. It was all right for us, we had time to get used to it, but poor Tom, it hit him like a hammer. I never seen him look so bad.' Mary's thin, serious face went distant. Hettie took her hand. 'He never got a chance to come to the funeral, see. He never seen her laid in the ground.'

Hettie sat with Mary, marooned in grief, waiting for the sad tale to continue. She said silent prayers.

'At any rate, the poor boy had to believe it in the end. Now he's up with the lark every day, off to Covent Garden, working his barrow to bring back the pennies.' Mary sighed. 'I'm proud of that boy, Hettie. And you'll not believe this, but his poor pa's found work as well. He heard of a job going down at Coopers', and he went across right that minute and they took him on. He came home grinning fit to bust, all swelled up with pride. Now he's bringing in a few shillings again.'

Hettie smiled. Her talk with Edith Cooper had eventually paid off.

Mary patted her friend's hand. 'Joe's not a bad man, only he's been down on his luck. What's a man to do without work, I ask you, except sit on his backside and get down?'

'And worry about rent day coming round,' Hettie agreed. She tried to imagine doleful Joe O'Hagan grinning fit to bust.

Mary nodded. 'We done many a moonlight flit, me, Joe and the kids, and I ain't ashamed to admit it to you. But please God, things will be different now. We turned a corner, thanks to you!' She returned Hettie's hand to her own lap. Through the doorway, six tousled, sleeping heads lay without pillows. The women sat on in companionable, peaceful silence.

A week later, on the 11th of November 1914; a day engraved on their minds for ever, Edith and Jack Cooper stood among the proud parents at Victoria Station, waving their son off to war.

Young men swung up into the carriages, feeling their importance, knowing their destiny. Individual differences faded, marked only by a tartan band on this soldier's cap, a line of gold braid around that sailor's cuff. To a man, they looked down from the open windows with a mixture of defiance and fierce bravado. Instructions from mothers centred on food and frequent letters. Fathers stood by silent, hands behind their backs, feet apart, heads raised to look at the gathering clouds of steam under the giant glass canopy.

'Write soon, Teddy!' Edith Cooper cried, strangled with guilt now that the moment had arrived. Perhaps it was too great a test, merely to restore their good name. He looked young and vulnerable, too fair and soft to face the harsh realities of war. But it was too late.

'Don't fuss, Mother.' Teddy frowned. His Flying Corps uniform encased him in a tough, worldly shell. He leaned out and shook his father by the hand. The train whistle shrieked, the wheels began to shunt. His mother cried along with all the rest.

Teddy leaned out until he lost their heads in a sea of waving hands. Then he ducked inside the carriage and sat down heavily on the buttoned cloth. Soon he was in conversation with an army captain, exchanging regiments, training camps, news of the front and so on. Edith and Jack sat in silence as they drove along suburban streets beneath skeletal trees all swirling in November fogs, between faint pools of gaslight.

Next day before dawn, a heavy knock on the doors of the Duke announced the arrival of a telegram.

Duke came down and slid back the bolts with dread certainty. It was Robert. He held the door open a fraction and took the envelope without speaking, then he closed the door and stood in the empty hallway. The paper shook in his hand.

'I'll open it, Pa.' Frances had come quietly down in her shawl. She put one hand on his shaking arm. The other girls had gathered at the top of the stairs, clutching the necks of their night-dresses. Florrie soon joined them.

He handed the telegram to her.

Frances tore it open. She read the official message and sighed. 'Robert's wounded. He's in the field hospital.'

'Alive?' Duke breathed.

'Wounded. It don't say how bad.' She had to lean on him for support now. She looked up at her sisters.

'But alive.' He took the message and reread it. 'They don't tell you nothing. What we supposed to think?'

Florrie, Hettie, Jess and Sadie came down to stand in the cold hallway. They crowded together for comfort. 'We gotta be patient,' Florrie said. 'They'll look after him and send him back for proper nursing when he's strong enough.'

Frances nodded. Her friend, Rosie Cornwell, took care of cases like that. 'Soon as he gets back, we'll be able to tell. We can go and see him for ourselves . . .' But she remembered the terrible injuries Rosie described; men without limbs, shell-shocked, scarred, with terrible stammers, or blind from exploding bombs. Sadie began to cry.

'Stop that, girl, we ain't lost him,' Duke told her. His hand still shook as he took hold of the banister rail. 'He's one of the lucky ones. We gotta remember that.'

Chapter Twenty-Three

A dark gloom settled on Duke and his family as they waited for news of Robert. A day went by. Hope flickered that his wound would be slight, that his recovery would be swift and complete. After all, he was a strong, fit young man with a good fighting spirit. If enemy shells had failed to finish him off, there was no reason why the doctors and nurses couldn't patch the wound and put him back together as good as new.

This was the opinion of people up and down Paradise Court. They read the bullish reports of battle and transferred the illusion of national invincibility to individual cases like Robert Parsons. He knew how to take care of himself, none better. He'd lived on his wits all his life, and no one had ever got the upper hand. They held in their minds a picture of the tall, strapping lad manhandling great barrels down into the cellar, and the girls remembered him in particular as brazen, handsome Robert Parsons, the ladies' man.

'Any news?' Annie Wiggin asked Florrie when she came into the bar for her evening drink. Though she still looked askance at Florrie's bossy ways, she preferred a quiet word with her rather than bothering Duke directly. Annie felt his unspoken hurt keenly, but she had developed the tact to keep her distance. She knew all too well the torment of waiting to hear news of a loved one. Her old man had put her through two whole years of it before she finally gave up hope.

'Who is it you want to know about this time, Robert or Ernie?' Florrie was up to her elbows in soap suds, washing glasses. 'If it's Ern, there's nothing new. We're moving heaven and earth to get him off. His trial comes up in less than a month.'

'It's bleeding criminal!' Annie said, fired up all of a sudden. 'That's what it is. Makes my blood boil to think of the poor sod banged up in some prison cell. What d'they think they're up to, accusing an innocent man?' She took a savage gulp from her full glass, then calmed down. 'You been to visit?'

Florrie nodded. 'Ett took me along with her last week. White as a sheet, he is, and pining for home. He don't know what's hit him, not really.'

'Any rate, he's in good hands.' Annie had kept in touch with Frances about the work being done by Mr Sewell on Ernie's behalf. 'We gotta hope for the best.'

'Ett says we gotta trust in Jesus,' Florrie said. She turned to lean across the bar and lowered her loud voice. 'Tell me if I'm speaking out of turn here, Annie, but Jesus by himself ain't enough, not to my way of thinking.'

'It's a start, though. With Him on your side, things is bound to get smoother.' Annie didn't consider herself religious, but she paid lip service to God's existence as a kind of insurance premium. 'I go along with Ett. I think we should trust Him.'

Florrie's eyes narrowed further. 'Don't get me wrong, I ain't against a well-meaning prayer or two, don't think that. All I'm saying is it's a good job we got Jess and Frances both doing their bit and all. And it's a good job we got

British justice. Twelve good men and true. I'd rather put my trust in them, if you want to know.'

Annie's mouth went down at the corners. She glanced sideways to make sure that Duke was well out of hearing. 'No, Florrie, I'd put my money on Jesus if I was you. Them other scales is weighted against the likes of Ernie, believe me!'

'No thanks,' Florrie snapped back.

Annie saw she'd put her man-sized boot in it. 'Don't mind me. Of course, we gotta hope for the best, I know that.' She took another swig from her glass. 'Anyhow, what's the news from France? Are they sending Robert home for a drop of Blighty?'

Florrie slung a damp tea-towel across one shoulder and picked up a wooden tray full of clean glasses. 'They are. We got word this morning. They put him on a train last night; he gets back within the hour.'

'Well, that's good, ain't it?' Annie's face lit up with genuine pleasure. 'That's what you all been waiting for.' She nodded at Duke. 'I hear you're getting your boy back tonight!'

He came across. 'We got a telegram. Hettie's going up to Guy's to see him.'

Annie faltered. 'He ain't coming home then?'

'Not straight off. He has to stay in the hospital.' Duke tried to keep a steady gaze and a level voice. 'They want to keep an eye on him for a bit, that's all.' He changed the subject. 'Now then, Annie, what's this I been hearing about you giving young Amy Ogden her old job back? I never knew business was that brisk these days.'

Annie shuffled on her seat. 'It ain't brilliant, I gotta admit. But she's been out of work a fair while now, and I promised her ma I'd keep her out of harm's way. It's coming up to Christmas; you gotta do your bit.'

'There's a lot wouldn't.'

'Well, she ain't a bad little worker. She keeps going on about the bleeding weather though, and I have to tell her to shut it or it gets me down. Otherwise I ain't got no complaints.' She finished off her beer.

Duke picked up the glass. 'Have another one, Annie? It's on the house.'

Annie beamed at sour-looking Florrie. 'Don't mind if I do, Duke. And you tell Jess and Hettie they can come down my stall and get special rates any time they like. Anything they need. I hear their own little business is taking off nicely these days. Cotton thread, darning wool, shoulder pads, bias-binding; I got everything they need nice and cheap. You just tell them that from me, you hear.' She settled in for a good evening. Trouble brought out the best in folk, she thought. If you couldn't trust Jesus or justice, at least you could be sure of your friends and neighbours.

When she heard the news about Robert's home-coming, Sadie went straight down to Charlie's house. Everything had been so gloomy lately that this ray of light made her jump up to visit, even though she knew Charlie didn't like her to call. 'Tell Pa I'm at Charlie's,' she shouted up the street to Frances, just coming home from work. 'Ain't it brilliant? Robert's been sent back home!'

Frances nodded quietly and went up to see Jess and baby Grace. 'I wish to goodness Sadie would calm down a bit,' she complained. 'She's a harum-scarum, and it ain't as if she's a little kid no more.' Frances's own mood had been thrown off balance by a chance word of Billy Wray. Rosie had called in to tell her that his wife, Ada, had been admitted to the women's hospital and was very ill.

Jess glanced up from the bed, where she sat cleaning and

changing the baby. 'Leave off, Frances,' she said. 'It's been tough on Sadie lately. She's only thrilled at Rob being sent home, that's all.'

Frances sighed. 'We ain't heard what's wrong with him yet, though, have we?' She sat heavily at the other side of the bed.

'Ett's just gone off to find out. We'll know before too long, at any rate.' Jess kept busy. She hoped it was bad enough to get him sent home for a good long time, not too bad to have done permanent damage. With luck, they'd have him at home for the trial. He'd be able to come and give evidence in person. Every cloud had a silver lining, she thought.

'Give me a cuddle of my favourite niece!' Frances declared with sudden warmth. She bent to pick up the child, gathering her close and breathing in the smell of clean skin and talcum powder. Grace, fully awake and curious, began to poke her chubby fingers against Frances's lips and nose.

Dolly came slowly to the door to answer Sadie's knock. 'Why, it ain't your birthday, is it?' She stood on the doorstep, arms folded. 'What's up? I ain't missed nothing important, have I?' She too knew that Charlie was funny about Sadie coming to the house.

'No!' Sadie laughed out loud. 'Not yet. But Rob's been sent back. He'll be arriving any minute. I came to tell Charlie!'

Dolly nodded and eased herself back down the corridor. 'In that case, you'd better sit in the front room while I go up and get him.' She smiled pleasantly in response to Sadie's infectious excitement, glad there was something to smile about at last. Maybe the girl would cheer up her moody, touchy son. 'He ain't at work with Mr Leigh tonight, so he'll have a long face on him if I know anything about it. You got your work cut out with him, girl.'

Sadie was shown in, and sat down on a rickety *chaise-longue* in the Ogdens' empty front room. The sofa was covered in torn black calico, with its horsehair stuffing sprouting through in places. It wobbled noisily on the bare, uneven floorboards. The grate lay empty in spite of the cold weather, and the walls, once decorated in fawn-flowered wallpaper, were patchy with damp, dark stains. Soon she heard Dolly's footsteps return downstairs and go through into the kitchen. Several nervous minutes later, she recognized the sound of Charlie's own scuffing feet.

As the door opened, she sprang up to greet him. 'Guess what, Charlie, good news!' she began, darting forward.

Charlie frowned and backed off against the closed door. He felt the bare, bleak meanness of his family circumstances more than he could put into words, but he turned it against Sadie herself. 'I thought I told you not to come bothering me here.'

She paused. The smile faded. 'I didn't think I was bothering you,' she murmured.

'You didn't think, full stop.'

'I thought you'd be glad, Charlie.'

He moved uneasily towards the window, avoiding her gaze. He didn't want to be deflected from saying what he knew he must say. Her big, dark, liquid eyes would put him off. 'Robert gets back tonight, Ma told me,' he said, his voice flat. He stared out at the row of identical houses opposite; no gardens, no railings, no net curtains, nothing. 'That's good.'

Sadie stood there unnerved. She looked a fool, she realized. Dolly could never keep her mouth shut, not even for a second. Sadie's insides started to churn. She clutched the buckle of her belt and began to back off towards the door. 'I just wanted to tell you myself, that's all.'

Charlie nodded. He had to say what he'd decided one night last week when he sat in the projection room at the Gem. Pictures of America flickered on the screen; a great train journey across the Wild West, depicting the exploits of cowboys and gun-slingers. The world was a vast, unexplored territory. The dusty little room was dark. It smelt of hot metal, it whirred as the film rolled past the bright lens. He was stuck in prison and the camera showed him freedom. 'I want us to stop walking out together,' he said in an empty way. 'It ain't no use going on, now the winter's here. It ain't as if we can ride out on Sundays, is it?' He glanced round to judge the effect of his words. The room fell quiet.

'But we can go again in spring,' Sadie said at last. She stared at the back of his head. 'Can't we, Charlie?'

'No, we can't.' He hated her docility. Didn't she realize he was chucking her? Why wasn't she angry?

'Why not? Do you have to give your bike back? We'll get you another one, then it'll be fine.' She came close up behind him, reaching out her hand.

'It ain't fine!' He turned on her. 'Ain't you heard what I said? I want us to stop walking out together, that's what. I'm sick of it!'

Sadie stepped to one side, averting her face as if he'd struck her on the cheek, half-turning away so that her long plait swung round in front of her shoulder. She clutched both hands together.

'What did you have to come here for?' he raged. 'Why can't you stay out of my way? You're always hanging round, showing me up. Can't I do nothing on my own? Can't I?'

His head was thrust towards her, then he rushed past her, pushing her off balance. 'I ain't ready to be tied down,' he said finally. 'Can't you see that?'

Sadie gathered herself. He still stood by the door, one hand on the handle. It seemed he wanted her agreement to break off on his terms. Well, he could think again. 'I ain't tied you down, Charlie Ogden. I enjoyed being with you, and either you lied to me or else you enjoyed being with me too. That ain't tying you down. I listened to all your big ideas and I never said nothing. But you never listened to nothing I said, I know that now. I listened while you rabbited on about being hard done by because you ain't got a garden or a room of your own. Well, poor thing! I ain't got a room of my own neither. I got one brother wounded in the war, no one knows how bad, and one other brother in gaol accused of murder. I got a sister struggling to bring up a baby on her own. And I think they're the bleeding best there is!' She paused, but only to draw breath. 'I love my family, Charlie Ogden, and I loved you too. Not any more. You don't know the meaning of the word, and I'm sorry I wasted my time waiting for you to find out!' She swept past him at the open door. 'Fine words and big ideas, Charlie. That's you from top to bottom. Well, you'd better just go off and do them fine deeds so you can live with yourself, and I wish you lots of bleeding luck!'

Charlie watched her go. The front door slammed.

'Blimey, where did that come from?' Dolly asked from down in the kitchen. She'd overheard every word. 'I got her down for a little mouse, but she put you in your place, son.' She sat sewing stockings. 'Not half!'

Sadie's feet hardly touched the pavement as she flew back up Paradise Court. For the first time in her life she'd been deeply hurt and angry, with Charlie and with herself. But she quietened herself as she pushed through the decorated doors and went upstairs. No one would want to hear her troubles, what with Robert due back tonight. She looked flushed and her heart beat fast as a cat's. 'Ain't Ett back yet?' she asked. Baby Grace was up with a touch of colic, being walked back and forth by Jess, who'd administered gripe water. Frances had the ironing board out by the fire. Freshly ironed clothes lay all around in warm piles.

Charlie waited to confide in Maurice Leigh when he arrived home from work. He came out of the bedroom on to the landing and waited for the older man as he heard his key turn in the lock. 'I had a word with Sadie and I put a stop to things,' he told him, his face grave. 'I told her I didn't want to be tied down.'

Maurice stood, hands in pockets, his hat tipped back. 'No complications?' He remembered his own old, confident motto.

Charlie nodded. 'It's one thing walking out every now and then, but I don't want her hanging around my neck, do I?'

Maurice agreed. 'Course not. But you thrown a good-looking one away there. You sure you know what you've done?' He kept his expression serious, though Charlie's tragic face was a bit over the top in the circumstances. He was young and intense.

Charlie frowned. 'Looks ain't everything.' But he had a sharp flash of memory; Sadie's perfect features stared out from a mass of rich, dark hair as his arms encircled her in the Turkey Trot. 'Brains is important too. She gotta be able to keep up. I ain't gonna be round here much longer, see.'

And then Maurice did smile at the forced bravado. 'Good for you. Beauty and brains. Sounds perfect.' He nodded. 'What would your ma say if I took you up the Duke for a quick drink before closing?' Maurice put a chummy arm around Charlie's shoulder. 'Let's go down and find out, shall we?'

Charlie hesitated. 'Mind you, I wouldn't want to bump into her, would I? Sadie, that is.'

Maurice tutted. 'Hair of the dog,' he declared. 'The sooner the better. Face up to things, come on.' He had his own reasons for wanting a last drink at the pub before closing time. Besides, Charlie had some growing up to do, in his opinion, and he didn't mind lending a hand.

That tea-time, Hettie had insisted on making the short journey to Guy's Hospital alone. 'They won't want crowds of people hanging around the first night,' she warned. 'There'll be a whole bunch of our boys coming home wounded on that train, and you know what Rob's like; he won't want a fuss.'

Reluctantly the others agreed. 'Be sure you ask him everything; how long he's got before they send him back. Every last thing!' Jess was most particular. 'Don't forget nothing.'

'No need to jump the gun,' Duke grumbled. 'Give the boy a chance.' He squeezed Hettie's hand as she set off. 'You look nice and smart,' he said. She was dressed in her greeny-blue outfit and feathered hat.

Hettie grinned. 'Yes, well, I didn't want him dying of shock on me,' she conceded. 'He ain't had time to get used to me being in the Army yet.'

'Me neither. But you go and cheer him up, girl.' The old man watched her step out along the dark street. It didn't seem five minutes since the big send-off. This was modern war, modern life. It moved along too fast. He shook his head clear of hopeless thoughts and went back to work.

Hettie entered the huge doors of the hospital and stepped into an alien world. Outside was the monstrous roar of traffic, the clerks coming home from work, builders clattering up and down scaffolding, factory hands streaming out to the shrill sound of hooters. Inside, all was calm, clean and quiet. Nurses glided down corridors, shrouded in white aprons and nun-like head-dresses. A doctor stuffed a stethoscope into his jacket pocket and went from one ward to another. There was a glimpse of dormitory-style beds and men in pyjamas sitting playing cards at a table by a radiator.

Hettie turned on the spot, wondering where to go next.

'Name?' An overweight man behind a desk inside a glass-partitioned room stuck his head through an open window. Visitors were an untidy intrusion, apparently.

'I want to see Robert Parsons.' She stayed calm, unbuttoning her jacket in the overheated atmosphere.

The cross man checked a list. 'He's in E Ward. Third on the right,' he barked. 'You a relative?'

'His sister,' she confirmed.

He nodded her down the wide corridor straight ahead.

Hettie trod quietly, chin up, refusing to look to left or right at the men in their beds until she reached the sign which told her that this was Robert's ward. By now the smell of disinfectant had seeped through her clothes and into her pores. Sickness, disease, pain were all around. She hesitated, then pushed the door.

She saw a man in a wheelchair, one leg stretched out and resting on a metal platform, his hands shaking, his dark head sunk forward on to his chest. Another lay immobile on his side, bedclothes up to his chin. Another was flat on his back, staring at the ceiling. Hettie looked quickly away from a fourth patient wandering slowly towards her, one side of his face a mass of burned flesh, scarcely healed. Then a nurse came quietly down the central aisle. She smiled at Hettie.

'Robert Parsons,' Hettie whispered, low and nervous.

The girl nodded and led the way down to the far end of the ward. 'Don't expect too much,' she warned. 'And try not to tire him.'

Hettie flashed her a look of panic, but met no response. Instead, the nurse gestured to Robert's bed and went on her way. Hettie approached the bed, afraid and at a loss.

Robert lay propped against pillows, his eyes closed. His face ain't been touched, thank God, was her first reaction. She would have nightmares about that other poor man's burned face. But second thoughts snatched away this reassurance. Robert opened his eyes and she saw that his face had changed beyond measure.

He was Robert, but not Robert, the same in form only. His moustache was shaved, his dark hair very short. His eyes opened in a blank stare which took in her presence but showed no recognition. His hands lay trembling on the folded-down sheet, a wire frame made a tent of the bedclothes.

'Robert!' Hettie rushed forward with a mixture of relief and apprehension. She wanted him to be the same, or at least have a sign that he would be the old Robert eventually. 'It's me, Ett!' She grasped one hand and kissed his cheek.

He submitted to the embrace. She felt his whole frame tremble. There was nothing in his expression to show he knew where he was or why.

'Pa sends his love, and everyone at home.' Hettie struggled for normality. She smoothed his pillow. 'Don't worry, no need for you to talk to me if you're not up to it.' He seemed to be looking at her in bewilderment. 'I'll have a word with the nurse on my way out. She'll put me in the picture.' She drew up a wooden chair and sat close by the bed.

Robert's head rested back on the pillow and he gave up the struggle to make sense of his surroundings. He gazed emptily at her face, unresisting as she stroked his hand, unresponsive to her news.

'We're all keeping well, and baby Grace is thriving. You should see her now. Pa keeps plodding on. Well, he would, wouldn't he? Auntie Flo's settled herself in good and proper, and Ern's just about bearing up.'

Robert sighed and turned his head to the wall.

After a few minutes, the same young, fair-haired nurse returned. 'That's all for today,' she suggested. 'Come back and see him tomorrow.'

Hettie jerked to her feet. She bent to kiss her brother and blindly followed the nurse up the aisle between the beds. 'He ain't always gonna stay like that, is he?' she pleaded. They'd reached the radiator where a group of men sat and played gin rummy.

'Shh!' The nurse glanced at her other patients. 'Your brother's suffering from shock, that's all.'

'It'll wear off, won't it?'

The nurse nodded. 'In time. He needs to rest.'

'He'll know us if we come back tomorrow?'

'Maybe. It might take longer, considering his injuries.' She studied Hettie's face. 'Weren't you told?'

Slowly Hettie shook her head. 'We ain't been told nothing, only that he's wounded.'

'Well, it was bad, I'm afraid. He lay in no man's land for quite a time, apparently. He lost a lot of blood.' The young nurse saw she'd better get the news over with. 'Someone went over the top to get him and bring him back. He owes his life to that friend.'

Hettie nodded. 'It's his legs, ain't it?' She remembered the wire cage that lifted the bedclothes high in a ridge shape.

'One leg in particular. The right one. They had to amputate it there and then. There was no hope of saving it.'

Hettie hid her face in her hands.

'There are deep shrapnel wounds to that side of the body as well. He was in a lot of pain, but he's well sedated now.'

'Is that why he don't know me? It's the stuff you give him for the pain?' Hettie clutched at straws.

'Partly.' The nurse was reluctant to commit herself. She touched Hettie's elbow. 'Listen, why don't you go on home now and come back tomorrow. Wait and see.'

Hettie nodded and walked mechanically through the doors up the corridor to the main entrance.

The porter at the desk spotted her. 'Bad news?' he asked.

Tears came to her eyes as she nodded. 'Worse luck.'

'Never mind, I seen it day in, day out,' the man said. 'Poor bleeders, won't none of them ever be the same again. It's a bad business, if you ask me.' He wandered from his office and saw her through the door. 'You get a cab, girl,' he advised. 'Blow the expense. You don't want to be walking home in this.' He stuck his hand out into the rain which pelted into the dark puddles. 'Here, I'll go and get hold of one for you.'

He signalled to a taxi idling at the gate, went up to the driver and thrust his head close to the window. 'Take the girl home. She's had a bit of a shock.'

The cabman nodded. Hettie saw the back door swing open and remembered it was Robert's ambition to own a taxi. She got in. 'Paradise Court on Duke Street,' she said. The taxi jolted forward through the rain. What am I gonna

312

tell Pa? Hettie wondered. This'll break his heart once and for all. The thought of it choked her with more unshed tears. All too soon the taxi rolled past Coopers' and drew to a halt outside the Duke.

Chapter Twenty-Four

Annie saw Hettie walk, head bowed, from the taxi to the pub door. She'd positioned herself by the window as lookout, and she could see from Hettie's bearing that the news wasn't good. She went out quickly to meet her in the corridor. 'How bad?' She grasped Hettie's wrist and stared anxiously into her eyes.

Hettie reported the bare facts.

Annie gasped and nodded. 'Poor bleeder. Now, chin up, girl. I'm right beside you. You think you can manage to tell your pa?' She had an arm around Hettie's waist for support. 'You go on up while I fetch him.'

Glad to be relieved of at least part of the burden, Hettie did as she was told. Her limbs felt heavy, her head light as she climbed the stairs looking pale and shocked. Frances, Sadie and Jess welcomed her in silence.

'I'll go get Pa!' Sadie stammered. She looked wildly at Frances.

'No, Annie's fetching him.' Hettie shook her head and stood as if in a dream. 'I can hear him now.'

They waited for what seemed like an age as Duke's heavy tread came upstairs.

'He ain't gonna die, is he?' Sadie cried, terrified.

Jess held her tight. 'Hush!' she said.

Duke appeared in the doorway, Annie hovering behind. He knew from Annie's manner that he should expect the worst, so he came up grim-faced but prepared. 'Sit down, girl,' he said to Hettie. Frances brought a chair from the table and sat her down. 'Now take your time, just tell us what he got.' He was determined to stay calm, whatever the news.

Hettie looked up at him and took courage. He was strong enough to take the blow, after all. She saw the set of his jaw, the broad shoulders. 'It ain't just a Blighty one, Pa. He never even knew who I was. He looked straight through me!'

Duke nodded. 'But what's he got?'

'Shrapnel down his right side.'

He nodded again.

'And his leg.' She pointed to her own right thigh with a shaking finger. 'They had to take it off.'

A shudder gripped them, but Duke was the first to recover. 'Anything else?'

Hettie shook her head. 'He's full of stuff for the pain. He don't even know where he is or nothing.'

Duke remembered his own fighting days; the wild, rolling eyes of men too close to bullet and blade, the death-haunted look of those who crawled back to consciousness as their shattered bodies were lifted on to stretchers off the battlefield. He knew enough to realize that the horror would fade. But he drew a choking breath and looked blankly at Annie.

Her eyes widened in a defiant challenge. 'Now don't you give way, none of you. It ain't like you, Duke Parsons!'

Her words were a key to action. Frances went straight down to Florrie to hand on the news. Jess took Hettie's hat and coat, Sadie went to make tea. Duke talked of Rob getting well enough to come home and told Hettie not to worry, the shock would wear off; Rob would soon be his old self again. Annie nodded in satisfaction.

'I'll be off then,' she said, as soon as Sadie brought in the tea.

Duke followed her on to the landing. 'Thanks, Annie,' he said. He bowed his head in embarrassment.

'Ain't nothing to thank me for,' she said, a touch too quick and sharp. There was a catch in her voice.

'Well, thanks anyway.' Duke rested his arm on the banister and stared down at the patterned carpet. 'Robert!' he said with a sigh and a shake of the head.

'Yes,' Annie agreed. 'Robert.'

Duke looked up. 'You know he was the best boxer around here, Annie. The best by a mile.'

'He was.' Her eyes filled with tears. Quickly she grasped his hand, then turned and went downstairs.

The round of visiting Robert in hospital began next day. They went in shifts, with a determined cheerfulness, bustling down the ward with fruit, flowers and messages from half of Paradise Court.

Robert gave a sign of recognition as Duke bent over him. Next time, he reached out his hand to Sadie. Then he asked to be propped up and he spoke to Jess. Each visit saw such an improvement that the good cheer grew less forced and began to spread to other casualties in nearby beds.

'Bleeding hell, mate, how many sisters you got?' The man with the burned face, a sergeant from a cavalry regiment, asked enviously.

'Four.' Robert looked up the length of the ward, waiting for the influx of visitors. It was his fifth day in the hospital. His head was clear now, but each day opened up fresh memories of the moment when the shell landed with a soft whistle and a thud before the whole world exploded in a cascade of mud and stones. He preferred to keep talking about other things; anything to keep his mind off that moment. So he looked for the day's visitors with visible impatience.

'Blimey. Ain't none of them married?'

'No. Why?' He was prickly with the other men. Their scars and injuries reminded him of his own.

'Nothing. You can lend me one if you like.'

Robert glanced at the man's disfigured face. We're all in the same boat, he thought. 'You'd better ask them, pal,' he grinned. 'Here they come now.'

Sadie and Frances hurried down between the rows of beds with bright hellos to right and left. Frances brought him a book on the motor car from the library. Sadie sat on the edge of his bed. She stared critically at him. 'I been thinking, Rob,' she began.

'Oh, don't do that,' he reproached.

'No, I been thinking. You should grow back your moustache.'

He laughed. 'You think so?'

'Yes. You look ever so much more handsome with it, don't he, Frances?'

The older woman entered into the spirit. 'You do, Rob. Irresistible.'

He felt the stubble on his chin. 'How about a beard to match?'

'Oh no!' Sadie gave a little shriek. 'That's old hat, that is!'

'Old hat, is it?' He winked at his neighbour. 'A great big bushy beard?'

'You'd look like some old grandpa, wouldn't he, Frances. Don't let him grow a beard.'

The teasing went on from visit to visit, though sometimes there was a more serious interlude. Hettie explained her decision to join the Salvation Army after Daisy's murder, and she gave news of the O'Hagans. Eventually, Robert asked Jess about Ernie.

'His trial comes up on the tenth,' Jess told him. She described her fruitless visits to Teddy Cooper and Freddie Mills. 'I ain't got nowhere, and the coppers are playing things close to their chests.' Now that Robert was prepared to talk about things, she leaned in close to the bed. 'Rob, there ain't nothing else that you can think of that might help, is there? I know you told it all once already in the written statement for Mr Sewell, but if you can bear to think again and go through it, not missing a single thing!' She spoke urgently. 'Ernie goes blank when he gets to the part about waiting for you outside the stage door. He keeps on saying he's sorry. That don't look good, you see. But we can't get him to remember what he did next. No one can. And then they're gonna ask him why he just ran off and left the place, instead of waiting till you showed up.'

'He can't remember that neither?'

She shook her head. 'And there's one other thing, Rob.' Jess checked up and down the ward. 'If they get me up on the stand, they gonna ask me how Ernie was when he got back home.'

'And?'

'I'm gonna have to say how I cleaned him up.' She explained about the blood on Ernie's boots. 'If I swear on the Bible, I won't be able to tell a lie, will I? Then they're gonna ask me why I ain't said nothing sooner.'

Robert threw back his head and pinched the skin on his exposed throat. 'Bleeding hell!' he said. Then he looked directly at her. 'How many weeks have we got? Two? Three?'

318

'Three.'

'Get me out of this bleeding bed!' he cursed. 'Tell Mr Sewell I'll get myself to that bleeding court if it kills me. Tell Ern not to worry, I'll be there!'

Jess soothed him and promised to give Ernie the message. 'It'll make a difference to him, Rob, honest to God. He'll want you there to help him.'

'I'll be there,' Robert promised. 'I'll be in a bleeding wheelchair, but I'll be there.'

Ernie's trial began at ten o'clock on Tuesday, the 10th of December; a peculiar cross between entertainment and reality. The newspapers had got hold of it as an example of what can go wrong in a family if rules of conduct are too lax and discipline not maintained. The *Express* in particular painted a picture of a motherless boy dragged up in rooms over an East End pub, daily witness to drunkenness and all kinds of brutish, hooligan behaviour. Duke was picked out for special blame. 'Modern parents should not allow the art of flogging to pass into the limbo of forgotten achievements,' the paper intoned. Flogging would have set the accused on the right track and prevented the tragedy at the Southwark Palace. Such families, knee deep in vendettas and street fights, were a hotbed for violent crime.

They printed a picture of Ernie above a caption which read, 'It's a fair cop!' It set the courtroom buzzing with expectation as people crowded into the public gallery, awaiting the arrival of the accused.

Quickly the court filled up. Men came in with bundles of official-looking papers, which they laid out along tables in precise order. A woman came to sit on a high stool behind a typewriter. The jury-box was soon occupied by two rows of serious men, more at ease behind shop counters or desks in banks and offices than in this heightened atmosphere where life and death was at their disposal.

There was a stir in the gallery as Duke Parsons entered below into the main body of the court. He pushed his son in a wheelchair, with all four of his daughters following behind. A ripple of identification ran through the ranks of spectators, then one of puzzlement. This didn't look like the ruffian family depicted in newspaper accounts.

Duke was dressed in a dark suit, a heavy watch chain slung across his broad chest. His starched collar, the shine of his boots could attract no whiff of disapproval. There was even something dignified about him as he manoeuvred the wheelchair down the central aisle, then stood to one side to let the women pass into a row of seats kept vacant for them.

Frances didn't allow her gaze to flicker. She looked straight ahead, as if in church. The story in the paper had sliced into her soul, then brought out her proud resistance. By her presence she would prove every word a filthy slur and a lie. Hettie followed, holding Sadie's hand, each taking their tone from Frances. They'd taken care to dress up, not flamboyantly, but decent and smart, to give Ernie a boost and to prove the reporters wrong. Even Hettie had shed her Army uniform, to appear in court in her best green outfit. She felt it would attract less attention, and she didn't want to risk offending some members of the jury with her teetotal stance. Jess bent to speak a word with Robert, nodded, then proceeded to her seat. Duke set the brake on the wheelchair and sat down at last, shoulders back, head up.

'Wounded in France,' ran the whisper around the gallery. 'Oldest son . . . volunteered for action . . . saved by a pal.'

Robert took the force of their concentrated gaze. He

wanted to meet expectations. How would a proud, wounded hero react? He felt unsure, aware of the gap between their perception and his sense of the truth as it happened, there amongst the roaring guns and stuttering rifles. So he resorted to a stiff glare at the empty judge's seat. It seemed to satisfy. You could almost hear and touch public opinion as it shifted and swung behind the whole Parsons family.

Up in the gallery, Annie Wiggin and Florrie Searles, strange bedfellows during this crisis, helped things along. They conferred over the quality of the jurors; one looked pinched and mean, another too full of himself, but one, two, three on the right looked solid, decent sorts. Dolly Ogden, standing behind, poked Annie to draw her attention as the lawyers came in. Then a door rattled out of sight and two police officers preceded Ernie out of the cells. They walked impassively ahead.

Ernie emerged from his lonely, dark wait and ducked his head away from the massive room full of strangers. He stopped dead, until a third officer moved him on from behind. Then he shifted on again into the dock. There was a sea of faces, a babble of voices as he climbed three steps and sat alone and terrified in the seat of the accused.

A warder jerked him to his feet as a gavel rattled down on a desk and the procession of crimson and fur robes and curled wigs approached the platform from the side.

The judge sat in the central carved seat, flanked by lesser court officials. As he settled, pulling his robes close around his legs, he glanced at Ernie. Removed by ritual and by long years of administering justice, his cold eyes simply registered the usual; a raw young man spruced up for the occasion, but with a downtrodden look. He flickered a second glance into the body of the court to where the relatives sat, tight-jawed and upright. He was impassive to the point of boredom, hoping for no nonsense and a swift conclusion.

The family hardly spared a moment to assess their chances with Judge Berry. Ernie claimed every scrap of their attention as he struggled to hold up his head. Once he'd spotted them, he kept his eyes glued to their bench, and as proceedings began, his every move was dictated by his pa's silent, patient signs. He stood when Duke stood for the judge to enter. He sat at Duke's firm nod. He swivelled his body towards the men in wigs when they began to talk, but his gaze never stole away from the reassuring sight of his family all lined up to help.

Robert meanwhile suffered badly from the stares of all his old friends up in the gallery, facing them for the first time since his injury. He knew they were judging the changes in him; the stigma of his wheelchair, his white, drawn look and trembling hands. But all protest was beyond him. Just as in the hospital, you had to submit. Here it was different rules and regulations, but they kept you tied down just the same. They prevented you from speaking out when your family was under attack, and people drove their knives of accusation into the heart of your existence. The very language shanghaied him; the 'm'luds', 'm'learned friends', 'aforesaids' and 'incriminating evidence'. Their posture spoke of privilege as they hooked their thumbs inside the front bands of their silk gowns and strutted down the centre of the court, wigs perched, pivoting on metal-tipped, polished shoes. He sat there angry and helpless as the prosecution presented their case.

Hettie took the witness stand first and swore her oath. She stood up high, recalling the night in question; the time, the place, the position in which she'd discovered her friend's body. In the corner of the gallery, almost hidden, stood Mary and Tommy O'Hagan. Hettie answered with honest simplicity and a touching faith in the truth. Earnest prayers had shown her the way; the blame would shift and rest on the right person if only she told the truth.

'Tell me, Miss Parsons, were you expecting to meet the victim, Daisy O'Hagan, on that particular night?' Charles Forster, prosecuting counsel, paused by the witness stand. He was a tall man with white hair and shadowy grey features. His voice was deceptively smooth and polite. 'It was your custom, was it not?'

Hettie nodded. 'Daisy never said nothing about going off by herself. That's why I went back to look for her.'

'Had you already looked?'

'Yes, and I asked around the whole place. One of the girls said she'd seen her go off to meet someone at the stage door, but that was earlier on.'

'She went off to the stage door, you say?' Forster sounded merely curious.

'That's what they said. I ain't seen her.'

'Did they say whom she'd gone to meet at the stage door?'

'I don't know. Some gentleman, I expect.' Hettie returned his stare.

'Did they say *which* gentleman?'

'No, sir. It could've been anyone.'

'Hm.' Forster's expression was disapproving. 'So it seems the victim had an assignation at the stage door.' He raised an eyebrow at the jury-box. 'Let's proceed. What did you do next, Miss Parsons, when you failed to find your friend?'

'I seen Mr Mills looking for her, and . . .'

'Mr Mills?'

'The manager. He had her wages. He wanted to get hold of Daisy to hand over her money.'

Forster nodded. Sewell, sitting beside another bewigged figure, wrote a short note and slid it along the table. 'But eventually you left the building, Miss Parsons?'

'Yes, sir.'

'Assuming that the victim had met her gentleman friend and gone off. Now tell the court why you returned and made the unfortunate discovery.'

Hettie gave a small frown. 'I met up with Robert out on the street.' She looked down at the barrister and answered his brief prompt. 'My brother, Robert. He asked me, had I seen Ernie 'cos he'd lost him. Ernie's my other brother.' She glanced towards the dock. 'I said we'd best go back. Ern was bound to be waiting at the stage door. He never went nowhere without us. So we went back.'

There was more urgent scribbling at both defence and prosecution benches.

'And was he at the stage door?'

'No, sir.'

'That was most unusual, you say? So where was he, do you know?'

'No, sir. It was after that I went in and found Daisy, like I told you.' Hettie's head went down for the first time. Her eyelids pricked with tears.

'And when in fact did you next see your brother, Ernie?'

'Back home, sir.'

'Not where, but when, Miss Parsons. That same night?'

'No, sir. He was already in bed when me and Rob got back. I never saw him till breakfast.'

'I see.' Forster backed off with raised eyebrows. He sniffed, checked the brief on his desk and finished with his witness with an air of quiet satisfaction. The case had begun nicely.

The sergeant and the inspector from Union Street cemented it firmly in place, identifying for the jury the time of events, the unusual amount of violence used against the victim, the position of the murder weapon after it had skidded across the floor away from the body.

'Thrown down in haste, would you say?' Forster suggested.

The sergeant nodded. 'I'd say so, yes, sir. Not very clever. Done in a panic before the murderer ran off.'

'What kind of knife, Sergeant Matthews?'

'Kitchen knife, sir. Ordinary type with a bone handle, a six-inch blade.' The sergeant performed his duty with minimum fuss. 'Available from any ironmonger's.'

'Including Powells' of Duke Street, Sergeant?' Forster loaded his voice with quiet significance.

Mayhew, the defence counsel, objected. If the type of knife was commonly available, he argued, the fact that it was on sale at Powells' could not be considered relevant. The judge agreed. Jess looked along the row at Frances and nodded.

Forster inclined his head towards the bench. Unfortunately, the police had not been able to pin down the shopkeeper, Powell, over the purchase of that particular knife. He had to let it go, but he turned energetically back to his witness. 'Did you subject the weapon to forensic scrutiny, Sergeant Matthews?'

'We did, sir, and we found fingerprints on the handle.' The sergeant rocked on to his heels as a ripple of renewed attention ran through the room.

'Could you identify those fingerprints for the court?'

'Yes, sir. They appear as item number three in evidence for the prosecution. They belong to the accused, Ernest Parsons.'

There was a gasp. Prosecuting counsel executed a turn and clipped his heels together. Then he dipped his head to the judge and returned to his seat.

Duke sat looking steadily at Ernie, while the others dropped their gaze under the dual weight of confusion and shock. Ernie had touched the knife. Fingerprints couldn't lie. Defence cross-questioning continued in a haze, and they were well into the inspector's testimony before the family could gather their concentration.

'Now, during your interview with the accused at Union Street police station, Inspector, did he give an indication as to why he had waited at the stage door in the first place?' Forster was in full swing.

'Yes, sir. He expected his brother, Robert, to join him there, to wait for the girls, Hettie Parsons and Daisy O'Hagan.'

'And did he? Did his brother eventually join him?'

'We don't know, sir. According to him, the last thing he can recall is arriving at the appointed spot.' The inspector turned a page on his notepad set down on the ledge in the witness-box. He looked up sharply to field the next question.

'But you found fingerprints belonging to the accused on the murder weapon, did you not? Do you have any other evidence to corroborate Ernie Parsons's presence at the scene?' Forster led him on, sure of his ground.

'Yes, sir. We found his cap, item number two in evidence for the prosecution, down in one corner of the girls' dressing room, as if it had fallen off and been kicked about a bit.'

'In a struggle? Is that what you suggest?'

'That's how it looked to my men, yes, sir.'

'And in his written statement, is it true that the accused admits to having done something he was sorry for on that occasion?'

This was another question guaranteed to raise the tension in the court. There was an intake of breath. Robert gripped the arms of his wheelchair until his knuckles turned white. Hettie, unnerved by her own time on the stand, stared down at her lap.

The inspector cleared his throat and picked up the notepad. He read in a loud, clear voice. 'Yes, sir. He said, "I never meant to do it. Tell Rob I never meant to!" He said it twice, sir. There was no doubt.'

Forster nodded and pursed his lips. '"I never meant to do it."' He repeated the phrase deliberately and looked accusingly at Ernie. '"I never meant to do it." We all do many things we never mean to do, on the spur of the moment, and often they give cause for regret. Our temper snaps, we lose control, isn't that so, Inspector?'

'In crimes of this type, that's true in my experience, yes, sir.'

'And would you say that the accused has a temper like anyone else? That he might be prey to jealousy if the girl he wants is seen taking up with another man, for instance? That he might very well lose control and snap, as we say? What would be your opinion on that, Inspector?'

'Like you say, sir, he ain't no different. Same as the next man, if provoked. Only not too bright and not open to reason, in my judgement. I can see a case of him choosing the wrong girl and having to stand by and watch her chuck him over for someone else. Well, it's obvious what might happen then.' The inspector gave a worldly shrug.

If his family could stand up and shout, right then and there, 'You don't know Ernie. He ain't the same. He's gentle as a lamb, there ain't no harm in him!' they would bring the trial to a shambling halt. But you had to live with him to know him; poor, gentle Ernie, just bright enough to realize his own shortcomings, ever anxious to make himself acceptable in spite of them. He never 'wanted' anything in his life and just took it; least of all Daisy, least of all a life. Yet he sat with a puzzled frown, shaking his head at his pa, seeing through a daze that things were not going well now.

Fred Mills came next, suave and sneering about Daisy. Yes, it was possible she was seeing more than one man at once. Yes, he'd seen her walk home with Ernie Parsons on more than one occasion, but that wouldn't stop her from going with other men. She liked the ones who gave her presents and she knew how to lead them on. Mills painted the picture of a cheap flirt who might provoke a man to violence. He seemed not to care that her mother stood in the gallery, and he cast a cold look at Hettie, sitting subdued and strained alongside her sisters.

Mayhew cross-examined him. Had he managed to find Daisy and give her the wages owed?

'No, sir. The other girls told me she must have gone off early, so I left it.'

'Was that normal, Mr Mills?'

'Not really, no.' The manager's mouth twitched side-ways. He looked disgruntled.

'And weren't you suspicious? That a girl should go off home without her wages?'

'I'm not her keeper,' came the flippant answer.

'Yes or no will do, Mr Mills,' Judge Berry interposed wearily. 'And we keep a civil tongue here.'

Mills breathed loudly through his nose. 'No, I wasn't suspicious. I didn't think it was my business.'

'Weren't you worried?' Mayhew pressed the point. He was dogged; a dark-haired, olive-skinned man, much younger than his opponent, Forster. 'Forget suspicion. Weren't you perhaps alarmed that a girl in your employ, not yet twenty years of age, seemed to have simply disap-peared into the maze of London streets, late at night, in the dark?'

'No,' Mills insisted through gritted teeth.

'So you stayed inside the building and forgot all about her?'

'Yes, I went back to my office.'

'To count the takings, no doubt. Did anyone see you during that time?'

The witness stared him out as he answered with a note of triumph. 'In my office, you mean? As a matter of fact, yes. I was with Archie Small.'

The gallery gave a deflated sigh. 'Just when he was getting his claws into the oily bleeder, he comes up with an alibi!' Florrie scowled her disbelief.

Annie grunted. 'Them two's thick as thieves,' she grumbled. 'Mills and Small. I wonder what they've got to bleeding hide!'

Mayhew, dashed but not defeated, came at his witness once more. 'Would you please describe your relationship with the victim, Mr Mills,' he said coolly.

'What are you getting at?' Mills was visibly rattled. His suave exterior gave way.

'Answer the question,' the judge commanded.

'I gave her the work. I paid her wages.'

'So you never took what might be called a romantic interest in Daisy O'Hagan, Mr Mills?'

The manager's laugh struck a dry, hollow note. 'Not me, mister. Strictly professional, that's me.'

Mayhew continued with his sceptical tone. 'And what about your friend and alibi, Mr Small? To your knowledge, was he in any way other than professionally involved with Miss O'Hagan?'

Mills turned to the judge. 'He's a married man, Your Honour!'

This time, some spectators responded with a laugh. Moral outrage sat absurdly on the cynical manager's shoulders. Berry's hooded eyes closed for a moment in exasperation. Mayhew, seeing that the judge's tolerance had reached its limit, backed off. But Mills was exposed as a nasty character. Set alongside Hettie, with defence evidence yet to come, Mills had come off badly. Archie Small would back up his alibi, no doubt, but first the court must deal with a witness whom no one in the gallery had expected.

Syd Swan came on to the stand to open disapproval. No one liked the blunt-featured, crude individual who took a sly interest in all the girls and had fingers in many of Chalky White's shady deals.

In the gallery, Dolly frowned at Amy for having taken up with such an unpopular figure. 'You can certainly pick them, girl,' she growled. Swan had never completely emerged from the pimply stage; there was something grubby and unappealing about him. His head hung slightly forward off hunched shoulders. He looked furtive even when trying to impress, as now.

'Hush, Ma!' Amy squirmed.

Down in the middle aisle, Robert's grip on his wheelchair tightened. His skin felt lousy, as in the trenches. Just looking at Swan made his flesh creep. But yes, he had been there that night, hanging around under a dark archway, giving chase when he spotted Robert. Now no doubt he'd have more 'incriminating evidence' for the jury to consider. Robert's throat constricted with rage and helplessness.

New spectators entered the public gallery as Swan swore the oath. Maurice Leigh and Walter Davidson had met up by chance outside the courtroom and made their way in together, discussing Ernie's case as they went. Maurice had come as early as he could, to lend Jess moral support. 'I only hope it goes the right way,' he said to Walter. 'It'll break Jess's heart if they go and hang him.'

The phrase stunned good-hearted Walter. It seemed out

of the question until you heard it spoken. 'They wouldn't,' he said quietly.

'They hung a flower seller in Shoreditch that time. Margaret Murphy, the one what done her kid in.' Maurice peered through the door to seize their time to enter. The court usher was handing the Bible to the witness. 'And they hung that farm boy last year. Eighteen years old. Then they found out he hadn't done the murder, too bleeding late.'

'Not this time, they won't.' Walter strode past Maurice into the mass of spectators. He spotted Chalky White coming in through an entrance opposite, then lost him in the crowd.

Forster's questions for Swan were brief and simple. He established his witness's rivalry with the older Parsons brother, Robert, which had come to a head after the performance at the Palace. He pictured for the court the chase that took place between them just at the crucial time when the accused had come out of the theatre in search of that brother. Robert listened, a bitter taste in his mouth, unable to look at either Ernie or Duke.

'Now then, Mr Swan, what did you do after Mr Parsons had given you the slip?' Forster could feel the initiative returning to him.

'We walked back to the Palace.' Syd stood gripping the ledge of the witness stand. He leaned forward, eager to lay the blame.

'How many of you?'

'Three or four.'

'For what purpose?'

Syd shrugged. 'I dunno. We was having a lark, that's all.'

'Looking for girls, Mr Swan?'

He leered. 'Could be.'

'But you didn't find any?' Forster pretended to condone the rough code of picking up fair game in the street.

'We left it too late, see.'

The judge sat back in his seat. Forster rolled his eyes at his witness's informality. 'Whom did you see outside the Palace after your return?'

This was Syd's star part. He leaned even further out of the box. 'We seen Ernie Parsons.'

'Where, exactly?'

'He was running up out of the side alley from the stage door, going hell for leather. Never seen nothing like it. He was moaning and yelling something, I couldn't make out what. First we heard him, then he comes pelting out on to the street, a proper bleeding mess.'

'In a panic, would you say?'

'Not half.'

'You say you couldn't make out what he said, Mr Swan?'

Syd paused. He caught Chalky's eye up in the gallery, certain that his standing had shot sky high with his leader and all the rest of the gang. 'Just one word,' he told the court. 'I just made out the one word.'

'What was that?' Forster stopped pacing and rested one knuckle on top of his pile of papers. He looked directly at Ernie as Swan gave his final answer.

'"Daisy,"' came the reply. 'Lots of times, over and over, before he runs off like a mad thing. "Daisy. Daisy. Daisy."'

Chapter Twenty-Five

An unofficial jury gathered that evening in the public bar at the Duke. Some felt that the first day of the trial had gone as well as could be expected. They liked Mayhew's style; he came across straight, unlike the puffed-up, insincere Forster.

'I reckon him and Sewell make a good team,' Dolly told Florrie, who stood staunchly behind the bar while the rest of the family pulled themselves together upstairs. Joxer too had come in as regular as clockwork through all this, steadily minding his own business and never missing a day. 'Frances did well to find them two.'

Florrie nodded. 'They got Ernie's best interests at heart. They're thinking of leaving well alone and not dragging him on to the stand as a witness.'

'Why not?' Amy couldn't see the point. Surely they'd want to get Ernie to stand up and say he wasn't guilty for all to hear.

'They think he might panic.' Florrie couldn't make up her own mind about this. On the one hand, she thought Ern could win the jury over, on the other hand he might well go to pieces.

'If that bleeding Forster gets at him,' Annie explained, 'he can twist things round and make them look bad. Poor Ernie ain't no match for him.'

Everyone nodded uneasily.

'But we'll have other witnesses speaking up for us.' Florrie tried to rescue the mood.

Arthur Ogden, well dug in by the pianola, agreed. 'We got Robert home for a start.'

'They'll take to him all right,' Dolly said. 'They're gonna have to see they ain't dealing with a pack of ruffians when he gets on the stand. He'll wear his uniform, I hope?' She glanced at Florrie for confirmation. 'Well, he still looks big and handsome, poor bloke, and very decent. He'll stand up for Ernie.'

Several bystanders picked up on the awkwardness of her choice of phrase, and stuck their faces deep into their beer glasses. Amy wondered privately how they would manage to get the wheelchair up the steps into the stand. Walter Davidson frowned and shook his head in Maurice's direction.

'Ain't Hettie done well?' Annie put in to change the subject. 'There ain't a drop of cunning in that girl. Nice and clean and honest, she came across. And not going on about Jesus neither, thank God.'

Dolly turned up her nose. 'It's all right, Annie Wiggin, everyone here knows you ain't been to church in a month of Sundays. If you ask me, Ett should've worn her Army uniform and all.'

Annie disagreed. 'It'd put them off. They're all fond of a drink or two, I bet.'

'Who is?' Arthur was slow to follow.

'Them geezers on the jury. They like Ett the way she was, an honest, good-looking girl.'

No one mentioned the police evidence and the weight it must carry. 'That Syd Swan's a bleeding smarmy bastard,' Walter said with unusual force.

Amy felt her face glow red. Walter realized he must have

missed something. When no one put in a word in Syd's defence, Amy stuck her head in the air and waltzed out.

'You put your bleeding foot in it there, mate,' Annie told Walter. She nudged him and looked over her shoulder at the swinging door.

'Serve her right,' Dolly said. Her relationship with her daughter hadn't improved of late. There were fewer rows, but each pretended she couldn't care less what the other thought. Dolly said Amy could go out with whoever she bleeding well chose and get herself done in, like poor Daisy O'Hagan. Amy said she could look after herself and do as she liked. 'Walter's right. Syd Swan's a nasty, creeping sort. Look how he tried to put the blame on Ernie today,' Dolly said. She looked at her beer as if it had suddenly turned sour.

Just then, the door opened again. Jess held it wide from outside to let Robert wheel himself through. The awkward silence broke as Walter moved forward to greet his old friend. He admired the man's nerve; shot to bits, just out of hospital, but wheeling himself in to see the old crowd. Walter caught Robert's eye and shook hands with genuine warmth. 'What'll you have to drink, Rob? The usual?'

Jess managed a smile as she joined Maurice at the bar. The deep affection between them grew day by day, despite the poor circumstances. An important step had been taken when they first allowed people to notice them as a couple at the Town Hall dance. Now, whenever Maurice called into the Duke for a drink, the shout went up to go and tell Jess that her young man was here. 'You on your way to work?' she asked him as he looped an arm around her waist.

'Yes, I got ten minutes though.'

'How do you think it went today?' She looked up into his face.

'We was saying, well as can be expected.' Maurice's own feeling was gloomier and perhaps more realistic than the general opinion. He'd picked up the police evidence from a fellow spectator, and seen the reaction to Syd Swan's dramatic testimony. But he didn't want to dash Jess's hopes.

'Hm.' Jess looked worried none the less.

They switched to safe small-talk, and as Maurice got ready to go, he crossed paths at the door with a crowd of new drinkers, including Syd Swan and Chalky White. They came in off the street with careless bravado. Instinctively Maurice ducked back into the room to keep an eye on things and to make sure Jess could cope with the unwelcome intrusion.

Chalky and Syd were all dressed up. They strode in as if they owned the place, knowing smiles passing between them. Whitey Lewis went up to Florrie to order drinks. Someone went over and fingered the keys of the pianola, setting up a tuneless sprinkling of notes.

Florrie's glance darted towards Robert. He'd picked up on their entrance right away, though his back was turned. His jaw was clenched tight. Walter put one hand on his shoulder. Behind them all, Duke came through the double doors.

'Give the men a drink, Florrie.' He sounded matter of fact, striding across the bar and lifting the counter flap. He reached up to a high shelf for clean glasses, lining them up for Florrie to fill. All the while he kept his eyes fixed on Syd Swan.

Some of the regular drinkers began to mutter. Dolly led an exodus of women away from the bar to the furthest corner of the room. But the gang enjoyed this demonstration in a thick-skinned, insulting way. It proved they were having an effect.

Duke switched his gaze to Robert. The boy's suffering

was too much to bear. 'Pa!' Jess cut in. 'You gotta get rid of them!'

He took a deep breath. A fight was the last thing he wanted. But he was landlord here, and he could sense everyone was behind him in slinging them out. He would keep it calm, but he'd get them out. He counted five of them, then nodded firmly in the direction of each one of his own supporters; Walter, Maurice, and if it came to it, Arthur Ogden and some of the older men. Joxer lined up alongside his boss. One look at his grim face and iron-hard frame would send most men running for the door.

Syd looked uneasily at Chalky for direction. He'd agreed to this for a lark, and because Chalky had been set on carrying it out. 'It's my local,' he'd bragged. 'Ain't no reason why we can't go in for a quiet drink, is there?'

'You want to set the bleeding cat among the pigeons, you do.' Whitey had woken up to the possibilities. He was keener on a good scrap than Syd.

'You're right there, Whitey. What's wrong with reminding them Parsons that they got themselves in a spot of bother when their boy done that poor girl in?'

Out on the cold street the gang had laughed at Chalky's false concern for Daisy. Majority opinion went with their leader's plan, so they dived into the Duke, grinning like monkeys, scattering the kids hanging round the doorstep for crumbs of news about the trial.

Now there was a serious possibility of a fight.

'You just drink that down, gents, and then you can leave the premises,' Duke said loud and clear.

'Or else?' Chalky checked around the room and guessed that numbers were evenly matched. 'You don't want to throw us out, old son. It won't look good when it gets out. More rough stuff. As if you ain't got enough bother already.'

Duke didn't hesitate. Chalky's cheap taunt roused him to anger at last. He slammed open the bar flap and moved out to face Chalky. 'I'm the one who decides that, mister, and I'm chucking you out, no matter what!' With Joxer, Walter, Maurice and Arthur lining up behind him, he stood his ground.

Chalky snorted. He took a long, slow pull at his drink, draining it to the dregs. All eyes were on him. Jess had crossed over to Robert, who wrenched at his chair, trying to drag it into the centre of action, restrained by Dolly and Annie. Chalky withered him with a pitying look, then he turned back to Duke. 'Listen, we don't want no trouble.'

Duke's fist ached to smack Chalky's jaw. He held it ready clenched, but he could see they would slither out of a confrontation now that they'd thrown the place into turmoil. He felt Walter drop his guard and Joxer shift to one side.

'We're on our way!' Chalky derided them with his insolent cheeriness. All five men put down their empty glasses and turned away. Arthur made a grab at Whitey's coat sleeve, but Maurice pulled him back. Someone spat on the floor as the gang left.

Duke went straight over to Robert for a soothing word. 'Easy there,' he told him, 'you gotta do your bit in court tomorrow.'

But the humiliation had been too strong. 'What bleeding good will it do?' Robert demanded. He pulled his chair out of their grasp. Walter and Maurice came over, while other customers resumed their drinking. 'They already made up their minds Ernie done it. And for all we know, he did!'

Duke turned sharply away. He looked lost for words.

'He don't mean it, Pa!' Jess leapt forward.

But Robert was hurting too much. 'We don't know, do we? Me and Ett was on the scene that night and even we can't say for sure that Ern never did it!' He was beside himself.

'He *never* did it!' Jess clutched both arms across her stomach and fended off all doubt. Her face went wild with shock.

'No, he never.' It was Walter's calm voice backing her up. 'It stands to reason, Rob. Ernie never done nothing like that.'

Jess grasped his hand with relief. 'See!' she said. 'We gotta keep hold. Ern's innocent!'

'Well, who did it, then?' Robert had subsided into sullenness.

Duke sighed, bent to unhitch the brake on his son's wheelchair and began to wheel him out. 'If we knew that, son, we'd be home and dry,' he said.

Frances's sense of duty had taken her along to the hospital to enquire after Ada Wray. It was the first evening of the trial; reason enough to get away from the Duke and to try to keep calm. She was averse as ever to bar-room gossip and found herself uneasy with her neighbours' sympathy, however well meant. So she hurried along the rainy streets, intent on seeking out her friend, Rosie Cornwell, for news of Billy's wife's condition.

But it was Billy himself she met first in the hospital grounds. She recognized him, thinking it odd that he should be sitting outside on a bench in the cold, dark evening, staring ahead. They'd not met alone together since that evening in the coffee room at the Institute, and at first she almost redirected her track so as to miss passing close by. But then she changed her mind.

'Billy?' She went and stood by the bench, waiting for him to stir. 'How's Ada?'

Billy sat forward, resting his arms on his thighs, his cap slung between his hands, head down. Without giving any sign of recognition, he told Frances that Ada had died that afternoon.

Frances sat beside him. 'Oh, Billy, I'm sorry.' To her Ada had been a shadowy figure whom she'd met only once at a social evening; a faded but evidently pretty woman with a plump, pale face and carefully arranged light brown hair. She was quite pleasant but uninterested in Billy's 'causes', as she called them. Her mother lived in the house with them, and the two women were friends and allies.

Billy nodded. 'You came a long way out of your way to ask after her.' He kept his head down. Any effort seemed too much.

'I wanted a breath of air and a talk with Rosie,' Frances explained.

He glanced up at last. 'How's the trial?'

'I don't know, Billy. We just had one day of it.'

'I been thinking about you.'

'Don't, Billy,' she interrupted. 'Thanks, but don't say nothing.' She stretched out her hand in the dark and put it over one of his. Then she quickly withdrew it. After a few moments more she stood and said goodbye. They parted in the glimmer of dripping lamplight, with no witness to their sad, lonely scene.

Next morning in court, Mr Sewell came and drew Duke to one side to inform him that they'd decided against calling Ernie to give evidence. 'We don't think he's up to it, Mr Parsons. I've had one last talk with him, and I'm afraid he still insists that he can't remember anything that took place beyond that stage door.'

340

Duke didn't look surprised. 'He blocked it out, I should think. When he's upset he goes into a world of his own; that's just Ernie.' He was aware of the crowd outside shoving down the corridor for the second day of the trial; idle spectators, newspapermen, supporters.

Sewell agreed. 'Yes, I understand that from my talks with him in prison. It's like getting blood out of a stone.' He sighed. 'No, we can't take the risk of letting the prosecution have a go at him. He's easily led, you see, into saying what he thinks you want to hear.'

'No need to tell me that,' Duke argued. 'He'd put his own head into the noose, is that what you mean?'

Frances slipped her arm through her father's. Sewell looked uncomfortable. 'I wouldn't put it quite like that, Mr Parsons. But tactically it's best if we rely on the evidence of others, don't you agree?' He disliked any whiff of defeatism until the case was finally over. 'It really is going as well as we expected.' His own confidence was vital once the family started to go downhill like this. He turned to Jess to check final details in her account. 'Don't let Forster frighten you,' he warned. 'Stand up to him. Don't let him think you've got anything to hide.'

His unwitting words followed her on to the witness stand, the first to be called that day. Everyone sat or stood in place exactly as before; all the court officials with their own special piece of ritual to enact, the all-important Judge Berry presiding in his crimson robes and white kid gloves.

Forster got to work right away. Jess was the final witness for the prosecution, with information relevant to the state of mind of the accused when he returned home. She felt her fingers tingle to the touch of the calfskin cover of the huge Bible with its big gold cross. Her voice emerged faint and unfamiliar to swear the oath.

'Now, Miss Parsons, we want to hear how your brother, Ernest, behaved when he got back home from the music hall. He was alone, was he not?'

'No, sir. He came in with Frances.'

This was a bad start. Forster looked irritated by the contradiction.

'Frances is my sister, sir.' Jess offered to help.

'Quite. You have a large family, Miss Parsons?'

'Yes, sir.'

'But it was you who dealt with your brother and got him to bed?'

'Yes, sir.'

'How did he behave?'

'He was upset.'

'How, "upset"? Was he raving and moaning?' Forster reminded the court of Syd Swan's last account of seeing Ernie outside the Palace.

'Oh no, sir. More dazed. Upset in a quiet sort of way, sir. Frances found him outside on the street looking lost, and she brought him on up. Then I took over.'

'Quite, again. You say he was dazed. Did he say anything to you?'

'Yes, sir. He said he'd lost Robert outside the theatre. He looked for him everywhere, but he never found him.'

'Is that all?'

'Yes, sir.'

'Now, Miss Parsons, what time did your sister, Frances, bring the accused upstairs with her?'

Jess faltered. 'About midnight, sir.'

'Speak up. About midnight, you say?'

'Yes, sir.'

'And we know that the audience came out of the music hall at five minutes to eleven.' Forster included the jury in his calculations by walking close to their box. 'Does it take

342

more than an hour to walk from the Palace home to Duke Street, Miss Parsons?'

'If you're lost, it could do, sir.' She wanted to point it out as a fact, but the barrister turned it into a facetious remark with a frown and a sigh.

'Let's say he was *pretending* he'd got lost, Miss Parsons. Let's just suppose. If you came straight from A to B, from the Palace to the Duke of Wellington public house, how long would it take you? Walking briskly, as the crow flies?'

'About twenty minutes, sir.'

Forster placed his fingertips together and looked directly at the foreman of the jury. 'More than forty minutes unaccounted for, by my reckoning, sir.' He raised his eyebrows, then turned with a swish of his silk gown. 'Now, Miss Parsons, we're almost there. We'll return to your brother's distress when he did finally make his way home. Didn't you think it might amount to something more than his simply getting lost?'

'No, sir.' She could feel Ernie's full gaze fixed on her. 'I never.'

'So you thought the best thing to do was to pack him off straight to bed? Did he object?'

'No, sir. Like I said, he was a bit dazed.'

'I imagine he was, Miss Parsons. Now think carefully, and remember your oath. We've learnt from fingerprint evidence, and the presence of the cap of the accused that he had indeed been in the room where the murder had taken place. He doesn't deny that outright, at least. He only goes so far as to tell us that he can't remember having been there! Now, did he mention this vital fact to you?'

'No, sir.' Jess fell into the same dull, monosyllabic replies. Her mouth felt dry. She looked up to the gallery for Maurice, but a sea of faces looked back.

'Hm. It would account for his distress, would it not? If

he had been in that room, I mean? No, don't answer that, Miss Parsons. That was merely for us to ponder. Now, he mentioned nothing about the murder. That suggests he was trying to conceal it from you?'

'Maybe, but maybe not.' This was where Jess knew more about Ernie than they did in this court. 'If he's upset, he goes quiet, sometimes for days on end. It's a kind of shock, I think.' She spoke eagerly, turning to the jury. 'He don't remember nothing till he comes out of it, then he's right as rain again.'

'Very convenient, Miss Parsons.' Forster stood and demolished her with a single look and phrase. 'Selective amnesia, I think they call it, gentlemen.' He shared a joke with the jury, then reached the pinnacle of his questioning of this particular witness. 'Let's say he was concealing it. We must ask ourselves, was there anything about him to suggest that he'd been in a struggle?'

'No, sir.' Jess looked down at her own trembling hands.

'He'd lost his cap. Did you not notice that?'

'Yes, sir.'

'Perhaps in a struggle?'

'It didn't strike me at the time, no, sir.'

'Was his clothing torn?'

'No, sir.'

'Were his boots dirty, Miss Parsons?' The tension in Forster's naturally high, thin voice rose a further pitch.

Jess hesitated.

'Yes or no, Missie!' Judge Berry barked.

'Yes, sir.'

'Was there blood on them?' Forster realized he had her. Honesty was such a flimsy commodity in these circumstances; it could be turned both ways.

'Yes.'

Forster's head went back. 'What did you do? Did you clean it off?'

'Yes.'

'Louder, Miss Parsons.'

'Yes.' She looked up for help. There was none to be found.

'You cleaned blood off his boots, yet you say there was no sign of a struggle on him?' He sounded shocked, disbelieving.

Jess's lip trembled. She hung her head.

'That's all, Miss Parsons.'

Forster sat as Mayhew stood, quickly rethinking his tactics. This was more damning than Sewell had led him to believe, and the witness was in no state to act as character reference for the accused. But there was one point he must make clear in the minds of the jury. He would get it over with quickly. 'Miss Parsons, I'm sorry to distress you further, but let's be clear about this matter of the blood.'

Jess fought to look him in the eye.

'It was on your brother's boots, you say?'

'Yes, sir.'

'Was it on his trousers?'

She frowned. 'No, sir.'

'Speak up!' Judge Berry snapped. 'So we can all hear your answers, Missie!'

'No, sir!'

'Was it on his jacket?' Mayhew picked up the thread.

'No, sir.'

'Was it on his hands or his face? Was it anywhere at all, except on Ernie's boots?'

'No, sir,' she said, loud and clear now.

'That's odd,' Mayhew remarked. He looked quizzically at the jury. 'This is an exceptionally neat murderer, whose hands and clothes carry not one stain of his victim's blood, don't you think?' He waived any further questions and watched Jess half-stumble from the witness-box, then he bent to confer with the solicitor. Numb and weak, Jess returned to her seat.

'Good for you,' Hettie whispered as she sat down. 'You stood up to them, and Mr Mayhew nailed them good and proper.'

They brought Frank Henshaw to the stand next, to provide a good character for Ernie. The defence case would rest on the clean record to date of the accused. They would dismantle press reports of bad living and poor family support, and ask how a young man of unblemished reputation and admittedly limited capabilities to think for himself could suddenly transform himself into a vicious, frenzied attacker of a defenceless woman. His employer was the first port of call in the journey to re-establish Ernie's good name.

Henshaw took the oath and acknowledged judge and jury. He stood full square, hands behind his back, a solid tradesman like them. Mayhew established him as a chapel-goer and a thriving businessman, with the pick of a dozen errand boys to deliver his groceries. 'So why choose Ernie Parsons, Mr Henshaw?' Mayhew sounded relaxed. The shopkeeper wouldn't let them down.

'I knew him as a reliable lad,' Henshaw explained. 'I've known the family more than twenty years, ever since they came to live on Duke Street.'

'But as a chapel man, a Methodist, we might imagine you to have objections towards the family who lived at the pub, surely?'

Happy to be drawn out, Henshaw contradicted this view. 'I ain't one to ram my religion down another man's throat, sir. Like I say, I get on well with the Parsons family.

I offered work to Ernie and he turned out like I expected, a steady, honest, reliable lad.'

'He presented no problems at all, Mr Henshaw?'

'None, sir. And my wife, Mrs Henshaw, she found him just the same. You tell him what to do and it's good as done. The best lad we had in years.'

Mayhew nodded. The words penetrated even Ernie's bleak misery, and those who watched him saw his head go up and a faint look of pride appear on his face. A lump rose to the sisters' throats. Sadie allowed her hopes to rise.

'No questions,' Forster said abruptly, hardly bothering to stand, dismissing the witness as a tiresome waste of time and unworthy of cross-examination.

A new figure took Henshaw's place. The reporters in the gallery licked their pencils and began to scribble anew as the woman's faint voice repeated the oath. 'I, Mary Kathleen O'Hagan do swear by Almighty God . . .'

Annie Wiggin shouldered people aside for a better view. 'Good for you, Missus!' she said under her breath. Who better to give evidence for Ernie than the mother of the corpse? She glared in triumph at the surprised prosecution bench, and hoped that the shrivelled scarecrow of a judge would sit up and take notice. Morale rose. Dolly came and settled close to Annie, shoulder to shoulder.

Mary found the ordeal truly terrible. Naturally reticent, and worn down by long years of struggle, her instinct at the best of times was to shy away from the limelight. And this was the worst of times. But she did it for Hettie. She put on her one worn and dowdy brown coat and she came to court. She knew she looked what she was; a poor washerwoman from an immigrant family, whom life had treated badly.

'Thank you for taking the stand, Mrs O'Hagan,' Mayhew

began gently. Sewell had done well to get her here. She was a strong weapon in the emotional argument. He said he really only had two questions for her. 'Firstly, did your daughter, Daisy, ever talk to you about the accused, Ernie Parsons?'

'She did, sir. She mentioned him to me every so often.' Mary swayed and grasped the brass rail which ran along the top of the witness-box.

'Did she like him? Would you say she got on well with him?'

'She did, sir. She told me there was no harm in the boy and she liked to have him come to see the show. She was a good-hearted girl, sir, and she knew she could make Ernie's day, just by being friendly and nice with him.'

'Did she like him better than some of the other men who came to visit her backstage?'

'She did.' Mary's voice grew stronger. 'Some she didn't care for at all, sir, but they could be difficult to shake off. She knew her own mind in these things, sir.'

'But Ernie?'

'She liked him a lot, in a friendly way.'

'Not a romantic way, Mrs O'Hagan?'

'No, sir. They was just friends.'

Mayhew nodded. 'She trusted him?'

'Yes, sir. We all do.'

'Good. Thank you, Mrs O'Hagan. Which leads me to my second question, and this is really very important. In your opinion, would the accused be capable of committing this brutal act against your daughter?'

They held their breath as Mary paused. Her face looked long and weary. There were dark shadows under her eyes, and a hopelessness at the centre of her being. But she pulled herself upright.

'Do you understand the question?' Mayhew asked softly.

'I do, sir.' She looked straight at Ernie and her whole heart went out to him. 'I don't believe he done it, sir. Whatever they say against him, I don't believe he killed my girl!'

Chapter Twenty-Six

Ernie's defence counsel hoped he'd judged the public mood right as he watched Robert Parsons swear the oath. A special provision had been made for him to give his evidence from the floor of the court, still seated in his wheelchair, and it was true that he cut a sympathetic figure. Poetic phrases gathered around the injured man's head; 'Cut down in the flower of his youth', or more gloomily still, 'Think not for whom the bell tolls'. And that was the problem. Robert stood for the frailty of the human condition as well as for glorious sacrifice. Worse still, his uniform was evidently useless on him now, except as an emblem of the supreme indifference of war. But this pessimistic knowledge lay deep under layers of brash patriotism. Although the generals battling it out in Belgium and France were now prepared to admit that the war might well continue beyond Christmas, the demon Kaiser remained a figure of intense public hatred against whom the British Tommy would willingly fight to the death.

Mayhew banked on this image of the common-or-garden East End boy giving his all for king and country as he began his even-paced questioning of the wounded soldier.

Robert listened, and explained why he liked to take his young brother to watch the shows at the Palace. 'To give him a bit of a break. He was always on at me to go and watch Hettie and Daisy with him.'

'Why was that? Couldn't he go by himself?'

'No, sir. He needs someone with him. He ain't too good by himself.'

'No confidence?'

'No, sir.'

'What would happen to Ernie out on the streets alone?'

Robert didn't hesitate. 'He'd get lost. Pa never let him go off, especially at night. And we wouldn't want him to neither.'

'He'd get lost, you say? So it was entirely consistent for him to do so when he was separated from you on the night of the murder? I mean, you weren't surprised to hear he'd got lost while trying to find his way home alone?'

'No, sir.'

'And what was the reason for your separation?' Mayhew let the jury get used to the sound and look of this, his last witness. Robert's deep, sure voice with its military overtones came across well.

'I came out ahead of him. I told him we had to get a move on if we wanted to nab the girls. They didn't know we was there. So I shot off. But Ern's a bit slow in a crowd. I never thought of that, so I lost him somewhere. Then I ran into a bit of bother of my own.' Robert was reluctant to tell this part of the story, knowing that it was his own hot temper that had caused him to make an enemy of the powerful Chalky White, and this had led directly to his altercation with Syd Swan that night. Still, Sewell had convinced him to tell the whole truth, after Jess's experience on the stand. 'I planned to give Swan and his mates the slip as quick as I could, then double back for Ern.'

'How long were you gone?'

'About a quarter of an hour.'

'So you arrived back at the Palace at eleven fifteen?'

'Yes, then I met up with Hettie and heard there was no sign of Ern, so we set off home together, then we thought better of it, so we cut back again and went inside to check.'

'Inside the Palace, using the stage door?'

'Yes, sir.'

'At what time?'

'I'm not sure exactly. Before half eleven.'

Mayhew nodded. 'Now we won't trouble the court with another description of events surrounding the discovery of the body. Suffice it to say that the disaster coincided with your enlistment into His Majesty's regular army, and that your brother's arrest for this murder occurred on the eve of the fourteenth of September, the very day that you left Duke Street to join your regiment?'

'Yes, sir.'

'It must have been a terrible blow, Private Parsons?'

'We was all staggered. Frances wrote me the news and I jumped right up and said, "Oh no, that ain't right!" They had to sit on me to stop me jumping on a train back home to put them right about Ernie.'

'What was so incredible?' Mayhew had taken off his gold-rimmed glasses and swung them from his forefinger. He nodded encouragement at Robert.

'I knew in my bones they got it wrong. That's the first thing. Now, if they told me Ernie killed a bloke to stop him laying a finger on Daisy; maybe, just maybe I could see that. He'd die for that girl.

'Second thing, like you said yourself, sir, why wasn't he covered in blood then? All right, so suppose he goes into the room and suppose he finds her lying there. The poor bloke goes to see what they done to her, don't he? He goes over and he tries to get her up. Only she don't get up, and he gets blood all over his boots, like we heard. But if he'd been the one, it'd be all over his hands and clothes and all. And there ain't no sign of that.' Robert followed the logic without flinching at the details. 'He ain't never seen a dead body before. I bet he's scared stiff. He finds the knife on the floor beside her, and he grabs it and throws it away 'cos that's what done the damage. Now he's upset. He knows she ain't gonna wake up and he goes wild. He gets up and he runs out of the place quick as he can. That's when he bumps into Swan. By the time Frances runs into him, he's practically back home, and he's trying to block out what he just seen.'

'Explain to us why he would do that, if you please, Private Parsons.'

Robert sighed. ''Cos if he talks about it and tells anyone he's seen Daisy lying in a pool of blood, then it's true, ain't it? If he locks it up inside his own head, it can still be a bad dream. He can wake up. Daisy'll waltz into the room like normal, and everything's fine!'

Mayhew let this version sink in before he finished off. 'Private Parsons, why did you enlist with the army?'

Robert registered slight surprise. 'They need blokes like me,' he said, more subdued.

'Blokes like you?'

'Yes. Fit and strong. We can do out bit.'

Mayhew left it at that. 'And did your family approve?'

Robert looked straight ahead. 'Pa was with the army in India. He says it's the making of a man.'

'So you did it in part for him? Your family has a strong loyalty to king and country?'

'Yes, sir.'

'And finally, Private, could you tell us briefly the extent of your present injuries and how they occurred? No need to go into distressing detail, of course.' Mayhew's voice was respectfully lowered. He wanted to finish with this strong emotional impact.

Robert recalled for them the place, the time, the circumstances of the order to go over the top. He didn't tell them of the bitter cold, the muddle of command and countercommand, the sprawled bodies of comrades face down in the mud, the soft whine and thud of enemy shells. He said he was knocked unconscious by the explosion, and woke to find himself snagged on barbed wire, being hauled back to the Allied trench on the back of George Mann, a private in his regiment. 'He went on his belly with me slung round his shoulders, lying on top of him. He could've left me, but he never. They got me on a stretcher and they took me off in an ambulance. I never got a chance to thank Mann. Everything went black again. Next thing I know I'm in the field hospital. I've lost my right leg from the knee down, and they've had to patch up my hip and side.'

Silence reigned. Mayhew thanked him sincerely for gathering the strength to appear in court. He folded his glasses into his waistcoat pocket and sat down.

Forster stood and manoeuvred himself into position alongside the jury-box. This mood of reverence required quick deflation. 'Private Parsons, what was your relationship with the deceased?'

Robert pulled himself round to answer the snappy question. 'We was friends, sir.'

'No more than friends?'

'No, sir. We had a lark. We grew up in the same street together.'

'But she was an attractive girl, would you say?'

'You could say that, yes.'

'Private Parsons, the question is not whether or not *I* would say she was attractive, but what *you* have to say about the matter.' Forster's urbane voice picked up Robert's speech mannerisms and played with them. 'Did you find her good-looking?'

'Yes, sir.'

'Have you had lots of girlfriends?'

Robert's resentment began to show through. 'A few.'

'You're a good-looking man.'

There was a muttering in the gallery at the overt insensitivity of this remark, but Forster wasn't out to win any popularity stakes.

'You were a favourite with the ladies?'

'It ain't for me to say.'

'Oh, come, no need to be modest. You had the girls practically falling at your feet, didn't you? Weren't you what we call a ladies' man, Private Parsons?'

'I went about with women, if that's what you mean.'

'But not with Daisy O'Hagan?'

'No, sir.'

'You never flirted with her?'

The momentary pause cast doubt on Robert's answer. 'No, sir, not really.'

'Be precise, if you please,' Forster drilled into his man, his voice dry and sharp.

'Only for a lark, sir.'

'Did your brother, Ernie, see you flirt with Daisy, "for a lark", as you say?'

'How would I know?' Robert felt himself being led helplessly into muddy insinuations. He reacted sullenly.

'Let's say he did. He saw you with your arm around her, let's say. Yet according to your own words, the accused would "die for that girl". Isn't that what you said? Wouldn't he then feel jealousy when he came across you two spooning together?'

'We never spooned!' Robert interrupted.

'Well, call it what you will. We reach the point where

Ernie, dimly perhaps, begins to realize that you're the sort of brother who will steal a girl from a fellow the moment his back is turned.' Forster allowed Robert to glare at him for a few seconds before going on. 'So he must seize his opportunity in double-quick time. The bees are buzzing round the honey-pot, you might say.'

Judge Berry, who until this point had sat resting his chin on his hand, forefinger to his lips, suddenly leaned forward. 'Where is this colourful metaphor leading us, Mr Forster? Bees and honey-pots; what's the point, if I may ask?'

'The motive, m'lud. That's where we're leading. "By indirections . . ."'

'"Find directions out." Yes, quite, Mr Forster.' Judge Berry sighed but allowed him to proceed.

'Now, Mr Parsons, we've reached the night of the murder. The accused loses sight of you in the theatre. But he heads for the girls' dressing-room in any case. You admit that he could view this as an unlooked-for opportunity?'

'What are you getting at?' Robert frowned and twisted a finger inside his uncomfortably tight collar. He felt hot and flustered.

'I mean, he has Daisy all to himself, doesn't he? We all know how much he adored her. But what would Daisy make of Ernie's advances, there in the dressing-room, all alone?'

Robert let out a short laugh. But before he could frame an answer, Forster forged ahead.

'Exactly! Let's just say, she wouldn't respond well. And who can blame her? She's a popular girl. She has the pick of all the East End scuttlers. Surely she would prefer you to your brother, Mr Parsons; a good-looking ladies' man like yourself? After all, wasn't it you she liked to flirt with? Wouldn't she make these feelings quite plain to Ernie? And then what?'

'Then, nothing!' Robert found his voice. 'I'm telling you, you're going about this the wrong way!'

Forster glanced sharply at the jury, as if to say, *Pay attention. The witness is rattled*. Then he concentrated his sharp gaze on Robert once more.

'Do you believe that Daisy O'Hagan would reject Ernie's clumsy advances, Mr Parsons?'

'Course she would!'

Forster cut back in. 'Would she laugh at him? Would she put up a fight?'

Robert looked helplessly towards Duke. The old man's gaze was fixed on Ernie.

'Does Ernie panic in a fight?' Forster insisted.

'How should I know?' Robert couldn't find the right answer to put his finger on and clear Ernie of these ridiculous suggestions. Everything he said just dropped him deeper into Forster's trap.

'Well. *We* know the murder is the action of a man who suddenly loses control. We can tell that by the number of wounds inflicted on the corpse. This is no professional, premeditated act.' Forster took time to glance around the court. 'Would you agree, Mr Parsons, that this murder was committed by someone who did not accurately judge his own power to inflict harm? Would you say that it was a frenzied attack, from what you yourself saw of the body?'

Robert took a deep breath and nodded. 'But Ernie never fights! He ain't never hurt no one!'

'Quite.' Forster's jaws snapped shut. He paused. 'He never fights. But he is a strong young man. Therefore he has no idea of how much damage his violent actions can inflict, when his temper is provoked beyond restraint. His thin thread of self control snaps when Daisy rejects him. A sudden idea takes hold; if he can't have her, then no one else will. Maybe she is laughing at him even now. He takes a knife he carries in his pocket; a common or garden kitchen knife available at the local ironmongers'. He advances. He's surprised by how easily the sharp blade plunges into the soft flesh. And by the blood. He steps quickly to one side. But there's no turning back. Again and again he plunges the knife into Daisy. Then the struggle is done. He releases her. She slumps dead to the floor.'

Hettie hid her head in her hands and wept at the description. Frances felt pure hatred for the prosecutor. Sadie and Jess sat holding hands, stunned as Robert began to shout; incoherent words of rage that offended the jurors' ears and challenged the authority of the court.

'He can't bleeding well say that! He's a bastard, he is, putting pictures in their heads. This ain't what I call justice!' Robert ranted, raising his fist in an impotent, destructive gesture as Duke rose from his seat, intent on being the first to reach his son's wheelchair. He spun the chair on the spot and rushed him down the aisle.

'Easy, take it easy.' Duke slammed the chair through the double doors at the back of the courtroom, to the sound of the gavel rattling down on to the desk and to the rising consternation of spectators in the gallery. Duke leaned his head back against the closed door. It had been too much to expect. 'I'm sorry I put you through that, mate,' he said.

Robert sagged forward in his chair, hot tears stinging his eyes.

'A pity,' Mayhew said to Sewell, shuffling papers into order on his desk. 'If he could just have kept his temper . . .' The gamble hadn't quite paid off. He cast a cool eye over the jury to assess the effect of Robert's outburst, getting ready to repitch his summing-up speech. Meanwhile, Forster was making his own last push.

The jury heard again the mountain of evidence pointing to the guilt of the accused; the time, the opportunity, the motive, the forensic reports. They would recall the words from the accused's own lips: 'I never meant to do it', and his intense secrecy after the event, so clumsily covered up by the sister, Jess. It was a poor defence, was it not, to simply 'forget' one's exact movements in the room where the murder occurred, but it was the typical defence of a guilty man, not too bright, who saw all the fingers of accusation lining up ready to point in his direction.

Forster polished off his final speech with a common-sense touch, a sad but true tone which spoke regret that these things happened when men of this type were pushed beyond their limit. Nevertheless, a conviction was imperative. 'Despite your inevitable softer feelings of sympathy, gentlemen, which are perfectly natural when you see the distress of the accused as he sits in the dock listening to horrific accounts of his own actions, do not lose sight of the decision you must reach.

'Do not believe, as defence counsel would have you believe, that Ernest Parsons is incapable of committing this crime. They say he is a simple man, unable to negotiate the streets of London alone. Certainly, he is simple, but not incapable, as we have seen from the testimony of Mr Henshaw. No, Ernest Parsons can hold down the very sort of job which requires detailed knowledge of these streets, as Henshaw's errand boy. Moreover, we are sure that he harbours the ordinary feelings of men towards the gentler sex; this much is clear. Those feelings include possessiveness and jealousy, do they not, gentlemen? No, you may discount the view proposed by Mr Mayhew that this is a saintly simpleton, a kind of divine idiot. This is a man; a man who snapped, who killed in a frenzy the woman whom he loved "not wisely but too well". Can there be any reasonable doubt left in your minds that this is so? And likewise any hesitation that this man must pay the ultimate penalty which the law demands? Your duty is not a pleasant one, gentlemen. No man here says that it is. But it is plain, and it is a duty which we must carry out without flinching, in the name of justice. We must find the defendant guilty as charged.'

There was a terrible hush in the courtroom. Forster's speech was delivered watertight. It sent hopes spiralling down in the public gallery. It numbed the Parsons women, so that Mayhew's own summing-up speech had to beat its way with heavy wings through the gloomy atmosphere of the court.

He must rely on the unblemished family history, he must recall for the jury the whole-hearted support showered on the accused by his own family and community, not least from the mother of the supposed victim. 'An unprecedented thing, in my experience,' Mayhew said. 'A brave and selfless act by a woman who has suffered much, yet driven here by her belief in the innocence of the man whom the prosecution would hang.

'He sits before you, as he has sat through all these long weeks in prison, more boy than man, in utter sorrow and confusion. He denies nothing that is true, yet he does deny this brutal murder. His statement takes you as far as his own memory can possibly take you, and what this amounts to is that he was simply in the wrong place at the wrong time. As a result, his entire world collapsed, wiping out any observation of detail which might have helped him escape this charge; a shadow in a corner of the alleyway, a struggle overheard, a name called out in terror.' Mayhew's gaze raked the courtroom and the gallery, seeking out the guilty name to no avail.

He lowered his eyes to the jury once more. 'No one can deny the hideousness of the crime you have to consider; the brutal murder of a beautiful and defenceless young woman by a man without a conscience, a man sufficiently cool and cruel to let another stand accused here, who would let *his* blame hang the man who stands before you now. Two victims of one crime, gentlemen; consider that. The shadow of doubt looms large under the hangman's noose, and so it should, for this is an irrevocable act. This is a decision which may colour the rest of your lives.

'Look around this court, gentlemen, and let your gaze rest on Ernie Parsons. Study him.' Mayhew led them with a gallant gesture to where Ernie sat looking at his sisters with a fixed stare, waiting for them to tell him what to do next. 'This man is no liar, this man is no murderer. He is simply trapped by circumstance.' His final appeal was low, almost inaudible to all except the jurors. 'For God's sake, gentlemen, release him from that trap, and find him not guilty!'

Forster turned to his own assistant, as Mayhew returned, head bowed, to his seat and the jury received the judge's directions. 'Heart versus head,' he said drily. 'Let's see which way they swing now.'

When word came back that the jury had reached a verdict, Sewell took Duke aside one last time. 'There is a procedure,' he warned. 'In all these cases it is the same.'

'The black cap? Is that what you're getting at?'

'Yes. Innocent or guilty, the cap will be there in readiness. You mustn't jump to conclusions.'

Duke nodded. 'I'll tell the girls,' he promised as they took their places in court. The unreality of the occasion was only heightened by speaking of these things, when in truth he thought his heart must stop dead at the awful irresistibility of it all.

The jury returned to complete silence, each man in

procession, his gaze set straight ahead, tight-lipped, narrow-eyed. They sat as three loud knocks announced the re-entry of the judge. The Sheriff and Mayor followed in robes of crimson and ermine. An official carried the square of black cloth ceremoniously outstretched, and last of all came the chaplain, all in black.

Then Ernie was brought up from the cells into the dock. He looked anxiously for Duke, found him in his usual place, and fixed his eyes upon him.

The thing was played out in a daze. They knew in their hearts by the grim, fixed look of the foreman what the verdict was to be.

At last the clerk to the court cleared his throat. 'How do you find the defendant?'

'Guilty, m'lud.'

A scramble began in the gallery. Reporters left to be first on the telephone to their editors with the news. Uninvolved spectators nodded and drifted off into the next courtroom. Friends stood stock-still. The morbid hung on for the last details.

Judge Berry placed the cap on his head. It was over. He was satisfied, reciting the words which sealed the man's fate.

'Taken from this place . . . Eight o'clock on the fifth day of January 1915 . . . hung by the neck until you are dead . . . and may God have mercy on your soul.'

Chapter Twenty-Seven

Ernie was taken stumbling from view, and life lurched on around the vortex, the black certainty that he was to die.

Mayhew came to shake hands with Duke. He felt it had come about partly through lack of other suspects. 'There's a strong urge to convict when public opinion is roused. They need to blame someone, and of course we were unable to implicate anyone else.' He shook his head. 'I am truly sorry, Mr Parsons.'

Duke couldn't trust himself to speak. The girls wept and clung to one another. Robert covered his face with his hand.

'Can I see the boy?' Duke said at last, turning to Sewell, who went off to arrange it.

Maurice came down to help Jess and the women. Walter came for Robert. Annie sat in the rapidly emptying gallery next to Florrie and Dolly. She'd sent Tommy off home with the news, and now she turned to comfort Duke's sister. 'You go ahead, have a good cry, girl.' The old woman's stricken face streamed with tears. Annie put an arm around her shoulder.

Florrie choked back the tears, for the family's sake. She didn't want to make a fuss. 'Only, when I think what they're gonna do to Ern, it breaks my heart!' she wailed, overcome once more.

Annie drew a sharp breath. 'Don't say that, girl. I can't bear it.'

And it was Dolly's turn to put her strong arms around skinny Annie and let her weep.

Duke was taken along dark, bare corridors to the cells below the courtroom. Two warders guarded the door to Ernie's cell, and they avoided the father's eyes as he was silently marched inside the room. One officer remained there with them.

The boy seemed bewildered. He sat hunched over the table, hands clasped. He looked up at Duke in mute appeal, then turned away. At last he realized that even Duke couldn't help him now. For the first time in his life, Ernie recognized the limits of his father's power; up till now he'd thought he was invincible.

The turning away was too much for Duke. He stood by the door immobile, as cold as stone. In that windowless room, where condemned men accepted their fate, the electric light glared.

Ernie looked back and saw his father's weariness; the shadows on his face, his weakness and age. He got up and approached him. 'Don't worry about me, Pa. Tell Ett I remembered my prayers. Tell them all to come and see me.'

Duke nodded. 'We'll be there, mate.' He held his son close to him. 'We won't let you down.'

The weeks in prison had taught Ernie new rules. You did as you were told and never spoke your fears. He glanced at the warder. 'I gotta go now, Pa.' He began to ease himself free.

Duke released him. 'We never let you down, did we, son?' He wanted to be able to walk out with Ernie's trust restored.

'You never, Pa. I let myself down. I never remembered what happened to Daisy. I think I should've.' Ernie had walked across to the warder, but he turned again for a moment. 'That's right, ain't it, Pa? I should've remembered?'

Duke nodded. 'I know you tried, Ern. But it ain't easy for you, and it don't do to think of it now.'

Ernie shook his head. 'Would it've helped her? Would my remembering wake her up?'

'No, son, but we could've helped you.'

Ernie sighed. 'I'm sorry, Pa.'

'Don't be, Ern. What's done is done.'

The boy bowed his head and submitted to being led away. Another warder came in for the old man, gave him one brief, sympathetic glance, turned and took him off up the corridor, up the stone steps back into the courtroom. Duke heard heavy doors slam and lock. They battered his heart with grief and loss.

There was no cheer in the court as Christmas week drew near. People drifted in and out of the Duke, but they lost their natural rhythm when talking of Ernie and the terrible outcome in court. Some, like Arthur Ogden and even Syd Swan, refused to mention it at all, though it must have preyed on their minds.

When Syd took Amy out to the Gem in the week after the verdict, her heightened sense of drama made her want to chatter to Syd about the awful prospects facing Ernie now; the hangman's noose and the condemned man's last request before he went to meet his Maker. Syd refused to listen, as he ushered her through the shiny doors, relieved when their turn came up at the ticket office and they could sidle in for the latest Keystone adventures. Amy was all very well, but she never knew when to stop. Maurice Leigh watched them take their seats without his usual courteousness, and at home, later, he openly warned Amy off her association with Swan.

Dolly Ogden treated the subject of Ernie with an outpouring of powerful sympathy. She went the opposite way to Arthur and Syd, but her interest wasn't prurient, like Amy's. 'You come and tell that girl how sorry you are,' she chivvied Charlie. 'You gotta act like a man. They need all the help they can get these days.'

So Charlie went up to the Duke and asked to see Sadie. He was shown up to the living room, where the women sat. He said his awkward sentence, cap in hand, aware of the inadequacy of the words. He wondered for a moment if Sadie would turn on him.

But Frances thanked him for her, and said they appreciated his coming. It was a kind thought. Sadie sat in a chair by the fire, looking young and lost.

'Is there anything I can help with?' he faltered.

Sadie looked up at him through her grief.

'I don't think so, Charlie,' Frances said softly. 'But we're very grateful for the offer.' She showed him downstairs and closed him out of their misery.

If Dolly talked too much, running through the trial time after time with Flo at the bar, pouring out venom against Forster and the prosecution witnesses, it was accepted in good spirit and taken as a sign that Dolly really did care. In one way, Flo was glad to talk about things. She trod on eggshells around the place herself, now that the verdict had sunk in, not knowing how anyone was going to react in the long run. 'I went up the Post Office and telephoned to my Tom,' she told Dolly. 'He couldn't hardly believe it, said for me to save the newspaper account for him to read, but

I told him I couldn't bear to have it near me. Not with the things they write!'

The *Express* had followed up its early reports on the case with an expression of righteous indignation on the subject of lawlessness and the evil of wrongdoers such as Ernest Parsons, who made it unsafe for respectable women to walk the streets at night. They looked forward to his punishment with ghoulish pleasure.

'Don't take no notice,' Dolly consoled her. Florrie's flamboyant style had taken a knock this last week. Her rouge was put on crooked, her black hair showed grey at the roots. 'They can write what they like, no one round here thinks he done it!'

Florrie raised her pencilled eyebrows. 'Thanks, Dolly.' In private, she thought the touching faith might make things worse. She heard Sadie sobbing her heart out night after night, and Hettie's prayers, and Jess questioning everything, urging Frances to work on Sewell for an appeal. Florrie sighed. 'We're worn out with worry, I don't mind telling you.'

To make things worse, she had noticed a severe falling off in trade at the pub, since the government had decided to restrict opening hours for the duration of the war. It was to encourage sobriety and to concentrate people's attention on the war effort, but Florrie's point of view was that folk needed to drown or share their sorrows up at the Duke. She worried about the empty bar stools and full barrels in the cellar, the dwindling takings in the till. But she wouldn't trouble Duke with it, as Christmas approached, and the dreaded New Year.

Annie was one of the customers who stayed loyal, and she dealt with Duke in a clear, matter-of-fact manner which encouraged him to talk things through. 'Ain't no need to put on a show for me, Duke,' she advised. 'I don't expect it.' A couple of draymen had just finished rolling fresh barrels along the corridor to the cellar, and Duke had helped heave them on to the gantry. Now he stood at the window watching the men jump on to the cart, taking up the reins and positioning the splendid shire horses, ready to set off and merge into the busy traffic on Duke Street. He didn't shift position as he felt Annie come up alongside.

'Will they get rid of them in the end and all? What do you think, Annie?'

'What you on about?'

'The horses. Will they put them out to grass and go for the motor car?' He watched them take the strain and lift their huge hooves. They were great dappled grey beasts, with creaking leather straps, silver bits, golden brasses.

'Not before you and me are six feet under, if you want to know. I say they can keep their electric tramcars and their motor omnibuses for all I care. No, them drays is a sight for sore eyes, and they'll see us out, Duke.'

'I hope you're right.' He seemed happy to reminisce, briefly caught up in the shallows of memory, ignoring the approaching tidal wave. 'My old man brought us up over a carter's yard up in Hackney. Did I ever tell you that, Annie? There was one old grey in the yard, a bit like them two out there, and we called him Major, and my pa would hitch him up to a cart of a Sunday and take us kids out in the country for a day, riding back high on a load of hay, just smelling the sweet smell of the countryside all the way between the factory walls, down the cobbled streets back home. I could lie on that hay at the journey's end and stare up at the stars. Then Ma would come out with a face as long as a poker and shout where the bleeding hell did we think we'd been. I remember once Pa told her we'd stopped for a dog that he ran over on the road. He tried to save it, but it was too far gone. He had to bury it. Ma said never mind burying no stray dog, our bleeding supper was burnt to cinders. She made us pay for that day out, make no mistake.'

Annie smiled. 'We never got no days out in the country when we was kids. My old man was a bootmaker, and poor as a bleeding church mouse, with eight mouths to feed.' She stared down at her old standbys. 'That's why I knows a good pair of boots when I sees one.'

'Ain't it time you gave those up to the rag-and-bone cart, Annie?' Duke turned and frowned down at Wiggins's ugly legacy.

'Waste not, want not, I say,' came the gruff reply. Then she drew a small, slim wallet out of her pocket and showed it to her friend. 'Now look here, Duke, I had an idea what Ernie might like.' She opened the small brass clasp on the blue velvet wallet. It opened to reveal a concertina of small, framed photographs. 'I went up and down the court and I asked your girls and all, and they dug out a photograph for me, and I stuck them in here so we could get Ernie to remember that all the folks round here are thinking of him and praying for him. What do you think?' She handed the album across. 'I know he ain't one for books or letters, or nothing like that. But I thought he might like photographs. He can sit and look at his friends in a picture, can't he?'

Duke studied the brownish photographs. There was Tommy O'Hagan standing behind his fruit barrow, a grin splitting his face. There was Charlie Ogden on the back row in a Board School picture, with Sadie, neat in her white smock and black buttoned boots, sitting cross-legged at the front. There was a hand-tinted, glamorous head and shoulders one of Amy. Frances had provided a photo of the whole family, taken four or five years earlier, of them standing on the front doorstep of the pub. Ernie stood in the centre of the group, between Duke and Robert. And Mary O'Hagan had given up her favourite picture of Daisy, onstage, with white flowers in her hair and a sparkling laugh lighting up her face.

Annie grew uneasy at the long silence. 'If you think it'll only upset the poor boy, I'll take it back,' she suggested.

But Duke shook his head. 'It's just the thing, Annie.' His voice was hoarse. 'I'll take it in to him tomorrow.'

Now Hettie prayed fervently each morning and night, and went over to Lambeth to see her Army friend, Freda Barnes, as often as she could. Freda still helped to run the industrial home, dishing out soup and blankets to the poor creatures who came in off the streets at night. She was a plain-featured, grey-eyed woman in her mid-thirties, broad-faced beneath her navy bonnet, very down to earth and not at all smug. She encouraged Hettie to throw in her lot with them. '"Yea, though I walk through the valley of the shadow of death, I will fear no evil; for thou art with me, thy rod and thy staff they comfort me."' Hettie clung to her belief, seeing that it bolstered Ernie in his hour of need. She even invited Robert to attend an Army meeting with her.

Robert went once, but he preferred his old haunts. He allowed Walter to wheel him down to the gym, where Milo devised some weights which Robert could lift from a sitting position in his wheelchair, and a special punch-bag to exercise with. The hospital hoped he would soon progress from chair to crutches, and they promised an eventual artificial limb which would restore him in many ways to his old lifestyle. He worked at his recovery with fierce fanaticism. Nothing, nothing in life could be as bad for him as being treated like a cripple. They looked down at him in a wheelchair, and saw him as something less than human, so his pilgrimage took him through terrible pain on to crutches, too soon, and with several relapses before he could stand face to face with the next man once more. Now they admired him at the same time as they shied away from him. His experience was too raw, too recent, and he raged against each day as it brought him closer to the one set for Ernie's execution.

Maurice came in whenever he could, and took over some of the heavy tasks in the pub which Robert had once helped Joxer with. It gave him time with Jess, when the doors were closed and she came down into the bar, sometimes with Grace, sometimes alone.

She'd relented in this run-up to Christmas over her intention to keep her life with her baby daughter separate from her life with her lover. Maurice was especially tender after the verdict. She decided to trust him with getting to know the child.

She brought Grace down one day when she knew Maurice was at work in the cellar. She called him into the bar. 'Shh!' she said. 'Try not to wake her.'

His footsteps were heavy on the stone steps. He stared at the child, who was indeed stirring in her sleep. She opened her dark eyes and turned her head towards him.

'She can see your watch chain shining in the light.' Jess smiled as Grace freed one tiny hand from her fine white shawl and stretched it out towards him.

Maurice, mesmerized by Grace's dark stare, dare not move. At last he reached in his pocket and released the chain from the watch. He swung it gently towards her and let her catch its cold, shiny links. He glanced shyly at Jess. 'She looks like you,' he said.

There had been a sudden and drastic change from his freewheeling, quick-thinking pattern of old, which still had to operate while he was at work, or out and about. With Jess, however, things took on an intensity; not because she made much of Ernie's tragedy, rather because she was determined not to be defeated by it. She battled on for him, and seemed to Maurice to be living and breathing in a different sphere from mere mortals, where all trivialities fell away, leaving only her true self, pure and unadulterated. He was in danger of worshipping her, he realized, and there was nothing he could do to stop himself.

One sunny weekday morning before Christmas, he took her and Grace off to the park. Then he invited her along to a new Gaumont talkie, and got Hettie to back him up in making her go. He told her he was worried she would make herself ill over Ernie. 'You done everything you could. You done your very best,' he said.

'And it weren't good enough.'

They walked together after the picture had finished, back up Duke Street in a world of their own.

'Jess, you gotta stop hurting yourself over it. Sewell's working on an appeal, ain't he?'

'We need new evidence.' She thought of Ernie in the condemned cell. He was gentle with visitors, asking for news, never talking of his own situation. He'd told Frances that, when it came to it, he'd want her to write down a letter from him to Duke.

Maurice held her close. They stood outside the lively yellow warmth of the Duke. Strains of music filtered through the closed windows and doors. 'Come home with me,' he said softly.

In the empty house they made love again, with great passion between them. The ache of grief made her cry in his arms, and her tears healed the loneliness of his youth. He loved her clean smoothness, the slant of her shoulders, the curve of her back. She took his strong body to her, a little afraid of its power. They entwined. She was all softness until she pressed back against him and returned her female desire for his longing. Then she vied with him for pleasure, stroking and kissing him, and sighing as he held her. He looked down at her; her eyes looked deep into him with full consciousness of what she desired. What he could give, he gave, overjoyed by their union, their clinging limbs, their warm touch.

This time, the way back to cold reality was slow and gentle. They lay in each other's arms, murmuring to one another. He told her she was the best thing to happen in his life, kissing her eyelids, her forehead. She said she'd been wary of him at first.

'Too pushy?' he asked.

Jess nodded. 'I ain't used to all that attention. I lived a life below stairs, remember.'

'And wasted you were too, girl!'

She laughed.

'What about your pa? Ain't he made a fuss of you when you was little?'

'Not much.' She remembered winning the school races for him and bringing home the prize. 'It was all Rob, Rob, Rob with him, 'cos he was the first boy. Who wants three girls on the trot?' She said it without bitterness. 'I ain't complaining.'

'Well, you got plenty of attention from me from now on, if you want it?'

'Is that a question?' She turned on her side and propped herself on one elbow.

'If you like.' He was teasing, stroking the corners of her mouth and reaching across to kiss it.

'Funny sort of question. What was it again?' Her laugh, so rare of late, lit her up.

'Let's get married, Jess.'

She fell suddenly serious. 'You mean it? You don't want no more time to think?'

'I been thinking about it since I first clapped eyes on you.' He wanted to sweep her along. 'Say yes, Jess. Just say yes!'

She sat up in bed, hair tumbling about her shoulders, spreading her arms wide. 'I ain't gonna say no, Maurice, am I?'

'What are you on about?'

'Ain't I sitting here in your bed thinking we're bound to get married some day?' Strangely, it hadn't been a large question in her own mind. Then she realized that it was because she trusted him. 'Just as soon as you got round to asking me!'

'Say yes!' he demanded.

'Yes'.

He lay back flat on the pillow, speechless. It was Jess who kissed him and got up, got ready to go home to Grace. 'It ain't all plain sailing,' she warned.

Maurice's arm circled her waist as she sat again on the edge of the bed. 'No need to remind me.'

'But I love you, Maurice. Just remember that.'

'Then I'm happy,' he said simply. In his direct, optimistic way, he didn't see what could possibly go wrong.

Frances had arranged to meet up with Sewell in the prison. It was the Friday before Christmas. She greeted him in a subdued mood, and, it seemed to him, defeated.

'Never say die, Miss Parsons,' he reminded her as the warder showed them to Ernie's cell. They'd come for one last try to break down the barrier in Ernie's mind about events on the night of the murder. 'The doctors tell me that sooner or later it will all click into place,' he said. 'Like a camera shutter; click, as sudden as can be. And it will all be in place in perfect detail.'

'I hope so, Mr Sewell.' Frances went and sat by Ernie's side of the table. His face lit up to see her. Then he fixed his attention on Mr Sewell, screwing his gaze on the solicitor's face.

Frances noticed that Ernie held the little photograph album sent in by Annie. It was open at the picture of Daisy with white flowers in her dark hair.

'Now, Ernie,' Mr Sewell began. 'You understand why we're here?'

He nodded. 'To remember what happened to Daisy.'

'That's right. Let's just think about that. We're standing outside the stage door. What colour is it, Ernie?'

'Green. Dirty green.'

'Good. Is it closed?'

'Yes.' Ernie's eyes crinkled with concentration.

'Good. Is there anyone there in the alley with you, Ernie? I know we've asked you before, but you're doing very well this time. Just take things slowly. Now, is there anyone in the alley?'

Frances put one hand over Ernie's and stroked it softly.

'No, I'm by myself. I'm waiting for Rob. I know he'll be mad at me.'

'He's not mad,' Sewell reassured him. 'He's worried about you, but he's busy. He'll be back soon. He won't be mad.'

Ernie nodded. 'I never meant to do it,' he whispered; the old refrain.

'Do what, Ernie?' Sewell too lowered his voice.

'I never meant to get lost. Tell Rob.'

'He ain't cross,' Frances said. She grasped his hand tight. 'You never meant to get lost. We know that.' She glanced up at the solicitor, a light in her eyes. 'Now, Ernie, what happened while you was waiting for Rob? Did something scare you?'

Ernie's own eyes fogged over. He sighed heavily.

'What do you see?' Sewell leant forward across the table. They'd met up with the same invisible wall, the boy was giving in.

'What can you hear?' Frances urged.

'A noise. Someone's screaming.' He gripped the photograph. 'Daisy. Daisy's screaming. I can tell it's her. She's shouting. There's something wrong!'

'Daisy's inside and she's screaming. The door's closed, Ernie. What do you do?' Sewell pushed hard.

'I open it. I have to go in there, even if Rob comes along and I'm not there waiting for him. That's right, ain't it? I have to go in. Daisy needs me.'

'That's right, Ern.' Frances could hardly breathe. There was a moment when she thought, No, we can't go on. We can't make him live through it all again. It's a cruel torment. Once was enough. But Sewell was firm. He pressed on.

'She does. She needs help. Do you run inside, Ern?'

Ernie nodded. 'The screams are loud now. I have to run. They're coming from her dressing room, where they get changed. No, now they've stopped!' Ernie jolted to a halt. He was trembling. His eyes filled with tears.

'The screams have stopped, Ernie. Where are you now?'

'In the corridor,' he said, dazed and slow.

'Good. Do you see anyone?'

'No. I can hear someone running off. I turn the corner. But I don't see no one.'

Sewell let out a sharp breath. 'What do you do now? Now that Daisy's stopped screaming and you've heard someone run off?'

'I go in.'

'Go in where?'

'Into the dressing room – ' He paused.

'Who's there, Ernie?'

'No one.'

Sewell nodded. 'How do you feel now, Ernie? Daisy's not there. How do you feel?'

'Scared.'

'What of? Is someone in there hiding?'

'No. He ran off. I heard him.'

'But you're still scared?'

'Something's wrong. Something's happened to Daisy. I have to find her.'

'Where? Where do you look?'

'All over. I can't see her. But I know she's still here.'

'Do you find her? Where is she?' Sewell glanced at Frances, willing her to keep her own nerve.

'No, I can't find her!' Ernie looked wildly round, his eyes streaming with tears.

'Not at first, no. But you keep looking?'

'Yes. And the rail with the dresses hanging, I see it move.'

'How? Did it move much, Ernie?'

'A bit. Not much. One of the dresses falls down. I have to pick it up.'

'You go over.'

'I pick it up. It's caught. It's soft and silky, but it's caught.' Ernie gasped. 'I'm pulling it hard. There's a noise.'

'What noise?'

'Someone hurting. A hurting noise. Behind the dresses. I have to kneel down to see. It's dark behind the dresses.'

Ernie paused again, but both Frances and Sewell stayed silent. They let him lead them on at his own pace now, through the terrible remembering.

'I can feel something move, like a little animal moving. Something grabs my neck and pulls me down. My hat falls off. I lose my hat, Frances!'

'It don't matter, Ern. We'll get you a new one.' She thought her heart would break.

Ernie went on. 'It's Daisy lying down there moaning. Daisy's holding my neck and moaning. Her face is all white. She says something. Twice. I have to bend right down to listen. I see all the blood. I'm kneeling on the dress, getting it dirty. I lost my hat. There's a knife. I have to get it out. I have to be careful. It hurts. I take it out, quick as I can. She's not moving no more. She won't get up. Oh, she won't get up no more. I know it now.'

Racked by sobs, Ernie's head went down.

'What next?' Sewell held steady. He put a hand on the boy's arm.

'I have to go to meet Rob,' Ernie said blankly. 'I have to go, don't I?'

'You do. But before that, tell me one more thing, Ernie.' The solicitor held on to his arm. 'This is very important. What did Daisy say to you when you found her lying there?' He was after a final incriminating detail; Daisy's revelation of the murderer as she lay dying.

Ernie stared down at the photograph. 'She said it twice. She said "Ernie" twice.' It broke him, the memory of Daisy whispering his own name as she died.

They stayed a long time to comfort him, and the warder didn't interfere. Frances told Ernie he was brave. Brave as Robert in the army. She said there was hope now. What he'd done had given them new hope. At last he sat quietly, his eyes full of trust.

They left the prison at last, and went straight away to Sewell's office. Frances allowed her own spirits to rise.

'This is very good, ain't it, Mr Sewell? Ernie would never

make it up.' She grew animated, standing up in his office and beginning to pace beneath the shelves of heavy, leather-bound law books. 'They'll grant us an appeal now, don't you think?'

The solicitor smiled and nodded. He too stood up. 'I think we have a very good chance. You can go home and pass on the news. I'll be in touch as soon as we have a date for the new hearing.' He was more than pleased with the outcome.

'Before Christmas?'

He considered her eager expression. 'I should say between Christmas and the New Year, Miss Parsons.'

Her face fell.

'Yes, I know. It must be a torture for you all.' He came and shook her by the hand. 'Never say die, Miss Parsons. We're doing all we can, believe me. This time everything will depend on the medical men, and on Ernie. So keep up his spirits as best you can.'

Frances promised and left the office. There was new energy in her stride as she walked past the clerk at his desk and the telephonist busy speaking into her mouthpiece. She took the first tram home and alighted outside Coopers'. Billy Wray stood selling the evening papers. He noticed her as she made a bee-line straight towards him.

'Mr Sewell's managed to get up an appeal, Billy!' She was breathless. 'He was marvellous with Ernie today. He got him to remember every single thing about the murder. We're so glad you went and picked him out for us.'

People threaded between them, around his stall, down the close, or waiting at the kerb to cross the street. He felt jolted out of his own dull misery, back into life. 'Listen,' he said. 'I'll finish up here and you slip home. Give them the good news. Then meet me at Henshaw's and tell me all about it.'

She nodded her agreement. The family must know as soon as possible. Then she'd come and share it with Billy.

'We owe it all to him if Ernie gets off,' she told Robert. 'We got hold of Mr Sewell on his recommendation, and he's the best there is.'

Robert let his own hopes revive. 'We ain't beat yet,' he agreed. He wanted to go along to the Scrubs with Duke to help give Ernie a boost. When the news had been entirely bleak, he could hardly face the ordeal of a visit. Before long, the whole pub was looking on the bright side, and Frances left them to it, to make her own way back to the coffee shop.

Bea Henshaw had the news from Billy. She rushed to the doorway to greet Frances in a state of real pleasure, flustered but determined to have her say. She was a brisk, prim woman as a rule, but hopes for Ernie had given her a high colour and a breathless manner. 'Oh, Frances, we heard! Such good news. Your pa must be thrilled. Oh, my dear, we pray for him every single day. We want Ernie back with us, believe me!'

She led Frances, by now exhausted, to the table where Billy sat. Frances joined him, aware that circumstances had removed formalities and plunged them in the deep end again. Still, she stopped to ask about Ada's funeral, and the arrangements he'd had to make. 'You don't think me selfish for not asking sooner, do you, Billy? I've got a lot on my mind.'

Likewise, he told her. His mother-in-law had decamped and gone to live in Bermondsey with another daughter, to his secret relief. 'But I must say it leaves the house feeling big and empty, so I've got a plan in mind to sell up and move into a room above the Institute. I want to give up the newspaper stand, all in good time, of course.' He said the market life no longer suited him, and there was a chance to help the printer on some of the Workers' Education Centre publications.

'Lots of changes,' Frances commented. 'And now a new chance for Ernie.' She tried in vain not to let her hopes fly too high. Billy understood more about the process of appeal in such cases, and pointed out the complications. 'Still, we're banking on Mr Sewell and the doctors,' she told him. 'And we're grateful to you, Billy. We really are.'

He nodded. Frances kept on upsetting his balance like this by giving him sympathy or gratitude when he wanted something else. He wished things weren't so complicated by protocol, or by guilt and grief. Still, he offered her his arm and walked up the street with her. He was glad above all to have been of use.

Chapter Twenty-Eight

The Christmas truce came in the trenches, when British Tommies listened in wonderment to the familiar strains of 'Silent Night' sung in a strange tongue across the battlefield, and emerged to shake hands with the enemy, so like themselves. It meant little to the Parsons family or to the inhabitants of Duke Street and Paradise Court.

Local drama pushed national interests to one side as the day of Ernie's execution drew near. They sat round their firesides late at night, connected by a taut wire of dread, talking endlessly about the progress of Sewell's appeal. A hearing had been granted for New Year's Eve.

But on the morning of Christmas Eve, another, unexpected disaster struck. Edith Cooper travelled into town on the train and made her way to her husband's department store. This was unusual in itself, and her pale face, her dazed manner alerted the shop-girls to expect bad news. She walked between the counters bright with Christmas gifts, decked out with red ribbon and glass baubles. She gave no response to polite greetings, so that word went up ahead to the office that Mrs Cooper was here and all was not well.

Jack Cooper came to the top of the wide stairs to meet her, then led her into the privacy of the office. There could only be one reason for her being there.

'I had to tell you face to face,' she began.

'It's Teddy.'

She nodded. 'Oh, Jack, he's been shot down and killed.'

The words sank in like a stain. In those seconds of disbelief, Cooper went and picked up an invoice from his desk to file it in a drawer. He saw the paper shake in his hand. He looked up at his wife. 'They sure it was Teddy?'

Edith took the telegram from her bag and handed it to him. 'I read it over and over, Jack. There ain't no mistake.'

Jack Cooper sat at his desk and sank his big head into his hands. They'd snatched his boy, his only boy. He knew on the instant that he would have given his own life for Teddy's, but no one had offered him the chance. He was old, Teddy had been young, with his whole life ahead of him. The world was turned upside down. 'How? How could it happen? I thought he said them planes were safe.'

Edith went and bent over her husband. 'He wanted to fly them. It was his decision. We didn't have any way of knowing the dangers; this is a terrible war, Jack.'

He looked up. Shock had stunned him, but a strong idea already broke through that Edith was to blame. She'd forced the issue and made Teddy sign up. Then he was struck by her own misery, as she no doubt took this blame on herself; a double burden of grief and guilt. So he reached out for her hand. They thought of bullets ripping through the fabric of moth-flimsy wings, the rattle of rifle fire against propeller blades, the man in his cockpit gripping the joystick, the sudden end.

From the hosiery sweatshop in the basement to the hat workers in the attic, news of Teddy's death swept through the building. There was no false sympathy for the man himself, but a sober awareness of the new family situation, bereft of son and heir. Most of the women felt quiet fellow feeling for the grieving mother. She'd always behaved well and done her best with her wayward son. Teddy himself might have turned out all right in the end. Hindsight already softened perception of his womanizing ways. A pity he'd had no real chance to prove himself in civilian life, they said. They craned at windows to watch Jack Cooper take his wife out to the car.

'Stop whining, Lettie,' Dora Kennedy snapped, as the women in the hatters' workshop got back to work. 'And don't snivel over that bolt of best silk neither.' She rolled back her sleeves and seized the hot iron. 'We all know them's crocodile tears.' Tall, bony Dora would in fact miss Teddy's bravado and quick wit more than most. She liked to watch him in action with the Amy Ogdens and the Lettie Harrises. But she wouldn't let on that her world was a greyer place without him. There was no room for sentiment in her grim armoury.

Lettie wiped the tears with the heels of her hands and sniffed loudly.

'Here.' Emmy handed her a grubby cotton rag. She knew that Lettie had got news yesterday that her older brother, Arnie, was missing in action. As it happened, most families had at least one worry of this kind; brothers injured or missing, sons killed. 'Lay off, Dora,' she warned, against the hiss of steam and the thump of the iron.

All day they picked on Bert Buggles for being too mean to buy the girls a Christmas box of chocolates, for lounging in the corner with his racing tips, and for sloping off early when there were still orders to finish and pack. They clung to normality, while the war relentlessly robbed them of their menfolk.

Down the court, Christmas came and went under leaden skies, amongst aching hearts. A few regular customers braved the swing doors of the Duke's public bar, but they soon drifted out again. No holly decked the fine mirrors, no tunes played on the pianola. The place was like a morgue, they said.

Two days before Ernie's appeal, Robert sat quietly over a midday drink at the Duke with his friend and saviour, George Mann. George had himself received a shoulder wound bad enough to get sent home to recover. By now he was on the mend, almost ready to return to the war. But he looked in on Robert and was introduced to his family, bashful in the face of their immense gratitude.

In his talk with Robert he took a different view of things. Losing a leg was bad, but not the end of the world. He'd seen poor bleeders with their faces shot away, unlucky enough to survive. These days you got the order to go over the top and you saw men running in the opposite direction. They were rounded up and shot like dogs. The end couldn't come soon enough for George, yet he'd always reckoned on being strong-willed enough to withstand anything they threw at him. 'It ain't like it says in the papers, you and me both know that, Rob. Some mornings you wake up and you think you've landed in hell.'

Robert agreed. He appreciated the visit. Duke had taken to George, with his brawny, strapping figure and modest, level-headed way. He spoke out plain and simple; saving Rob from the battlefield was what any man would do for another.

Duke offered open house to George as soon as the war was ended, when he hoped to return to his old job on the docks across the water. 'Drop in any time, mate. You'll always find a welcome here.'

As George shook hands again and got up to go, a

message came with Joe O'Hagan. Would Robert be kind enough to call in on Mrs Cooper at the shop? Or would it be more convenient if she came and visited him here?

Robert sent back the message that he would find his own way there, and went up the street with George. There was a pea-souper of a fog, so acid and thick that it caught in their throats and enveloped the passing traffic, which roared and rattled past almost invisible. Swinging himself forward on his crutches, Robert welcomed the fog, for it hid his awkward, maimed figure. He parted with his comrade at Meredith Close. 'Look after yourself.' He freed one hand from the crutch by leaning heavily on the other.

George shook him warmly by the hand. 'Don't worry, mate. They ain't made the bullet yet that's got my name written on it!' He winked, nodded and walked off, smart and upright in his immaculate khaki uniform. The fog soon swallowed him, and Robert turned to go into the store.

Edith felt she simply wanted to talk to someone who'd been in the war like Teddy, someone who knew the suddenness and randomness of death. She wanted to hear that her son's end had been quick and sure.

Robert explained the job of the Flying Corps pilots. It wasn't quite as simple as flying overhead to determine enemy positions, for of course the enemy wanted to stop them and sent up his own planes to scare off the allies. They had gunners in the cockpits, sitting tight up behind the pilots, with machine-guns mounted on swivelling rests, and these gunners were highly trained and deadly. It depended on the skill of the pilots to dip and weave out of the line of enemy fire, but there was bombardment from below too. Robert had watched the dog fights in the air and counted himself lucky to be ankle deep in mud and filth, protected by sandbags and barbed wire.

'I hear the Hun's got hold of something new; a forward-mounted gun that fires between the propeller blades, specially timed to the split second. It means they can come straight at you, instead of sideways on.'

Edith sighed and nodded. 'Teddy never wrote and told us that.' They were in her husband's empty office. Robert looked uncomfortable, but he spoke calmly. She was grateful to him for putting himself out. How opposite to Teddy he was; dark and solid, very earnest.

'He ain't allowed to. It's all very hush-hush. But we knew them boys took a terrible risk every time they set off. You'd see them go up in flames and drop like a stone, straight down. They got plenty of guts going up there on a wing and a prayer to get shot down.'

Edith nodded again as tears welled up. 'Thank you.'

'No, I mean it. You wouldn't get me up there in one of them things, I can tell you.' He leaned forward. 'Will you tell Mr Cooper we're very sorry the way it happened. It ain't easy.'

She registered the pain the other family must be going through. She said she was glad there was an appeal for Ernie; it must surely succeed. They sat and looked at each other, caught between despair and hope, bitterness and nobility; the handsome, maimed young man and the gracious, grieving mother.

Ernie appeared at the appeal looking thin and unwell. The flesh had fallen away from his face, giving the brown eyes a wide, startled look. Prison pallor had settled on him and his movements were more stumbling than ever. Still, he put on a brave face for his family as he finally came on to the witness stand.

His account of the discovery of Daisy's body was consistent with the version he'd given to Sewell and Frances in prison. The memories were still painful; they were often broken by long pauses, to the obvious irritation of the judge. Many times the family longed to step in to save him his agony.

Though fewer onlookers had gathered in the gallery, stalwarts like Annie, Florrie and Dolly remained. They'd nodded their heads wisely during the evidence offered by the eminent medical men, remarking that it had been obvious from the start. The poor bloke had been shocked out of his wits, anyone with an ounce of common sense could see that.

Then came the vital summing up. Mayhew approached the jury as humane, decent men. They would recognize truth as it had been presented to them here. They would see that Ernie Parsons was sincere. 'You cannot hold it against a man for caring too much, for holding Daisy O'Hagan so dear in his simple heart that the discovery of her murder led to a state of complete shock and amnesia lasting several weeks, until the impact of her death gradually settled in his confused mind. You will surely believe him now.'

He walked along the row, appealing to each juryman in turn. His voice carried conviction and understanding. 'Remember, gentlemen, the law tells us that to convict a man of murder you have to know! You have to *know* that a man is lying when he protests his innocence. More important still, you have to *know* that there is no other possible explanation, no other possible culprit.

'New evidence has been brought to light here in this court today which shows us that there was indeed someone else present at the scene: a cry, a struggle, a frantic attempt to escape without being seen, and then a cold-blooded willingness to let another man hang for a crime he did not commit. All changes in an instant, does it not, gentlemen?

And the horror of the guilty verdict rears up to confront us as our worst nightmare.'

Characteristically, Mayhew lowered his voice as he came towards the end of his plea. He rested both hands on the lapels of his gown and stood full square before the jury. 'Consider the condemned man for a final moment.' The heads of the jurymen all swivelled at his bidding. They kept Ernie in their sights as they listened. 'No pressure in the world could make this man confess to the murder of Daisy O'Hagan. No police interview, no energetic cross-examination by my learned friend here today has brought about the slightest deviation in his account. And this is not because you see before you an accomplished liar and a fraud. No, this is because your man is innocent.' He paused. 'I was going to say as innocent as the day he was born, because in this case it would not be inappropriate. In this country we do not hang a man as a scapegoat for the heinous crime of another. That is not justice, gentlemen. Consider him once more, and I beg of you, go off and grant his appeal against conviction.'

Ernie sat mute in the dock. Duke and his family prayed with all their hearts. Forster could say what he liked; surely he could not sway the jury now.

But prosecuting counsel adopted a condescending tone. He could understand the softer feelings called out by the defence. How easy it was to feel sorry for someone under the shadow of the noose. 'We would be hard-hearted men indeed if we did not balk momentarily at such a punishment. But, more surely still, we would be weak-willed cowards to back off from our original conviction.' Forster twisted them to his point of view; the patrician whose sophisticated ideas they must accept.

'After all, what does this "new evidence" amount to? No more than a simple change of story; an invented scream, an invented attacker and an invented loss of memory. As for medical opinion, gentlemen, take that as you will.

'Our eminent doctors would freely admit that amnesia can be faked. They tell us that memory loss is possible in such a case as this, they do not tell us it *is* so. And as my learned friend so wisely pointed out, "You have to *know*." We do not know that the accused is sincere. We have only his word. Yet we have his fingerprints on the murder weapon. We have his bloody footprints leaving the scene of the crime. This is what we *know*, gentlemen!' He paused before he finished his man off. 'So let's have no more nonsense about changing our minds and such like. Let us have the courage to stick by our decision and to see justice done.' He bowed, then went to sit, lips pursed, eyes busily scanning the papers on his desk.

'The devil!' Annie muttered.

Florrie and Dolly looked down anxiously at Duke and the rest. They felt the spider snares of abstract justice entangle them.

Once again the judge and jury retired. Once again the endless wait, the fluctuating hopes and fears. The family scarcely talked, their minds fixed on Ernie's own feelings as he sat in his cell and awaited the verdict.

The announcements were made. The appeal was lost.

Ernie was taken from them a second time and they were plunged into the pit. Hopeless, speechless, defeated, they filed from the court.

That evening, Duke sat at the living-room table and addressed a letter to the most eminent man in charge of law and order throughout England: the Home Secretary. Sewell said it was the only avenue left open; a plea for mercy and a stay of execution. They had four days.

Duke's letter flowed on to the white page. It spoke of the difficulty the family had in understanding the ins and outs of the law. He did see how bad it looked for Ernie, and how his simplicity could be turned against him. It described his son's character as loving, obedient and gentle.

'Ernie has lived an honest life and I hope we taught him the same, since the death of his poor mother when he was little. Ernie ain't like other boys. He needs more help with things, and it breaks my heart when I think of him trying to cope with this latest piece of bad news.

'He ain't never committed no criminal acts in the whole of his life, and you have to believe me when I say he ain't no murderer. I swear on the Holy Bible in front of me.

'But the law is the law, and they seen fit to convict my poor boy and turn him down on appeal earlier today. His sisters, his brother and me know they mean to hang him before the week is out, so I write to you now, sir, for you to step in and stop this terrible thing before it is too late. If you don't help us, it don't bear thinking about.

'The boy accepts it all, and I left him calm when we came away from court. But his sisters and his aunt ain't coping, and we're all broken-hearted.

'Like I said before, sir, we want you to stop the hanging. We know you can do this for us, and save our boy from the noose.'

Duke signed himself as 'obedient servant'. He pushed the letter adrift into the middle of the table. Sadie, Hettie and Robert read it through with dull eyes. Jess came out of the bedroom carrying Grace. She nodded; yes they should send it straight off. Florrie and Frances agreed. The light was turned down low, the embers settled in the grate as Duke sealed the white envelope, set it down, then bowed his head over clasped hands and prayed.

Chapter Twenty-Nine

Sewell took charge of the delivery of the vital letter. For the family at the Duke, time passing became a nightmare, like having hideous foreknowledge of an assassin lying in wait around a corner, but being powerless to stop him. The minutes ticked by on the living-room clock.

In the cold first week of the New Year, business was almost at a standstill in the pub and out on the market stalls in Duke Street. Liz Sargent stamped her feet and blew on to her hands behind her boxes of fish. 'Might as well pack up here and sod off home,' she complained to Nora Brady.

Nora looked up at the heavy grey sky. 'It's gonna bleeding well snow if we're not careful.' She tried to cheer herself up by changing the subject. 'You thinking of going up the Duke tonight for a singsong?'

Liz shrugged. 'Ain't gonna have the time of our lives up there, are we? Like a bleeding morgue, according to Dolly Ogden, and I ain't a bit surprised.'

Nora jutted out her bottom lip. 'Who'd want the job of hangman in this day and age? It ain't natural. Do you think he has kippers for his breakfast the day he does it?'

'Don't.' Liz shuddered. 'I heard he has to have a chat with the poor bleeder and shakes him by the hand. Just think. You know you're for the chop, and you have to act matey with the geezer what does it.' She shook her head. 'How they taking it?'

'Who?'

'The family.'

'Bad. They sent a letter off to the Home Secretary, asking him to lift the noose from round the poor boy's neck. But they ain't hopeful.' Nora had spoken with Annie. 'They ain't letting on to Ernie though. They tell him he's bound to get off, trying to keep his spirits up.'

Liz looked doubtful. 'I think I'd tell him the score if it was me. How long they gonna go on fooling him?'

'Long as they can. They only got two days to go.'

This and similar conversations were held in hushed voices up and down the street. Snow threatened, trade was bad. The war lumbered on and Kitchener wanted more men. People said times were so bad that all the able-bodied young men flocked to enlist. 'And they come back home in a box, or not at all, like poor Teddy Cooper. Or useless, like Robert Parsons.'

Amy Ogden, standing freezing behind Annie's haberdashery stall, overheard such remarks. It brought back memories of when Teddy was alive and she had a steady job at Coopers', before all this trouble. She lapsed into self-pity; she'd only done what any girl would, making the best of her looks and setting her cap at the boss's son. She knew there were those who still blamed her, but they didn't see how she herself had been badly treated by a so-called toff, and her own family had ditched her over it. A girl had to make her own way now, and she didn't expect to have to freeze to death over a load of glass buttons and stay-hooks. Amy snivelled. Life looked bleak on this early January day.

'Bleeding misery,' Annie grumbled. 'If you don't cheer up, girl, I'm gonna have to lay you off work again. You're scaring my bleeding customers.'

Amy glanced up and down the half-deserted street. 'Ain't no bleeding customers.'

'No, that's because you scared them all off, like I said. What's got into you, anyway?' Annie, like Nora Brady, was deciding to call it a day. She began to reach under the stall for the lids to the cardboard boxes full of needles, thread, ribbons and lace.

'Nothing.'

'Here, catch hold of these.' Annie handed her the lids. 'If this is "nothing", I don't want to see "something".' She considered that Amy might make a bit more effort and think of someone other than herself for a change. 'What's the problem, girl? You gonna let on?'

'I got something on my mind, Annie. Just leave it, will you?' Amy found the right-sized boxes for the lids. The cold had pinched her nose and cheeks and chilled her to the bone. She felt truly miserable.

'Ain't we all?' Annie sighed. She thought of Ernie.

Amy hesitated, then took the plunge. She had to get it off her chest. 'Syd let something drop last night. It keeps bothering me, I don't know why.'

Annie stood with an armful of boxes, ready to load them on her small handcart. 'Come on, spit it out, girl.' She'd no liking for Syd Swan since his gloating performance at the trial.

'Oh, it's nothing. Forget I said anything.' It was a small niggle; something not quite right in Syd's recollection of the night of the murder. He was always going on about it, boasting how he'd helped to finger the killer. Last night, on the tram home from the Gem, he'd let slip a fact he'd never mentioned before.

'What did he say exactly?' Annie insisted. The slightest thing was worth knowing.

'Nothing much, Annie, really. He just dropped Chalky's

name into the conversation, like he was there at the Palace that night.'

'Chalky White?' Annie looked puzzled. He'd never entered the picture during the trial. She understood that Robert had flattened him earlier that day, and he'd had to hide away in his room. The police had never even had him in the picture, as far as she knew. 'Weren't he busy licking his wounds?' she asked.

'That's the way I saw it. So I says to Syd, "I thought Chalky stayed home that night?" And he says, yes, he did. He says I must have made a mistake; he never mentioned Chalky's name. I said he did. We had a blazing row on the tram. Syd just blew up at me.'

'But you still say he did mention it?' Annie seized the suspicion like a terrier. She dropped her boxes on to the cart and turned to grab Amy's hand. 'Syd did say Chalky was up the Palace the night of the murder?'

'Let go, Annie, you're hurting!' Amy withdrew her hand. 'Yes, he did. Then he turns round and tells me I must have gone round the twist; Chalky's name never passed his lips. Give me a bad fright, he did.' Feeling sorry for herself, she sniffed and turned on the tears. 'He said for me to keep my mouth shut, or else. Now he's gonna have a go at me again.'

'Never mind, you done the right thing, girl.' Annie quickly put her thoughts in order. 'You pack up here and take the cart on down the court. There's something I gotta do.' She nodded and set off up the street.

'Annie!' Amy's terrified voice called after her.

Annie turned.

'Don't say it was me. I'll get a beating off Syd if he finds out.' She stood in dismay at the chain of events she seemed to have unleashed.

Annie agreed, then hurried up to the Duke.

Duke stood behind the bar as usual. He'd just opened

up for the evening, determined to go through the motions. There'd been no word from the Home Secretary. Two days had gone by, and no word back. Each hour on the hour he went to the door and looked for the cream letter with the House of Commons seal. It never arrived.

'Duke!' Annie clattered through the doors and across the nearly empty bar. 'I got something to tell you!' She gasped and clutched the edge of the counter for support. Her hair had come loose from under her hat, her dark eyes were fired up. 'I knew things weren't right, and now I put my finger on it, thanks to a certain person!'

'Calm down, Annie.' Jess had come straight downstairs to see what the fuss was about when she saw and heard Annie make her frantic entrance. She wanted to spare Duke any extra trouble, so she took the older woman by the arm and looked to Florrie for help. Her aunt came over from the window, where she'd been busy wiping down tables. They got ready to walk Annie out smartly through the still swinging doors. 'We know how you feel. None of us is taking it that well. But it don't do no good making a fuss. You gotta let Pa be. So come on, Annie, girl. Let's get you home.'

Annie shook herself free and pushed them to one side.

'Act your age, woman,' Florrie said severely. She pulled her blouse straight. 'You can't barge in here like this.'

'Shut your mouth, Florrie Searles! And you, Jess, you listen to this!' Annie reached across the bar and laid hold of both of Duke's hands. 'It's the night of the murder, right? Your Rob's come out of the Palace and he has to hang around for Ernie. He sets eyes on that nasty piece of work, Swan, and two or three of his mates, and he gives them a run for their money.'

Duke nodded and sighed. 'What is this, Annie? This ain't nothing new.'

'Not yet, it ain't. But you just hold on. Rob seen Syd
and that bloke, Whitey, and one or two other hooligans.
But he ain't never mentioned Chalky White, has he?' Annie
delivered her news at a gabble. 'And Syd Swan ain't
mentioned him neither. So we think he ain't there that
night, and no one gives him a second thought.'

Jess came forward. 'What you saying, Annie?'

'I'm saying he *was* there. There at the Palace. But he
weren't hanging round with the gang, or Rob would've
spotted him, see!'

Jess nodded. She looked quickly at Duke.

'So where was he?' Annie demanded.

'Backstage.' Jess's two simple syllables, delivered flat and
deadly quiet, set up a flock of suspicions.

'Chalky White,' Duke said. He looked Annie in the eyes.
'You sure?'

She nodded. 'Think about it. They never go nowhere
without him, and he ain't one to stop home for a couple of
cuts and bruises. He was there all right!'

'And he'd fallen out with Daisy, Pa.' Jess had been
carried along by Annie's reasoning. 'I can just see him
getting his own back.'

'She threw him over. Ask Ett. You seen her in here with
him, ain't you? And he didn't like it one little bit when he
said she didn't want nothing to do with him. Ask Rob. I
think she had a bellyful of trouble with him.' Annie refused
to calm down. She released hold of Duke and shook Jess by
the arm. 'What we gonna do?'

'I don't know. I'll go and get Maurice for a start. You
stay here and see who else we can round up. Tell the others.
Ett's upstairs working. Tell her to find Rob.' Jess flew
towards the door. 'That's right, Pa, ain't it?'

Duke hesitated. 'It ain't much to go on.' He narrowed
his eyes and thought it through. 'But it's better than

nothing. You spotted something there all right, Annie. And when we lay hands on Syd Swan, he'll squeal, don't you worry. I know his sort.' He nodded at Jess, then went down into the cellar to fetch Joxer. They would gather all their help, then decide what to do.

Maurice was setting off for the Gem when Jess tracked him down. He handed over the cinema keys to Charlie and told him he was trusting him to open up the box-office. He'd get to work as soon as he could. Charlie walked on, but he stopped on Duke Street to let Tommy O'Hagan know what was going on. 'They're after Syd Swan. Anyone know where he is?'

Tommy had finished work for the day, and eagerly took up the cry. He ran up the street and passed the word. Soon all the kids on street-corners and doorsteps swarmed off down the alleys. Word was out; Syd Swan was wanted. Don't let him know, but go back and tell them at the Duke. There was trouble brewing; big trouble.

Tommy knew the gang's usual haunts and he was quick on his feet. He used all the short cuts, looking in all the likely places. It was he who landed back at the pub with the first news. 'Syd's down at Milo's,' he reported. 'With Chalky.' His breathless message provided the key.

The men left the pub straight away. Florrie was glad that Duke had decided to stay put and let the others deal with it. It was a young man's game, he realized. Walter Davidson said they didn't know what to expect exactly, but that he would keep an eye on Rob. Duke sent Joxer and Maurice to back them up. 'Don't do nothing stupid,' he warned. 'We want the truth, not a bloodbath.'

'We want Ernie out of that place,' Rob reminded him. 'Whatever it takes.'

Sadie, Hettie, Jess and Frances came out into the dark

street to watch them go. They stood in silence. It was a last chance for Ernie; no one else could help him now.

Milo came up the long, shabby room to greet Rob and his friends. 'Good to see you out of that chair, mate.' His smile wavered. 'What's up? You ain't had no more bad news, I hope?'

Men exercised and trained in all corners of the room. Iron weights rattled against the wooden floor, there was the thud of punch-bags, the scrape and squeak of shoes on canvas. The raised platform of the ring was occupied. Inside its ropes, Chalky White and an opponent were sparring.

'There's Swan, over there!' Walter pointed him out. He was standing fully dressed, with his elbows hooked over the low rope bordering the ring, shouting encouragement to Chalky and measuring his form.

Maurice took Milo to one side and quietly explained their mission. The small Irishman nodded. 'I wish you luck, mate.' He stood by and watched as the newcomers closed in on Swan.

Chalky spotted them first, as he moved his sparring partner round the ring and came into a position which gave him full view of the intruders. He went flat on his feet and dropped his guard, eyeing them warily. They looked an ill-assorted group: Joxer in his waistcoat and shirt-sleeves, Robert on his crutches, Maurice dressed up smartly for work and Walter buttoned up inside a greatcoat. But he could see it was trouble. Syd turned to investigate.

Robert stood forward of the group. They were framed by the long, black windows of the gym which reflected the yellow glare of electric bulbs. Curiosity had brought other men up close, their attention on Syd and Chalky to see what they would make of the interruption. Many breathed heavily. They stood about idly, their hands still strapped with tape, their singlets damp with sweat.

At a signal from Robert, Maurice and Walter moved in on Syd. 'We hear you've got a new story,' he began, 'about who was where when Daisy got done in.' He kept his eyes on Chalky, as the other two moved Syd up against the nearest wall. 'You might be interested to hear this and all,' he told Swan, without deflecting his gaze from Chalky.

'I ain't said nothing, Chalky!' Syd protested. They'd caught him off guard. Maurice and Walter had backed him right into the corner.

'Shut it!' Chalky warned. He stooped under the ropes and vaulted down to floor level. 'What the bleeding hell do you think you're up to?' He was face to face with Robert, aware of Joxer's bulky figure in the background. A taut nerve flicked in his cheek and pulled down one corner of his almost lipless mouth. He saw Robert give another signal to the two who'd cornered Syd.

Walter laid into Syd's body with well-rehearsed skill and timing. Syd aimed a return blow but missed, as Walter ducked. They heard the air expelled from his lungs by Walter's second, thudding punch. He collapsed forward as Chalky began to move in to join the fight. But then Joxer loomed up from behind and hooked a massive arm around Chalky's neck. He locked his elbow in position, forcing the man's head back, half-strangling him.

Maurice caught hold of Walter. 'Wait! See if he's ready to talk!'

Syd gasped and clutched his stomach, then he swung out, dribbling saliva, coughing, catching Maurice on the side of the jaw, so that Maurice had to lunge back at him to prevent him from running off. Joxer held tight to Chalky, keeping him pinioned against his own chest. Soon he ran him straight at his accomplice, like a battering ram, and bundled them back into the corner. He was so powerful that both men went sprawling.

Chalky looked up from his humiliating position. His hand slipped sideways into Syd's jacket pocket and he pulled out a knife, gleaming silver, long and sharp. He crouched, and a sneer came on to his face. Syd came up beside him. They edged forward, mocking and jeering as Maurice and Joxer were forced to back off.

'Go on, Syd, tell us why you never said Chalky was there.' Robert held his nerve. 'Couldn't be that he was busy backstage, could it?'

'Prove it,' Chalky snarled. He sprang at Robert with his knife, slashing through mid-air in wild, stabbing movements. Robert raised one crutch to protect himself.

The onlookers backed away. Milo ran to his office to use the telephone to ring Union Street station.

Joxer saw Chalky come at Robert with his knife. He put one shoulder down and charged, so heavy and strong that he knocked the attacker off course. He reached down for the knife as Chalky's arm flailed backwards, then grabbed his wrist and shook the weapon free. It clattered to the floor. Robert swung at it with his crutch and knocked it out of reach. Now Joxer was enraged, and he punched at his man's body and face, letting go a battery of blows.

Syd crouched back down and watched in dismay. Walter wrenched him to his feet and throttled him against the wall. 'Spit it out!' he ordered. 'I'm not stopping Joxer until we get what we want from you!' They heard Chalky groan under the weight of the cellarman's punches.

'All right, all right, he was there!' Syd broke down. 'So what? Call him off. He'll bleeding well kill him!'

Chalky groaned again. He'd fallen on the floor and tried to curl up, but Joxer rolled him over with one foot and bent to drag him upright again.

'Right, he was at the Palace,' Maurice challenged. 'We got that. Now what?'

'Now nothing.' Syd winced as Joxer landed another blow to Chalky's body.

Walter flattened him against the wall again. 'He went to see Daisy, didn't he? You was hanging around waiting for him. He went backstage and done her in!'

'No!'

They heard Chalky slump to the ground as Joxer let him go. The big man moved across towards Syd.

'Come on!' Robert urged. There'd be another murder committed before long. He saw Syd cower in Joxer's shadow, and realized he couldn't take punishment like Chalky. 'It was Chalky, wasn't it?'

Syd's nerve broke down. 'Yes!' he gasped.

Robert heard the confession. His head went down and he took a deep, shuddering breath. Maurice held him up. Joxer towered over Syd, while Walter kept an eye on their murderer, still lying half senseless on the floor.

'Call him off,' Syd pleaded. 'I said it was Chalky, ain't I? He went looking for trouble, said she had it coming. I thought he was gonna smack her about a bit, that's all. I didn't know he was gonna do her in!'

Chalky groaned and lifted a hand in protest. They pulled him to his feet. Vivid bruises already stood out on his cheekbone, a trickle of blood ran from one corner of his mouth. He knew it was all over.

'Get the police,' Maurice said.

Milo hovered in the background. 'They're on their way.' There was a stunned silence throughout the gym.

'Ask him why he did it,' Robert said, his voice shaky. 'Tell him I want to know.'

Daisy had laughed at him, it was as simple as that. He'd called her out from her dressing room into the dark alley, and she'd put her hand to her mouth and laughed at his black eye. She said she was glad Robert had given him it; it was no more than he deserved. She didn't want to go round with his sort, how many times did she need to tell him? He'd better make himself scarce. She laughed in his face and went to call Fred Mills for help.

That was when he followed her inside, after all the others had left. Fred Mills spotted him and left him to sort the girl out. It was none of his business, the manager said. Daisy wouldn't stop laughing. She'd gone hysterical when he started to push her about. Then he drew the knife. It was over in seconds.

'You done the girl in because she laughed?' Robert repeated. He shook his head in disbelief. 'And I bet that Fred Mills seen you at it. I bet he knows.'

Chalky stared sullenly back.

'Bastards, they were all in on it. They let Ernie get it in the neck without lifting a finger!' Robert stammered.

'Not any more.' Walter put an arm around his shoulder. 'We nailed them this time, mate. We nailed them good and proper.'

Chapter Thirty

Tommy O'Hagan was proud of the part he'd played in the arrest of Daisy's true murderer. He'd come a long way since he used to hang about Waterloo Station on the off-chance of earning a penny or two cab-ducking, or pestering the carters' yards to cut up hay. He'd seen life in the raw and been to sea. He'd set up his own barrow. He'd officially left school. 'No more Miss Sweetlips for me,' he told Sadie, remembering all too well Mr Donaldson's less-than-affectionate use of the cane, the books thrown as missiles, the hog-tying of boys to radiators. 'School's a mug's game for the likes of Charlie Ogden, not for me.'

Sadie appreciated how much Tommy had come on. He worked for himself and was doing very well. He was even thinking of hiring a lad and taking on Billy Wray's stall as well. He'd been practising the newspaper vendor's raucous, incomprehensible cry. And he'd filled out to fit his new jacket; no longer the skinny, ragged-arsed kid. He combed his hair, used a razor at least once a week, and prided himself on his valuable contribution to the family budget.

'You know something, if I'd been around when our Daisy got herself done in, they'd never have nicked Ernie in the first place,' he bragged.

'Oh, bleeding Sherlock Holmes now, are we?' At the

moment, Sadie would forgive Tommy anything. He'd slung his arm around her shoulder, leaning back against the bar with his other elbow. The room was crowded out with all their friends and family. Ernie sat at a table, the smiling centre of it all.

Tommy polished his nails against his chest. 'You just gotta keep your eyes peeled, that's all. You gotta be one step ahead.'

Sadie shoved him sideways and broke free. She stood, hands on hips, studying his white neck scarf, his bold brass buckle. 'Talk about big-headed!' She flashed him a challenging look. 'You're still nothing but a peaky blinder, Tommy O'Hagan, with that stupid cap and everything. Who you trying to kid?'

Tommy exaggerated his disappointment. 'Oh, Sadie, don't say that. Here's me thinking we'd clicked.'

'The day I click with you, Tommy, is the day they cart me off and throw away the key.'

'I'll go and chuck myself off London Bridge, you heartless girl.'

'And spoil your nice new jacket? Don't do that, Tom.' Sadie was aware of Charlie sitting with his family at a nearby table. She flirted with Tommy for all she was worth.

Maurice's words about throwing over a good-looking girl came back to haunt Charlie now. Sadie, restored to high spirits by Ernie's last-minute reprieve, sparkled. There was a time last year when he'd sat on a grassy bank with his arms round that girl, taking for granted the nearness of her creamy, smooth cheek, the soft intensity of her dark-fringed eyes. He'd showered her with bluebells and run laughing with her across a sweet-smelling carpet of flowers under branches newly green. He'd given her up, and now he must watch her flirt with Tommy. He frowned.

'Serves you right,' Dolly said. She followed his gaze and read his thoughts. 'You made your own bed there, son. Now you gotta lie on it.'

'Leave the boy alone.' Arthur cottoned on to his son's regret. 'No need to rub it in.' He pulled at his pint, ready to play the man of the world. 'Love them and leave them. That's my advice, Charlie. Ain't none of them worth losing no sleep over.' He winked and drank again.

Dolly laughed uproariously. 'Look who's talking; love them and leave them! A proper little Romeo, ain't you, Arthur Ogden? If you want to know the truth, I think you chucked over a real gem there, Charlie.' She waved at Sadie and called her over to join them. 'Just sit tight and be nice to the girl. I'll try and bring her round for you. You never know your luck.'

But Charlie blushed red to the roots of his hair. 'No, Ma. I told Mr Leigh I'd go ahead and open up.' He pulled a big bunch of keys from his jacket pocket. 'I gotta dash.' He leapt for the door as Sadie approached.

Amy grinned. 'Mister Leigh this, Mister Leigh that,' she mimicked. You'd think the sun shone out of that man's backside.

'Hush, Amy.' Dolly stood up to embrace the youngest Parsons girl. 'Sadie, we're over the moon for you, girl. We can't hardly believe it. This is the best bit of news we had in ages.' She held her close and patted her on the back. 'When they took Ernie away it was as bad as losing one of our own, I can tell you. The whole street was cut up. But now he's back!' Even Dolly ran out of words at last. She held Sadie at arm's length, eyes glistening. 'How about organizing a singsong to celebrate?' she asked. 'Go on, you got a voice like a canary when you get going. And Amy here. You girls get over there and sort it out for us, put us in the mood.'

Sadie smiled down at Amy. 'Come on,' she said. She linked arms and they threaded their way through the crowd gathered to join in Ernie's home-coming. When they reached the pianola, she turned to the older girl, who still looked downcast after the strain of recent events. She had put on an unconvincing show of dolling herself up for the occasion with flowers and feathers in her hair, but her conscience was uneasy. 'What's up, Amy?' Sadie wanted to know. 'You don't look yourself tonight. It ain't Syd, is it?'

Syd Swan was in deep trouble for concealing material evidence from the Crown. Chalky was firmly behind bars and without its leader the gang had disintegrated. In fact, Whitey and a couple of others had moved across the water until the fuss died down, and Syd was rumoured to be holed up in his ma's place in Walthamstow. Amy knew she was safe from him at present, but she didn't underestimate his long-term resentment. She felt no regret about his absence from Duke Street. 'No, it ain't Syd,' she confessed.

Sadie softened towards her and took her by the hand. 'Has any of us said thanks to you yet, Amy?'

'No, what for?'

'For fingering Chalky for us. That took plenty of guts, that did.'

Amy inhaled deeply. It took her a while to realize that Sadie meant it, then she shrugged.

'It did. And you was on the ball to pick it up in the first place, from what I hear. We got a lot to thank you for.'

'Oh, I ain't been too clever on the whole,' Amy protested. Not really.'

But Sadie wouldn't hear of it. Her gratitude bubbled over, and soon everyone within earshot was saying, yes, Amy Ogden was the one to thank. Without her, Chalky and Syd would have got away with it. They wouldn't all be sitting here now celebrating if not for her.

'You know,' Dolly said to Arthur, surprise registering in her voice, 'that girl of ours done us proud.' She sat nodding. 'All right, so she put a foot wrong here and there. Don't we all? But her heart's in the right place, ain't it?'

Amy's head had gone up, pleased as punch. She was getting ready to sing alongside Sadie Parsons.

Arthur breathed a sigh of relief. 'Blimey, you mean you two ain't gonna be at each other's throats no more?'

Dolly smiled blithely back. 'If they can climb out of the trenches for a Christmas truce, I reckon Amy and me can call it a day. That's what I say. Anyhow, I been thinking.'

'Oh, bleeding Nora!' Arthur hated it when Dolly schemed. It usually cost money.

'No, seriously. I been thinking. I want to send the girl to learn how to be one of them typewriters. I been talking to Frances, and she says it's the up-and-coming thing; girls working in offices.'

'Clackety-clack, bleeding machines,' Arthur grumbled. But he could see the writing on the wall. Dolly had ambitions for Amy. Well, it was better than open warfare in the house. 'Where's the money coming from?' he argued.

Dolly eyed him severely. 'You gotta get a job, Arthur. That's where the money's coming from.'

Arthur definitely drew the line at that. Moving with the times was one thing, and having ambitions above your station. But sending a sick man out to work to pay for it was quite another. He wheezed into his beer. He and Dolly would bicker about it for weeks, then Dolly would work miracles to find the money and send Amy off to college. There was no stopping her.

Before Amy and Sadie could get the singing into full swing, Hettie and her friends came round with the collecting tin for the Salvation Army.

'Cashing in, eh?' Robert winked. He hadn't got used to

this transformation in his fun-loving sister, but he respected her decision. He tipped a few coins into her tin.

'Why not?' Hettie retorted. 'Don't you think God deserves a bit of the praise and some thanks round here?' She held out the tin and rattled it under the noses of some of Rob's friends. Walter Davidson dug deep in his pocket. 'It's God kept us going through the darkest hours, ain't it, Ern?'

Ernie heard her shout and nodded back. He wanted to wallow in the moment, to agree with everyone, see the smiles on people's faces. He still couldn't believe the moment when the key had turned in the lock and Duke had come into the cell specially set aside for the condemned man. He was with Mr Sewell, who delivered the news. They'd caught the real murderer. Ernie was free to go.

Duke had confirmed it; it was true. Rob and the girls were waiting outside at the prison gate, all of them. The warder held the door wide open. Ernie was reprieved. He had remembered to thank God, and the warder who'd looked after him without harshness or contempt.

'Good luck, mate.' The warder clapped him on the shoulder and sent him on his way. At the gate, he fell into everyone's arms and they took him home in a taxi. He slept in his own clean bed.

'All right, all right, less of the Onward Christian Soldiers, thank you very much,' Robert murmured. 'It used to be Frances what was bad for business, but she turned out normal lately, and you stepped in for her.'

Walter kicked him under the table. 'Give it a rest, Rob.' He was fascinated by the change in Hettie, knowing there was a good-looking, vivacious woman lurking under that poky bonnet. He could understand her turning to the Army, though, and thought Robert was being too hard.

'She don't mind, do you, Ett?'

'Not if you cough up all the coppers you got in your pockets, Robert Parsons; I don't care what you say.' She asked after Walter's bruised hands and said thank you to him for the hundredth time. Her combination of natural warmth and zeal for the cause was irresistible. She and Freda took record amounts, before they set up the singsong with Sadie and Amy, turning their faces to the ornate ceiling and bursting with praise for the Lord.

Walter grinned at Rob. 'I wouldn't argue with her if I was you, pal.' He was happy to sit and talk things over with his friend. For the first time since his return from the Front, it seemed Robert wanted to look ahead and make plans. They brought up the old dream of owning a taxi.

'Whoever heard of a one-legged taxi-driver?' Robert complained. 'Or a one-legged docker when it comes to it.'

'How about a one-legged motor-car mechanic?' Walter didn't see that his injury would stop him in the long run from learning how to take care of car engines. 'We could still be partners; Davidson and Parsons, Hackney Motor Carriages.'

For a few minutes, their conversation took off; men who knew about the combustion engine would be in high demand after the war. Modern transport was going along those lines. Robert recalled his brave friend, George Mann, having to heave the horse-and-cart munitions wagon out of the mud. 'It's had its day, that kind of thing. From now on it's going to be motorized everything.' He agreed it would be a good line of work to get into. 'Only one problem,' he pointed out.

'What's that?' Walter was reluctant to fall back to earth just yet. He fancied a whole fleet of taxis, shiny and black, with running-boards and big chrome bumpers. He wanted an office with a telephone, and people ringing up to be taken into the West End.

'It's the little matter of pounds, shillings and pence, mate.'

'Ah.' Walter sighed. 'Ain't no harm in dreaming.' Then there was one other problem he thought it only fair to point out. 'It ain't on the cards right away in any case. I been thinking, Rob. I ought to join up.'

Robert's mood switched in an instant. 'Enlisting?' He tried not to give away his own doubts and fears.

'I think I ought.' Lord Kitchener's face with its black moustache and piercing eyes had begun to appear on posters. The finger of accusation pointed at those who still thought to let others lay down life and limb for their country, but not themselves. Walter had too much pride to resist the call for long. 'I ain't keen on aiming at the Hun down the barrel of a gun, don't get me wrong. I ain't one for all that. But I'm fit and strong, Rob, and it don't seem right to hold back no more. This jamboree's going on longer than they thought, ain't it? If I join up straight off, do my bit and come home a hero, there'll be a job waiting for me at the end of the line, won't there?' He attempted a confident grin. 'Then we can start saving for that taxi.'

Robert found it hard to look him in the face. 'Good for you, mate.' He shut out the mental pictures of mangled bodies, blank terror, the insanity of slaughter for ten yards of mud.

'I'm off up the Town Hall on Monday morning,' Walter promised. 'Then you won't have one up on me no more.'

'Well, drink up,' Rob said. 'It's on the house.' Awkwardly he took the two glasses by hooking his thumb through both handles and dangling them from one crutch.

Duke served the beer and looked straight at his son. 'You sit down, mate. I'll get Joxer to fetch them across.' The cellarman had reported for duty as usual the minute Chalky had been taken into police custody. He said nothing as he

411

buttoned his waistcoat and left the gym, and he didn't intend to discuss things thereafter. He knew he had a job for life with Duke, and they'd each mind their own business. His face was expressionless as he brought Robert the two pints of beer.

Duke stood happily behind the bar, back in charge, his old, unflappable self. With Ernie at home and enjoying the limelight for once in his life, he felt that nothing could dent his sense of all being right with the world; not earthquake nor calamity nor war. Thanks to family and friends, he added to himself.

He sent extra drinks over to Frances and her friends, Billy and Rosie. Even Frances had let her hair down and sat there having a good time like the rest of them. She was human, after all, in spite of all that nonsense about the suffragettes.

Billy was in the middle of telling them how the Workers' Education Movement was putting its shoulder behind the war effort, especially as far as women were concerned. 'Just like Mrs Pankhurst and the suffragettes,' he said. 'We gotta unite against the common enemy.' The women's movement had ceased hostilities against the government; no more window-smashing or burning of post-boxes. And since women were beginning to form the nation's workforce – on the buses, in the factories, out in the fields – the Workers' Education people were putting together leaflets and holding classes especially for their benefit.

'Talking of workforces,' Rosie said, standing up and preparing to go. She gathered her cloak around her nurse's uniform and put on her gloves. 'My night shift starts in half an hour.' She bent to kiss Frances on the cheek and told her to give her love to Ernie.

So Frances was left sitting face to face with Billy Wray.

She told him how the chief pharmacist, a married man, had just joined up. 'That leaves me in charge.'

'About time too.' He said he had great faith in her abilities. 'You got the right frame of mind,' he told her. 'Very particular in everything.'

'A fusspot, you mean?' She blushed, feeling a strong urge to throw off her finicky spinster image.

'Very precise. Very neat.'

'Oh Lord, Billy, don't I wish I weren't sometimes!' She confessed she wouldn't mind a bit of Dolly's free-and-easiness, a touch of young Sadie's rebellious high spirits. 'It ain't that much fun being the responsible one, day in, day out.'

Billy smiled at her. 'It don't mean to say that's all there is to you.' He paid her the compliment of implying a hidden depth and intensity to her character, calling to mind their one stolen kiss under the watchful bound volumes of Ruskin and Sidney Webb.

It was too soon for him to make any move. He wanted to do the decent thing by Ada's memory for a start. And he was no moonstruck youth. He had just enough confidence in himself to realize that Frances was playing the same waiting game; observing convention and biding her time. She for her part was no mere flighty girl.

Frances sighed. 'Sometimes it does take a catastrophe to pull out the best in us, like they say. I mean, it's the war that'll give me the chance I want in the pharmacy. And it was the trouble over Ernie that pulled me and Pa back on to the same side, acting as a family again. And take Jess over there; having the baby really proved her mettle. There's times we'd all have given up over Ernie if it hadn't been for her, I don't mind telling you. It's funny, she's my sister, but I don't think I ever really knew her till now.'

Billy liked to hear these things. An only child himself, he envied her her large family. 'Jess should count herself lucky and all,' he reminded her. 'She ain't never gonna be on her own.'

A sudden gust of cold air and an influx of women from the market and from Coopers' turned the tide of conversation. The pianola thumped out another tune, second nature to Hettie from her days at the Palace. Liz Sargent encouraged her to sing up. Little Lettie Harris jumped in to do the Huggie Bear with Sam the leather worker.

'Nothing like a good knees up.' Nora Brady sidled up to Robert. 'Just what the doctor orders.' She picked up her skirts and made him do away with his crutch. Then they swayed along to the music, arms around each other's waists.

'What's your old man gonna say, Nora?' Rob asked, his good humour restored. He pulled Ernie to his feet and made him link up with Nora's free arm. 'Now you've got two new beaux?'

'He ain't gonna say nothing,' came the bold answer. 'Not when he's banged up in Parkhurst for six months, now, is he?' She laughed like a drain. 'While the cat's away, you know the rest!' And she took Ernie by both shoulders to give him lessons in the latest American dance craze.

The noise rose as the evening got into full swing. The dreary tenements at the bottom of Paradise Court spilled out their occupants, and the poor but respectable terraced houses emptied in turn. Older children were left to care for infants and little ones. Keys turned in locks. Even the penniless unemployed turned out tonight to call in at the Duke and help Ernie celebrate.

'Annie, you don't half look a treat!' Nora shrieked at the late arrival. The music played on, the bar was alive with bright lights, curling smoke, reflections in mirrors, the clink of glasses. There was the uproar of competing conversations.

Annie had lingered in front of her own glass, making a special effort. She'd been in and out of first this blouse, then that. Finally she'd chosen a smart one of shiny green and white striped poplin. She arranged her hair in softer, more flattering folds, put rouge on her cheeks, then scrubbed it off again. At last she set off for the pub.

Robert Parsons gave a cheeky whistle, Liz passed by with a nod of approval. Annie crept nervously towards the bar.

'Blow me!' Florrie said in a voice laden with sarcasm. 'Look what the wind blew in!'

'I see you're done up like a dog's dinner as usual, Florence.' Annie didn't wait for the full force of Florrie's scorn to land on her before she returned the insult. 'I keep on telling you, girl, but you ain't got the sense you was born with. Them magenta ribbons ain't you at all. And I should tone down the black dye a bit and all, if I was you. In fact, I'd say it was high time you gave in gracefully.'

'Who asked you, Annie Wiggin? Any rate, this ain't magenta, it's scarlet!' Florrie took the bait as usual. She rushed across to serve Annie so that Duke didn't need to stir himself. As she pushed the porter towards her, she leaned over the counter and her eyes popped. 'Blimey, Annie!' She clutched the bar for support. 'I think I must be seeing things!'

'Very funny, ha, ha!' Annie began to beat a retreat, but Nora too broke off dancing and came and seized her by the arm.

'Do you mean what I think you mean?' Nora said to Florrie. She gazed down at Annie's feet. 'Or is our eyes deceiving us?' She fluttered back into someone's arms, as if in a faint.

'Very funny, very funny!' Annie grumbled. She wished now she hadn't taken the plunge in such public fashion. It was true; she'd bought herself a pair of brand new boots.

'My, but they're a pair of bobby dazzlers.' A group led by Nora gathered round, to Florrie's satisfaction. The boots were black and pointed, with neat raised heels and dainty scalloped edges where the laces threaded through. They were immaculate.

But if they thought they could get one over on her, they'd another think coming, Annie told herself. 'So what? Ain't you never seen a new pair of boots before?'

'Not on you, Annie, no.' Florrie's tone kept up the derisory note. 'You mean to say you finally thrown over the memory of old man Wiggin after all these years?' She arched her eyebrows in the direction of Duke, but her brother stolidly refused to join in the taunting of Annie.

Annie gathered herself. She felt ladylike in her new boots, and well above Florrie's low aim. They gave her movements new snap and vigour. 'As a matter of fact, yes, Florrie. I thought it was time I laid his old boots to rest along with him, God rest his soul. Me and Duke's been in mourning long enough, ain't we, Duke? We think it's time to liven things up.'

Florrie gasped at Annie's audacity, and was even more surprised when Duke seemed to happily concur in the use of the first person plural. Annie evidently wasn't using 'we' in the royal sense.

Duke smiled awkwardly and came out from behind the bar. He felt himself moved by a sense of destiny. 'I see you took my advice about them old boots, Annie!' He took her by the arm and led her to a seat in a corner.

Annie retaliated as of old. 'Ain't nothing to do with your advice, Duke. I spotted these down the market. They was too good a bargain to miss.'

The hum of celebration continued all around them; the soaring girls' voices, the lively conversation, an outbreak of laughter. 'Too good to miss, eh?' Duke said meditatively.

'Yes, some things are too good to pass by.' Suddenly Annie's voice dropped. She realized that neither of them were talking about boots any more.

'That's it, we'd be fools to pass by certain things in this life.' He sighed. 'I'd go a long way before I found a friend like you, Annie.' He took her hands in his own large, work-worn ones.

She struggled to reply. 'Now, don't you go all soft on me, Duke Parsons. Just 'cos I bought myself a new pair of boots.'

He cleared his throat. 'Annie Wiggin, I think you and me should get spliced!' It was hasty, he knew.

'Blow me down!' was Annie's reply.

'Come on, Annie, you can't kid me you never knew what I was leading up to!' he protested. She'd gone coy on him.

'I never! You could knock me down with a feather!' Her heart fluttered. Her hands still rested in Duke's.

'Well?'

'I thought you'd never ask!' she answered at last, her face radiant. 'Blimey, Duke, you certainly took your time!'

Duke and Annie stood up and linked arms, then went across to the table where Jess and Maurice sat in self-conscious conversation. He held up his hands for quiet.

'Now as you know, I ain't one for public speaking,' he began. His voice rumbled into the newly created silence. He gestured for Ernie to draw near. 'You're all friends here, not just customers. We grown up and we grown old together, some of us.' He had a tone of deep tenderness, his arms around Ernie's shoulder. 'So I don't have to tell no one here what it means to have Ernie back home.'

A cheer went up for Ernie, and an outburst of applause. Once more, Duke put up his hand.

'Without you we'd never have come through this like we have, still in one piece, and we ain't never gonna forget what we owe you, as long as we live.'

Sadie, standing at the pianola with Tommy and Amy, sighed happily. Hettie stood proud and smiling by the door. Frances squeezed Billy's hand. Robert stood shoulder to shoulder with Walter, while Jess hung on to Maurice's arm.

Duke took up the thread, his voice thickened with emotion. 'Now, I aim to do this whole thing right and make it a home-coming to remember.' He cleared his throat. 'Ernie, I got one more bit of news for you. Frank Henshaw sent word he wants you back at work on Monday, eight o'clock sharp.'

Ernie nodded. The last shred of doubt about his future fell away.

'And more than that. Jess here, and Maurice have asked me to announce their news.' Duke raised her up to stand alongside him. 'They asked me to tell you they plan on tying the knot just as soon as they can.'

A buzz passed round the room, then another cheer.

Duke continued. 'We ain't known Maurice long, but we say welcome to the Parsons family.' He turned to shake his prospective son-in-law vigorously by the hand. 'As long as you think you can put up with us, that is.'

Maurice grinned sheepishly and put an arm round Jess's shoulder. 'You mean I'm stuck with the lot of you?' He had no qualms now. Once he'd decided, he went ahead. He was already talking of finding bigger lodgings down the court, or nearby on Duke Street, so Jess and Grace would still be on the doorstep. He'd approached his employer for a rise in wages, describing his plans to marry and settle down.

He'd been offered more money in return for helping to set up another new cinema down the road in Dulwich.

Jess basked in the contentment spreading through the room. She was the luckiest woman alive, with Maurice and Grace, the one to pour her hidden passion upon, the other on whom she could dote so tenderly. She felt like a passenger rescued from the wreck of the great *Titanic*; she'd kept her head in the icy waters and climbed into a lifeboat with those she loved. She reached out and kissed her father, then Ernie, then Maurice.

But Duke hadn't reached the end of his own long, unaccustomed journey into speechifying. 'Now, girls,' he said to no one in particular, 'I expect you're all thinking of buying a new hat for Jess's wedding, and I ain't one to force you into no unnecessary expense.' He paused to look round and clutch hold of Annie's hand. 'So Annie and me, we thought we'd better make it worth your while and follow up with a wedding of our own. No need to buy another hat, see, Dolly. You can wear the same one to both!'

Annie stood beside him, looking small and spry, like a preening bird. She dipped her head and looked sideways up at him, then stared straight at Florrie with a new sense of territory. Her head went back, her chest out. Until this moment she hadn't really believed in Duke's proposal. His announcement of it had stunned everyone in the room. Well, that was one in the eye for his sister, Annie thought with undisguised triumph.

Florrie shook her head as if a bee had landed on her nose. Of all the foolish things. After all these years. Annie Wiggin, of all people. She couldn't pull one sensible thought together. Then it came with startling clarity; Annie had wormed her way under Duke's guard and into his affections when he was at his lowest point over Ernie. Of course, that was how she'd managed it. Otherwise, how could it be explained?

There was not a single thing about Annie that cut her out from the common crowd of middle-aged women whose husbands ran off and left them in the lurch. She was no beauty, that was certain; thin as a whippet, all skin and bone, and her mouth needed a permanent muzzle. No, it wasn't romance that had drawn Duke in her direction. She'd just wormed her way in, out of spite against Florrie.

But if she thought Florrie would pack her bags and toddle meekly back to Brighton, she was making a big mistake. She, Florrie, was made of sterner stuff, and there was many a slip between this moment and, 'Do you take this man to be your lawful wedded husband?' Florrie chuntered on to herself. She had of course turned down umpteen decent offers in her own time. It was the only dignified course for women in their situation.

Still, congratulations for both couples poured in. 'I ain't gotta call you Ma, have I?' Robert winked at Annie.

'You do and I'll knock your block off,' she said.

'I see marriage ain't gonna soften you up none,' Arthur Ogden observed. 'Not that it does in most cases, if you ask me.' He looked ruefully at Dolly.

'It ain't gonna change nothing,' Annie insisted. 'I'll run my stall of bits and bobs, and Duke will run this place like before. We ain't gonna live in each other's pockets, don't you worry.'

The men slapped Duke on the back, bought him drinks and admired his nerve.

'Well, we're living in dangerous times,' he told them. 'It makes a man feel reckless, don't it?'

Hettie, Frances and Sadie came across to complete the family group. The Parsons were back together and the heart had been restored to Duke Street and Paradise Court. They might have been posing for a picture as the music struck up. They stood, arms intertwined, a fading photograph in an album, seen through a haze of smoke, features already beginning to blur. They held position for a moment in time, in harmony, completely happy.